GRAND
CENTRAL

**LARGE
PRINT**

DEAD MOUNTAIN

A Nora Kelly Novel

DOUGLAS PRESTON & LINCOLN CHILD

GRAND
CENTRAL

LARGE PRINT

DEAD
MOUNTAIN

Copyright © 2023 by Splendide Mendax, Inc. and Lincoln Child

Cover design by Faceout Studio, Molly von Borstel. Cover images by Shutterstock. Cover copyright © 2023 by Hachette Book Group, Inc.

Grand Central Publishing
Hachette Book Group
1290 Avenue of the Americas, New York, NY 10104
grandcentralpublishing.com
twitter.com/grandcentralpub

First Edition: August 2023

Grand Central Publishing is a division of Hachette Book Group, Inc. The Grand Central Publishing name and logo is a trademark of Hachette Book Group, Inc.

The publisher is not responsible for websites (or their content) that are not owned by the publisher.

The Hachette Speakers Bureau provides a wide range of authors for speaking events. To find out more, go to hachettespeakersbureau.com or email HachetteSpeakers@hbgusa.com.

Grand Central Publishing books may be purchased in bulk for business, educational, or promotional use. For information, please contact your local bookseller or the Hachette Book Group Special Markets Department at special.markets@hbgusa.com.

Library of Congress Cataloging-in-Publication Data has been applied for.

ISBNs: 9781538736821 (hardcover), 9781538736838 (ebook), 9781538765975 (int'l edition), 9781538756874 (Canadian edition), 9781538742532 (large print), 9781538757109 (B&N signed edition), 9781538757116 (signed edition)

Printed in the United States of America

LSC-C

Printing 1, 2023

Douglas Preston and Lincoln Child
dedicate this book to
the Authors Guild,
America's oldest and largest association
of authors, journalists, and poets

DEAD MOUNTAIN

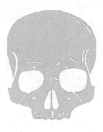

1

Brandon Purdue and his frat buddy Mike Kottke sat on a rock underneath a big fir tree, near where their Jeep had skidded off a Forest Service road into a ditch and run over a sapling. They were passing a bottle of Captain Morgan Spiced Rum and a joint back and forth between them. There was no cell service this far up in the mountains, and it was getting dark. But they were already too drunk and stoned to hike out, and besides it was a good ten miles to the nearest paved road. There was no chance someone else would come along the road they'd taken on their drunken joyride—it was closed, and they weren't supposed to be there. The only thing to do, Brandon told his buddy Mike, was to sit under a tree and get messed up.

"Don't bogart that joint, my friend," sang Kottke in a cracked voice, holding out a hand.

"Get wrecked, dude." Purdue handed it over to

Kottke, who took a toke while offering the bottle in return.

"Dude, you let it go out!" Kottke complained, holding the reefer out at arm's length and staring at it disapprovingly.

Purdue handed him the lighter. Kottke fussed with it, swearing as the wind picked up. He finally got the joint fired up and sucked in a lungful of smoke.

"It's getting cold, man," said Purdue, tilting up the plastic bottle of rum.

"No shit, Einstein. We're only at ten thousand feet above sea level." Kottke looked at the roach. "This is finito." He tossed it. "Got another?"

"Suck on this." Purdue fumbled in his day pack and drew out a big bertha, lit it, and held it out to his friend. God, he was high. The big trees around them were all moving in the wind, or maybe they weren't moving at all and it was just his brain that was moving. But it was getting colder by the minute. It was Hallowe'en, and it might go below freezing that night. Definitely would go below freezing. They couldn't spend the night in the Jeep, tilted as it was in the ditch, its windshield broken, the interior strewn with glass. On top of that, there was a smell of gasoline that made Purdue guess the sapling had punctured the tank. If they tried to start up the Jeep for warmth, they might blow themselves up.

What were they going to do? They couldn't stay

out here in the open, drinking and smoking until they passed out and froze to death. Purdue pushed the thought out of his mind as he took another pull on the bottle of rum. That would warm him up, at least temporarily.

"Brandon, you feel that?" Kottke yelled.

Purdue's head swam back into focus. "What?"

"Rain. I felt it on my face. A drop of rain."

Purdue took another gulp from the bottle. As he did, he felt something cold touch his cheek.

Kottke reached into his day pack, pulled out a flashlight, and turned it on. He shone it up into the sky. "It's *snowing*!"

"Oh, Jesus." Purdue let out a groan. Snow. Of course. In the Manzano Mountains at ten thousand feet. In late October. They were screwed.

"Hey," said Kottke. "We've got to find some shelter. Seriously."

Purdue groaned again. Shelter? They didn't have a tent, sleeping bags, nothing. Just light jackets. Was there a blanket in the Jeep? He couldn't remember but didn't think so.

"Light a fire?" Purdue finally said.

"That's not going to stop the snow. We gotta find, like, *shelter*, man."

Now Purdue could feel the cold sting of snow against his face. The wind was rising. Kottke stood up and circled the area with his flashlight. The ground sloped down into a forest of fir trees. Kottke shouldered his pack and took a few steps forward, shining the beam left and right.

"What are you doing?" Purdue said.

"What do you think? Get up and let's go find a place to spend the night. We can hike back down in the morning."

Purdue lurched to his feet, fighting a sudden rush of dizziness. He followed Kottke down the slope into the forest, stumbling and shuffling. The temperature was plunging and snowflakes swirled around them. Far below, Purdue could see the distant lights of Albuquerque's South Valley, dissolving in the haze of snow.

"Dude, you see those big rocks down there? We might find an overhang." The flashlight played into a ravine that didn't look promising to Purdue at all. The slope got steeper. The smooth, pine-needled forest floor gave way to rough stones and small outcrops, interspersed with dense bushes and roots. It looked, in fact, like a good place to break some bones.

"I don't know about this," said Purdue.

"Come *on*!"

Purdue followed reluctantly, angling down into the ravine. The snow was accumulating now, and the ground was getting slippery. Purdue forced himself to focus on where he was putting each foot, but even so he felt unsteady and slipped constantly, swearing and grabbing for handholds. His butt was already soaked from skidding down and sitting in the snow.

The slope continued plunging toward the bottom of the ravine, which was filled with boulders dusted with fresh snow. Purdue felt like he was sobering up fast. "I'm not going down there," he said. "All you're going to do is get our asses flash-frozen."

"Hey! Check that out!" Kottke yelled, pointing.

Purdue looked over. The flashlight beam, piercing the swirling snow, vaguely illuminated the far side of the ravine. About ten feet from the bottom it revealed a small, dark triangular hole—the opening to a cave.

"You see that?" Kottke asked.

"We can't fit in there, man," said Purdue.

"Yeah? Watch me."

They slipped and slid to the bottom of the ravine and climbed up toward the opening. The rock here was rough lava, with lots of hand- and footholds, and in a few minutes they had reached the cave mouth. Kottke shone the light in. The beam revealed a space opening up beyond—a cavern with a sandy floor.

Kottke crawled through the opening and Purdue followed.

"Oh, man!" said Kottke, staggering gingerly to his feet. He raised his arms. "This is righteous. And *I* found it!"

His flashlight beam probed the space. It was, Purdue had to admit, an ideal shelter, tall enough to stand up in although narrowing in the back to a crawlspace.

"I'm freezing," said Kottke. "Let's light a fire."

"Yeah." Purdue peered back out the cave entrance. The ravine had been scattered with dead and fallen trees and branches. It meant going back out.

"You go back out, hand me up the wood," Kottke said.

Reluctantly, Purdue crawled out. While Kottke held the flashlight, Purdue gathered a bunch of kindling and branches and handed them up. He had no gloves and his hands were wet and freezing, but in very little time he'd amassed a heap of sticks big enough to do the job.

Purdue crawled back in while Kottke lit the fire. Even though the wood was a little damp from the snow, dry grass and leaves had blown into the cave, and he soon had a fire going, the smoke being drawn out through a crack near the front. It was close to perfect—a miracle.

Purdue warmed his hands at the blaze. "You got another doob for us? I need something after all that work."

"Coming right up." Kottke unzipped his pack and took out another plastic bottle of rum, a small jar with a couple of buds, a hand grinder, some rolling papers, a Kit Kat, a Snickers bar, a bag of Peanut M&M's, and a large can of Pringles.

"You came prepared, bruh."

"If I carry weed, I also carry munchies. Straight-up rule."

Purdue grabbed the new bottle, cracked the cap, and took a deep swig, trying to revive the warm feeling he'd enjoyed earlier, before the snow began to fall. He watched as Kottke stuffed a bud into the grinder and gave it a good twist, the smell of herb drifting in the air. Then he proceeded to roll a fat one.

The fire was now throwing off so much warmth that Purdue unzipped his jacket. He took another long pull on the bottle. His head was whirling pleasantly once again, he was warm, and they had found themselves a cave. The wind howled outside, the snow falling. Tomorrow would be crap—but that was tomorrow, and for now they had shelter and they were buzzin'.

"Whoooo, this the shit!" Kottke said, firing up the blunt. They swapped the rum and the doobie. Purdue sucked in a hit, then another, then a third.

"Hey, check that out!" Kottke said.

Purdue turned and saw what Kottke was pointing at. In the light of the fire, near the narrow back of the cave, was a long flat surface of stone, and on it were pecked several designs. Petroglyphs.

Purdue squinted. In the firelight he could see a spiral, several faces, a zigzagging arrow, a bird, and a hunchbacked figure playing a flute. Hallowe'en.

Being here, tonight of all nights, he felt a bit creeped out despite his buzz.

But Kottke, unfazed, just picked up a rock. "Two points if I hit that spiral." He threw it and missed, striking one of the faces. "Three points for that!"

"No points for that," said Purdue, determined not to act like a wimp. He picked up a rock of his own. "Five points for the bird." He lobbed it and smacked the bird right in the middle, leaving a gash. "Yes! Five points!"

Kottke picked up a bigger rock. "This is a ten-pointer." He heaved it at the spiral and it struck with a crash, shaking a few pebbles loose from the ceiling. "Ten points!"

Not to be outdone, Purdue began prying a bigger rock out of the side of the cave, wiggling it loose. Then he took a step closer.

"Hey, that's cheating!"

"The hell it is." He chucked it at the bird, where it impacted with a big hollow boom. Now a bunch of small rocks fell from the ceiling. "Fifteen points!" he cried, laughing uproariously.

"Fifteen points, my ass." Kottke pried out an even bigger rock, so heavy he could barely carry it, then shuffled all the way to the back and slammed it against the flute player. It jarred the stone wall so hard that it moved, and a sudden grinding noise came from the ceiling. With a yowl, Kottke leapt back as a torrent of rocks were shaken loose and came down with a clatter, raising a cloud of dust. Kottke, who had barely escaped being brained, fell into the dust settling from the small cave-in. He was laughing hysterically.

"Enough of that shit," said Purdue. "I don't want to be buried alive."

Kottke kept laughing. Purdue settled back and took another swig of rum. The bottle was almost empty. God, how much had he drunk? For a moment he forgot where he was, lying on the ground looking up at the firelight on the ceiling, unable to organize his spinning thoughts. He heard more hysterical laughter—was that him or Kottke? The laughter turned into the sound of vomiting, but now he was so tired he didn't care. He just wanted to close his eyes and go to sleep. But he was cold. He managed to crawl nearer to the fire and lay down again in the sand, trying to get comfortable, but the sandy floor had some lumps in it, and he twitched and wriggled. Something was digging into his back, right where he wanted to sleep.

He vaguely heard more retching—Kottke puking again. He flopped over onto his stomach and dug his hand into the sand to move the thing poking his back. As he scraped and dug, he saw that it wasn't the rock he'd assumed, but something smooth and light brown, like a dome. Even with his head spinning and his eyes barely able to focus, as he brushed and fumbled he saw two dark hollows appear, followed by grinning teeth and a clump of braided hair attached to a dried patch of flesh.

"Holy shit!" Purdue screamed. "There's a dead motherfucker in here!" He pushed himself backward with his feet and hands, trying to get away from the thing that stared at him out of the sand, black eye sockets and gleaming teeth. "Mike! *Mike!*"

But Kottke was lying sprawled on the other side of the fire, unconscious, his shirt covered in vomit.

Purdue tried to get up, but, unable to maintain his balance, crawled backward instead, pushing with his feet. Finally, when he had gotten as far away from the thing as the cave would allow, he eased onto his side and curled himself up into a ball, shutting his eyes tight, hoping this would all go away, that it was just a nightmare, while his drunken brain sank into unconsciousness.

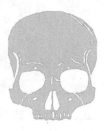

2

Special Agent Corinne Swanson stopped at the secretary's desk outside the door—the closed door—of the SAC's office. The young man glanced up at her.

"You can go in," he said, pressing a button on a terminal on his desk.

Corrie grasped the doorknob of the corner office with more than a little apprehension. It had been almost four months since her last big case: a case involving, among other things, the murder of Hale Morwood, the senior agent who'd been mentoring her since her arrival at the Albuquerque Field Office a year ago. She was still traumatized by his death. Not a day passed without something reminding her of Agent Morwood, a dull, stubborn ache that never went away. Corrie was slow to respect people, and even slower to trust them... but Morwood had earned both from her before his death.

Her last big case. For the past four months she'd

attended the various boards of inquiry, sat for lengthy debriefings, and submitted to several lie detector tests. Given the craziness of that case, the blowback was not surprising. She'd brought the investigation to a successful conclusion, if unconventionally... But as soon as it was over, almost the entire project had been classified, which, she realized belatedly, meant she wasn't going to get much public recognition or the chance of a commendation. Even more troubling was that Special Agent in Charge Garcia had not yet assigned her a new mentor—technically, she was still an agent in training—or even given her a new case of any note. She wasn't being punished—she would have been told that—but Garcia had kept her on low-profile, low-risk tasks like surveillance, and she couldn't help wondering if she was under some kind of clandestine evaluation.

Shoving these thoughts aside, she entered the office.

SAC Julio Garcia rose from behind his desk and stretched out his hand to shake hers. Although it was some time since she'd been in his office, it looked exactly the same. The only thing that seemed to vary was the amount of traffic on the freeway beyond the windows.

"Agent Swanson," he said, "thank you for coming. Please take a seat."

As always, she was surprised by how such a brawny guy could be so soft-spoken. As she took a seat opposite the desk, he sat down again, pulled a folder close, opened and scanned it.

"So, Corinne," he said without looking up. "Ready to get your hands dirty again?"

"Yes, sir," she said, the words almost tumbling out. She felt a rush of gratitude.

He nodded, then looked up at her, neither smiling nor frowning, as was his way, his brown eyes taking her measure. "In that case, I'd like you to meet your new mentor."

"My new mentor? Yes, sir." Was the head of the field office going to ghost her himself? But no—Garcia pressed the button on his desk comm and the door opened. A lean, middle-aged man stepped in.

"Agent Swanson, this is Supervisory Special Agent Clay Sharp."

She rose. The man extended his hand and she shook it briefly. His skin was cool, his grip firm but not ridiculously so—not like some agents who seemed to enjoy crushing knuckles. Agent Sharp was of average height, late forties, with sleepy-looking eyes. He had a handsome, even delicate face, and was dressed impeccably: although his suit was standard-issue FBI blue, it was of a sharper cut than usual and well tailored to a trim and athletic body, complemented by a tightly knotted, expensive silk tie. Rather than a military buzz or the standard side-part, Sharp's long brown hair was combed back in a smooth coif, completing the picture of a man attentive of his personal appearance but not a slave to FBI style. Corrie couldn't decide if this was a good thing or not.

She had seen Sharp around the office from time to time but had never interacted with him. He was quiet and somewhat enigmatic, and the other agents seemed to treat him with a combination of respect and wariness. She'd gotten the sense he was what was called a "brick agent": terse, no bullshit, impatient, and capable.

"Agent Sharp has agreed to guide you through the rest of the mentoring period," Garcia said briskly. "Since he's never mentored before—and since you need to get your feet wet again, Swanson—I've given you an easy one." He closed the folder and held it out to them both, ambiguously. Sharp indicated she was to take it, not him—and she did, appreciating the gesture.

"Last night," said Garcia, "two frat boys from South Valley Tech got stuck in a snowstorm up in the Manzano Mountains. They took shelter in a cave—and found some human remains."

"Prehistoric or historic?" Corrie asked.

"That's what you're going to find out. The information we got from the boys was not very coherent."

"So it might be a Native American burial," Sharp said, speaking for the first time in a quiet voice, with an accent Corrie couldn't quite place. "Or—" he paused— "something more...interesting?"

"Exactly," Garcia said.

It seemed to Corrie there was a hint in Sharp's comment that Garcia had picked up but she had not. She glanced at Sharp. His pale hazel eyes— more amber than green in the slanting sunlight— looked even sleepier than before. She had the feeling that the sleepier he looked, the more alert he actually was.

"Seems they might have vandalized the site, too," Garcia added. "Charges might be filed—but that's not our problem, thankfully."

Sharp nodded slowly. He glanced at the file in Corrie's hand, to which an address had been clipped. Then he turned toward her. "Shall we get started, Agent Swanson?"

"Yes. Of course." As she headed toward the door, she stopped momentarily and looked back at SAC Garcia. "Thank you, sir."

The head of the field office looked back at her, one hand rubbing his chin speculatively. "Good hunting," he said.

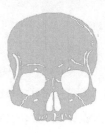

3

"WHAT DO YOU know of the Manzano Mountains?" Agent Sharp asked as they drove south on Highway 337, followed by the FBI's Evidence Response Team van.

"Beyond seeing them from far off, not much," Corrie replied. "I haven't been in New Mexico very long." She'd felt guarded and nervous when she first met Sharp, and the feeling had yet to go away. He was a difficult person to read, with his slow manner of speech and inscrutable demeanor. Her previous mentor, Agent Morwood, had also been reserved, but she'd managed to connect with him. She was trying not to compare the two men and let that comparison color her perception—but she wished her new mentor wasn't quite so reticent. At least now he was talking.

"Your file indicates you've been pretty busy. And there's a part of the file that's classified...even I don't have clearance to see it. Intriguing."

Corrie had taken a look at his file, too—at least, what she could glean from it without raising eyebrows. Sharp had been with the FBI almost sixteen years and, unlike Morwood, who'd been sidelined into the mentoring position by an injury, had risen through the ranks as a lone wolf. Before joining the FBI, Sharp had been military, in positions of such high security that only the countries were identified: Yemen, Iraq, and Turkey.

"The Manzanos are part of the Rio Grande Rift—layers of rock that got fractured and heaved upward starting twenty million years ago. There's a steep western face along the Rio Grande, and a more gradual eastern face. The highest peaks of the range are over ten thousand feet."

"I see, sir," Corrie said.

"The Kirtland Air Force Base occupies the entire northern part of the mountains. Largest storage facility for nuclear weapons in the world, overseen by the Air Force Global Strike Command."

"The largest?" Corrie had had no idea.

Sharp nodded. "South of Kirtland lies a strip of Indian land: part of the Pueblo of Isleta. And south of that is a quarter million acres of national forest and wilderness, one of the least visited areas in the Southwest."

Corrie wasn't sure what to say. Sharp seemed to enjoy imparting this information. Asking a few questions, Corrie thought, would probably make a good impression. "What will they do with all those nuclear weapons? Don't they have enough already deployed?"

"Most of them are intended to replace weapons that have been fired after a missile and bomber exchange—in a war."

"You mean, to reload the bombers after the world has been destroyed?" Corrie immediately regretted the comment and wondered how Sharp would take it. She found Sharp looking at her curiously. His eyes, which she'd noticed rarely blinked, blinked now—with the slow deliberation of a lizard. Then he issued a low chuckle. "That's the idea, Agent Swanson, illogical as it may sound."

They drove in silence while Corrie got up the nerve to ask the question she'd been wondering about ever since the meeting with Garcia. "Sir, just to be clear: Am I officially the agent in charge of the investigation, or are you? Just so I know who's taking the lead," she added, stammering.

He looked at her with those sleepy eyes. "Why, you, Agent Swanson. I thought that was understood."

"Thank you, sir. I hope to earn your approval."

God, did she sound like too much of a toady? She wished she could get a better handle on this guy.

Sharp took a right on Route 55, and soon they

had passed through the tiny hamlet of Tajique in the foothills and were climbing up a series of dirt Forest Service roads. In the investigation folder was a paper map, and now Sharp asked Corrie to navigate, which she did using her cell phone GPS and the map. On the map someone had drawn in pencil the spot where the car went off the road and the location of the cave. Fresh snow had fallen in the high mountains overnight, but the storm had blown over and it was a cold late fall day with a cloudless sky. Soon they were above the snowline, bumping along a terrible road made worse by melting slush. The Tahoe was handling it well, but the ERT van was struggling, which slowed them down.

The piñon and juniper trees had given way to ponderosas, which in turn were replaced by fir and spruce. There were so many branching roads, and so many turns, and it was taking so long, that Corrie began to worry she might have taken a wrong fork somewhere. But she kept her doubts to herself. At least she could see fresh muddy tracks of previous vehicles, which was encouraging.

Finally, they arrived at a spot where the road had been blocked with a berm of earth but with vehicle tracks working their way around it. This had to be the closed road the two subjects had taken. Sharp worked the Tahoe around the berm as well, then waited for the van. In another half mile they arrived at the scene of the crash, where several vehicles were parked: two green National Forest Law Enforcement pickups, the Torrance County sheriff's truck, and a flatbed wrecker on which sat the crashed Jeep.

Corrie got out of the passenger side, carrying her FBI cell phone and a notepad. She had found the FBI-issued iPad awkward, and she preferred the solidity and permanence of pen and ink. It seemed paper notes were coming back into favor at the FBI, since electronic records could be altered and juries were increasingly suspicious of them.

Sharp shut the driver's door while the van pulled up. The ERT piled out and started unloading their gear. A man in a sheriff's uniform came over, hand outstretched to Sharp. "Welcome," he said. "Deputy Sheriff Baca, Torrance County."

"Special Agent Clay Sharp." He shook the deputy's hand.

"Special Agent Corrine Swanson," Corrie said, trying to sound crisp and professional. Baca was wearing a cowboy hat, had a big black mustache, and was about forty years old with a genial smile. She looked around to see where the sheriff himself was. This, in turn, reminded Corrie of her friend Sheriff Homer Watts, and she wondered what he was up to. Watts's county, Socorro, was adjacent to Torrance—they were no doubt all acquainted.

"Glad to meet you both," said Baca. "And welcome."

The ERT leader, a big guy named Nate Findlay, came over. Corrie had met him a few times in the office: a wisecracker, but one with a reputation for competence. "Agent Sharp, we're ready to roll," he said.

Sharp raised his eyebrows and gestured toward Corrie.

"Oh. Right." Findlay turned to her expectantly. "Ma'am? We're all set."

Ma'am was the FBI equivalent of *Sir*, but Corrie hated it. Couldn't they come up with a word that didn't make her feel like a wizened old lady? "Thank you, Mr. Findlay, let's go take a look." She turned. "Deputy Baca, could you please escort us to the site?"

"Of course." He hesitated. "It's rough going."

When nobody said anything, he set off down the slope, picking his way on bow legs. There were about four inches of snow, trampled from people coming and going. The slope quickly grew steeper and rockier. It amazed Corrie that two drunken kids could have come this way after dark without breaking their necks. A quarter mile of cautious walking brought them to the edge of a small ravine. There were a couple of officers at its bottom, passing around a thermos of hot coffee. A retractable ladder had been placed against the opposite side of the ravine, and its top end rested against a cave opening.

Again, Corrie was amazed. Those boys were lucky—they could easily have missed that cave and died of exposure.

"Deputy," she asked, "where are the individuals now? Are they still around?"

"No, they were taken away for a medical evaluation—they'd had a pretty tough morning, hungover from a lot of drinking the night before—and then we let them go."

"We—you mean the sheriff's department?"

"Yes."

"Why not question them?"

"We'll do that if necessary, after we evaluate the site and see if there's any reason to press charges."

"Right." She made her way down to the bottom of the ravine, through some slippery boulders covered with ice. Sharp and the ERT followed. There wasn't a lot of space at the bottom. "I don't see a perimeter," she told the deputy.

"We figured the FBI would want to set that up themselves."

She nodded. "Let's string some tape here, and here." She directed Findlay to block off the bottom of the ravine below the cave, then turned to the others. "You guys go ahead and suit up. And I'd like a suit for myself."

"Of course, ma'am," said Findlay.

A head suddenly stuck out of the cave entrance. "Hey, Baca, we got a second body up here."

Corrie stared up at the man. "Who are you?"

The man looked down at her. "I'm Sheriff Hawley—and who are you?"

Corrie held up her lanyard and shield. "Special Agent Swanson, FBI." Distantly, she could hear another voice from behind Hawley.

"Sheriff, could you and your men please exit the scene?" she said.

The man had a fleshy face and aviator sunglasses pushed up on a shaved dome. "We're working. We'll let you know when we're done."

Who was actually in charge at the site? Was it the county sheriff, FBI, or National Forest LE guys? It just wasn't clear. Corrie made a quick decision: she was going to take charge. If that turned out to be wrong, it was still better than not taking charge when it was her responsibility—especially in front of Sharp.

"Sheriff Hawley," said Corrie, "you and your men are at a potential crime scene without protective covering."

He stared down at her, his face darkening. "Don't you tell me how to do my job."

Corrie was afraid to glance over at Sharp—she needed to handle this on her own. She took a deep breath and tried to muster an authoritative tone of voice. "Sheriff Hawley, according to standard law enforcement protocol, you should not be in proximity of a potential crime scene without protective covering until an evidence team has processed the area. So I would respectfully ask you to vacate the site so our Evidence Response Team can enter and perform their work."

The sheriff continued to stare at her. He didn't look very bright, and Corrie realized she might have thrown too many big words at him, too fast.

Nevertheless, he'd gotten the message. "Who the heck are you, young lady, to tell me and my deputies what to do on our own home ground?"

For a moment, Corrie was taken aback by this open defiance. Then she felt a surge of anger. *Young lady.* But before she could say anything, Sharp spoke up.

"Sheriff? You are going to have a very serious problem with the FBI if you don't come down from there. Now. Is that understood?"

Sharp's voice was not loud, but somehow remarkably full of menace. Almost immediately, the sheriff pulled his head back, spoke to the other person in the cave, came out, fat-ass-backward, and climbed down the ladder, a deputy following. They said nothing as they slipped under the fresh tape and stood to one side, arms crossed. Corrie looked down, feeling the burn at the thought of Sharp needing to intervene—but the senior agent had retreated once again and was standing behind her almost deferentially.

Findlay, meanwhile, handed a monkey suit to Corrie. She slipped into it, followed by booties, hood, and mask. "I'll go first, if you don't mind," she said, then climbed the ladder, the team following.

Lights had been set up inside the cave, hooked to a battery. The place was a mess. On one side a recent fire was now dead, soot smudging the ceiling. In a sandy area nearby were two exposed human skulls, with some loose bones scattered about. It appeared that someone—maybe the sheriff, maybe the frat boys—had partly dug them up. There was the sour smell of puke, and she located the offending puddles on the far side of the fire. Broken glass lay scattered about, along with cigarette butts, marijuana roaches, and some toilet paper. There were footprints everywhere, so numerous it would be impossible to separate which were the boys' and which belonged to the sheriff, his deputy, and whoever else had been in the cave. To the rear a portion of the roof had fallen in, with a bunch of fresh rocks and debris scattered about, and to the right of that was a wall containing some prehistoric petroglyphs, with fresh gouges, dents, and scratches made by thrown rocks that littered the cave floor beneath.

"Can you believe those jackasses?" murmured Nate.

"Asinine," said Corrie.

She turned her attention to the human remains. She could see right away, from the deep mahogany color of the bones, that they were old—almost certainly prehistoric. A piece of desiccated flesh clung to one cranial dome, a partial braid of hair attached to it: more evidence of antiquity.

An edge of fabric was just exposed in the sand. She gestured to Findlay. "Can you hand me a brush, please?"

With short, careful strokes, she exposed a woven fabric that, as she uncovered more, was clearly part of a prehistoric blanket. A little more brushing revealed that the backs of the two crania were ritually flattened: a dispositive indication that these were Ancestral Pueblo Indian burials. This was further supported by the ancient petroglyphs. She brushed some more and soon uncovered the rim of an ancient painted pot—freshly broken.

She looked at Nate. "Prehistoric."

He nodded.

"So what we should do now," she said, "is, since we're here, we'll collect evidence of vandalism to support local law enforcement—photos, documentation, samples of trash, footprints, whatever might be needed as evidence if they decide to prosecute."

"Gotcha," said Findlay.

She went back to the mouth of the cave, descended the ladder, and took off the monkey suit. She was glad to see the sheriff and his deputy had gone. This would be a good reason, she thought, to call up Sheriff Watts: say hello, inquire about Hawley.

She found Sharp looking at her. "It's a prehistoric burial site," she said.

She was surprised when the phlegmatic Sharp looked deflated—even disappointed. "Definitely prehistoric? No chance of it being more recent?"

"Not a chance. Those kids damaged ancient petroglyphs. And it looks like they may have even triggered a small cave-in with their shenanigans. I told the ERT to collect evidence in order to assist local law enforcement." She hesitated. "I hope that was the right call."

He nodded. "It was."

"Bottom line," Corrie concluded, "it doesn't appear to be a case for the FBI." She hesitated. "Thank you, though, for straightening things out with the sheriff."

He gave her a long, appraising look. "When jurisdictional issues are unclear, the FBI's in charge. Always."

Corrie felt herself color. "Yes, sir."

"You say it's not our case. Probably right. But we're here now, and our reputation is in play—and there's the possible desecration of a Native American burial site to be considered. That has a tendency to turn into a hot-button issue." He paused. "So, Agent Swanson—do you have a recommendation on how to proceed?"

"I think we should interview the two students. I'm not sure I trust the sheriff's department to handle that properly."

He inclined his head in agreement.

Corrie asked, "How far are we from Isleta Pueblo land?"

"Six, maybe eight miles to the north."

"So they'd be the NAGPRA-designated tribal custodian of these remains?"

Sharp nodded.

"We should be in touch with them right away. And we also need to get a trained archaeologist out here to document the site and confirm for the record that the bones are prehistoric."

Another nod.

"I have a recommendation along those lines. Dr. Nora Kelly, Chief of Archaeology, Santa Fe Archaeological Institute. I've worked with her before."

A beat. "She sounds pretty high-powered for a small job like this."

"Yes," she agreed, "but I think it's our call to make. When jurisdictional issues are unclear, we're in charge."

At this, Sharp's sleepy face broke into a smile. "Carry on."

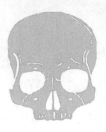

4

Wᴏᴀᴛ sᴏᴏᴜʟᴅ I do with these?" Bob Rotherhithe asked, pointing to the two framed Salvador
Dalí reproductions that, until five minutes ago, had
graced the wall of Nora Kelly's new office. While
Nora had no objection to Dalí, she wondered why
Connor Digby had felt pictures of melting clocks
would be appropriate for the office of a curator of
Southwestern archaeology—especially when there
were so many more appropriate decorations close at
hand.

"Ask Connor if he wants them," she said. "If not,
donate them to Goodwill."

"Yes, Dr. Kelly."

She had tried many times to get Rotherhithe to
call her Nora, but he politely refused. So, given her
strong streak of egalitarianism, that meant her calling him Mr. Rotherhithe instead of Bob, like everyone else did.

Her new office was modestly sized, but utterly charming: hand-plastered adobe walls, a kiva fireplace, hand-adzed lintels, and a ceiling of vigas and latillas. Dr. Marcelle Weingrau, the president of the Institute, had offered her a much bigger office in the front of the main campus building. It was impressive, with a wall of windows looking out over a courtyard with a rose garden and fountain. But Nora had opted for something smaller, quieter, and harder to find.

As part of the Institute's open collections policy—items were arranged in storage to be seen by visitors, rather than tucked away in darkness—curators were encouraged to display items in their offices for public viewing. Nora had taken advantage of this philosophy by selecting a beautiful Acoma olla, a painted water jug dating back to the 1910s, for placement in a niche near the fireplace, beside a Navajo eye-dazzler rug. For the opposite wall, she had selected two 1930s paintings by the Taos artist Albert Looking Elk. They would replace the two Dalís. Otherwise, the office would be spare and minimalist: Nora did not like clutter.

Rotherhithe began hanging the two Looking Elk paintings, while Nora advised him on placement.

Next came the rug. This was more involved. She watched as Rotherhithe measured out the wall, made marks, drilled two holes, and affixed a hanging bar, which slipped through a sleeve in the rug.

"Will that be all, Dr. Kelly?" he asked when he'd finished.

"Yes, thank you, Mr. Rotherhithe."

He left and she settled back in the old, creaky leather chair, took a deep breath, and enjoyed the moment of peace and quiet. She thought how grateful she was to be working at the Institute, in such a beautifully appointed space. The eye-dazzler rug was spectacular, and she knew she'd never tire of looking at it. It was November and the field season was over, but she'd already started formulating plans for next year. Big plans, financed by the new field school endowment set up by Lucas Tappan. Next season's expedition would involve one of the most enigmatic locations in the Southwest. North of Abiquiu, in the Jemez Mountains, lay a spectacular Ancestral Pueblo ruin called Tsi-p'in-owinge, dating back to the 1300s. She had first hiked to Tsi-p'in as a child, when her father had taken her and Skip to see it. He had loved taking his two children around to remote ruins in New Mexico, far off the tourist trail. Tsi-p'in was one of the most impressive. It was built on a high mesa, surrounded by cliffs, with only a single point of access. Constructed of carved stone blocks, it had once risen four stories and contained at least two thousand rooms, with additional scores of cave dwellings hollowed into the cliffs below. There were thirteen kivas, in addition to one great kiva, carved into the stone bedrock of the mesa. The ruin had never been excavated, and only one survey had been done—and that one was inadequate, poorly conducted, and half a century old. Because it was so remote and inaccessible except by a difficult switchback trail on a steep mountain face, Tsi-p'in had been largely ignored by archaeologists.

The lone path to the citadel lay along a narrow ridge, across which the inhabitants had built no less than three massive stone walls with arrow ports, creating a maze-like pathway that invaders would have to thread even before reaching the massive outer walls of the city. In its day, Tsi-p'in was a most powerful and populous fortress. But there were many unsolved questions about it. First, why was the city built like a stronghold when there was no record of violence or warfare during the 1300s? What were they so afraid of that they built their city far, far above their irrigated fields, requiring difficult daily climbs to access? Were they under threat—or were they themselves the threat to everyone else in the region? Adding to the mystery, the city had been abruptly abandoned around 1475. It seemed all the citizens had just walked away, leaving everything behind. No lasting theory for this had ever been put forward.

Tsi-p'in-owinge was a place of many mysteries, Nora thought, and a meticulous, well-financed survey of the ruin—done without excavating or disturbing the site—would shed a great deal of light. The survey she'd proposed had already been permitted and provisionally staffed, and it would begin in late May, as soon as the mountains cleared of snow. Such expeditions were what she loved most about archaeology—getting out into the wild, away from cell phones and the internet, living in a tent and spending each day uncovering more of the past in all its complexity and fascination.

"Knock-knock?"

Nora's reverie was interrupted by a head poking around the door, covered by a mop of hair and a cowlick. "Hey, Sis."

It was her brother, Skip. He had recently taken a position at the Institute as a collections manager. Or rather, retaken the position, after a stint working for Tappan on a special project.

"Come to see my new office?" she asked.

"Yeah." He eased in. "Cute. Cozy." Without asking, he took a seat in the chair opposite her desk, leaned back, and put his feet up. "I could get used to this."

"Off, Brother."

He dropped his feet. "Has Lucas seen it yet?"

"No. He's in Massachusetts, dealing with the Marblehead kelp-huggers."

"Kelp-huggers?"

"You know, the environmentalists who want to break our addiction to fossil fuels—"

"What's wrong with that?" Skip interrupted.

"*Nothing's* wrong with that. Just the opposite. Except now that clean energy is being proposed offshore, where they'll see it, they're going all NIMBY." Tappan was trying to build a windfarm in the Atlantic, fifteen miles from Marblehead and its million-dollar seaside homes, and it was not getting off to a good start.

Skip laughed. "Kelp-huggers. That's a good one. When's he coming back?"

"A couple of weeks, I hope. But you never know—he's got one hearing after another, and those people can talk."

"Yeah, well, Tappan's a pretty good talker himself." Skip placed his hands on the arms of the chair and rose. "Got to get back to work, but I just wanted to check out the new digs. See you for supper."

The door closed and silence descended once more. Nora rested another moment, then roused herself: she had to get back to work as well. She went to the filing cabinet that had just been moved in from her old office, opened the drawer labeled "Tsi-p'in-owinge," and removed a rolled-up piece of paper. She flattened it on her desk and examined it. It was a rough map she'd made herself of a curious site on a mesa next to the ruins. It was a circle of stones, around what were four taller standing stones, since toppled, that she believed might have been designed to mark the solstices. She'd taken compass readings and measurements, and now she was trying to determine whether the tall stones, if raised again, might prove her theory true.

Her phone rang. She was tempted to ignore it, but then she glanced over and saw it was Corrie Swanson, calling on her office phone.

"Corrie, how are you?"

"Good! All good! And you?"

She sounded just a little too chipper. "Just settling into my new office. Come by sometime and take a look."

"I will. Sooner than you think, perhaps." Her voice trailed off.

Nora sighed. "I notice you're calling from your FBI number, so you might as well cut to the chase."

Corrie laughed. "Okay. Two prehistoric burials in a cave in the Manzano Mountains. Vandalized. We need a quick survey to assess the damage and report to Isleta Pueblo, the NAGPRA custodians. You won't need to excavate the burials, just do a quick survey. It's a day's work—promise."

Nora smiled despite herself. *A day's work*—Corrie's favorite line. It was what she'd said last year, when she discovered a seventy-five-year-old mummified body in a ghost town. A day's work that ended up taking weeks and almost got them killed.

"Vandalized how?"

"A couple of drunk frat boys were joyriding in the mountains yesterday evening, crashed their car, then took refuge in a cave where there were human remains and some petroglyphs. And naturally trashed the place."

Nora thought a moment. "I've got a terrific field archaeologist, someone who just joined the department, PhD from UNM. His name is Stan Morrison. Lot of energy and smarts. He'd be perfect for this."

This offer was greeted with a silence. After a moment, Corrie said, "What about you?"

Subtlety was not one of Corrie Swanson's strong points. "Stan could really use the experience."

"Well," said Corrie, "here's my situation. I've got a new mentor who's replaced Agent Morwood." There was a brief silence. "The thing is, I want to bring in a top person to make a good impression— and that person would be you."

Nora understood immediately. A day's work— she could spare the time to help out a friend. "Okay. I'll do it."

"Thank you, Nora! By all means bring Stan, too. I'm emailing you a bunch of photos now."

Her computer started dinging as the photos came in: Corrie must have had them all lined up and ready to go. Nora began scrolling through them as Corrie described the site and its location.

"Hold it," Nora said. A photograph showing the broken rim of a pot was now on her screen, and she increased the magnification. "That broken pot—did you uncover more of it?"

"No. Those photos show the site as we left it. Why?"

"I think that's a golden micaceous pot."

"Is that important?"

"Golden micaceous pottery happens to be one of my specialties, and it's never been found in this area—only in Utah. It's made of clay with countless tiny pieces of mica in it that are unaffected by the firing process and give it a golden sheen. When do you want me to come out?"

"Um, tomorrow morning? We can't sign off on the evidence gathering until you do your thing, so the sooner the better."

"Tomorrow is no problem. How shall we meet?"

"Come by the Albuquerque Field Office at nine, and we'll go from there."

"Will do."

Nora hung up the phone. Golden micaceous pottery, found so far south of its usual range? This could get interesting, she thought.

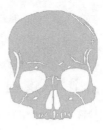

5

CORRIE LOOKED DOWN at the two ID sheets in front of her, then up at the two young men awkwardly taking seats opposite her and Agent Sharp at the metal table bolted into the floor. They were inside one of the interview rooms at the Albuquerque FO, a spare cinderblock cell painted gray. The ID sheets had been put together in haste and neither had pictures.

"Brandon Purdue and Michael Kottke?" Corrie asked. "Which is which?"

"Brandon," said one of the young men, raising his finger.

"Kottke," said the other.

"I'm Special Agent Swanson, and this is Special Agent Sharp."

The pair fidgeted in their seats, looking nervous.

She took a moment to appraise the two. Even though they had obviously showered and changed their clothes, and it was three in the afternoon, they still looked brutally hungover. Brandon had light brown hair cut short, thin lips, barely of shaving age—a follower for sure. Mike was the alpha male here: black curly hair, beefy, with bloodshot eyes and no doubt a pounding headache to accompany them. According to the ID sheets they were both nineteen. They looked scared—as well they should be. Prior to the introduction, Corrie had been undecided as to what tack to take—sympathetic and understanding, or hard-ass scary bitch. But as she looked at them, she realized they were intimidated enough and pushing things might cause them to shut down, lawyer up, or—worse—get their parents in. It was still too early to know if they'd committed a serious crime or not. Much would depend on Nora's examination of the burials—if they'd been deliberately vandalized and dug up, or accidentally disturbed.

She glanced at Sharp. He looked sleepy as ever, his eyes half-lidded.

"All right, gentlemen," she said. "We're recording this interview. Do you understand you're here voluntarily to answer questions, and that you've waived the right to an attorney?"

They agreed.

"We're just gathering information at this point."

"Right," said Kottke. "We're okay. We didn't do anything wrong."

Corrie nodded. "So what happened? Start with the road accident."

Kottke looked at Purdue. "Well, we were driving around the national forest, and I guess we took a wrong turn."

"Were you drinking?"

A silence. "No."

A lie, but Corrie let it go.

"So anyway, we took a wrong turn and skidded off the road into a ditch. There was no cell reception up there and it was after sunset, so we decided to look for shelter."

"And how did you find the cave?"

"It was totally by accident. When it started to snow, we went downhill looking for an overhanging rock or someplace. We came to a ravine, saw the cave, climbed up, lit a fire."

"And then you began drinking?"

"We had some rum to help warm us up."

"Marijuana?"

"It's not illegal. I've got a medical card."

"Please just answer the question. We're not going to charge you with possession. Were you both smoking marijuana?"

"Yeah."

"What else did you do?"

"Nothing."

Corrie turned to Purdue. "Is this also your recollection?"

"Yes."

"How did the petroglyphs in the back of the cave come to be damaged?"

The two young men looked at each other. "No idea," said Kottke.

"Did you throw rocks at them?"

"I don't remember."

Corrie let a beat pass while they did some more fidgeting. Then she said, "I told you we're not going to charge you with possession. But keep in mind, it's a felony to lie to the FBI. That includes claiming you don't remember something when in fact you do. Now: Would you care to strain a little harder to remember?"

They stared back with pale, frightened faces. If it hadn't been for the damage she'd seen in the cave, she might have felt sorry for them.

"Maybe we did throw some rocks," Kottke said. "We got pretty messed up by the end of the night."

"Did you trigger a cave-in?"

"No cave-in, not at all, it was . . . just some rocks that fell from the ceiling."

Corrie paused briefly. "You found the cave, got

drunk, got stoned, then began throwing rocks at the petroglyphs."

"I guess," said Purdue. "But I didn't know they were anything important—I just thought they were graffiti someone had left in the cave."

"How far back into the cave did you go?"

"Not beyond that point where the rocks fell. It didn't look safe."

"How did you discover the burial?"

At this question, both young men grimaced involuntarily.

"That was Brandon," said Kottke. "I was sleeping."

She turned. "Brandon?"

"I was trying to go to sleep and this thing was poking me in the back. I looked, and it was the skull."

"And then?"

"I freaked out. I moved to the side of the cave and…well, I guess I must have passed out. Next thing it was morning."

"So you didn't try to dig it up?"

"No. No, I didn't. I didn't want anything to do with it."

"And your friend? He didn't disturb it?"

"He was passed out, too."

"Was he the one who vomited?"

Brandon looked at his friend. "Yeah."

Corrie nodded. She was glad it was going to be up to the sheriff whether to charge these kids. She believed what they said about not intentionally disturbing the burial, which would have been a class C felony. Vandalizing the petroglyphs—she wasn't sure what the statute on that was. It probably fell under ARPA, the Archaeological Resources Protection Act.

She turned. "Agent Sharp, any questions?"

"Thank you, Agent Swanson." He glanced over at the two and let a silence settle in before speaking. "Mr. Kottke, why did you deface those petroglyphs?"

"I don't know. Like Brandon said, I didn't know what they were. You've got to understand, we were pretty drunk."

"You didn't know they were petroglyphs?"

"I didn't, sir. They didn't look old. I guess...I mean, I know that we weren't thinking very clearly."

"No more questions," said Sharp after another pause.

Corrie said, "Thank you, gentlemen, you're excused."

Neither one rose. "What's going to happen to us?" Kottke asked. "Are we in trouble?"

"We'll turn this information over to the Torrance County Sheriff's Department. What happens next is in the hands of the sheriff's department and National Forest Law Enforcement."

Now the boys stood up and shuffled out, still pale and scared.

When they were gone, Agent Sharp turned to Corrie. "I don't know about you, but I've become distinctly aware we both missed lunch. Would you like to head down to the cafeteria for coffee and a snack?"

Corrie was hungry herself—and she could hardly say no. "Yes. Of course."

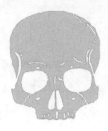

6

Thoughts?" Sharp asked as they sat down for coffee, Corrie with a donut, Sharp with an egg salad sandwich.

"I think we've dotted the i's and crossed the t's," Corrie said, "and now we can let the capable Sheriff Hawley take over."

Sharp chuckled. "Do you see any criminal culpability in their conduct?"

"Hard to say. Deliberately disturbing the burial might have been a felony, but I believe them when they say they didn't mess with it. I bet if any digging was done, it was by Sheriff Hawley or his deputy. There might be a criminal mischief charge for damaging federal property, but I think it's a stretch—especially with their asserting they thought the petroglyphs were graffiti."

Sharp nodded. "I agree on all points. You've done a responsible and thorough job, Agent Swanson."

"Thank you." It was funny—Sharp was a true enigma, but already she felt herself growing more at ease in his presence, less worried about her every move. It had taken a lot longer with Morwood.

Sharp said nothing more until he'd finished his sandwich. Then he took a sip of coffee and turned toward her. "When I first heard about the remains in the cave, I thought perhaps we'd finally discovered a few more Dead Mountain victims."

Corrie stared at him. "Dead Mountain?"

"You don't know what I'm talking about."

"No." Dead Mountain...It rang a bell somewhere in the back of her mind, but beyond that only a blank.

"Curious," Sharp said, looking at her appraisingly. "Next to the Roswell Incident—which I know you're all too familiar with—it's perhaps the biggest campfire legend in New Mexico."

"What was it?"

"Fifteen years ago, nine grad students from the New Mexico Institute of Technology disappeared up in the Manzanos. Six bodies were found, but three are still missing." Sharp leaned back in his chair. "You've really never heard of Dead Mountain?"

"Fifteen years ago I was in a Kansas high school," Corrie said, "and not really keeping up with the news of the day." She was pleased she'd been able to put this out there without sounding defensive. Not only had she been ignoring the news at the time, but she'd been dealing with an absent father and an alcoholic and abusive mother, spending her time stealing paperback books from the travel center on the interstate, avoiding the sheriff, and dreaming of escaping the hellhole that was Medicine Creek, Kansas.

"That's what comes of not fraternizing with your fellow agents," said Sharp. "It's quite a story. I'd just arrived at the Albuquerque FO in 2008 when it happened. I didn't work on the case directly, but it consumed the office for months. It's never been solved—still officially open."

Sharp didn't seem exactly the fraternal type himself, but Corrie was surprised he knew this personal detail. Beyond that, however, she found herself growing intrigued. "Where is this Dead Mountain?"

"There isn't an actual Dead Mountain in the Manzanos—it's just the name the media gave the case."

"So what happened?"

Sharp glanced at his watch. "You have a few minutes?"

"Yes, if you do." Sharp, despite his mellow demeanor, enjoyed telling stories—or, more likely, wanted her to hear this one.

Sharp leaned back in his chair, sipped his coffee, and began to tell the story in much the same manner as a camp counselor might spin a ghost story around a campfire, a faint, laconic smile playing on his face.

"The year was 2008," he began. "Nine grad students in the engineering department at the New Mexico Institute of Technology took a Hallowe'en backpacking trip into the Manzano Mountains. They left on October 27 and planned to hike south to north following the spine of the mountains. Their return date was set for November 3. They chose that high-country route because, as far as anyone could tell, no one had done it before. The students belonged to an outdoor hiking and wilderness club at the university, and they were all highly experienced backpackers and mountaineers. They were well aware that in late October, sudden snowstorms or other extreme weather might occur at that altitude—and they came prepared. There was no cell coverage anywhere in the Manzanos back then, or even today, and they knew they'd be cut off during the week they'd be gone.

"They were to report in to the head of the wilderness club on their return, but November 3 came and went without a word. There had been a snowstorm in the Manzanos on Hallowe'en into Hallowe'en night, so it was initially assumed they'd gotten snowed in and delayed. Nobody was particularly worried, because they'd all had a great deal of snow-camping experience. But by the afternoon on November 4, that began to change. The mother of one of the campers started to raise hell, the other families got into the act, and search and rescue parties were organized. The New Mexico State Police coordinated all search and rescue operations in the state, and on November 5 they put two birds in the air to survey the high Manzano ridges. The hiking club at the university also put together a search.

"On November 6, one of the helicopters spied the hikers' tent, partly buried in snow. They sent a ground team up there in snowmobiles."

Here Sharp paused to take another sip of coffee.

"What did they find?" Corrie asked after a moment.

"Something utterly bizarre." He looked at his empty cup. "Want a refill?"

"No. No."

"I'll be right back."

Corrie watched Sharp as he casually walked over to the coffee machine. She couldn't be sure, but it seemed he'd staged this interruption deliberately.

"The tent had been set up on one of the highest ridges in the Manzanos," he said as he sat down again. "Above the tree line, just below the summit of Shaggy Peak. The tent had been dug into the snow in the wind shadow of the peak. The snowstorm struck around noon on October 31, and the snow had accumulated significantly by the time they camped.

"The tent was only partially collapsed from the snow. It was of a large backpacking design and weighed around thirty pounds, with a zippered front and back door. The snowshoes of the entire party were found neatly stacked next to the tent. Photographs show the front door was unzipped and open. The back door was not. There was no sign of the nine hikers.

"When the rescue party looked inside, they found everything to be in good order. Hiking boots were lined up inside the vestibule of the front door. Packs were laid out along one side. Sleeping bags were all unrolled on their mats. A small stove stood in the vestibule, apparently left on, a pot of burned food upon it. Plates of half-eaten food were found abandoned mid-meal. A later inventory discovered that only two things of importance were missing. The first was a camera and film carried by one of the hikers, who was an avid photographer and the person assigned to chronicling the trip. The second was the group's expedition journal."

Sharp paused to sip his coffee. Corrie realized she was still holding a small arc of her donut, and quickly popped it in her mouth.

"I mentioned that the front of the tent was unzipped and open. However, the side of the tent had been slashed open—slashes that went through both the inner tent and the fly. A careful examination showed they had been made from the inside. Further investigation revealed footprints leading away from the tent. The prints made it clear that most of the hikers were barefoot or wearing socks. One seemed to be wearing both boots; another had on a single boot with a sock on the other foot; a few had on the felt footwear known as valenkis."

Sharp looked down at his cup. "Interesting, don't you think?"

"I'll say. Sounds crazy. Did an investigation determine the temperature and conditions outside when the students left the tent?"

"It was ten degrees below zero, the blizzard was at its height, and the wind was gusting to forty to fifty miles an hour."

"Going out in that weather barefoot would be suicide."

"It would be. And it was."

"Why did they do it?"

"An excellent question. Why do you think?"

As Corrie looked at Sharp—head still down, watching the coffee swirl languidly in his cup—she suddenly realized he had turned this into a forensic challenge of sorts. The story was riveting, and Sharp was a skillful storyteller.

"The front door of the tent was unzipped, but they nevertheless cut their way out the side?"

Sharp nodded.

"The front entrance must have been blocked— by someone or something. What about prints?"

"The search and rescue team trampled all around the tent before anyone had the sense to rope it off and take photos. But beyond the immediate area, prints made it clear that the hikers had run down-hill into a deep thicket of small fir trees about a mile from the tent, in the center of which was a tall cedar. Beneath the cedar they found the remains of a fire, and around this fire were three of the hikers— frozen solid. In addition to lacking boots, they were wearing only underwear and T-shirts. All three had burns on their legs and feet—one had the right side of his head scorched and his hair singed. Searchers also noticed there were freshly broken branches on the trunk of the cedar, about ten feet from the ground. On closer examination they found pieces of human skin scraped on the bark."

"Someone had climbed it to break branches off for firewood," said Corrie.

"So it would seem. In any case, shortly thereafter, a searcher managed to find a female body about a quarter mile beyond the campfire, heading along the northward ridge. The autopsy showed she had died of exposure and was wearing clothes cut from one of the other bodies.

"In any case, winter had already closed in pretty fiercely by then, and though the search continued by air, with dogs, and by ski and snowmobile, no more bodies were found. When it became obvious nobody could have survived, the search was suspended until spring.

"It resumed in early May 2009. It had been a harsh winter, and there was still a lot of snow in the mountains.

"Then, in a ravine covered with snow about two miles beyond the campsite, another discovery was made: two more bodies, slightly better dressed than the others, but still lacking boots. The eyes of both victims and the tongue of one were missing. An autopsy indicated both bodies had been crushed so badly that, in one case, bone fragments from the chest cavity had pierced the heart. Despite the terrible trauma the bodies had suffered, there were—oddly enough—no external wounds."

Sharp finished his coffee, placed the cup back in its saucer.

"My God," Corrie breathed. "That sounds almost unbelievable."

"It gets better. Someone, somewhere, requested that the clothing of the victims be tested for radiation. The tests showed low levels of contamination from plutonium, uranium, and tritium, among other radioactive isotopes. None of these isotopes are natural—in other words, they must have come from a man-made source such as a reactor or nuclear weapon."

"Could that account for the burn marks on the bodies?"

"No. As I'm sure you know, radiation burns present very differently from normal burns. The burns on these bodies were caused by normal heat and included charring."

Corrie nodded as she digested this. "So the State Police conducted the initial search and rescue operations?"

"Yes—until it seemed obvious they were dealing with a criminal case. Then the FBI got involved."

"Who was the agent in charge?"

"Robertson Gold."

"What did he say about ordering those radiation tests? That's way outside the normal evidence protocols."

Sharp looked at her from beneath hooded eyes. "Another excellent question, Agent Swanson. Gold claimed he hadn't asked for the tests to be done, and he had no idea who sent the samples off for testing. After the results came back, they were promptly classified—removed from the case files—so nobody was able to review them further."

Corrie shook her head. "No idea what government agency requested the tests?"

"If an agency made such a request, it was redacted from the files even before they were classified."

"Is Gold still alive?" she asked.

"Yes. Long retired. Lives in Silver City."

Corrie thought a moment. "What about the other three victims?"

"The other three victims were never found."

"And you thought the remains in the cave might have been one of them?"

"Under the circumstances—had you known your local history—wouldn't you?"

"I think so." She remembered the short exchange between Garcia and Sharp during their preliminary briefing—and Sharp's expression of disappointment when she'd come down from the cave.

"In any case, the evidence of blunt force trauma was enough to open a homicide investigation on federal land, which is why it became an FBI case, taking over from the State Police and forming a task force with the local sheriff's department—but neither suspect nor motive could ever be established. It was assumed one of the three missing victims had been carrying the camera and journal, which if found might go a long way toward solving the mystery. But diligent searching never turned up camera, journal, or bodies."

"Is the cave we visited near where the tent was found?" Corrie asked.

Sharp plucked a napkin from the holder, took out a pen, and began to draw. He took his time, and when he reversed the napkin to show it to Corrie, she saw a remarkably professional-looking sketch of a line of mountain peaks, complete with crosshatching and stippling for added clarity.

"This is a north-south representation of the Manzano mountain range," he said. "Here is the approximate location of the tent. There's a memorial marker there now, just below Shaggy Peak. And here—" he made a mark to the north— "is where the first three bodies were found. The fourth body was here, the fifth and sixth here. The distance from the tent to the ravine where the last two bodies were found is roughly two miles."

Corrie watched the point of the pen move over the sketch. "A straight line, going north."

"Exactly. And the cave is here, also more or less in that same line: another mile north of the ravine." They both stared at the sketch a moment longer. Then Sharp crumpled the napkin and placed it in his empty cup. "So I was hoping that maybe—just maybe—those bodies in the cave would be two of the missing victims."

Corrie pondered this. It was indeed a crazy story—so unusual she was surprised she hadn't heard it before. "Based on the evidence you've described, I would guess something appeared that so terrified the hikers they slashed their way out the side of the tent and fled to certain death in the storm rather than confront it."

"That's what almost everyone assumed. Some argued it might have been a very large bear. Others, of course, claimed a Yeti, or aliens. The photos and scientific reports are in the file, if you're interested."

"In the file? Aren't they on somebody's desk?"

This time, Sharp's smile was a little different. "Not anymore. They're just sitting in cold case storage, waiting for more evidence to turn up."

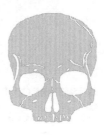

7

THE BLACK TAHOE carrying Corrie, Agent Sharp, Nora, and her assistant Stan eased around the now-ineffectual Forest Service berm and back onto the dirt road, drove down it a brief distance, then pulled off to the side. The snow from two nights ago had already started to melt, and the road was a muddy mess. Having shown her the route the day before, Sharp let Corrie drive today, apparently preferring to ride shotgun. That was unlike her previous mentor, Morwood. But maybe that had just been his style, and he'd preferred driving himself in that confiscated candy-apple-red pickup.

They all got out, Nora and her assistant removing their tools, backpacks, and equipment. Stan was an eager-beaver type, nerdy in a good way, clearly thrilled to be part of the team. Even though he'd recently completed graduate school, he looked about sixteen. Corrie reminded herself that she, too, looked young for her age, and this was something she had to push back against all the time.

She was disappointed to see a Torrance County sheriff's vehicle also parked at the turnoff. She hoped it wouldn't be Hawley at the cave.

Nora and Stan were soon kitted up, and the four of them began hiking down the slope along the muddy trail formed from the comings and goings of the past twenty-four hours. After a quarter of a mile the ravine came into view, followed by the cave and ladder. The yellow crime scene tape was still in place, and two Torrance County deputies were there: Baca and another man, seated on folding chairs outside the tape at the bottom of the ravine. The other guy was smoking.

They jumped up. "Hello, Agent Swanson," Baca said. "Agent Sharp."

"Thanks for watching the site." Corrie introduced the two specialists. Since the site had now been forensically processed, there was no need to wear monkey suits. Corrie led the way up the ladder, Nora and Stan following with their gear.

"I think I'll stay down here," said Sharp. "Don't want to crowd your work."

Once in the cave, Nora made a beeline for the two exposed skulls. She and Stan began taking photographs and examining the area as Corrie watched.

Nora was clearly excited. She leaned over and took several close-up photos of the exposed pot.

"What a tragedy," she said.

"Was that pot broken by the vandals or already broken?" Corrie asked.

"This just happened, unfortunately. These broken edges are very fresh." She stepped back. "This pot is rather interesting. Years ago, I led an expedition in Utah that uncovered a large cache of these micaceous pots. I believe they were at the heart of the myth of Quivira: the fabled lost city of gold. The Spanish conquistadors carried samples of gold to show the Indians, and they asked where more of it could be found. The Indians talked all about pots and plates made of gold—but they turned out to be not of gold, but this micaceous pottery. A distinction lost in translation, apparently."

"That's fascinating," said Corrie. "I'd like to hear more about that expedition."

At this, Nora's face momentarily clouded. "That's when I met my late husband, Bill. I'll tell you the story sometime, although it might take a few drinks."

"I'd love to hear it," Corrie said. "Or not. Up to you."

Nora turned her attention back to the two skulls and assorted scatterings of bones. She and Stan continued brushing away sand from the burial site and clearing the area. Then Nora took out a large drawing pad from her backpack and opened it up. Grabbing a pencil and tape measure, she began to map the site by hand, jotting down various distances on her sketch.

After a while, she glanced over at Corrie. "Let's have a look at those petroglyphs," she said, pointing to the back of the cave. Corrie followed while Morrison continued to work on the burials, humming to himself under his breath.

"What a shame," Nora said, running her finger over the gouges and scratches. "I hope you throw the book at those assholes."

"That's up to the sheriff."

Nora took a suite of photographs. "Is there anything farther back in the cave?" she asked. "I'd be surprised if there weren't more burials back there."

"Nobody's been back there, as far as I know—at least not beyond where those rocks fell from the ceiling."

"We'll take a look in a moment."

Corrie shone her light beyond the pile of fallen rocks and into the space behind. The cave was made of rough lava that had filled with sand on the bottom, but the roof was still fractured and riddled with cracks. Although the ceiling sloped down, the cave itself seemed to go back farther than she'd originally assumed. She could get a better view if she moved aside a couple of the fallen stones. She looked back at Nora, busy again with the petroglyphs, and Morrison, stabilizing the burials. With both hands she grasped a fallen rock and rolled it out of the way, then another, and then crouched, shining her light into the cavity she'd just exposed.

"Got another body back here," she said to Nora.

Nora looked over sharply. "Just as I thought. Could you please back away? It's vital that we don't disturb any more prehistoric burials—the Isleta people will decide what to do with the remains."

"I don't think the Isleta people are going to care much about this particular body."

"Why wouldn't they?"

"Because the foot of this one's rocking a North Face hiking boot."

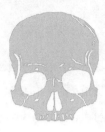

8

Corrie leaned out of the mouth of the cave. Sharp was chatting with the two deputies, getting along well.

"Agent Sharp?" she asked.

He glanced up.

"There's something you should see up here."

She waited while Sharp climbed the ladder and crawled into the cave entrance, then stood up. He looked at Nora and Stan Morrison, then at Corrie, his face expressionless. "Yes?"

"Back here." Corrie led Sharp to the rear of the cave. He stopped abruptly, staring down at the booted leg sticking out from underneath the rubble. The other foot was covered only in a felt bootie—a valenki. Corrie watched as his eyes widened.

"Holy mother of God," he breathed.

"Yeah," said Corrie. "Looks like we found one of…"

She didn't finish the sentence. She didn't need to.

Sharp nodded. A long silence ensued while he stared at it. And then he looked up. His surprised expression—the first she'd seen—slowly fell away, like ripples on a pond. He glanced once again at Corrie.

"It's still your case...for now, at least." He let the sentence hang in the air.

"Right." Corrie—who until this moment had been merely excited by the ramifications of the discovery—felt a sudden sense of panic, as if she'd been thrown into the deep end of the pool and ordered to swim. She looked at Nora and Stan Morrison. "Fortunately, we have two archaeologists already on site—we ought to make use of their expertise in excavating the body and any others that might come to light. And we need to get the Evidence Response Team back in here to process the rear section of the cave."

Sharp looked at her, face unreadable once again.

"Dr. Kelly," she asked, "are you able to do a little more work for us? I realize you're busy, but it would be a great help."

She found Nora looking back at her with a half-amused, half-exasperated face. "On the ride out, you mentioned Dead Mountain. You think this is one of the missing victims?"

"You know about the Dead Mountain case?" Corrie asked.

"Everyone in New Mexico knows about it."

Except me, thought Corrie.

Sharp spoke quietly into the silence that followed. "According to the footprints that were originally found, one of the hikers fled their tent wearing a boot on one foot and a bootie on the other. This corpse fits that description perfectly. It beggars belief this isn't a Dead Mountain victim—and there's a good chance the two others still missing are in the back of the cave as well."

"So," Corrie asked Nora, "would you consider expanding your work here?"

"Of course. This is an amazing discovery and I'd be grateful to be part of it."

"You can get the time off from the Institute?"

"I have no doubt they'll be happy to let me assist the FBI, pro bono—our field season is shut down for the winter. But it's going to be awkward with the Indian burials in here. We're almost done with them: we'll finish up and then cover them to make sure they aren't disturbed any further."

Corrie felt a surge of relief. She glanced at Sharp and thought she could now detect approval, or at least satisfaction, in his gaze.

"Thank you," said Corrie. "Tell us what you'll need to protect the burials."

"Some sheets of plywood; two-by-fours to build a structure that will keep the plywood off the ground;

stakes; caution tape. I'll do some more measuring and get you a detailed list."

"We'll see that you get everything you need," Sharp assured her.

"Once we've built a cover of sorts to protect the burials, Stan and I will begin working on the body in the back of the cave. Sound like a plan?"

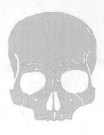

9

By one, Nora Kelly had finished putting the last screw into the pitched roof structure she and Stan had built over the Native American burials, with materials brought to them in a second FBI Tahoe. Now she was looking down at the two legs sticking out from underneath the rubble: one with a boot, one without. She remembered vividly fifteen years ago, when the Dead Mountain disaster had occurred. She was an assistant curator at the Institute—her first paying job out of graduate school. It had been a huge deal: the disappearance of the hikers, the search, the discovery of the tent and the first three frozen bodies— and then the bizarre developments in the months that followed as additional bodies were found, each circumstance seemingly stranger than the last. Since then, dozens of theories had been advanced, some reasonable but most improbable or even preposterous. Russian spies, UFOs, a homicidal cult…the list went on and on, filling the vacuum left by the absence of real evidence. Until now.

She had moved the lights farther back in the cave and was contemplating the scene. The illumination revealed that the back of the cave went on another twenty feet or so before narrowing to a crack. There was a lot of rubble on the floor of the cave that could be hiding more corpses.

She would start with this one and take it from there. She knelt to take photographs and a few more measurements.

"I hate to say this," Corrie said, "but both of you are going to have to put on monkey suits before going any further."

It took some time to bring the protective suits and several body bags from the Tahoe. While Corrie and Agent Sharp stood well back by the cave opening, Nora and Morrison returned to the body sticking out from under the rubble.

"Let's shift some of these rocks," Nora said.

They got to work. Morrison was stronger than he looked, and as he began picking up rocks and placing them to one side, the rest of the body was gradually revealed. It was desiccated, nearly free of decay, and its clothing looked rummage-sale fresh, save for some chewing and nest-building by mice. The altitude and dry atmosphere were almost ideal conditions for preserving a body.

"Interesting," said Sharp, looking on from the mouth of the cave. "This victim appears to be more fully clothed than the ones found originally."

He was right: Nora noted the body was wearing a pair of snow pants, a down vest but no jacket, a woolen hat, no gloves. It lay on its stomach, arms tucked underneath, legs splayed, head turned to one side. It was a grim sight, the desiccation having drawn the lips back from the teeth and left the eye sockets empty, giving the corpse a grinning, Hallowe'en-like aspect. A faint smell of decay arose.

After about forty minutes the body was fully uncovered. Nora turned to Stan. "Could you please bring over a body bag?"

Stan quickly returned with the body bag, unzipped and open, which he and Nora laid out next to the corpse. Then she turned toward the mouth of the cave. "We're going to need four pairs of hands."

Nora lined Corrie and Agent Sharp up on either side of the corpse, showing them where to grasp. "On the count of three, we lift, rotate the body face up, and lay it down in the body bag. Gently."

Corrie slipped her hands under the body's hip and thigh, while Sharp took the shoulder and head.

"One, two, three, *lift*. Turn. Now: lower."

The body was surprisingly light, and the operation went perfectly—but it was followed immediately by a shocked silence. The body's two mummified hands were clutching a knife, buried to the hilt in its breast.

"What the hell?" Stan Morrison blurted out, stepping back in involuntary horror. "The guy stabbed himself to death!"

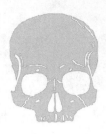

10

CORRIE STARED AT the body. The face was frozen in a rictus of pain and suffering, its skin drawn so tight it had cracked in several places, the facial bones coming through. The eyes were dark hollows. It was hard to tell what he might have looked like in life, but her experience with forensic facial reconstruction helped her form a mental picture: a narrow, handsome face, longish hair, very white teeth. Tall, over six feet.

"Do you know which victim this is?" she asked Sharp.

"I'm fairly confident it's Paul Tolland. He was, ah, six foot two, brown hair." A pause. "I'm sure it's him, in fact."

"Any idea why he might have stabbed himself like that? It's a hell of a way to commit suicide."

"Why is everyone assuming it's suicide?" Sharp asked.

Corrie thought about that. "I guess someone else could have stabbed him in the chest, and he died trying to pull the knife out."

"That scenario is just as likely."

Corrie nodded. "Nora, with your okay, let's get this body out of the cave and into the back of the Tahoe before we proceed further. As I mentioned, we'll need to get the ERT back here, but in the meantime Dr. Kelly should probably look for more bodies."

Sharp nodded.

Corrie zipped up the body bag. Sharp took one handle and she took the other, then they lifted it. The corpse crackled as they carried the body bag to the mouth of the cave, then lowered it gently. After reaching the bottom of the ladder—and the astonished deputies—they carried it back up to the Tahoe and placed it in the rear. By the time they returned to the cave, they found Nora and Stan Morrison in the back waiting for them.

"There's another body," Nora said. "Also recent."

Corrie nodded. "Could you please excavate it? I want to make sure we've thoroughly searched this cave for bodies before we leave."

"It's over here," said Nora.

They had to get down on their hands and knees to reach a spot where Morrison had cleared more of the small cave-in. Wedged into the narrow passageway, the second body came into view—a body that, it appeared, had wriggled deeper into the cave, perhaps in hopes of finding better shelter. It too was dressed in outdoor clothing: a down jacket, snow pants, and boots—this time on both feet. It also wore a warm woolen hat. Corrie speculated that these two individuals had been able to make it farther from their tent because they were more warmly dressed. But why were they traveling north at all? Were they looking for something? Or escaping something? Why hadn't they gone west, toward a lower altitude? The discovery only seemed to deepen the mystery.

Sharp played his light over the corpse's face. The body was lying on its side, hands drawn up to its chest, knees flexed almost to a fetal position. It had a thick black beard and a mouth gaping wide as if screaming. Corrie knew that could be misleading— in death, the mandible often fell open and remained that way.

"That's Gordy Wright," said Sharp.

It was a tight spot to work, and Nora had to lie on her side, moving stones and brushing away sand and gravel near the head, while Stan Morrison worked at the far end. In half an hour the body was free.

"We're going to have to slide it out," said Nora. "It's wedged in pretty tight." She grasped the jacket and Stan a pant leg, and they carefully eased the corpse out of the slot. Corrie brought over another body bag, and the four of them put it in.

"Are there any more back there?" Corrie asked, almost hopefully.

"No," said Nora. "It's clear."

Corrie glanced at Sharp. "I guess we still have a body missing."

"I believe you're right about that."

"I'd also guess this means the FBI is back in the game."

"I *know* you're right about that." And Corrie could detect a definite gleam of interest behind the sleepy eyelids of Agent Sharp.

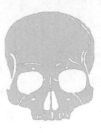

11

Corrie decided to ride with the body bags in the ERT van back to the Albuquerque FO. The FO's forensic lab director had recently retired in disgrace, and the job was still open—which meant there was no one at the lab Corrie trusted to receive and process the two bodies. She'd do the job herself. Sharp had said he would join her later.

The ride out of the mountains was bumpy, jostling the cadavers, which occasionally emitted dry, crackling protests. Corrie hoped they weren't falling apart. The cadavers were husks, as fragile as eggshells. When the van finally reached a paved road, she breathed a sigh of relief.

Two hours later, the ERT van pulled up at the rear entrance of the FO. The head ERT guy, Nate Findlay, came around to the back and flung the doors open. With his red beard and long hair, he looked more like a Viking marauder than an FBI crime scene technician.

"Sorry about the rough trip," he said. "Stiffs make it okay?"

"They complained about riding in coach."

He laughed. "Just tell us where to take 'em, Agent Swanson."

"To the forensic lab," she said, as she climbed out of the back and stood aside while the team rolled out the gurneys with the body bags, unfolded the wheels, and pushed them into the building. With Corrie following, the ERT guys cracked more corpse jokes as they trundled the gurneys along, wheels squeaking. There was a jocular, almost festive atmosphere among the team—this case was a big deal, and everyone knew it.

They came to the double doors leading into the lab vestibule, and Corrie unlocked them with her key card. The laboratory and surrounding area had been rebuilt after a fire four months earlier, transforming it from a shabby, rather outdated space into a state-of-the-art forensic lab, with an adjacent morgue, two operating rooms for autopsies, and a brand-new biological evidence storage area.

"Where do we park them, Agent Swanson?" asked Findlay.

"Can you take them directly to OR 1, please?

Transfer them to the two empty gurneys under the lights. I'm going to start work on them right away."

"Gotcha, ma'am."

They wheeled them through and transferred each body bag onto a lab gurney. An evidence container holding items retrieved with the corpses was placed on an adjacent table.

"Anything else?" Findlay asked with a grin.

"I'll take it from here. Thanks, guys."

He bowed and they left, wheeling away their gurneys. The door shut and silence fell, leaving Corrie alone in the lab.

She exhaled, gazing at the two body bags, then glanced at the clock. Four PM. This was going to be a big job, and she'd better get started. She wished she had someone experienced to work with, but the lab director position hadn't been filled yet. She could call on Nate if needed.

She laid out the steps to follow in her mind. The remains had to be treated with the utmost dignity and respect, of course—but at the same time, her objective was to extract every possible morsel of evidence from them. The two goals—evidence extraction and dignity—were at odds, since the cadavers would need to be stripped, autopsied, and cut to pieces, then have the organs removed, toxicology tests done, and much else besides. By the end of the process, very little would remain intact. On top of that, the extreme desiccation of the cadavers would make everything more difficult.

Corrie had a degree in forensic anthropology, but her expertise was in the analysis of bones. These were not bones, but fully intact, naturally mummified bodies, and they would be engaging a medical examiner to conduct the autopsies. The Albuquerque FO did not have one on staff, and that meant calling in the state's Office of the Medical Investigator, located at the University of New Mexico. But before an OMI pathologist could be contacted, she had to do the preliminary examinations and then get the corpses legally identified.

She went to the wardrobe and suited up in full surgical scrubs, gown, gloves, mask, goggles, and haircover. And then, with a certain trepidation, she unzipped both body bags and gazed at the cadaver of the person Sharp had informally identified as Paul Tolland. She had removed the wallet from his back pocket while still in the cave, and it was now in the adjacent evidence container. While that seemed to check all the ID boxes, it wasn't sufficient for a legal identification. As she gazed at the mummified face illuminated under bright lights—withered cheeks, shrunken neck cords like a hangman's noose, dark craters where the eyes should be—she knew there would be no point in asking the family to identify it. Which meant either fingerprints or dental records would be necessary.

She sighed again. Part of her was curious as to what she might find, but another part shrank from the gruesomeness and invasion of bodily privacy. She reminded herself she'd seen more than her share of cadavers: time to suck it up and get to work.

She turned to a small A/V console and started the video. A red light went on in the camera mounted above her head. She walked around Tolland's gurney, commenting for the record on what she observed, focusing on the blade that was protruding from his breast. It sure looked like a fatal blow, having gone through the ribs and probably into the heart. The fingers clasped around the hilt of the knife looked like cheroots.

She took a step back. Wright was wearing boots on both feet, while Tolland had a boot on one foot and a valenki on the other. Wright was wearing gloves, but Tolland's hands were bare. As she turned to lean over Wright's corpse, she noted aloud that he had what appeared to be significant defensive knife wounds to his hands, cutting and slashing through the gloves. Tolland's bare hands, clutched around the knife that was buried in his own ribs, showed no defensive cuts. His body showed no obvious cuts or slashes either—just the one fatal blow.

What had happened here? Only one knife had

been recovered at the scene, and it was sticking out of Tolland's chest. Had a third party attacked and stabbed them to death? Or was it possible they'd fought with each other? If the latter, the defensive wounds on Wright implied Tolland had attacked him first, cut the hell out of him, before Wright managed to wrest the knife from Tolland and kill him with it. Of course, that assumed the attacker wasn't someone else. Corrie knew these questions couldn't be answered until the autopsies were completed, but she couldn't help pondering them as she walked around the cadavers, keeping her commentary strictly observational, without evaluation or speculation.

It took about thirty minutes to complete the anterior examination of the dressed corpses. Now she had to turn them over and describe the posteriors. The corpses were much lighter than they would have been if fresh, but they were still too heavy for her to properly roll over on her own. She'd have to get help. She was about to exit the lab to find Nate when the door opened, revealing Agent Sharp.

"Good afternoon, Agent Swanson. How are you faring?"

"Very well," she said. "I'm in the middle of the preliminary examinations."

"Interesting?"

"It certainly is, although it's too soon to draw conclusions. Would you, ah, care to watch?"

"That's why I'm here."

"In that case, sir, would you mind gowning up? And then I could really use your help flipping these cadavers."

"Flipping them?" He smiled at the terminology. "Gladly."

She watched him eye the two bodies for a moment, one eyebrow raised, then he turned to get gowned up. It didn't surprise her in the least that he wasn't squeamish.

He returned looking a lot less intimidating in the puffy white outfit than when dressed in one of his elegant suits. Above the mask, his eyes looked, as usual, sleepy yet disturbingly alert.

"Show me how to flip a cadaver," he said. "I can only assume no spatula is required."

"Put your hands underneath, here and here," she said. "We'll gently but firmly roll it over, then slide it back to the middle of the gurney."

He nodded, placing his gloved hands where indicated. The body of Tolland was rolled over neatly, the posterior side now revealed. Since it had been lying on its stomach all these years, the back showed less deterioration, with the exception of rodent and insect activity.

"Turn the next one?" Corrie asked.

"There's nothing I'd rather do."

This body was more complicated because Wright

was frozen in a semi-fetal position. But with Sharp's help, she managed to turn him over with minimal trouble.

"Thanks," Corrie said. "Now, I need to finish the preliminary examination under the watchful eye of *that*." She pointed at the camera. "Then after the examination, I'll have to cut off the clothing and do it all over again."

"What about legal identification of the remains?"

"Since we already more or less know who they are, I think dental X-rays are the best way to go. We could rehydrate the fingers, but because of their youth and lack of criminal records it's less likely their prints will be on file. As you can see—" she pointed to their mouths, gaping in profile— "they've both had dental work."

Sharp nodded. "And you'll X-ray them here?"

"Yes. We don't have a dental setup, per se, but the new X-ray machine will do just fine. We'll have to send the X-rays with the old dental records off to Quantico. Once we ID them, we'll have to inform the families." She hesitated. "Um, sir, I've not encountered that situation before. Who will do that?"

Sharp gazed at her. "The families will each be paid a courtesy visit."

"Yes, sir."

He didn't say who'd be making those visits. Perhaps he didn't yet know.

"And the autopsies?" he asked, intruding on her thoughts.

"We'll need to call in OMI."

Sharp nodded. "Very good. Please carry on."

He stood back while Corrie resumed her walk-around, once again describing what she observed. She was acutely aware of Sharp's presence, and his evident interest made her nervous. The Dead Mountain case would of course be revived, and she wondered who would be put in charge. Certainly not her, an agent still on supervised probation. Maybe not even Sharp: there might well be other agents in the field office with seniority, or relevant experience from the original case. Reflecting on the pressure and exposure that would come with the assignment, she felt only relief.

She completed the second round of observations, then went to the supply cabinet and removed a pair of cloth-cutting shears. Sharp remained silent as she cut off the clothing, one piece at a time in methodical fashion, using tongs to remove each piece and lay it on an evidence table, where she tagged them and slid them into envelopes, sealing and labeling each. The process was long, tiresome, and unpleasant. A smell rose more insistently from the corpses, faint yet vile. There was something, Corrie thought, about the smell of decaying human flesh that was infinitely worse than any rotting animal.

Slowly she undressed the bodies, exposing the skinny, shriveled limbs, the skin wrinkled and colored like an old apple, the genitals shrunken almost to nothing. A lot of blood had come from the wounds and, drying, had glued the clothing to the skin in areas. Corrie had to gently work the clothing away from the papery skin, trying not to pull up flesh along with the fabric. Five o'clock came and went. Finally, two and a half hours after she'd followed the gurneys into the lab, the cadavers had been fully inspected and were ready for X-rays.

She glanced up at the clock.

"Six thirty," said Sharp. "I would say it's quitting time—what do you think?"

"I think so, sir."

"Good. We can leave the building together. That should be a bracing experience."

"Bracing? What do you mean?"

Sharp just raised an eyebrow and smiled.

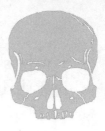

12

THEY WALKED TOGETHER through the deserted corridors of the building, most of the staff having already left for the evening. As they went through the lobby toward the smoked front doors, Corrie could hear a muffled sound, which grew louder as they approached, and through the doors she could see what looked like reporters with cameras and mikes.

"What's this?" Corrie said, halting.

"The media," said Sharp.

"How the hell did they get the story so fast?"

"It's their job. Police band radio, informants, pals in various nooks and crannies of law enforcement."

"Let's go out the rear entrance."

Sharp turned agreeably and began following her back through the lobby. After a dozen steps, he said, "Are you sure?"

She stopped. "What do you mean? We don't want to talk to them."

"We don't?"

She stared at Sharp. This was new. In her limited experience, the FBI hated to talk to the press and usually avoided them at all costs. Morwood certainly had drilled that into her. "Sir, are you suggesting we go out and engage the press?"

"What I'm suggesting is you weigh the pros and cons before making a knee-jerk decision. The media are not our enemies, and they serve an important role in our society...although, lest I sound like a PR flack, they can admittedly be a huge pain in the ass. We always have the opportunity for misdirection or even silence—where appropriate. But this is a high-profile case, with intense public interest. Might it not be worth showing our faces, saying a few words, and establishing that we're in charge and moving forward with all possible dispatch?"

Corrie considered this. The last thing she wanted was to run interference through a media scrimmage. What if she made a mistake, said something stupid, or stumbled over her words and looked like an idiot?

"We don't have anything yet to give them," she said, a little feebly.

"Perhaps not. But I'm not sure that's the impression we want to give the public at large. This case is still coming together...and you have an opportunity here." Sharp gave her a thin smile. "So what's it going to be, the hard-charging Eliot Ness or the secretive J. Edgar? I'll leave it up to you to decide— exit here or sneak out the back."

Sneak out the back. Corrie could sense he wanted her to deal with the press—perhaps to "toughen up her calluses," as a guitar-playing friend at the Academy liked to say. Sharp was proving as enigmatic as the Buddha. She found herself wishing for Morwood's straightforward guidance.

"Okay, let's go," she said, striding forward, pushing the crash bar, and opening the door. As they emerged into the portico, the crowd surged forward, boom mikes swinging toward her, video lights switching on, accompanied by the shouting of questions. Corrie was temporarily stunned by the activity, but took a deep breath and kept in mind that Sharp was beside her. They made eye contact and he gave her an amused smile, as if to say, *You've got this.*

She looked back at the crowd. On second glance, it didn't seem so big after all, or so overwhelming. She held up her hands.

"Ladies and gentlemen!" she said. "If you could please quiet down, I'll make a statement."

It was amazing how quickly silence fell.

"I'm Special Agent Corinne Swanson, one of the initial agents on the scene." She tried to muster a tone of gravitas. "First: I can't answer any of your questions right now, because it's far too early in the investigation for details. What I can say is that we're fairly confident we've found two more victims of the so-called Dead Mountain incident of 2008. We are currently in the identification and evidence-gathering phase, and I can assure you that the FBI are devoting all necessary resources into solving this case once and for all—after fifteen years."

She paused. The lights were dazzling, as was her growing realization that this was probably being broadcast live on TV. She ought to close it down. "My colleagues and I will supply you with additional information as soon as we are able. Thank you."

This was followed by an upswell of questions, but Corrie braced herself and moved forward, the crowd parting reluctantly to let them pass. Some of them continued following as they walked across the tarmac toward their cars, but they soon melted away, realizing they would get nothing more. By the time she reached her car door, she and Sharp were alone.

"You have to admit," he said in an undertone, "the walk from the back exit is longer."

Now that it was over, she could feel her heart pounding, the adrenaline still coursing through her veins. "Sir, did I establish that we're in charge and moving forward with all possible dispatch?"

This wasn't meant to be insubordinate, and a

lazy crinkling around Sharp's eyes made it clear he hadn't taken it that way. "You gave them just enough to pick over, while respectfully representing the Bureau. I'd say it was just about perfect. When you get home, I would recommend treating yourself to a stiff drink."

"I will. Thank you, sir."

Sharp went off to his own car while Corrie climbed into her vehicle, drove across the lot and out onto Leucking Park Avenue, her pounding heart settling back into a normal rhythm.

13

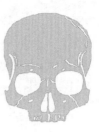

Nora Kelly parked her Jeep in the increasingly muddy area beside the Forest Service road. She noted that the Torrance County sheriff's Ford Explorer was also parked there, which meant Deputy Baca was still standing guard over the cave. The temperature had warmed to above freezing, and a chilly mist drifted among the black tree trunks.

A second Jeep pulled up alongside, carrying Darren Tenorio, a member of the Isleta Pueblo Tribal Council. They all got out, Nora and her assistant Stan Morrison hefting small daypacks with tools and equipment, Tenorio slinging a worn leather bag over his shoulder.

"It's this way," said Nora, indicating the now-established trail leading downslope.

Tenorio nodded. He was a middle-aged man with two long salt-and-pepper braids, wearing a down jacket over a traditional Pueblo shirt, jeans, and hiking boots.

They gingerly picked their way down the slippery terrain, finally arriving at the ravine. Nora was surprised to see someone she assumed must be Sheriff Hawley there with Deputy Baca, sitting in chairs, smoking and passing a thermos of coffee back and forth. All that was missing, she thought, was a beer bucket and a portable grill, and they'd have a tailgate party for a Jets game.

Hawley rose as they arrived. "What's this?" he asked, looking at Tenorio and Nora. "Who are you?"

"Dr. Nora Kelly, Santa Fe Archaeological Institute," she said. "I'm here at the request of the FBI."

"That so? You got ID?"

Nora was surprised by the challenging tone of his voice, but she reached into her back pocket for her wallet and fished out her SFAI identification card.

The sheriff took it and scrutinized it, grunted, and handed it back. He turned to Tenorio. "And you?"

Tenorio handed him his driver's license.

The sheriff took it. "What's the nature of your involvement, Mr. Tenorio?"

Tenorio said, his voice low and calm, "I'm here to inspect the two burials, which we believe are ancestral to Isleta Pueblo."

"And who authorized this?" the sheriff asked.

"I did," said Nora sharply. "With the approval of Special Agent Swanson, who asked me to liaise with Isleta Pueblo over these burials."

"Swanson?" he said, a note of disrespect in his voice.

Nora wondered what Hawley was doing there anyway: the cold, damp mountain was not exactly Monet's field of poppies. She had a sense something was up.

"This is an active crime scene," said the sheriff, returning the driver's license to Tenorio with insolent slowness. "Ten minutes."

Tenorio put away his license. "This is a burial ground of our ancestors, it is sacred to us, and for that reason I'll take all the time I need." He spoke in the softest voice, but there was an edge to the words.

Hawley stared at him. "I understand completely. Like I said: ten minutes."

Nora pulled out her cell phone to call Corrie but quickly realized there was no service. She looked at Hawley and—after the briefest of deliberations—decided to call his bluff. "Like Mr. Tenorio said: we're going up there for as long as necessary. If that's a problem, Sheriff, then go ahead and take us into custody." She stared at him. Why was he being so hostile?

Hawley stared back. "Don't think I won't make note of this defiance of a lawful order."

Nora was on the brink of responding but, since it seemed they were going to get their way, decided against it. She gestured toward the ladder. "After you, Mr. Tenorio."

They ascended the ladder, Nora following Tenorio, and Stan Morrison bringing up the rear. Nora switched on the lights, still set up within the cave's mouth, and the interior jumped into illumination. After a moment of silence, Tenorio said a prayer in Tiwa, removed a small ceramic vessel from his bag, took out a pinch of what was evidently corn pollen, and sprinkled it around while continuing to chant. Then he put it away and turned to Nora. "Show me what you found."

She and Morrison went over to the temporary wooden cover and removed it, exposing the two skulls, the fringe of blanket, and part of the micaceous pot. Tenorio came over and knelt. He removed a whisk from his leather bag and brushed away at the ancient blanket, gradually revealing more of the woven black border and a band of red. Then he cleared away the pot, eventually exposing an incised decoration along the side Nora recognized as a geometric lightning symbol.

Tenorio straightened up. "The remains," he said, "are certainly those of our ancestors. I want to thank you for notifying us so promptly and for your respect in protecting the site." He walked toward the back of the cave and examined the petroglyphs, running his hand over the gouges and scratches. "These are ours also. What a shame."

"They were vandalized by the two kids who found the cave. Hopefully, they'll be prosecuted. The FBI gathered plenty of evidence and turned it over to the sheriff—it's apparently his jurisdiction."

"The sheriff will not prosecute them." Tenorio shook his head. "This isn't the first time we've had dealings with Sheriff Hawley. He has no jurisdiction on Pueblo land, of course, but he's not exactly made himself a helpful presence outside our boundaries. Fortunately, only a small corner of our pueblo is in Torrance County."

Tenorio took out his cell phone. "I'll take some pictures now."

"Of course."

Tenorio took a suite of photos from a variety of angles, first of the burials and then the petroglyphs. Just as he was finishing up, Nora heard loud voices outside the cave. The metal ladder rattled, and then a head popped up in the cave entrance. "Hello in there! Incoming!"

Nora stared. The head rose, revealing a man holding a large video camera emblazoned with the logo of a local television station.

"What the hell is this?" Nora asked.

"Press!"

"Stop right there," said Nora, moving to block his view. "No one's allowed in."

"What do you mean? The sheriff granted us access." He began to shoulder the camera.

Now Tenorio took a step forward. "This is a sacred burial site. Please get down off that ladder."

"But this is a big story. The sheriff said—"

"The sheriff is not in charge here. I consider this now to be Isleta land."

"Come on, man, you know it's national forest land. I'm just going to get a shot from here—"

Tenorio strode over and covered the lens of the camera with his broad hands. "No, you're not. Please do not profane this place."

"Jesus! Get your hands off my camera!"

Now Nora could hear the sheriff's voice shouting from below, raised in anger. Suddenly she understood. He'd arranged for a photo op. Of course—it was November 3, with the election just a few days away. Stepping back to the cave's mouth, she could see the television crew down in the ravine with their equipment, staring back up at her. It was a small group—for now—but they had a second camera, and it was trained on her.

She took a deep breath. "Ladies and gentlemen, you probably heard Councilman Tenorio of Isleta Pueblo just explain this is a sacred burial ground. As an archaeologist employed by the federal government, I can confirm that. As much as we all believe in freedom of the press, you have no right to violate sacred ground."

"And *you* have no jurisdiction here!" Sheriff Hawley cried, and all the cameras swiveled to him. He collected himself and modulated his voice. "As sheriff of this county, I'm in charge. I've given permission to KWOW to cover an important news story, of legitimate interest to all citizens of Torrance County!"

Tenorio spoke down to them in a calm, almost gentle voice. "Do you really want to ride roughshod over my people's religious values and traditions...for the sake of a story? What will your viewers think?" He paused. "I know your camera is capturing my words, so—if you do decide to come in here and trample my ancestors' graves—will you at least have the decency to present our point of view as well?"

A silence fell as the camera crew below shifted uncomfortably. Finally, a woman—evidently the producer—spoke up. "Okay, everyone, pack up. No more shooting. And my apologies, Councilman, for this intrusion. We weren't—" she shot a glance at the sheriff— "fully informed as to the situation. We didn't know there were Indian burials here."

"Thank you," said Tenorio.

The sheriff said nothing as they began to pack up, but he was clearly speechless with rage. His deputy, Baca, looked exceedingly uncomfortable.

The cameraman went down the ladder, and Nora and Tenorio retreated into the cave. Tenorio gathered up his tools and put them into his leather bag. Then he turned to Nora. "The Tribal Council will take this matter up and make a decision whether to disinter and rebury these remains on Pueblo land or leave them here. In the meantime, thank you for protecting these remains. We might ask if you'd appear in front of the council to answer questions."

"Of course. I'm just sorry about all the disrespect."

Tenorio smiled. "We've had four hundred years to get used to it."

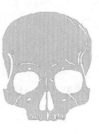

14

It was late afternoon when Corrie looked up to see Agent Sharp leaning his head into her cubicle: hair slightly tousled, the brown strands shining faintly in the fluorescent light.

"Come with me, please," he said.

She locked her computer screen, rose, and followed him into the corridor and along the wall of cubicles, until they arrived at the open door to Garcia's office. It looked crowded inside.

They walked past the secretary in the outer office. Sharp stepped aside to let her go first, then followed, closing the door behind him. And now Corrie saw something new in her experience: at least a dozen senior agents, standing in a half-circle before the big desk. Garcia sat behind it, playing with a pencil. She and Sharp took a place at the far end of the group, nearest the glass that normally looked onto the cube farm beyond. The horizontal blinds were closed, shuttering the view.

Garcia looked at each agent in turn, and it took many seconds before he got to Corrie. His gaze displayed no emotion, but it was penetrating and severe, and she tried not to wilt like an orchid under a heat lamp. Then he pushed back from the desk and addressed the group as a whole.

"None of you need to be told why I've called you in here," he said. "The Dead Mountain case, on ice for years, is as of right now active—and hot."

Nobody said a word. Corrie could feel tension rippling through the group.

"As you all know, the story has broken in the local press," Garcia said, looking for the briefest moment at Corrie. "I wish to hell we could have had a couple of extra days to work this quietly, but there we are. Our first priority is to formally identify the victims and notify next of kin. You can bet the national press will be here soon, and they yell a lot louder than the locals do."

Garcia looked around the group again. "I'm assigning Dead Mountain to Supervisory Special Agent Sharp." He paused to let this sink in, his gaze quelling any murmuring. "I know there are some among you who assisted on the original case under Agent Gold, now retired. Agent Sharp will undoubtedly call upon you for background." He paused again.

"I've got a warning for the young eager beavers among you: catching a case like this is nothing a law enforcement officer should want. You're going to be under a microscope. You'll be inundated with lies, false leads, bullshit, and craziness. Conspiracy theories will spring up like mushrooms after a rain. You screw up, and the press and public will be merciless. This goddamned puzzle defeated our best efforts fifteen years ago. Now that it's raised its head again, we have to solve this bitch once and for all. Because this is the kind of case that's going to stick to a career—all down the line. Now, Agent Sharp wasn't chosen just because he and Agent Swanson discovered the bodies. He has a unique skill set, and perhaps more importantly the ideal disposition to prosecute this inquiry. But he'll need help, and I know he'll be reaching out to many of you. I expect you to give him a hundred percent. That's all."

Garcia finished so abruptly that it took a moment for Corrie to realize the meeting was over. The semicircle of agents around the desk began to break up, turning for the door. Several of them glanced over at Sharp as they left. Corrie, who had heard her name mentioned once and once only, felt a little dazed, as if she'd just been unexpectedly smacked across the face. She started to leave—only to feel Sharp's subtle restraining touch on her arm.

When only the three of them were left in the

office, Garcia stood up and came around the desk and walked up to Sharp. "I think you know why you're still lead on this case."

"Sir," Sharp said. Corrie wasn't sure if this counted as an answer.

"You know what's involved. This case isn't old enough to be in the history books, but old enough for every jackass out there to have a theory. Just keep your head down. Never speculate, never explain. You don't want to feed the conspiracy machine."

He fell quiet again: a hesitation more than a pause. "Just one more thing, Agent Sharp...Do I need to remind you of it?"

"No, sir," Sharp said quickly. "You don't."

Garcia nodded slowly. "Then get to it."

As the two walked out of the office, Corrie felt the dazed sensation fade and her cheeks begin to burn. Just yesterday, she'd been congratulating herself that she was too junior an agent to be involved once this case ramped up. Then again, she'd been out there at the site, done as much as anyone—but when Garcia had stepped up to Sharp, he hadn't even spared her a glance. Was she on the case or not? It seemed not. And under the circumstances, there was no way Sharp could continue mentoring her now. She took in a shaky breath, then let it out. She reminded her-self she was still technically a trainee, and this was obviously a big case. She had to accept that if she had a role in this case—which seemed unlikely—it would be small.

They were approaching her cubicle now, and Sharp had remained silent. Corrie did her best to tamp down her feelings. The fact was, she didn't know *how* to feel.

She stopped in front of her cubicle, and Sharp halted with her.

"I just wanted to say thank you, sir," she told him. She was relieved to hear that her voice remained calm and professional. "I appreciate your mentoring, brief as it was." She took a deep breath and screwed up her courage. "If you need any help on this case, maybe I could...you know, lend a hand." She didn't trust herself to say anything more, so she turned to her desk.

She paused when she realized Sharp was still there. "Lend a hand?" he asked.

Corrie waited. She was confused enough as it was and had no idea what he could mean.

"As your mentor," he said, "I decide when an assignment is finished—not you."

"But this case, isn't it going to take up all your time—?"

"Yes. A slight readjustment is necessary. Going forward, you'll be my junior partner on Dead Mountain."

Corrie felt dazed all over again.

"I know, it feels like you've just been thrown out of the plane with no parachute—doesn't it? But don't worry, we're going to rope in several extra agents up front and more as we need them." He reached into his jacket, pulled out an envelope. "Memorize this."

She took it. "But did Garcia request—"

"Request what? Did he take you off the case? No. What he did was assign it to me. And my first decision as lead agent is to remain as your mentor and elevate you to agent number two. If...you feel ready." He raised an eyebrow at her.

"I'm ready, sir. Absolutely." She tried to sound confident, but her voice squeaked a little.

"One priority," he said, "is to find that final body. We're going to expand the search team already at work in the mountains—that's going to be your bailiwick. And while you're at it, have them establish more effective barriers around the cave."

"Yes, sir."

"Stop by my office at five and bring your ideas for a plan of investigation."

When he said nothing else, she at last looked at the envelope. It was unmarked and contained a single sheet of paper that, she realized, was a list of all nine victims of the Dead Mountain tragedy.

Victim	Cause of Death	Location of body	Next of kin
Andrew Marchenko	Exposure	Fire	Dmitri and Ann Marchenko
Henry Gardiner	Exposure	Fire	Thomas Gardiner
Michael Mastrelano	Exposure	Fire	Adele Mastrelano
Amanda Van Gelder	Exposure	Quarter mile north of fire	Terry Van Gelder
Lynn Martinez	Chest fracture; heart trauma; missing both eyes and tongue; radioisotopes on clothing	Ravine	Ray Martinez
Luke Hightower	Skull and chest fracture; brain trauma; missing one eye; radioisotopes	Ravine	Fred and Doris Hightower
Paul Tolland Jr.	Autopsy pending	Cave	Paul Tolland Sr.
Gordon Wright	Autopsy pending	Cave	Cosmo and Cassy Wright
Rodney O'Connell	Missing	Missing	Melody Ann O'Connell

Had Sharp been planning to give this to her all along—even before the announcement? But then again, had he known about the announcement in advance? She felt a twinge of anxiety as she thought about her high-profile new role in the case, especially the resentments it might cause among more-senior agents. Sharp had given her the opportunity of a lifetime—or maybe the match to ignite her own immolation.

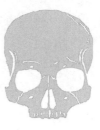

15

CORRIE WATCHED FROM a desk in the rear of the lab as Nate—still suited up in the morgue area—zipped the body bags closed and made the final preparations to put the corpses of Wright and Tolland, already lying on rolling metal slabs, into storage for the night.

Wright and Tolland. It was ironic—they pretty much knew the identities, but they still had to wait for the Quantico dental expert to do an X-ray verification. Only then could they proceed with notifying the families. Clothing samples had been sent off to check for radiation contamination. The autopsies were still to come, which she hoped to God would answer some of the riddles these bodies posed. The more she'd examined the corpses of the two young men, the more mystified she'd become. Had they been attacked by a third party? A murder-suicide?

Given the strange history of the Dead Mountain case, she couldn't take anything for granted.

Her cell phone rang. Corrie glanced down and—almost thankful for the disturbance—saw it was Nora Kelly.

"Hi, Nora. What's up?"

"I'm just on my way down the mountain. Finally got cell service again."

"You're just heading back now? The sun's down already."

"Yeah, well, my associate and I have been busier—like my brother would say—than a one-legged man in an ass-kicking contest."

"How so?"

"The Isleta Tribal Council is going to take up the matter of what to do with the prehistoric remains."

"Okay."

A pause. "That Sheriff Hawley called in KWOW."

"Wait—the local news channel?"

"Yup. Hoping to get his fat mug plastered all over television—just in time for the election."

Jesus, now she had another television spot to watch. "How much did they get?"

"Nothing useful. We stopped them from getting any shots inside the cave. Once they realized the situation, they packed up and left. But you know damn well that sooner or later, they're going to be back—in bigger numbers."

"We're putting a stop to that. We're establishing a larger perimeter around the cave."

"A bunch of dark SUVs with flashing lights passed me a while back—guess they were part of the cavalry."

"Too bad they didn't get there earlier," Corrie said, more to herself than the archaeologist.

"Well, you can blame the sheriff for that. Somebody should teach him that law enforcement comes before self-promotion."

"Nora, listen—I really, really want to thank you for your assistance on this. I mean, not only with the bodies, but liaising with the local tribe, fending off the press... everything."

A pause. "Why does this sound like the lead-up to yet another request?"

"Because it is. Would you please take a look at the site where the old tent was pitched?"

"You mean, as in fifteen years ago? There's a monument there now. Souvenir hunters have probably scrubbed that place cleaner than the latrines at Parris Island. That's another imperishable line of my brother's."

"Look—I know it's a big ask, with you still having to work with the Tribal Council and everything, but you said it yourself—those were souvenir hunters, not archaeologists. There's no telling what you'll find. Or what fifteen years of rain and snow might have unearthed."

Another pause, followed by a sigh. "All right. I guess Stan and I could do a survey."

"Thanks a lot, Nora. Get home safe."

As she hung up, she heard one slam, then another, as Nate rolled the corpses into their berths and shut the steel doors. "Guess that's it," he said, climbing out of his suit, going through the usual wash-down procedures, then turning off the morgue lights and stepping into the main lab. "You coming?"

"I'll be along in a moment, thanks."

Nate pulled on his coat. "Okay. See you tomorrow." And he slipped out the door, leaving Corrie alone in the lab.

She sat at the desk, the light in the lab now relatively dim—just her and the two bodies hidden in the alcove beyond. She wondered for a moment why she'd lingered, rather than leaving with Nate. Then she realized what it was: that slam of metal upon metal had stirred a memory—a deep memory she hadn't recollected in years.

She'd been thirteen, and five months had passed since her father had left home without leaving a note—or so she'd thought. Five months and two weeks, give or take. And in all that time, her mother hadn't spoken a word to her. The first night, her mother had manhandled the old TV from the living room of their trailer into her bedroom, and after that, Corrie had to be content amusing herself with library books and used paperbacks. Her mother drank—a lot—as she knew from the clink of all the vodka minis she smuggled home from work. A sixth sense had always warned her from asking any questions when her mother was drinking. Questions like when her dad would be coming home, or what she should make for supper. So she lived on cornflakes and bagged dry ramen while she endured the teasing and bullying of her schoolmates and waited for her father to return.

During those middle and high school years, she hadn't realized how much anger was building up inside her—directed in an unfocused way on Medicine Creek and Kansas and the whole world—until one afternoon when she'd passed the Wagon Wheel Tavern. Inside, she could see the local sheriff at the bar. He was drinking a rum and Coke, though no one would ever admit there was any rum in the red plastic glass, and eating an éclair. And no doubt talking trash about her father, as he did at every opportunity—or so his son, the local bully, informed her: how her dad was a no-good easy rider who, when he'd grown tired of banging his hag of a wife, had hopped a freight train out of town.

Without waiting, without thinking, she'd deviated from her intended path, crossing the street to where Sheriff Hazen's dusty cruiser was parked. She didn't know a lot about cars, but she knew how to let air out of tires. She was on the last one when Hazen came out of the tavern.

Ten minutes later, after struggling and biting his finger, she was sitting in the lone holding cell of the jail, her body still shaking from the slam of the cell door.

Metal on metal. Just like the two corpse lockers.

She sat in the cell for hours. For a while, the sheriff's son came in to mock her, but eventually he got bored and left. She wondered if it was even legal to keep someone her age locked up so long. But she did her best not to show her fear, consoling herself with the knowledge that her mom—who had a mean streak as long as your arm—would let the sheriff have it for making her come into town after work to bail her daughter out of jail.

Finally, she heard voices out in the main office: it was her mother and that new deputy, Tad Franklin. The sheriff must have gone home for the night. Five minutes later, the deputy appeared, unlocked her cell, and led her out into the office. Her mother stood there waiting, her face dead and expressionless. As soon as she saw Corrie, she turned and walked out of headquarters, letting the screen door bang loudly in the Kansas night.

Corrie trailed after her as they walked toward the AMC Gremlin. "Mom," she began, "that sheriff keeps bad-mouthing Dad and—"

Her mother turned— faster than Corrie thought possible—and smacked her across the face. Hard. Corrie sprawled into the dirt. Tears sprang into her eyes, as much from surprise as from pain.

"I just had to pay forty bucks to spring you loose," she said, standing over Corrie. "That's two weeks of food money."

You mean drinking money, she thought, but said nothing.

"Which means two weeks of you getting your own food. And if you mention that bastard father of yours to me again, you'll get the beating of your life. Now get your ass in the car."

Thirteen-year-old Corrie, ears ringing and one hand instinctively rising to her aching cheek, stood up and got into the car. And in the present day, Agent Swanson rose from the desk and—after a final walk around the lab—snapped off the lights and locked the door behind her.

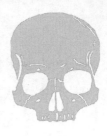

16

Tom Gardiner sat in the Barcalounger, in the far corner of Adele Mastrelano's living room. Her house had by now a comforting familiarity, like that of a favorite in-law's residence: the high-ceilinged entranceway in fashion when the Briargate subdivision was first developed; the Native American décor, domesticated for suburbia; the *World Book Encyclopedia* and Folio Society books lined up on the shelves, along with the fading family pictures. A few more pictures had been added, Gardiner noticed: mostly of Ralph Mastrelano, Adele's husband, who'd passed away eighteen months ago after a long struggle with colon cancer.

The potluck food was now spread out on the long dining room table, and through the living room columns Gardiner could see people lining up to get plates. In recent years, these meetings—now just annual—had become increasingly ritualized. People brought the same dishes: ranch lasagna, cheddar bacon jalapeño poppers, Lady Bird Johnson's Pedernales River chili. Now, with every meeting, there was almost always some recent death to console or retirement home transition to talk about. After dinner, the ritual would begin: the lighting of the candles, the naming of the victims—followed by those still missing. And always, a period of silence and prayer after each name.

Gardiner looked around the dining table, instinctively checking for anyone missing or for any unexpected additions. As always, he found himself doing this in the order their children were found. Besides himself and Adele, there were the Marchenkos, Dmitri and Ann, as always dressed in black. Next, Terry Van Gelder, once an outgoing high school math teacher, now a widower. Then the Hightowers, Fred and Doris, always sitting alongside Ray Martinez. Their children, Luke and Lynn respectively, had been found in May of the year following the tragedy, the bodies lying on top of each other in a ravine, with horrible and inexplicable injuries. Doris Hightower never spoke, and Gardiner wondered if this was some sort of stroke or product of grief, or if she merely chose to be silent at their meetings.

Now his eye moved to Paul Tolland Sr. and Cosmo and Cassy Wright. Fate had dealt most harshly with these three—fifteen years of not knowing, not having a body to bury. Torture. Paul, a dental surgeon, was now widowed. Cosmo and Cassy, plump and sad, both retired.

And then finally there was Melody Ann O'Connell, a real estate lawyer. The odd one in the group. She had joined the group four years ago, the widow of Harry O'Connell, who himself had been widowed after the tragedy and remarried her. That made Melody Ann technically the stepmother of Rodney O'Connell, the ninth victim, although she had never met the young man. Melody Ann was a powerful personality who had quickly become the most active, most organized, and most vocal of the Manzano Families Memorial Association. She had given the group its official name, gotten it 501(c)(3) status, drawn up bylaws, and made it official. While she could be abrasive, a lot of the families felt that after all this time a little abrasiveness was needed, and they were all grateful for her organizational abilities, even if they felt little affection for her as a person.

In the immediate aftermath of the tragedy, Gardiner's life had been a blur of confusion, followed by endless, unrelenting anguish. It was in that early period—after the first three were found—that the families had come together in an ad hoc group. His own wife, gone these five years now, had been instrumental in organizing this support group. It was after her death that Melody Ann arrived on the scene and made the group official.

What a fifteen years it had been. The investigation had started with a roar of promises, furious activity, proclamations of progress, pressers and releases, news programs, and eventually documentaries and a made-for-TV movie. The FBI were everywhere, Agent Gold's serious, careworn face ubiquitous on television. And then came the long, slow, gradual trickling down of the investigation as it stalled and cooled and finally iced over.

The Manzano Families Memorial Association had not, however, given up. Under Melody Ann's leadership they gathered petitions, wrote letters, went en masse to the state capitol, and created a web page with biographies and photos of all nine students. They collected donations to help fund the cause and keep the search alive. But over the years, their raw grief and anger had faded into sorrow, and the get-togethers had become solemn reunions rotating among the three or four houses closest to the university and the mountain range that had taken their children.

On this evening, however, things felt different. People had now helped themselves to food and taken their places on the living room sofas, and Adele had brought in more chairs and trays to accommodate the rest. Instead of getting a plate for himself—Gardiner never had an appetite at these affairs—he looked around, taking an almost subconscious count. Twelve people, including himself. Originally the number had been more than double that, with siblings and other family joining in solidarity. Among those twelve, though, the small talk that usually went around the room—the murmuring, occasional sobs, infrequent laughter—was missing tonight. People just seemed to push food around their plates in silence. It was, Gardiner knew, the return of the old specter, thanks to the recent news: still vague and uncertain, but promising renewed investigation and grief to come. Right now, it seemed nobody had the heart to rake off scars only partially healed.

"Well?"

A woman's voice had punctuated the silence. Melody Ann's.

"An hour has gone by, and I can't believe everyone is just dancing around the subject. It's as if a ghost were sitting here and we're all pretending not to see it."

"We" was an interesting term to use, Gardiner thought. Three years after the tragedy, Harry's first wife, Ruth, had fallen down the basement steps after one too many and broken her neck. Harry had quickly remarried—to Melody Ann—and then just as quickly died too, taken from this earth by a massive heart attack, which to Gardiner was just another expression of his grief.

There was silence for a moment.

"What are we supposed to say?" This was from Paul Tolland, whose son was among the missing, perhaps now found.

"Anything. Everything. I mean, you must have heard about what's been *found*. And the FBI's surely going to reopen the case. You've all heard that!"

Of course they'd heard. It had been all over the news. Two bodies had been discovered in a cave several miles from the site of the tent. An FBI agent had just confirmed this much, but she'd given no further details other than they were probably victims of the tragedy. There was the brief television spot at the cave where the discovery was made—but no further details, which simply added to the agony.

Suddenly confronted by this development, everyone appeared paralyzed...everyone, that is, except one.

Melody Ann O'Connell put her plate down and went on. "I look around, and...what? It seems like we're half-asleep."

When nobody said anything, she continued. "I mean, I don't want to be the one to bring this up, but—why aren't we, of all people, hearing anything? Why haven't they been in contact with us? Doesn't it seem *suspicious*?"

You love bringing this up, Gardiner thought. She was just the type—with her braying Long Island accent, botoxed face, too-skinny limbs, and frosted blonde tips—to be the center of attention. She hadn't lived it; she was late to the party. He tried to be charitable, telling himself she'd been incredibly helpful with both her time and legal expertise. And she was a fighter. They needed a fighter.

Terry Van Gelder said in a low voice, "We've been through this before. We can't do anything but wait."

At least Terry tried. But it made little difference.

"Of course we've been through it before," Melody Ann went on. "They're expecting us to wait. They're *counting* on our passivity."

Van Gelder, whose daughter had been found near the campfire, said nothing.

"Look, for quite a while now I've wondered why the case was shelved so fast—given it was never solved. Anyone else had those thoughts?"

There was a vague murmuring.

"Maybe they didn't want to solve the case. Now two more bodies turn up and they have to do something. Or at least *look* like they're doing something. Am I right? Harry told me about Agent Gold, that guy in charge of the first investigation. Sounds like a Mister Do-Nothing to me. He may be gone, but the FBI's the same."

Gardiner had heard this before from Melody Ann and didn't really buy it. Although he didn't think Agent Gold, for all his promises, had done a very good job, he'd always considered him an honest man. But now a tiny doubt crept into his mind, which he quickly pushed away. Over the fifteen years, members of the group had floated, discussed, and argued over a hundred theories. They were drowning in theories, paralyzed by theories—not one of which seemed to fit the facts.

"I took an undergrad course in poli sci at Levittown Tech," Melody Ann went on. "And the professor gave a lecture on the subject of propaganda and social influencing. This is how they do it: they keep saying the same things again and again. *We don't know much at this time. Information is still coming in. The investigation is making progress. Sorry, the details are confidential.* How often have we heard that?"

Gardiner could hear some low murmurs that sounded like agreement. He also wondered if, despite her shrillness, she wasn't right.

"And now and then," she said, "they drop a little crumb of hard information to deflect or mystify." She paused. "We're only people. But they're a machine. They don't get tired."

"Tired of what?" Fred Hightower asked. Everyone was listening now.

"Of keeping their secrets. Of manipulating

us into believing their lies. Whatever. That's the method and it works every time. If you don't know what questions to ask, you exhaust yourself guessing. That's why we have to start with simple questions *and demand answers.* For example: Why haven't we been contacted yet? Not just over the last fifteen years...but the last fourteen hours. Does it seem right that the press is given this information first? That we find out what's going on from a television screen?"

Now everyone was nodding and agreeing.

"These questions we need to ask," she went on, arms stretched wide, skeletal fingers spread. "They're not hard. They're easy. And we deserve answers— let's be honest, we've *earned* them."

Gardiner chewed this over. He was reluctant to admit it, but again she had a point. Two more bodies found—their own children's, almost certainly— but no notification. At least he'd had a body to bury. He knew what Paul, Cosmo, and Cassy— and, at least indirectly, Melody Ann herself—must be going through right now.

As more people began to express agreement, Melody Ann raised her voice over the noise. "And when they refuse to answer those easy questions— and they will—we escalate to the hard ones. Was it really a couple of drunk kids who found these two bodies? How could ordinary people stumble by accident on something the government, the *military*, has been searching for now a decade and a half? Is it sheer ineptitude? Or is there something else going on? Something... perhaps intentional?"

Now she moistened her throat with a drink of water. The word "intentional" had quieted the group. And into this quiet she spoke again, in a low voice.

"The FBI are covering something up. I'm certain of it—and so are you. As a group, we now need to focus on a single goal: *to learn the truth of what that something is.*"

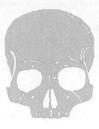

17

Go past the church and keep heading straight," said Stan Morrison, fiddling with his phone while sitting in the passenger seat of the Institute car Nora was driving. They were navigating a warren of dirt streets in the old section of Isleta, just now passing the iconic whitewashed church in the center of the pueblo, one of the oldest mission churches in America.

"In half a mile, Tribal Road 40 crosses a bridge, and it's on the right."

His directions brought them to a modest stucco building with a dirt parking lot, surrounded by bare cottonwood trees—the office of the governor. She parked in front and they got out. It was a cold, sunny fall morning, and a steady wind blew skeins of dust along the ground.

They went inside. A friendly receptionist in the small waiting room directed them to the back, where a short hall led to a conference room. Even though they were early, the Tribal Council had already assembled and were seated around an oval table.

As they entered, the council members rose and came forward. Darren Tenorio introduced everyone in turn and they shook hands. The council consisted of only six people in addition to the governor, and they all soon took their seats again, along with Nora and Stan Morrison.

"Welcome to Isleta Pueblo," said the governor as he sat down last. He spoke in a soft voice. "We appreciate you coming and answering our questions. Councilman Tenorio said you were supportive yesterday at the cave."

"I was glad to help," said Nora. "I'm sorry it was even necessary."

The governor nodded and opened a file in front of him, sliding out a piece of paper and holding a pen, getting ready to take notes.

Nora was curious how this would proceed. The meeting seemed informal and friendly—that was the Pueblo way, she'd learned in previous dealings—but she knew the subject was one of the utmost seriousness.

"Please tell us the full story," said the governor. "It would be helpful to hear it firsthand, from an unbiased source. So if you don't mind, start from the beginning."

"I'd be glad to." She told the story of the drunken frat boys, the car accident, taking shelter, the vandalism, the discovery of the bodies both ancient and recent, and the involvement of the FBI, while the Tribal Council listened in respectful silence and the governor jotted down some notes.

She tried to keep it succinct. "And that," she concluded, "is where we are now."

The governor turned to the group. "Does anyone on the council have questions?"

Polite hands went up.

"The two recent bodies in the cave," one councilwoman asked. "How certain is it that they're from the Dead Mountain incident?"

"The FBI seem to be almost a hundred percent certain."

"The newspaper report indicated violence."

"That's correct. One body had a knife sticking into its chest."

This caused a brief silence.

"Was it a murder?" another asked.

"I can't say until they're autopsied, but it seems likely."

"And these two hooligans—will they be prosecuted?" This was from the governor himself.

"I don't know. It's up to Sheriff Hawley—that's his jurisdiction."

This was met with a chilly silence and several frowns.

"How much longer will the cave be roped off and considered a potential crime scene?"

"That's hard to say. It may be a while." She hesitated. "It's a real problem that the media found the location of the cave and tried to gain access. Mr. Tenorio and I were able to turn the first group away, and the FBI is setting up a bigger perimeter, but I imagine others will be back sooner or later."

"How disturbed were the burials?" asked a council member.

"The main disturbance was the scuffing of one of the skulls and the breaking of the rim of a micaceous pot buried with the remains." She described how she'd covered the burials with a plywood frame to protect them. "And, as you know, the petroglyphs in the rear of the cave were gouged and scratched."

Another uncomfortable silence.

"Could there be more burials under the surface?"

"It's doubtful," said Nora.

"How about elsewhere in the cave?"

"I would say unlikely. We surveyed the cave quite thoroughly."

Another hush followed. Then the governor said, "If there aren't any more questions, we've reached the point where we have to make a decision as to whether to move the remains and rebury them here, on Isleta land, or leave them in their original location."

He turned to Nora and Stan. "Would you mind stepping out? I doubt this will take long."

Nora and Stan went into the waiting room. Ten minutes later, Tenorio ushered them back in.

The governor spoke. "Due to the profanation of the cave, the vandalism, the presence of what might be murder victims, the publicity, and our inability to protect the location, we've decided to disinter the remains and rebury them on Pueblo land."

Nora inclined her head; she wasn't the slightest bit surprised. "I think that's a sensible decision."

She found the governor looking at her. "According to NAGPRA," he said, "we need to establish that these are Isleta ancestral remains. Do you believe we've done so?"

"Beyond question."

After a hesitation, he continued. "Would you be willing to disinter the bones on our behalf? Councilman Tenorio will help you make sure it is done properly."

This surprised Nora, but she quickly recovered. "I'd be honored to help," she said.

"When can we disinter the remains?" the governor asked.

"I'm not absolutely sure about the protocol," said Nora, "but at the very least it would mean getting a federal permit, and that would mean interacting with the Forest Service and possibly also the sheriff's department. Basically, it boils down to a lot of governmental red tape."

At this the governor smiled broadly. "We at Isleta are no strangers to red tape. Any guess as to how long before we can get clearance?"

Nora hadn't given the question a lot of consideration, but she knew how long it took to get even the simplest permit from the Forest Service or Department of the Interior. "Returning Kennewick Man to the related tribes took over twenty years. This will be a lot quicker, but I wouldn't be surprised if we're talking six months or even a year."

Nora could see the wheels turning in the governor's mind. He finally spoke.

"The site has been desecrated. The individuals buried there have had their rest disturbed. They are spiritually suffering."

Nora inclined her head in agreement.

"We've established, with your help, that those remains belong to us under NAGPRA. Do you think it's just, asking us to remain patient for months or years while our ancestors are in distress?"

"I would say not," Nora replied. She was acutely aware, from previous experience, just how serious Pueblo Indians were about the spiritual rest of their dead.

"We have no way to protect the cave. Its location is now known, and has—or will—attract substantial public interest. There won't be any feasible way for us, or you, or even the FBI to protect it night and day."

Nora nodded.

The governor leaned forward in his chair. "Will you go up there tomorrow and disinter the remains for us?"

Nora was speechless for a moment. "You want me to dig up the bones tomorrow?" she asked. "No permit—just like that?"

"As an archaeologist, you know how to do this respectfully and professionally. Councilman Tenorio will go with you to perform the proper ceremonies. He'll bring a van. You'll simply put the remains in the van, and he'll drive them back here for reburial."

"I ... I don't know," Nora stammered.

"We've determined the remains belong to us. NAGPRA law says once that happens, the bones are ours to do with what we wish. I assert that taking them now would be perfectly legal."

"I'm no lawyer..." Nora hesitated. "But you might be right."

"Would it be unprofessional for you to do this?"

Nora thought about this. The request was not out of line. Professionally, she would not be violating any standards—far from it, in fact. The feds might not like cutting a few bureaucratic corners, but would they object? Probably not. The ownership of the bones was clear, and there were innumerable legal precedents to back this up. Certainly, popular opinion in New Mexico would overwhelmingly side with the Isleta Indians and their efforts to protect the remains of their ancestors. Nobody at the Archaeological Institute would object—in fact, given how the treatment of indigenous artifacts had evolved in recent decades, they'd applaud.

"I think my professional responsibility as an archaeologist would be well served in helping you preserve those remains from further desecration," she said, keeping her tone measured. "The Institute works closely with the Pueblos all the time: the remains are yours and we'd simply be helping you repatriate them."

"So, Dr. Kelly—will you help us?"

Once again, Nora paused. The National Forest people might object, and the sheriff probably would. But she could disinter the remains in an hour, and then it would be a fait accompli. That was the key: moving the bodies before the local authorities could jump in and muck up the works. Once it was done, who could object?

But trumping these considerations was something else: it was the right thing to do. Just thinking of all the permissions, the hearings, the blowhard expert witnesses, and the attention-seeking politicians who would weigh in with uninformed opinions made her head reel. Meanwhile, the cave would be a target for looters and vandals. And at a fundamental level, the governor was right: there was nothing illegal about it. NAGPRA case law was clear: the remains belonged to Isleta and had to be returned to them.

She was aware of a more selfish motivation as well. If she did the work herself, she might be able to glean some important archaeological data—perhaps even involving the micaceous pottery.

"I'll do it," she said.

"Good. We can provide diggers."

"Not necessary, I'll be able to do it with Stan—if he's willing." She turned to him. "Sorry, I should have asked you before. What do you think?"

Morrison shrugged. "I'm fine with it."

She turned back to the governor. "I'll enlist my brother to help us—he works for the Institute and has archaeological field experience. The three of us will be sufficient. Mr. Tenorio will be there to make it crystal clear—should that prove necessary—that what we're doing is officially sanctioned by and at the behest of Isleta Pueblo."

The governor laid his palms down on the table and looked around, smiling. "This is good news. Are we all agreed to this plan?"

When everyone nodded, the governor turned back to Nora. "What time tomorrow?"

"It'll take me the morning to get my tools and equipment together. Let's say, two o'clock?"

"Very good. Mr. Tenorio will be there at two PM with a Pueblo van, carrying an official letter from me authorizing your work. He will bring the remains directly back here after exhumation."

"Agreed," said Nora.

The governor rose, and she and Stan did as well. "I know I speak for the entire Pueblo in thanking you, Dr. Kelly, for helping us bring peace to our deceased ancestors. We will never forget your service to our people."

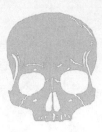

18

Socorro County Sheriff's Office, Homer Watts speaking."

"Hello?" came the old-crone voice.

"This is the sheriff. Can I help you?"

"Hello?"

"Ma'am, can you hear me? This is Sheriff Watts."

"Speak up, sonny. I'm just a mite hard of hearing."

"Can you hear me now?"

Corrie held the phone away from her ear. "You don't have to shout. I may be hard of hearing, but I ain't deaf."

"How can I help you?"

"There's a rattlesnake under my trailer, and I'm afraid to go out."

A pause. "Ma'am, did you say a rattlesnake?"

"Are you hard of hearing too? Yes—and I want you to come get him."

"Come *get* him?"

"Sonny, do you always repeat everything another body says to you?"

"Ma'am, how...how do you know it's a rattlesnake?"

"'Cause I done shot his head off before I ran into the trailer."

"So...he's dead?"

"I reckon he must be, with his head blown clean away. Unless he's some kind of zombie."

Another pause—longer this time. "Ma'am, I don't understand. If the snake is dead, why are you afraid to come out of your trailer?"

"'Cause I can't stand the sight of blood."

"But...wait..."

Corrie had hoped to string the sheriff along another minute or two, but the croaking was starting to hurt her throat and, instead of speaking, she burst out in laughter.

"All right, who is this?" Watts's voice turned indignant. "It's you, isn't it, Gus? When I catch your ass, I'm going to—"

"Why, Sheriff," Corrie said, stifling her mirth. "That's no way to speak to a lady."

Another perplexed silence, this one briefer. "Corrie?"

Sitting in her car in the field office lot, she again dissolved into laughter.

"Corrie Swanson, *a la maquina*! You're a little devil!"

"A big-time sheriff like you has to keep on his toes."

"Well, you got me, all right. I can't deny that." And they both laughed for a moment.

To be honest, Corrie hadn't quite known how best to say hello to Homer Watts. They'd worked together twice before on law enforcement cases, and . . . well, she wasn't really sure if they were now associates, friends, or perhaps on the way to being something more. All she knew was that she felt awkward calling him up out of the blue, and messing with him was the first thing that came to mind.

"Any idea why I'm calling?" she asked.

"You miss me desperately and want to ask me out?"

"No." She said this too quickly and immediately regretted it.

"Oh." A beat. "Then I'll bet it has something to do with those two bodies they found up in the Manzanos. I saw you on TV."

"That's right. I've been assigned to the case."

A whistle.

"The thing is, I feel like I'm five steps behind everybody else—you know, being new to the area. I hadn't even heard about the Dead Mountain hikers until my new mentor told me."

Another whistle. "You *are* a greenhorn."

"Yeah, well, I was hoping you could rectify that,

fill me in on all the rumors and chatter that won't be in the FBI files."

"Sure. I'll buy you dinner."

"I'll buy you lunch."

A resigned chuckle. "All right. I know just the place."

Jaramillo Eats was a shabby, dusty joint with swinging doors, just like in an old Western. Watts got there first, and as he saw her and stood up from the booth, Corrie caught her breath. She'd almost forgotten how young he was, and how handsome, with his brown eyes, curly black hair, and teeth straight out of a dental advertisement. As usual, he wore his two-gun rig...but there was something different about him. Then she realized what it was: the expensive silver-belly cowboy hat he always wore. It had been ruined in the last case they'd worked on together, and now he had a new one: in black.

"You gone over to the dark side?" Corrie asked as she sat down, nodding at his hat.

He chuckled. "I've always wanted to be the bad guy," he said. "You're looking great. Seems the FBI suits you."

"Thanks," she said. "So what happened to that old scorched wreck you used to wear?"

"It's in my office now, hung on the wall along with my other retired hats." He took off his new one and placed it on the table, brim up. "These Resistols are a bit like mustangs: you gotta break 'em in slowly."

They laughed as a waitress came over and dropped two menus on the scuffed table. "Two coffees," Watts told her. "One black, one sweet and thick."

Corrie smiled inwardly, pleased he remembered. "How did you pick out this town for us to meet? Not that you could call it a town: it's more like two speed limit signs five hundred yards apart."

"Veguita? Why, it's a bustling metropolis with a post office, two churches, a volunteer fire department, and a Dollar General. What else could you ask for?"

They glanced at their menus a moment, laminated in plastic. "Actually, this is just about as far north as my jurisdiction extends," he explained. "We're a stone's throw from Valencia County. Besides, I figured it was a shorter drive for you. And the chuck here is pretty damned good."

"Thanks, Homer—that was thoughtful." And it was. There was something about the sheriff that always made her feel self-conscious.

"So you've been assigned to the Dead Mountain case," he said. "I wasn't involved in the initial one, of course—I was twelve at the time—but it sure stuck in my mind. Tell me what you know and I'll fill in the missing pieces."

Corrie couldn't argue with this request from a fellow law officer. After all, there wasn't all that much to tell, and the only important information being withheld—the identities of Wright and Tolland—would be formally confirmed by an expert the next morning, with autopsies set for the following day.

Watts listened in silence as she told him, in a low voice, about the drunken students, the ancient burial site they trashed, and her investigation with Nora Kelly that located the two bodies. He listened with rapt attention as she described the bizarre knife wounds.

He sat back. "Whew," he said, running a hand through his hair as the waitress came over to take their orders. He waited until she'd walked off before speaking again. "Well, it seems you're pretty much up to speed on the backstory. I remember the stories we told in the schoolyard were pretty crazy."

"What were they?"

"We were sure that an Abominable Snowman had appeared in the door of the tent and they freaked out and ran."

"You still believe that?"

"Naturally." He smiled. "There have been dozens of Yeti sightings up in those high mountain areas. None confirmed, of course."

"Seriously—do you have a theory?"

"Those peaks have mountain lions and black

bears. I used to think that maybe a hungry animal poked his nose into the tent and scattered everyone. But that theory kind of falls apart when you consider how far some of them went. No bear would chase them for miles like that. And they were experienced winter mountaineers. To run out into that blizzard in bare feet and underwear, or whatever—they would have known that was certain death. Better to face the bear. So, to answer your question—I really have no theory. What about the last missing body? The ninth student? Any idea where that might be?"

Corrie shook her head. "We're doing a thorough search of the area, and I've asked Nora Kelly to take a close look at the tent site as well as the cave where the two were found."

"Where exactly was this cave?"

"More or less along a line due north from the tent." Corrie paused. "That's one thing I'm still getting familiar with—the geography of the area. It's nothing but a maze of forest roads and muddy paths—and then that huge wilderness area."

"You got a map?"

Corrie took out her phone, and he came around to her side of the booth to look, while she brought up the USGS topo map, acutely aware of his thigh touching hers.

"So here's where the tent was," she said, "and

that's the location of the fire where three bodies were found. Here's the ravine. And here's the cave."

"All in a line due north."

"Right. So we're focusing our search for number nine on that same corridor. You know the area?"

"Not really. I've hiked up in there a few times, but there are a hellacious lot of mountains."

Their lunches arrived and Watts returned to his side of the booth. "So I was wondering," Corrie continued, "if they weren't heading for something in particular, why did they keep going like that? Were they trying to get somewhere specific in those mountains?"

"There must also be natural caves up in that area like the one those kids recently found." He shook his head. "Shame they desecrated the place."

"If they hadn't, Sheriff Hawley would probably have finished the job for them."

Watts suddenly frowned. "Hawley? Christ, he's not involved, is he?"

"Yup. He was rooting around that cave like a pig in a truffle patch until I put a stop to it. He also did us the favor of calling in a camera crew. Only thing he forgot were the neon signs and reelection buttons."

"Figures." Watts took a bite of his sandwich.

This response surprised Corrie. "Tell me about him."

Watts swallowed, shrugged. "There's bad blood between the sheriff's departments of Torrance and Socorro—has been for a long time. Hawley's the reason."

"How so?"

"I ..." Watts hesitated. "Sorry, I don't feel right talking trash about a fellow sheriff."

"I'm a fed. We're colleagues. I need to know."

Watts sighed. "That county, Torrance—well, Hawley's been sheriff there forever. Always gets reelected, greases palms, kisses up, kicks down. There's only fifteen thousand people in the whole county, and so it's like a little fiefdom for him. He's uneducated, a clown, morally unfit—and a bully. But he has this uncanny ability to sniff out a person's soft underbelly and rip into it."

Corrie rolled her eyes.

"First term as sheriff," Watts went on, "he was in a gunfight with a bank robber. Hawley took a bullet. He returned fire and slowed the perp down long enough to nab him. Hawley's been living off that gunfight for twenty years, and you gotta give him credit for it. Only—"

Watts stopped abruptly.

"What?" Corrie asked.

"I've said enough." It seemed to Corrie that, for a moment, Watts was struggling to maintain a straight face. "Anyway, he's got friends, so his job is secure unless he does something really stupid. But be careful—he may seem like a dumbass, but he's crafty as a mongoose and a person with absolutely no principles. And that makes him dangerous."

"I'll remember that. And I'll let Nora know."

"Lucky her." Watts laughed as he turned to signal the waitress to refill their coffee mugs.

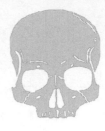

19

NORA, HER BROTHER, Skip, and Stan Morrison arrived in the cave turnout at 2 PM, virtually at the same time as Tenorio pulled up in a van emblazoned with the symbol of Isleta Pueblo on the side: a flying bald eagle inside a circular fan of feathers. Nora saw, with a sinking feeling, that a Torrance County sheriff's vehicle was also there. She hoped it was only Baca, the deputy. He didn't seem like a bad guy, just cowed by Hawley, and she believed she could handle him.

Tenorio got out, slinging the same old leather satchel across his shoulders. He raised his hand in greeting and came over. "Dr. Kelly. Good to see you."

"Call me Nora, please," she said.

"Of course. And I'm Darren."

"This is my brother, Skip, and you know Stan Morrison."

"Hello," said Skip, seizing Tenorio's hand and giving it an enthusiastic shake.

The previous evening, when she had enlisted Skip in this little expedition, he had showed such gusto for it that she'd been a little taken aback. She'd explained it was going to be a quick, low-key operation—no fuss, no confrontation, just in and out. If there was any problem, Skip was to stand back and let her and Tenorio do all the talking— not lose his cool, as he had a tendency to do.

Skip had agreed to those conditions. "I promise," he said. "I'll be as meek and mild as Mister Rogers."

Taking a deep breath of mountain air, Nora hefted her pack and headed down the increasingly well-worn trail, following Tenorio, with Skip and Stan taking up the rear. It was another cold, sunny day, and the ground crunched beneath her feet.

When they arrived at the site, they found Deputy Baca, sitting in a chair and smoking, thermos of coffee by his side. When he saw them, he lumbered to his feet.

Nora nodded at Tenorio and they went up to the deputy. They had already agreed Tenorio would take the lead: this was his show.

"Good afternoon," Baca said, looking nervously at their packs.

"To you too," said Tenorio. "Hope all is well here?"

"Oh, sure, yes," said Baca. "No problems."

"Glad to hear it." Tenorio slipped a letter out of his pocket. "We're here to recover our ancestral remains. Here's the authorization from the governor of Isleta. That's your copy."

Baca started reading the letter, his face clouding with doubt. "I wasn't told about this."

"It's all routine," said Tenorio. "NAGPRA law. We'll be out of your hair in no time."

Baca kept reading. "You're going to dig up the bones? I don't know. NAGPRA?"

"Native American Graves Protection and Repatriation Act. We're going to repatriate these remains, as permitted under the act. Dr. Kelly and her two assistants will be doing the work for us." He turned to Nora. "Ready?"

"Ready."

Tenorio turned back to Baca. "Are we good?"

He was still staring at the letter. "I'd better check with the sheriff."

"You do that," said Tenorio. "We're getting to work."

"Maybe you should wait for the sheriff," said Baca.

"I'm sorry, but we're on a tight schedule," said Tenorio, moving past Baca. He grasped the ladder and began climbing. Nora followed, then Skip and Stan. In a moment, all four of them were inside the cave. Nora could hear Baca talking loudly on his radio—bad connection, it seemed—telling the sheriff what was going on.

Tenorio turned to them. "Before we start, I'd like to say a few prayers."

"Of course."

Tenorio began to sing softly as he sprinkled some pollen from a pouch in his bag, then lit a sage bundle and waved the smoke around with an eagle feather. The sweet perfume of burning sage arose, and the low musical murmur of Tenorio's voice gave Nora a momentary feeling of peace.

After a few minutes his voice died away. "All right," he said. "Let's get to work."

"Hey!" came Baca's voice from below, shouting up to the cave. "Hey, you up there!"

"Skip, Stan, go ahead and get to work," Nora said. "We'll talk to him."

"Righty-ho," said Skip, opening his pack and laying out tools, trowels, brushes, and two body bags for the remains, while Stan—humming "Between the Devil and the Deep Blue Sea" under his breath—began removing the plywood protection frame.

Nora and Tenorio returned to the cave entrance. Baca stood below, still holding the radio. "The sheriff hasn't authorized this! He says you have to stop right now!"

Tenorio spoke. "I'm sorry, but we're fully within our rights."

"You've got to stop now! That's an order!"

Nora heard Tenorio's low-pitched answer. "This discussion is over."

"But the sheriff—!"

Tenorio turned away and walked back from the entrance, his face dark, while Baca continued to yell up at them from below. "I'm warning you! The sheriff's coming up here himself!"

"Who the hell is he to tell you what to do?" said Skip angrily. "This was all Isleta land once, right? Before the Europeans stole it?"

"Yes," said Tenorio. "But let's just focus on the work."

"He can kiss my ass!" Skip said loudly.

"Easy now," said Nora.

They put on knee pads, masks, and gloves, then got to work, loosening the sand with small trowels, brushing it away, and piling it to one side. The sand was dry and the work went quickly. The two skulls were exposed first, with their strands of braided hair. The rest of the skeletons swiftly came to light, along with the micaceous pot. It was a beauty, and Nora was sorry that, as a grave offering, it would have to go with the remains back to Isleta for reburial.

"Too bad your boyfriend Tappan is mired in red tape back on the East Coast," Skip said, exhaling and wiping his brow. "We could have used a few grunts from his company for some extra muscle."

"It's patience and delicacy we need," said Nora. "Not muscle."

The two skeletons were lying on their sides, in the traditional flexed position of prehistoric Pueblo burials. Both had once been wrapped in blankets, but only fragments of them remained, which they picked up with tweezers and placed in the two body bags. The yucca fiber sandals had survived better, along with some scraps of leather clothing.

An hour later, both skeletons lay completely exposed. Tenorio photographed them with his cell phone, sprinkled pollen on the bones, said another prayer. "They're ready to be transferred," he told the others.

Nora and Stan used tongs to pluck out each bone and place it in its bag. They worked fast and carefully, recovering every trace of human remains, until both shallow graves were empty. The micaceous pot and its rim fragments went into a plastic container.

"Now," said Nora, "we need to screen this sand for anything we might have missed."

She instructed everyone to put on N99 dust masks. Skip expertly set up the screen and they began troweling sand into it, shaking it slightly, picking out the last small bone fragments and placing them with the others. In another ten minutes, their work on the first skeleton was complete.

"Okay," said Tenorio, sprinkling more pollen on the remains. "You can close it up."

Nora zipped the body bag shut.

"Why don't you and Skip take the first set of remains down to the van," said Tenorio, "while Stan and I finish packing up this second body. We want to be out of here before the sheriff arrives."

"Good idea." Nora and Skip picked up the remains, carried them to the mouth of the cave, and carefully brought them down. Then they picked up the bag by its handles, fore and aft, and began carrying it up the trail to the van.

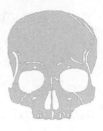

20

As they approached the parking area, Nora saw another Torrance County sheriff's vehicle come tearing in, slewing around, spraying mud and dirt. The door flew open and Sheriff Hawley jumped out.

"Just what the hell do you think you're doing?" he cried out, hustling down toward them and blocking the trail.

Baca, who had been waiting in the parking area, fell in behind him.

"Put that down!" the sheriff said.

"Sheriff," said Nora, speaking as calmly as she could, "NAGPRA authorizes these remains to be repatriated to Isleta Pueblo—which everyone agrees they belong to."

"Everyone? I sure as hell don't!"

"You're not an archaeologist," said Nora dryly.

Hawley stared at her, his face raddled and flushed. "So the FBI authorized this."

Nora hesitated. She had thought of calling Corrie but knew it would put the freshman agent in a difficult position. Better to ask forgiveness than permission.

"The FBI authorized me to take charge of these remains," she replied.

Hawley's eyes came alive in his face as he saw what seemed like an opening. "That isn't what I asked you. Did they specifically authorize you to *remove* them?"

"Not specifically. But like I said, I was given general authorization to do what I thought was correct."

"In other words, they *don't* know what you're up to. I thought so!" He waved the governor's letter, which Baca must have given him, triumphantly. "This is just some Indian gobbledygook! Listen to me: this is federal land, and those bones are federal property. You leave them right here."

Nora stepped forward. "Sheriff Hawley," she said, "NAGPRA law—a federal law, by the way— gives the Isleta people every right to repatriate their remains from federal land."

"Bullshit. You drop those bones, and drop them now."

"I'm sorry." Nora turned to her brother. "Skip, let's get this in the van." She took a fresh grip on the handle, but Hawley was still blocking their way.

"Are you going to arrest us?" she asked.

"Wouldn't you activists just love to get your asses arrested? I'm not going to give you free publicity—but I'm ordering you to put down that federal property, *now*."

"Federal property?" Skip burst out. "This is a sacred Native American burial! These people were here when your ancestors were still drinking poteen in some damp bog halfway around the world!"

"Whoa, Skip—" Nora began.

The sheriff turned savagely on Skip. "Just who the hell are you, sonny?"

"Skip, *can* it," Nora said. "Let's go."

She tried to go around Hawley, but once again the sheriff blocked her path. She hesitated, realizing that if she so much as touched him, he'd claim assault. And that, it seemed to her, was what he hoped would happen.

"Are you going to step aside?" Nora asked.

"Not while you're stealing federal property." The sheriff was about to say something else, but then he suddenly pointed at Skip. "Hey, you, cut that shit!"

Nora turned to see Skip shooting the scene with his cell phone.

"Stop that!" the sheriff cried. He lunged forward in an effort to grab the phone, roughly shoving Nora aside in the process. She stumbled backward on the slope, lost her balance, and dropped the body bag as she fell.

"You motherfucker!" Skip cried as the sheriff charged him. He seized the sheriff by the shoulders and, using the man's own momentum, grabbed him with one hand, checked him with his shoulder, and threw him to the ground. The sheriff fell with a loud grunt, landing sideways and rolling onto his back in the mud and snow.

"Skip!" Nora cried as she got up. "What the hell?"

Skip, realizing the implications of what he'd done, froze with horror, phone still in his hand.

With a second grunt, this time of effort, the sheriff staggered up, drew his weapon, and pointed it at Skip. "You're under arrest!" he bellowed, the gun shaking in his grip. "Show your hands!"

Skip, terrified, raised his arms.

"Drop the phone!"

He dropped the phone.

For a moment, Nora thought Hawley might shoot Skip, and she scrambled to throw herself in front of him. But the sheriff was more interested in the phone. He snatched it up, holstered his weapon, and then grasped Skip's upraised arm, spun him around while yanking the arm behind his back, grabbed the other arm, and slapped a pair of steel cuffs on him.

"You're under arrest for assaulting an officer of the peace," Hawley bawled. "And...and attempted murder!"

"What are you talking about?" Skip cried.

"My head grazed that rock, there, after—after you decked me." The sheriff pointed to a small rock protruding from the snow and dirt. "I could have been killed."

"Skip didn't 'deck' anybody!" Nora said, while the sheriff, one shoulder and part of his face covered in mud, recited Skip's Miranda rights at high volume. "You didn't even hit that rock!"

"You assaulted my sister!" Skip cried. "I've got it on video! Give me my phone back!"

"Not a chance," said the sheriff. "Evidence."

"That's my phone!" Skip said.

The sheriff gave Skip a hard shove. "Shut the fuck up and get going—unless you want to get charged with resisting arrest as well."

"What are you going to do with him?" Nora asked in a panic.

"He's going to jail, to get processed, fingerprinted, photographed, arraigned. The whole nine yards." Hawley rubbed his shoulder. "Assault and attempted murder of a police officer."

"That's completely false!" said Nora. "You assaulted me first!"

"Bullshit, lady. I didn't touch you. You lost your balance and fell on your own."

"It's on video!" cried Skip.

"Really? The phone will be entered into evidence,

and we'll see. Anyway, I've got a witness here. Deputy Baca will swear I didn't touch you."

Nora looked at Baca, who didn't meet her eyes.

"I *said*, get moving." The sheriff gave Skip another push.

Skip looked back at Nora, his face full of fear mixed with receding bravado.

"Skip," she called out to him, "for God's sake, keep your cool and *shut up*."

The sheriff shoved Skip into the rear seat of his vehicle, Baca getting in the front passenger side. They backed up with a roar and skidded out down the road. Nora watched them disappear into the forest, trying to get control of her fury and dismay, savagely wiping away a tear. She was afraid Skip might still do something stupid that would get him shot.

Silence soon returned to the forest, the only sound the whispering of wind in the firs. The body bag lay on the ground where it had been dropped, forgotten by the sheriff in his eagerness to arrest Skip.

She stood there, heart pounding. It was just like Skip to get himself in trouble. But...at the same time, she'd been the one to ask for his help; they came here to do something important—and they were going to do it. She picked up the bag in both arms, took it to the Isleta van, and placed it inside. Then she hiked back down to the cave, just in time to find Tenorio and Morrison bringing the second bag out of the cave.

"What's going on?" Tenorio asked when he saw her face. "We heard shouting."

She recounted what had happened.

Tenorio's face darkened when he heard the story. "I'm very sorry to hear this," he said.

She swallowed. "My brother . . . is a bit impulsive."

"Your brother is a good man," said Tenorio, "and he was only protecting his sister. The sheriff assaulted you first."

"Yeah. And he got it on his phone."

Tenorio looked grave. "The sheriff will have erased the video by the time they're off the mountain—and Baca will back up his lies in court."

Nora stared at him. "You really think so?"

"I *know* so. We've been dealing with Hawley for twenty years."

She wiped away another tear. If the video was erased, Skip was screwed.

"What do you want to do now?" Tenorio asked.

"We came here to repatriate these remains," said Nora. "So let's finish it. Gain at least one measure of justice."

Tenorio nodded. "Thank you. I'm going to bring this matter before the Tribal Council—we're not powerless in this state, I can tell you that. You and your brother are true friends of the Isleta people."

"I appreciate that."

They worked in silence, Nora trying not to think about Skip. As soon as the second body bag was loaded, Tenorio shook her hand and Morrison's, reiterated his promise of help, and drove off.

Nora turned to Morrison. "I'll take you back to the Institute, and then I'm going to head down to Estancia to bail my brother out of jail."

"I'll come with you," said Morrison.

"No need."

"Look, I want to. You could use some support, just the same."

Nora felt a rush of gratitude at this unexpected gesture. "Thank you, Stan."

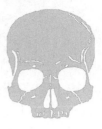

21

THE FILES AND photographs were spread across two long plastic tables in the cavernous evidence room of the Albuquerque FO. This, Corrie knew, was only the tip of the iceberg. There were at least forty more boxes that had been pulled and stacked along the wall beside the tables. She'd never seen a case that had generated even a tenth this much material.

"A bit overwhelming?" asked Agent Sharp, at her side.

"A bit, sir."

"Do I need to introduce Agents Bellamy and O'Hara?" Sharp had pulled six other agents onto the case, including Bellamy and O'Hara, and Corrie was pretty sure that before it was over there would be more.

"We've met, thanks," said Corrie, nodding at the two of them, who nodded back with murmured greetings. Bellamy and O'Hara were more senior to her, having graduated from the three-year mentoring process. She had seen them in passing, and they seemed like nice, eager-beaver agents—Bellamy a buzz-cut, blue-suited guy and O'Hara similar, only taller and thinner with slightly longer hair. Both were fit, blond, and Nordic looking—so similar they might almost be brothers.

"Since I'm a lot more familiar with the case than you all," Sharp said, "I took the liberty of making a quick pass through this material and extracting the most relevant files."

A murmur of thanks. Sharp walked alongside the first table and leaned over the head of it. "I've arranged the material in chronological order, and I'm going to go through it as a way of bringing you up to speed. Please feel free to interrupt me with any questions you might have."

Everyone indicated their agreement.

"You all know the basic story: Nine hikers on a mountaineering trip through the Manzanos. They're caught in a blizzard that hit peak intensity on October 31, 2008—Hallowe'en. When they fail to return on November 3, a search is organized. On November 6, their tent is discovered. Here are photographs of the site as it was found."

A half dozen photos, laid out on the table, showed the tent from various angles. It was dark green, easily large enough for nine people, partially collapsed and covered in snow. The front zipper door was open, and the tent had been slashed open on the downhill side.

"Unfortunately, you can see the initial searchers trampled everywhere before any of these photographs were taken. But farther away, footprints were discovered."

Another set of photographs showed footprints in the snow, distorted by wind and time, but several clearly showing bare feet with the imprint of toes. Others showed socks; some felt booties. One set of prints showed a lone hiking boot, and another, a pair of hiking boots.

"This one," Corrie said, pointing, "must be Paul Tolland—the corpse in the cave wearing only one boot."

"Very likely," said Sharp. He tapped on a piece of paper. "Here's a chart summarizing the footprints. We have two with both feet bare, two with socks, one with a bare foot and a valenki, two with valenkis on both feet, one with a valenki and a boot, and one with both boots."

He paused. "It appears one of the hikers with both boots, the ninth victim, is the one that hasn't yet been found. Rodney O'Connell."

Corrie noted silently to herself that having two boots would have allowed O'Connell to travel farther.

"They all left the tent together and headed down-hill, to the tree line."

"Any Yeti footprints?" asked O'Hara, to a small chorus of chuckles.

"Believe it or not, they looked," Sharp replied. "The tent was just below a ridgeline, on the eastern side in the wind shadow. The snow had accumulated to a great depth on that side—and that was the side they ran down. But the western side was scoured clean of snow by high winds. So there *could* have been prints on that side—we just don't know. Anyone who came up that western slope would have had their footprints erased. Chuckle all you want, but we can't just discard the theory: something or someone appeared in the door of the tent so terrifying that they cut their way out and ran. That bear, mountain lion, human, Yeti—" he gave a brief smile— "may have come up the bare slope."

Sharp moved down the table to another set of photographs and documents. "In any case, the searchers followed the footprints to the tree line, about a mile away. There, they found the remains of a fire built underneath a cedar tree." He pulled out a photograph showing the snowdrifted remains of the fire. "And around it were three bodies, frozen solid."

He pulled out three more photographs and lined them up. Snow had been cleared from around each corpse, leaving them in the grotesquely contorted positions they had been found. They were horrible looking: eyes wide open, white with frost, hands clutching nothing, faces frozen in grimaces, wearing nothing but underwear.

"Andrew   Marchenko…Henry   Gardiner… Michael Mastrelano…," said Sharp. "The first three victims found."

He picked up a nearby folder. "Here are the autopsy reports. I'll just touch on the main points. The right side of Marchenko's head was badly burned, his hands and torso covered with cuts and scrapes, and the side of his lower leg badly burned as well."

He shuffled out photos from the autopsy. Corrie made an effort not to react or, God forbid, turn away.

"Here's a study in muted tones of the cedar tree, and another showing pieces of skin on the rough bark. It appears one of the victims climbed the tree to break off some lower branches, scraping his skin. DNA established that person was Marchenko.

"Now to Henry Gardiner. Both his shins were badly burned. He had a long, very shallow knife wound down the outer side of his right thigh. Done post-mortem, by the way. And some of his clothes had been cut off."

More close-up photos.

"Michael Mastrelano had third-degree charring on the soles of both feet."

Sharp paused. "Any questions?"

Corrie had a million, but she decided to wait until the end of the briefing. The others remained silent.

"Moving on, then. The searchers then followed six sets of tracks in the snow, going due northward from the location of the fire more or less along the spine of the mountains. The trail was hard to follow, but a quarter mile on they came across another frozen body: that of Amanda Van Gelder."

More photos showing a grotesquely distorted body.

"Van Gelder had hair badly burned on one side of the head."

Still more photographs. One showed a woman with long black hair, stretched out facedown in the snow, and another showed her frozen body turned over. She was wearing valenkis and long-john bottoms, a sports bra, a tattered woolen shirt, but no gloves. "See how that woolen shirt is sliced on the side? It belonged to Gardiner and was apparently cut off his body in an attempt to add more warm clothing to herself."

Sharp wasn't done brandishing photos. "Now we come to the last two of the original victims. The initial search could not find more bodies, as they were hit with more snowstorms that obliterated the tracks and made further searching impossible. These two were not found until early May, six months later, when the heavy snows began to melt. Lynn Martinez and Luke Hightower. The bodies were found lying facedown, one across the other, in a rocky streambed at the bottom of a ravine."

The photos showed the bodies in that position, then turned over. Martinez was missing her eyes and her mouth was open, showing that she was also missing her tongue. Hightower was missing an eye as well, and his cranium seemed oddly distorted. Both of them were wearing more clothes than the previous victims—valenkis, pants, and down jackets.

"Here are the highlights of the M.E.'s reports for these victims. Both experienced powerful crushing injuries. The M.E. noted, and I quote, 'injuries sustained of the kind normally only seen by a person struck by a speeding truck.' Martinez's chest was crushed, the ribs driven into the lungs and heart. Hightower's head was also crushed, pieces of the skull driven into the brain. Both injuries would have been disabling if not immediately fatal—yet the skin was not broken. These injuries must have occurred on the spot where the bodies were found, unless of course someone moved them—of which there was no evidence. The M.E. was unable to propose a proximate cause of the injuries."

He moved to the end of the first table. "Which brings us to the new victims discovered by Agent

Swanson. They have not yet been autopsied or formally identified, but there is little doubt they are Paul Tolland and Gordon Wright."

Corrie was startled, then pleased, at getting the credit. She was careful to cover up any reaction.

He looked slowly at each agent in turn. "Any questions?"

"What about the radioactivity?" Corrie asked.

"For some reason that has never been made clear, samples of the first six victims' clothing were sent out for radioactive testing. Plutonium-239, uranium-235, polonium-210, and tritium—in very low concentrations—were detected. Not dangerous... but also decidedly not natural."

"Were any theories put forward to explain it?" O'Hara asked.

"You mean, legitimate theories? Only one: that it was contamination from Kirtland AFB, where nuclear weapons are stored. It just so happens those radionuclides are the classic components of a thermonuclear weapon. One of the theories held that the air force was testing some classified weapon, the tests went awry, and—somehow—contaminated some of the hikers' clothing."

"Did the FBI investigate if there was weapons testing?" Corrie asked.

Sharp looked at her for a moment. "Yes, we did.

There was nothing: no tests, no evidence of tests, no secret weapons development."

"But if it was highly classified?" Corrie pressed.

"In other words, the air force lied to us?" He shrugged. "That's a possibility. Here's what we do know: they don't test weapons at Kirtland at all—never have, never will. All weapons testing is done at White Sands Missile Range, a short flight south from Kirtland."

"Did the FBI really consider a Yeti theory?" asked Bellamy.

"We considered every theory. In fact, we made a catalog of them. It's right here." He tapped a fat binder. "All seventy-four of them."

"Seventy-four?" asked Corrie in surprise.

"And counting. I'll tick off some of the more salient. You can read up on them later—some are quite entertaining.

"One: UFOs. That would explain their terrified flight, the radiation, the strange burns on parts of their bodies.

"Two: Avalanche. The tent was covered by a small avalanche; they were frightened and cut their way out the side, then took refuge in the trees. They tried to warm themselves at an improvised fire, but the cold and wind was too intense. Some froze to death, the rest cut off the clothes of the dead and went north, dying along the way. But there was no evidence of an avalanche at the scene."

"Why did they go north?" O'Hara asked. This was the same question Corrie had asked Watts.

"We were never able to answer that. There's nothing to the north except a strip of Indian land and Kirtland, itself surrounded by double chain-link fences.

"Moving on. Three: Drugs. The nine hikers all ingested some powerful hallucinogenic substance that drove them crazy. But their systems were tested for all manner of drugs and toxins, with negative results.

"Four: Murder. Perhaps they intruded on sacred land and were attacked, chased, and killed as retribution. Or perhaps Russian KGB agents spying on Kirtland or the nuclear arsenal came across their tent, then chased and killed them.

"Five: Katabatic wind. This is a rare kind of abrupt, extremely cold hurricane-like wind that can occur in the mountains. It could have struck the tent, forcing them to flee.

"Six: Infrasound. High winds, swirling around the peak above them, may have created what's known as a Kármán vortex street, producing terrifying, low-frequency sound that drove them out into the storm to escape it."

"Kármán vortex street?" Bellamy asked. "What the hell is that?"

"If you don't like the name, take it up with the meteorologists. Seven: Gravity fluctuation. A sudden violent local fluctuation in gravity disturbed the group, possibly dragging them upward or even out of the tent.

"Eight: Carbon monoxide poisoning. The backpacking stove they were cooking on produced carbon monoxide, which could have filled the tent, driven them out, and poisoned their nervous systems to the point of irrationality. Result: madmen in the storm.

"From there, the theories grow more outlandish. A time vortex, a teleportation experiment, Arctic hysteria, *folie à neuf,* a fight among the group, methanol poisoning—plus fifty-nine other scenarios, all summarized in this binder."

"There were two women in the group," Corrie said. "Were either of them dating any of the men?"

"Interesting question. There was no evidence of romantic interest or attachment among the members of the group. No evidence of prior conflict or problems, either. By all accounts, they got along well and had gone camping together before. And they weren't amateurs: they were all highly experienced winter mountaineers, hikers, and skiers. They knew the weather in those mountains was dangerous in November, and they'd come prepared with all the necessary clothes. But most of those were left back in the tent."

"That's one crazy story," murmured Agent Bellamy.

Sharp raised one eyebrow as if to say, *A perspicacious observation indeed.* Instead, he merely cleared his throat and went on. "Now, this new discovery—two bodies, with evidence of a knife fight—hasn't cleared up anything; on the contrary, it's only deepened the mystery. If we could find the body of Rodney O'Connell, the ninth and last, we might gain some insight into what caused them to bolt. We know from old interviews that he'd been appointed the expedition's chronicler, and since neither the camera nor the expedition's journal have been located, it seems possible that, if they still exist at all, they may be with his body. And insight is what we desperately need, because that's the central problem here, at least as I see it: something appeared in the door of the tent—something so terrifying that, rather than face it, they cut their way out and fled in panic to certain death."

He paused. "So, ladies and gentlemen, let's outline a plan of action—and get to work."

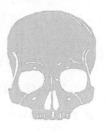

22

NORA SAT FUMING in the parking lot outside the Torrance County Sheriff's Office. She and Stan had driven from the mountains straight to Estancia, the county seat, to find out what was going on with her brother. She'd never been to the town before—it lay eastward of the mountains, where the Staked Plains of New Mexico began, flat grasslands dotted with dry lakebeds and covered with white alkali deposits. The town unnerved her: a windswept grid of pre-fab homes, surrounded by chain-link fences with snarling dogs. Many houses were abandoned and in ruins. It was 6 PM and the sun was setting in a dirty gray sky, the wind picking up. She watched a greasy McDonald's wrapper skitter and tumble across the lot.

She had tried to enter the sheriff's office and been brusquely turned away. They would tell her nothing, beyond confirming that Skip's arraignment and bail hearing in magistrate court would be the next morning. Stan, saying goodbye to her, hitched a ride back to Santa Fe with an electrician. Skip, it seemed, was going to spend the night in jail—and there was nothing she could do about it.

She sat in her car for a long time, looked at her phone, before she dialed Corrie's number.

"Hi, Nora," Corrie answered. "What's up?"

"I'm calling because I've got a problem."

"What kind of problem?"

Nora could hear the immediate concern in Corrie's voice. She felt a twinge of apprehension; she didn't know how Corrie was going to react to this complicated bit of news. They'd become friends after a fashion, but at times still found themselves in opposition to each other—at least professionally.

"I had a meeting with the Isleta Tribal Council yesterday," Nora said. "They asked me to help them repatriate the remains from the cave."

"Right," said Corrie.

"So I did."

"You did what?"

"I went up to the cave this afternoon with a Tribal Council member, excavated the remains, and he took them away."

There was a long silence. "And this was authorized by . . . who?"

"Listen, Corrie. In retrospect, I realize I should

have called you. But I also know it would have put you in a difficult position if I'd told you ahead of time."

Another long silence. "Okay. But you got the Forest Service, or Interior, or some other federal agency to greenlight it—right?"

"No. I didn't. In my experience, it takes months or more for tribes to repatriate remains found on federal land. The red tape is nuts. This is a clear case where the Isletans are the custodial tribe and NAG-PRA rules apply. The cave had been desecrated by those frat kids, not to mention the violent deaths of the two Dead Mountain victims. The spirits of their ancestors were in a disturbed state. Corrie, they take their religious beliefs as seriously as any priest does. It was my moral responsibility to recover those bones before they became even more disturbed—or stolen."

"So you just went up there, dug up the bones, and turned them over to the tribe?"

"Yes."

She heard a long sigh on the other end of the phone. "Well, I'm not sure this is something that concerns the FBI. I'll talk to my supervisor, but I think our position is going to be this is an issue between you and—I don't know—the Forest Service or local law enforcement."

"There's a complication," Nora said.

A short silence. "Go on."

"The sheriff physically tried to prevent us from removing the remains. He claimed they were federal property. When he blocked our path, my brother, Skip, began videotaping him. He knocked me down and lunged for the phone. Skip pushed the sheriff down, and then Hawley arrested him and confiscated his phone."

"The sheriff knocked you down? Are you all right?"

"I'm fine. But Skip's in jail, and they have his phone. I'm worried they'll erase the video, since the sheriff is already claiming he never touched me. Skip only acted to defend me, but Hawley claims his head hit a rock and he's threatening an attempted murder charge."

Now the silence went on for a good thirty seconds. Finally, Corrie spoke. "What a shit show. Nora, this is so unlike you. You're supposed to be the steady one, the one who follows the rules. *I'm* the impulsive one. And yet here you are, stealing bones and getting in a tussle with a sheriff."

"I didn't steal anything! What I did was well within the NAGPRA law. And it was the right thing to do."

"Of course it was the right thing to do," said Corrie. "But, Nora, we live in the real world, where the right thing is not always the smart thing. Believe me, I've found that out the hard way. I thought you were savvier than this."

"I'm not going to apologize for ethically correct behavior," Nora said hotly. "Especially when it comes to the dignity of Native Americans and their religious rights!"

"Whoa, don't lecture me like I'm some retrograde. I'm totally in sympathy with those views, but, for God's sake, Nora—your brother got in a fight with a sheriff!"

Nora swallowed, trying to collect herself. "Look, I know I've created a problem, but I'm going to need help. Skip's in a lot of trouble. You're FBI— I'm hoping you'll be able to intervene, calm the situation down, use your influence to get the charges dropped."

"Are you kidding? The FBI can't touch this with a ten-foot pole. I'm really sorry, but we're going to have to disavow this rogue operation of yours—and in no uncertain terms."

"You're not going to help? What if the sheriff erases the video? I mean, he's a corrupt bastard. You know that."

"We can't intervene in any way. I'm sorry. I really, really wish you'd come to me first. This is going to be all over the news—and I'm going to look bad for bringing you in."

"*You're* going to look bad? I'd like to remind you

that if you hadn't asked for my help to begin with, my brother wouldn't be behind bars right now!"

There was a brief, brittle pause. "I'm sorry. You need to get Skip a good lawyer, because if Hawley follows through on that attempted murder charge…" She paused, and Nora heard her speak to someone in the background. "Nora, I've gotta go. Quantico's about to send us the dental labwork on the two bodies."

Nora lowered her cell phone. Her hand was shaking, and she felt sick to her stomach. She looked out at the parking lot in time to see the greasy McDonald's wrapper come back around in a circle, scraping on the asphalt, carried by the endless wind of the Staked Plains.

She raised the phone again and called Councilman Tenorio.

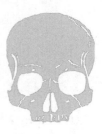

23

Take a right at County Road 69," Sharp said, "and follow it north for a mile or so. The entrance isn't far past the Masonic Cemetery."

Once again, Corrie was driving the Tahoe and her mentor was riding shotgun. It was a three-hour drive from Albuquerque up to Trinidad, Colorado, and Sharp hadn't said more than a few dozen words over the last hour—most of those involving directions. She'd told him about Nora's rogue disinterment and Skip getting arrested, and his reaction had been opaque to say the least. A curt nod, a vague murmured phrase about "not our problem," and then he'd fallen silent. As the ride went on, she'd given him a few covert glances, and he appeared fast asleep—but she didn't think that was the case. At times like this, he reminded her almost of a lizard: a wiry lizard that could stay motionless forever, only to strike abruptly and with lightning speed.

Just one more thing, Agent Sharp...Do I need to remind you of it? She recalled Garcia's final words. Once again, she wondered what that had meant.

Most of the first of kin of the Dead Mountain victims lived in or around Albuquerque. Paul Tolland Sr. was one of the few who, bucking the tide, had moved farther away. He and his wife had relocated to Colorado to a condominium community about five years after their son went missing. Five years later, his wife had passed away as well.

The Wrights were also on their list to visit, but they lived closer to Santa Fe, and Sharp had thought it best to talk to them on the ride back. Meanwhile, the other lead agents, Bellamy and O'Hara, with some others Sharp had corralled, were doing the grunt work of re-interviewing everyone associated with the case—starting with the families of those whose bodies were first to be found. Corrie wasn't sure which of these tasks she'd rather have been assigned to.

Trinidad proved a pleasant town, with a historic district and enough mesas, trails, and art galleries to satisfy day-tripping tourists. Up ahead now, she saw the well-groomed entrance to Tolland's gated community—Piñon Canyon Estates—and she pulled up to the guardhouse. She gave her name to the woman inside, waited while she phoned ahead, and then followed the directions. She knew they could have just shown up unannounced and flashed their badges, but Sharp had vetoed that idea. "It's better if he knows we're coming," her mentor had said. "He'll know why. It'll give him time to prepare."

Corrie pulled into a spot reserved for visitors and they got out. Tolland's townhouse was an end unit, tidy and understated except for the expensive-looking bow windows on two sides. It was painted in community-approved colors. As she looked it over, Corrie thought back to the question she'd asked Sharp earlier: why exactly they were here now, before the coroner had conducted his autopsy. "The FBI are servants of the people, and we need to show we care" was his response. "And the fact is, we do care. Now that we have an ironclad ID, it's our immediate duty to inform the next of kin—in person and without delay."

He climbed the front steps and pushed the doorbell. Corrie, following behind, saw a series of painted-over holes beneath the nearest bow window that made her think a planter had once hung there, perhaps before Tolland's wife died.

"Agent Swanson," Sharp said quietly, "I'm going to handle this interview myself—if you don't mind."

This was unexpected, and although Corrie hadn't exactly been looking forward to delivering the news, she realized that, in fact, she did mind. Why hadn't he told her before? She'd spent a good part of the drive running over in her head just what she'd say. But then the doorknob turned, there was a faint chuff of weatherstripping, and a tall, stooped man stood in the entryway looking out at them.

He'd been an endodontist, she recalled, and a very successful one. In middle age, he would have stood six foot one or perhaps a bit taller. But age, kyphosis, and tragedy had shrunken his frame. He wore a cardigan with a dress shirt and tie beneath, along with well-pressed wool trousers. As Sharp made the introductions, Corrie looked the man over as inconspicuously as possible. His eyes were red, and a little rheumy, but she didn't think this was from tears. She wondered if he'd put on the tie for their benefit.

"Is there anyone else at home—a relation, perhaps—that you'd like to have as part of this conversation?" Sharp asked.

The man shook his head. Using few words—like many doctors, Tolland seemed used to speaking with brevity—he ushered them into a neat and well-appointed living room. He offered them tea and coffee, which they both declined. Glancing around, Corrie didn't detect what she would once have called a woman's touch.

Tolland waited until they were both seated, then

sat down himself in what was obviously his favorite chair—the stand beside it held a couple of magazines and a book on Roman history, lying with its spine open.

"Dr. Tolland," Sharp went on, "I'll skip the small talk and get to the point, as you seem to be someone who would respect that."

Tolland gave that a nod.

"No doubt you're aware that two bodies were recently found in the Manzano Mountains in the general location of the Dead Mountain incident." He paused for only a second. "We're very sorry to inform you that one of those two has been identified as your son, Paul Jr. Agent Swanson and I extend our sincerest condolences."

Corrie glanced at her mentor. He was sitting on the far side of the couch, legs folded—not as if he'd made himself comfortable, exactly, but neither in the hands-clasped position of attention she would have adopted. He spoke in his usual manner, a little formally but without needless filigree. The approach seemed to work: as Sharp spoke, Dr. Tolland relaxed visibly in his chair. His hands, which had grasped the armrests, lost some of their stiffness.

Sharp went silent, allowing their host to digest what, in his heart, he'd already known. This, too, surprised Corrie a little—she might have let the facts, such as they were, come tumbling out to fill an awkward gap. But Sharp allowed—or at least, appeared to allow—Tolland to direct the conversation.

After a minute, the dental surgeon cleared his throat. "It's been five days since the bodies were found—or six, maybe, as nobody has given us a clear timeline."

Sharp nodded.

"If my son—if Paul—was one of the two who were discovered, why am I learning about it only now?"

"Because, Dr. Tolland, it's our policy not to inform next of kin without a positive identification. That only came last night."

"Dental records?" Tolland asked abruptly, his hands stiffening again on the arms of the chair.

"Exactly. That's when our lab at Quantico completed matching the dental records to the remains. You're the first person we've informed, and until such time as there's an official press release, we will tell no one else." He paused. "Naturally, I'm willing to answer any questions you might have."

Corrie marveled at the concise yet relaxed way Sharp presented the information. It seemed unredacted, logical, cool, and smooth as marble—but, like marble, slippery and leaving little room for questions.

Tolland slowly nodded as this sank in. "You say you didn't make a positive identification until last night?"

"That's correct."

"What took you so long?"

Sharp took this blunt question in stride. "Dr. Tolland, it's hard to describe the process we must go through in such cases without seeming—well, a little cold and robotic. Our first concern, of course, was that the remains be treated with the utmost care and dignity. That alone—removing them from the cave where they were found—took more than a day."

"That still leaves four days." Tolland's voice quavered slightly as he made this statement. He'd been so composed up until now...Corrie hoped to God he wouldn't fall apart.

"To be precise, three—or slightly less. Then we had to retrieve your son's dental records from years back, which took two days, and finally have our lab compare them to the X-rays we took of the remains."

"Surely you found some ID with the body?"

Sharp continued in the same voice, the same semi-relaxed posture. "We did, yes, but in an investigation of this nature, evidence like a driver's license can't be considered official or legal. You can imagine the unnecessary pain we'd cause if we made an error."

"You didn't ask me to identify the body," Tolland said.

"It was not in an identifiable condition."

Tolland was very still for a moment. Then he said, "Can you tell me how he died?"

"Not yet. That must await the autopsy. We'll know more within twenty-four to forty-eight hours. This case is our highest priority."

"Can't you tell me anything more?" Tolland said.

To Corrie, he seemed increasingly agitated. She wondered if this was a normal reaction. It seemed like Tolland had something on his mind.

"Certainly." Almost imperceptibly, Sharp quickened the pace of his speech. "Now that your son has been identified, I can give you a few more facts—although I'd ask you not to share them, since they're preliminary and also confidential to the investigation. He and another of the hikers found shelter in a cave, which lay about two miles north of the makeshift fire circle where the first three victims were found."

"Did they, I mean my son and the other one, freeze to death?"

"Not likely. It appears there was a struggle."

"Struggle? What kind of struggle?"

"A knife was involved."

"So my son was stabbed to death?"

"He was found with a fatal knife wound, yes."

The color rose in Tolland's face. "Who did it? The other person? Which one was he?"

"We can't tell you the identity of the other person just yet, and we don't know what happened. We have to wait for the autopsy. I'm unable to say more. The other victim in the cave also had knife wounds."

"They were both attacked?"

"It seems more likely they fought each other, but that's again speculation."

Tolland stared in disbelief. "My son...He hasn't come near a knife since...since what happened in eighth grade! He could hardly bear to *touch* one!"

At this, Sharp said quietly, without missing a beat, "What happened in eighth grade?"

Tolland was almost shouting. "He was playing mumblety-peg and put a knife through his best friend's finger!"

"I'm so sorry," said Sharp, and then went on as if the information were of little importance. "As I said, we won't be able to state a cause of death or fully reconstruct what happened until the autopsies are completed, but you'll be the first to know the results. Now, I have to ask you, Doctor: I know you were interviewed years ago, but we may—in fact we will—want to speak to you again. Would you be willing to help us?"

Tolland listened to this. Finally, he took a deep breath, then nodded again—very slowly. "Of course," he said. And then after a hesitation, "Thank you for coming to tell me."

The two agents got back into the Tahoe, drove out of the subdivision, through town, and onto I-25 before Sharp spoke. "Thoughts, Agent Swanson?"

"Interesting story about the knife. What's mumblety-peg?"

"It's an old-fashioned kids' game in which two people compete. Kind of like jacks, but with a knife." He smiled wryly. "You face each other, take turns throwing the knife into the ground between, trying to get it to stick. It's not played much anymore, for pretty obvious reasons."

"I was sorry to see how much he's still suffering after all these years."

"Yes. But, as I told you before: we are servants of the people, and we need to show we care. We did that just now. Hopefully, Dr. Tolland will derive some comfort, or finality, from what we were able to tell him. Also," he said after pausing significantly, "in addition to showing our concern, valuable information can arise from such meetings. In their grief and shock, bereaved people sometimes reveal things they otherwise might not."

"I understand, sir."

"We might look into that knife business further. If there are criminal records, they would most likely be juvenile and sealed—but then again, possibly not. But if what Tolland said is true, his son seems hardly the type to be wielding a knife in anger." He glanced toward her. "Were you aware of any other fresh revelations?"

Corrie frowned. She wasn't sure what, specifically, he might be getting at. "Sorry?"

"For example, though he obviously lives alone, he used the plural: 'nobody has given *us* a clear timeline.' That 'us' means the Dead Mountain support group has begun to stir again. They caused quite a lot of trouble during the initial investigation. No surprise, but we'll need to prepare ourselves."

And with that somewhat ominous statement, he went silent.

They had passed Raton before Corrie could stand it no longer. "What about you, sir?"

Sharp bestirred himself. "What about me?"

"Did you come away with any fresh revelations?"

Damned if she wasn't going to interrogate the interrogator.

"Nothing beyond what we've already touched on." He let a few miles of road go by before continuing. "Relating to the case, at least."

"What, then?"

"Every now and then, Swanson, when I least expect it, something reminds me of my humanity. It happened again, during this conversation."

"Sir?"

"When Dr. Tolland stiffened so abruptly in his chair."

Corrie didn't need reminding—the movement had been obvious enough. But so what? He was in the middle of having tragic news dumped on him. She thought a moment. "It was right after he guessed the ID was made by dental records."

"Precisely." When Corrie didn't reply, he added, "I could be wrong, of course. But remember that before he retired, Tolland was an endodontist. I think at that moment, he was imagining making that dental identification of his son . . . himself."

Jesus. Corrie took one hand from the steering wheel and wiped it on her sleeve.

Now that he'd been disturbed, Sharp took advantage of it to reach for a folder on the seat behind him. "As Job said, we humans are born to trouble as the sparks fly upward. And now we find ourselves bearers of trouble to the Wrights." He opened the folder and perused it for a moment. "You can take the lead on this one, if you'd like."

Corrie pressed her lips together as she drove southward, reminding herself in the future to be more careful what she wished for.

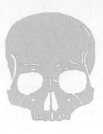

24

Nora parked in the cracked asphalt lot and then entered the Torrance County Sheriff's Office: a flimsy structure made of brown stuccoed panels, standing under gray skies. Snow was in the forecast, and Nora wanted to get Skip home before the flurries began.

Skip had spent the night in jail—there wasn't anything she could have done to change that. The arraignment had been this morning, thank God. If it weren't for the lawyer hired by Isleta Pueblo to represent him, Skip would still be sitting in jail.

She found Skip with his new attorney waiting in plastic chairs in the tiny lobby. When she came in, he jumped up and hugged her like a child—and she suddenly had memories of him doing exactly the same when coming home from school after sitting in the principal's office for some infraction, hugging her for comfort.

He released her and she turned to greet his attorney. He was dramatic looking, tall and lean, with long black hair all the way down his back, dark brown skin, and a craggy face, wearing an expensive-looking suit and tie.

"Edward Lightfeather," he said, taking her hand in his. "Glad to meet you. I've heard much about you from Councilman Tenorio."

Nora had a dozen questions to ask, but even before she could speak, he smiled and held a finger to his lips. "Let us go somewhere quiet and secure to chat." He emphasized the word "secure" ever so slightly.

"Yes. Thank you."

"Is that agreeable to you, Skip?" the attorney asked.

"Sure, fine. Look, Nora—"

Lightfeather pressed Skip's shoulder. "Later."

They went out into the parking lot of the godforsaken town, and Lightfeather paused at the door of his car—a Porsche 911—to hand Nora a card. "I've arranged for us to have lunch in Albuquerque at the Cervantes Club on Aztec Boulevard. One o'clock." He reached into the car and pulled out a tie. "For you, Skip."

He took it. "What kind of place is this?"

"Quiet. Private." Lightfeather got in and took off with a roar, leaving a cloud of dust. Nora walked over to her pickup and Skip followed her. Sliding into the driver's seat, Nora turned to look at him.

"I'm so sorry, Sis," he said, his voice breaking, eyes filling with tears.

She sighed. "You were defending me. How could I blame you?"

He held up the tie. "Do we *have* to do this? I just want to go home and sleep. I was stuck in a cell with a rancid drunk who farted all night. At least he didn't try to—"

"Skip, TMI! Let's just do what he says. Lightfeather's top-notch."

He nodded glumly.

It was a one-hour drive up to Moriarty and through Tijeras Canyon to Albuquerque. The Cervantes Club—Nora had heard of the place but never been there—was at the top of one of Albuquerque's tallest buildings. In the elevator, Skip put on the tie. Nora was glad she had dressed up for the drive to Estancia, but Skip looked like hell—unshaven, hair messy, clothes filthy from digging in the cave. Well, so be it. If Lightfeather didn't mind, she wouldn't either.

They entered the hushed confines of the restaurant. Lightfeather was already seated at a table by the window. He waved them over, rose, and held Nora's chair for her. Skip took a seat on the other side.

"Sorry," said Skip. "I must look like a bum."

"Don't worry," said Lightfeather with a smile. "I often take my clients here to help them recover from a night or two in jail. Now, before we start, I have to ask: May we speak freely about the case in front of your sister?"

"Of course."

"Good. But first, let's get drinks." He waved his finger and a waiter hurried over. "Nora?" he asked. "Your preference?"

"Coffee, black."

Lightfeather looked disappointed. "Nothing else?"

"No thanks."

Skip said, "I'll take a beer. Nuckolls lager."

"My usual," Lightfeather told the waiter, who then left them alone.

"How was the food in the jail?" asked Lightfeather. "Did you order Betty's strawberry shortcake?"

Skip had to laugh. "You know I didn't." He turned to Nora. "The jail doesn't have a kitchen, so they let you order from Betty's Café. The only thing is, you're not allowed to order the strawberry short-cake for dessert. Jail rule. The rest of the offerings are...godawful."

The drinks arrived—Lightfeather's turned out to be a martini, straight up with two olives, which arrived frosty with chips of ice. They ordered lunch from the menu. Nora didn't feel particularly hungry and chose a salade niçoise. Skip wanted the cow-boy steak—the most expensive item on the menu, his usual practice when someone else was paying.

Lightfeather had the same. Nora wondered who, in fact, *was* paying—Isleta Pueblo? She'd better check into that.

After the waiter left again, Lightfeather said, "I hate to interrupt a good lunch to talk shop."

"I was only defending my sister," Skip began, all in a rush, "and it's on tape; I recorded it on my cell phone—"

Lightfeather held up his hand. "It would be best if I first went over the charges against you. I'm afraid they're serious class three and four felonies. The first is 'Willfully and intentionally assaulting a peace officer while he is in the lawful discharge of his duties with intent to commit obstruction of justice.' Two: 'Intentionally fleeing, attempting to evade or evading an officer of this state when the person committing the act of fleeing, attempting to evade or evasion has knowledge that the officer is attempting to apprehend or arrest him.' Class four felony. Three: 'Larceny in the third degree, the value of the property being over two thousand five hundred dollars and below twenty thousand dollars.' And four: 'Tampering with evidence with intent to prevent the apprehension of the suspected person.'"

"Bullshit!" Skip burst out. "I may have pushed him away, but I never tried to run. And what's this crap about tampering with evidence and resisting arrest? Jesus Christ!"

Again, Lightfeather held up his hand. "I know. You've already described to me what happened, and I believe you. Nora will corroborate it. The problem is proving it in court."

"But I recorded the whole thing!"

"I've filed for all evidence on the phone to be turned over." He hesitated. "You really believe that recording still exists?"

Skip stared. "You think they erased it?"

"Of course they did," Nora said.

The lawyer nodded. "I would have to agree. That recording most likely shows the sheriff trying to assault you in an attempt to illegally seize your phone, knocking down your sister in the process. If they didn't erase that recording, you'd not only be acquitted, but you could probably win a significant damage award."

"But—erasing it would be illegal! Is that how they operate around here?"

"Most county sheriffs in New Mexico would never do anything like that. Unfortunately, Hawley's the exception."

"I've got my phone set to upload all images to the cloud," said Skip triumphantly. "So it's there."

"There's no cell or data service in those mountains," Nora said.

"Shit!" said Skip.

The lawyer nodded his agreement. "'Shit' is right.

You can be sure the recording was erased long before they brought the phone back into cell range."

"But even if you erase something, isn't it still there?"

"Not if you know what you're doing. I'm afraid we have to assume that video is gone forever." He leaned forward. "And they have an unimpeachable witness in Deputy Baca, who's no doubt going to testify as instructed. I hate to be the bearer of bad news, but we're in a tight place."

"But *I* saw it," said Nora. "*I'm* a witness."

"You're his sister. A jury is going to be skeptical of your testimony. And Skip, Hawley's fall left a visible bruise on his shoulder. They've got photos and a hospital report. On top of that, a Torrance County jury is going to be in the pocket of that sheriff. They love him over there, at least most of them. The ones that don't, well, they keep their heads down. Sheriff Hawley keeps getting reelected, year after year, and his buddies run that county like a good old boys' club."

Skip groaned. "I'm totally fucked."

Lightfeather went on. "If we don't play ball and plead out, they've threatened to add attempted murder to the charges."

"Attempted murder? What the hell?"

"The sheriff claims his head hit a rock when he fell, and that he could have been killed. Is that true?"

Nora and Skip looked at each other. "There was a bit of rock sticking up from the ground," Skip said. "But I don't think it hit him. I don't think it even glanced his head."

"Attempted murder alone could bring you fifteen years—and since the supposed crime involved a law officer, the punishment could be escalated. We don't know what Hawley's hospital records will indicate, but he's playing with a strong hand here, and the rest of the deck is stacked against us."

"Fifteen *years?*" Skip groaned again. "This just gets worse and worse." He gripped his head in his hands and rocked back and forth. "What do we do?"

"I've laid out the problem as baldly as I could. There's still much I can do and much research to be done. The good news is we got you out on bail, despite their efforts to get pretrial detention. You can remain in your sister's custody, go to and from work, even travel for work-related purposes—within the county, of course. No need for even an ankle bracelet."

The steaks arrived, along with Nora's salad. She had lost what little appetite she'd had. Skip was looking at his steak, a sick expression on his face. Lightfeather, on the other hand, immediately tucked into his. After a moment, he stopped and looked at the two of them.

"*Bon appétit*," he said, finishing his martini and cutting a hunk of bloody meat. "One thing you learn as a defense attorney is to enjoy every moment you can...because you never know what tomorrow will bring."

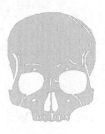

25

Tom Gardiner looked around the den with curiosity. He hadn't been in the O'Connell house for years. He could see that Harry's widow had been busy since his death. The carpet, wood paneling, unassuming furniture, and paintings by local artists had been replaced with marble tiling, chrome, glass shelving, and a huge piece of abstract art set into a mirrored frame. The chairs and sofas were all of white leather, angular with low-set legs. Gingerly, Gardiner took a seat on a sofa next to Paul Tolland. The retired dental surgeon looked his way—slowly, like somebody waking from hibernation—and gave him a nod of welcome.

Gardiner didn't imagine the den normally looked this way, with the tables gone and the seats arranged into something like a circle. But then, nothing about this meeting was normal. There was no pot-luck dinner, no small talk, just a hushed group of people sitting around restlessly in their chairs, waiting... for what? The friendly jocularity—forced or otherwise—was gone, and there was a feeling of trouble in the air.

Trouble, he decided, was the right word for it. He'd gotten the email just four hours earlier—it had come from Melody Ann, and he could hear her shrill voice in its capitalized letters. The group was to convene again, that very night, for an EMERGENCY MEETING!!!, as Melody Ann had described it in her online summons.

He had an inkling of what it was about. This had contributed to the vague sense of dread he'd felt on the way here—and what he saw around him did nothing to assuage it. Whether it was the recent events, the "reunion" a few days before, the tone of the email, or some combination of these, he could see in people's faces a mixture of looks—confusion, dismay, apprehension, anger, belligerence, indignation.

Melody Ann O'Connell, as hostess, seated the last to arrive—Terry Van Gelder—then closed the door to the den. But instead of taking a seat, she remained standing, as if about to give a speech.

"I got a call," she finally began, "from Cassy Wright around three this afternoon. The FBI had just left her and Cosmo's house after delivering the news." She paused a moment, then looked over at

the Wrights, who were sitting together on a loveseat across from Gardiner. Now she came forward
and stopped before the loveseat, stooping slightly
and putting her hands on her knees, as one might
when addressing a child, looking at Cassy Wright.
"Would you like to tell the group what they said?"

Cassy, who was grasping a tissue in her hands,
looked down. It was obvious what she and Cosmo
had been told—why was it necessary for her to
repeat it? The Manzano Families Memorial Association had been founded for emotional support, of
course, along with advocacy and other things—but
one thing it had never been was impromptu group
therapy.

"Go ahead," Melody Ann cooed comfortingly.
"After all, you called me. You needed to talk. It will
help if you tell the others."

"I...," Cassy began, then stopped.

What was Melody Ann trying to accomplish?
For the moment, however, she knew the most about
this situation, so Gardiner forced himself to sit back
and keep his mouth shut.

"They told me...," Cassy began again, dabbing
her nose. "They told me one of the bodies they
found...was Gordy."

A low gasp rippled around the room: the news
was no less horrifying for being expected. There
was a momentary outpouring of condolence and

sympathy. When that died down, Melody Ann resumed. "We're all so, *so* sorry for your loss. But I hope it helps to remember this is exactly why this group was formed: to get you through such a trying time."

That wasn't the main reason it was formed—and this woman wouldn't know anyway. But Gardiner held his tongue. He looked at Cosmo, Cassy's husband. He was sitting very still, avoiding eye contact with anyone.

"Why don't you tell the group what else the FBI said?" Melody Ann urged.

Another silence.

"Did they, for example, tell you anything else that might give you closure?"

"They told me Gordy appeared to have been involved in a knife attack," the woman blurted out, twisting the tissue around and around her finger. "A knife fight with the other person in the cave. They wouldn't know for sure until they did the autopsy."

This time, the gasps circling the room were far more audible.

"Did they tell you *who* he was found with? Who that other person was?"

Cassy dropped her head. "They refused. They said it was confidential."

"We all know the reports spoke of two bodies. And yet they *refused* to tell you who else was found?"

Cassy Wright simply shook her head, breaking into tears.

Melody Ann rose again to her full height, then turned away to face the rest of the group. "I can't speak for the rest of you," she said, her voice trembling now, "but when I got that call from Cassy, I didn't know what was more awful: her loss . . . or our *not hearing about Rodney!*"

More gasps, followed by a murmur.

"A week ago, three of our children were missing. Now, it seems, two have been found. I called the FBI. They refused to tell me if Rod was one of them. They wouldn't tell me anything. Anything!"

She stopped, and the murmuring ceased.

"God help me, but, when they refused to tell me if my boy was one of the bodies . . . I couldn't help myself. I called Paul."

Gardiner froze, willing himself not to look at Paul Tolland, sitting directly beside him.

"I asked him if he'd had a visit today." She swiveled toward Tolland, as if willing him to speak. "Paul, do you want to tell the group about that visit?"

By now, the rest of the room had turned their gazes to him as well.

"It seems," said Tolland, "that my son was the other body they found in the cave."

Another outpouring of sympathy began, but Melody Ann stilled it by raising her hands. "Here's what we know so far. The FBI visited Paul and the Wrights earlier in the day. Two agents, a man and a woman—that same young woman, it seems, who refused to answer media questions outside the FBI office. And...well, I'll respect Paul's privacy in the matter, of course...but they told him basically what they told Cassy. That his son had been found. Under the same conditions: vague talk about violence, a knife fight—God knows what. In other words, they drove all the way from Albuquerque to tell him more riddles—but they refused to come out and give him the cause of death! Meanwhile, two other agents disrupted the peace of Terry and the Marchenkos, asking yet again the same questions they'd asked fifteen years ago. What I want to know is, What about Rod? My boy? Why can't they find him? But nothing. *Nothing!* You want to know the saddest thing? The answers are right on the internet, for anyone to see—and the feds are just hoping we're too stupid to see them."

"What answers?" somebody asked.

"Oh my *God*!" Melody Ann said in disbelief. "Half a dozen of the theories I've studied—maybe more—fit all the facts. But for my money, our kids were victims of the Boston Project."

"The what?" Ray Martinez asked.

"The Boston Project. It was started back in the fifties, like so many other lame-brained government initiatives. They wanted to create super-soldiers that could fight, and conquer, in the third world war they assumed would break out at any moment. They tried a lot of different things—including crossing humans with Yetis."

"*Crossing* humans? You mean..." The voice faded as the implication, and perhaps a mental image, apparently became clear.

"There used to be Yeti sightings all the time in the mountains," Melody Ann said. "Why do you suppose they stopped? The ones still left are up there at Kirtland, waiting to be put out to stud. Now: Do you really think the authorities are going to admit to *that*?"

Gardiner couldn't stand it any longer. He took a deep breath. "We've all heard our share of speculations. Once the authorities know something for sure, they'll tell us."

"Will they?" It was Cosmo Wright. Up until now he'd remained silent, head turned away. But now he was looking at Gardiner, eyes like coals. "Easy for you to say. You put it all behind you fifteen years ago. Well, we didn't have that luxury. We've been waiting fifteen years without knowing."

His voice was loud, uneven. "Cosmo," Gardiner began again, "that's not what I'm saying. I know what you're going through—I've been there too, even if it was years ago. But after all this time, shouldn't it be...well, more of a consolation than anything else?"

"Maybe that's enough for you!" Cosmo said, almost shouting now. "You had someone to bury. But we had nothing, waiting for the FBI to do something, anything, promising us the truth but never delivering. Oh, that Agent Gold put on a show, didn't he? All the promises he made."

"He looked sincere to me," Gardiner said.

"Sincere?" Wright cried. "I've been waiting fifteen years for the truth and now I'm done. We all asked questions, wrote letters, got some petitions going. And God knows we answered all their questions, so many questions—over and over. And for what? Nothing. And now it's starting up again. Maybe all along, we've just been as meek as a bunch of frigging sheep. We meet like it's some annual holiday, eat casserole, sing kumbaya...Well, guess what: that's what they're counting on. And now: coming back again fifteen years later, asking the same questions over again, evading any meaningful answers...Jesus H. Christ!"

"You think they're covering something up?" Gardiner asked.

Wright stared at him. *"Hell, yes."*

There was startled silence. But then whispers of assent began rising from around the room.

"What really happened to my boy?" Wright

looked around. "What happened to all our kids? The fact is, what we've heard about their deaths makes no sense—undressed, radioactive, eyes missing, crushed, knife wounds—and the FBI won't even give us the first clue as to what *really* killed our children! I've waited for fifteen years, but what I heard from the government today...well, I'm not going to just keep eating the shit they're shoveling us. I'm going to get to the bottom of this—I swear to God."

For a moment, the background chatter ceased. And then Doris Hightower said, "He's right."

"We need answers, not evasions," said Ray Martinez.

"I've tried to move on, but I can't. It just feels wrong—and, to be honest, it always has!" This was from Terry Van Gelder, who just a couple of nights before had been a voice of reason. "I'm tired of being brushed aside. Something's been fishy for a long time—and I think what happened today only proves it. We've just never had the guts to face the truth. The problem isn't just our personal tragedies—the real problem is the contemptuous disregard for our right to hear the truth!"

The discussion grew in volume, everyone speaking at once, until Melody Ann raised her hands again. When silence finally fell, she looked around and spoke, quietly for a change.

"Nobody's going to help us," she said. "You all understand that, right? We're on our own. We need to find out what they're trying to bury—and expose them. This is what we owe our children. We, and only we, can do this. I'm with Cosmo. Are we all in this together? The Manzano Families Memorial Association has a new mission now, one we should always have put at the forefront: to learn the truth. So who'll join us? Raise your hands!"

All was quiet. A hand went up, and another, and soon they were all up, except Gardiner's. He looked around and, finally, raised his as well, feeling a flush of emotion as he thought of his son Henry, half-naked, terrified, and freezing to death in a blizzard. And as his eyes misted over with tears, he could still make out Melody Ann O'Connell standing in the middle of the circle, somehow looking less and less like a bereaved parent—and more like a triumphant general.

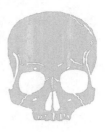

26

THE MONUMENT MARKING the site of the Dead Mountain tent was a mile walk from a Forest Service road that ended at the edge of the Manzano Wilderness. Nora had parked at the small turnaround and exited the Institute vehicle with Stan Morrison. The well-traveled trail to the site ran northward along a high, alpine ridgeline, with spectacular views looking east over the New Mexico plains and west across the Rio Grande Valley. It was a gray, windy day, with snow forecast in the afternoon. Nora was anxious to get to the tent site before the snow began to fall. Most of the snow from the previous storm had melted, creating a window for her to do the survey of the tent site she'd promised Corrie. But up here, the weather could turn ugly in a flash—given the altitude and the mountainous terrain, not even Skip would think of riding a snowmobile in this remote spot.

Thinking of Corrie reminded her of why she was

doing this survey in the first place, which in turn reminded her of Skip and the fix he was in. As much as she respected and even liked Corrie, it seemed like every time she did the FBI agent a little favor, it drew her into a gigantic mess. She closed her eyes and exhaled deeply, trying to rid herself of these distractions. But this time the mess was with her brother, and that made it worse. She'd tried so hard for many years to keep him out of trouble, and now this.

The trail to the monument circled just below the crest of Shaggy Peak, a barren knob of broken granite. It had lately seen traffic, no doubt a result of the fresh news on the case. Stan trailed behind Nora, humming as was his wont. It was one of his characteristics, or maybe quirks, that Nora had learned to live with. Stan would hum songs from the Great American Songbook under his breath, but what came out was more a series of grunts and quavers, with many of the notes left out or wrong. Nora usually tried to tune it out, but on occasion she found herself attempting to identify what song he was endeavoring to hum, or quaver, or whatever.

On the far side of the peak, where the shoulder of the mountain temporarily leveled out, stood a cairn of cemented stones ten feet high. A bronze plaque set into it recorded the grim event, and around the base were scattered the remains of various offerings, from withered flowers to beads and semiprecious stones, along with a large miscellany of other items: a glass Buddha, a string of jingle bells, coins, keys and locks, and other weird offerings of uncertain meaning.

Nora looked at the site in dismay. Time, weather, and curious visitors had spread the offerings everywhere.

"Some archaeological site," she said.

"How are we supposed to distinguish all this stuff from artifacts left by the hikers?" Stan asked.

Nora looked at him. "We can't."

"So what do we do?"

"I don't know."

She slid off her pack and took a turn around the monument, taking photographs. Then she paused to read the plaque:

On this site, on the evening of October 31, 2008, nine hikers from the New Mexico Institute of Technology set up camp. That night, a tragedy of an unknown nature drove all nine expedition members from their tent and into a blizzard, where they perished. This monument was erected by the Manzano Families Memorial Association in July of 2010 to honor the memory of those who lost their lives:

HENRY GARDINER
LUKE HIGHTOWER
ANDREW MARCHENKO

LYNN MARTINEZ
MICHAEL MASTRELANO
RODNEY O'CONNELL
PAUL TOLLAND JR.
AMANDA VAN GELDER
GORDON WRIGHT

She glanced up at the snow clouds advancing out of the west. She looked again at the memorial, strewn not only with offerings but also bits and pieces of trash from thoughtless visitors—gum wrappers, old cigarette butts, aluminum foil, a discarded water bottle, even toilet paper. People could be such pigs.

She felt a wash of irritation. They could make a huge collection of all this stuff lying around and take it back to the archaeology lab, of course, but there would still be no way of telling offerings or trash from something left by the original hikers. And what could they find now, fifteen years later, that hadn't been recovered before?

She turned to Stan. "I know we promised the FBI we'd survey the site, but it's hopeless. Wouldn't you agree?"

"I would."

What a waste of time. There must be something they could do to salvage the long trip out here.

Suddenly she had an idea: it was so simple, so

obvious, that she was amazed no one had thought of it before.

She paused, looking around. The tent had been pitched out of the wind, with the ridge sloping down northeast to the tree line and a saddle, about a mile away. That was the direction the hikers had fled, and in those trees was where they had tried to build a fire. Under a cedar tree. But as she looked down, she realized most of the trees were not cedars but Douglas firs.

"Let's hike down to the saddle," she said, "and see if we can find the cedar tree they built a fire under. And survey that area instead."

"Is this something the FBI asked you to do?" Morrison asked a little dubiously.

"No. I don't think they've even thought of it. But it's a good idea—don't you think?"

"Sure. If we can find it."

They hoisted their packs and headed down the ridge, Stan resuming his humming. After a while the tree line loomed up, seemingly a solid wall of firs, with small, wind-twisted ones at the edge and taller ones farther in.

Nora followed the edge of the trees, looking for a cedar and trying despite herself to figure out what tune Stan was massacring. Just as she decided it was "On the Sunny Side of the Street," she stopped.

Damned if there wasn't a cedar, standing all by itself just twenty yards into the fir forest.

She pushed through the scrubby firs, and in a moment she and Stan stood under the tall cedar. The area underneath was fairly open, and it seemed like a perfect place to take shelter. As she looked up, she could see that some of the lower, dead branches showed signs of being broken years before.

"Okay. Let's look for charcoal."

She paused to take stock, trying to imagine what it would be like here at night, in a blizzard. The wind had been from the west—she remembered that from the meteorological files—so they would have started their fire on the eastern side of the tree. Since naturally they'd all want to huddle around, the fire would be back from the trunk a bit. Her eye settled on an area of ground thankfully free of snow and covered by cedar duff.

"Let's start here," she said, dropping her pack and taking out a small trowel. Kneeling, she used the edge of the trowel to gently move aside a layer of duff, then another, and then a third, moving linearly from one side of the possible campfire site to the other. On the fourth swipe, she turned over a small chunk of charcoal and some black-stained earth.

"Bingo," she said.

Stan was looking at her, mouth agape. "How the hell did you do that?"

Nora couldn't help but smile. "Let's stake out a four-meter-square grid here, with corners there, there, and there."

Taking Day-Glo pegs from the pack, Morrison drove one into the ground, then measured off two-meter distances at right angles, and soon had completed the grid, strung across with orange string. Nora photographed it.

"You start on that quad; I'll start on this. Go down only as far as the charcoal horizon—no deeper. Photograph every trowel section. And pile the tailings here, please."

"Got it."

They began work. Mercifully, Stan remained silent. Nora carefully removed a layer of duff from the charcoal stain, the smells of cedar, pine resin, and damp earth filling her nostrils. Gradually, they exposed the full extent of the fire, which was so well preserved there were still some pieces of partially burned wood embedded in the ground. They were fresh, and far different from the prehistoric hearths she was used to excavating.

Once they had uncovered the charcoal area, she began to go down, millimeter by millimeter, scraping with the edge of the trowel, while Stan worked outside the perimeter of the fire stain.

A gleam came to light at the edge of the old fire. She halted, looking closer. Then she put the trowel aside and took out a small paintbrush, with which she swept back crumbs of soil and charcoal. For a moment, she stared in amazement at the object she had uncovered. Then she took a series of photos with her phone.

"Have a look at this," she said.

Morrison came over. "Wow. You think one of them dropped this?"

"I do. Hand me a Ziploc bag."

Morrison went over to the pack as Nora stared at the object: an open penknife with a wooden handle and brass bolsters, slightly scorched. It was in remarkably good condition for having been buried in the dirt fifteen years. It gave her an odd feeling, a sense of connection to the nine desperate hikers who had huddled around this fire, trying to stay warm in a monstrous blizzard. Three of them had died here, while the six others went on—but not before cutting off the clothes of the dead. Why did they leave the shelter of the fire? Was the storm too powerful for the fire to keep them warm? But if they left the fire...six of them did...then where, exactly, were they going?

Morrison returned with the bag. "Record this, please," Nora said, handing him her phone, "while I remove it."

"Got it."

While Morrison filmed, Nora took a pair of

wooden tongs and loosened the knife from its bed of charcoal, then gently turned it over. A small silver plaque was inlaid into the handle, with initials engraved into it:

M H T

Using the tongs, she slipped the knife into the bag and placed it inside a plastic container.

"MHT," said Morrison. "I don't recall one of the victims having those initials."

In her head, Nora went over the names she had just read on the memorial plaque. The only one whose last name began with "T" was Paul Tolland Jr. She wondered if the knife belonged to his brother or some other relative.

That was worth looking into.

The knife—whoever had brought it along on the expedition—had probably been used in the frantic attempt to gather branches for fuel, and afterward dropped and forgotten. And as she stared at the remains of the fire, she realized it had not been small. They must have piled wood into it, almost making a bonfire.

And yet, for some reason she could not speculate about, six people had still left its warmth.

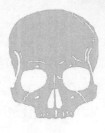

27

Nora took a seat in the restaurant. She was a few minutes early, and she took a moment to look around the dim interior, the hand-troweled adobe walls, the kiva fireplace in which a real fire was burning, the low ceiling of vigas and latillas, the small tables set close together. It was one of Santa Fe's famous old restaurants, in which nothing had changed in decades, including the menu. The restaurant had been Corrie's idea, and she had insisted on taking Nora out as a sort of apology for the way she'd reacted when first learning of Skip's arrest.

Corrie entered the dining room, saw her, and came over. She took a seat and the waitress handed them their menus. "Still or sparkling?"

"Sparkling," said Corrie.

"Me too."

"Bring us a bottle, please."

"Drinks?"

"Hendrick's martini, straight up, dirty, two olives," said Corrie.

"Glass of Chablis," Nora said.

"Coming right up." The waitress went off.

"Dirty martini?" Nora asked. "I didn't know you were, ah, such a robust drinker."

Corrie laughed. "I just came from the autopsy of the two victims and, Christ, I need a stiff one."

"What did you find out?" Nora asked.

"Crazy. Just crazy. I'll tell you in a minute." She leaned forward. "But first—I'm sorry about my reaction to hearing about Skip's arrest. I'm really grateful for your help, and this whole thing with Hawley is awful. I wish there was something I could do, but you understand there's just no way."

"I understand," said Nora. She was tired of worrying herself sick about Skip. If there was a way to get into trouble, he would find it, no matter how good his intentions. But he'd never found trouble like this. "He's out on bail and has a top-notch lawyer, which is all we can do. But let's not talk about that."

The waitress came back with their drinks. Corrie practically seized hers, the gin slopping over the rim, and raised it. "Cheers." She took an alarmingly long pull.

"Cheers." Nora sipped her Chablis. "Hey, don't eat that glass!"

Corrie opened her menu with a smile. "What's good?"

"The steak Dunigan is the classic here—a New York strip smothered in green chile and mushrooms."

"Perfect," said Corrie, closing her menu. "I like it rare. And my treat, remember."

"Are you sure? This place is expensive."

"After everything you've done? This is the least I can do."

"So tell me about the autopsy," Nora said.

Corrie took another gulp. "It was kind of strange. Both bodies were thoroughly desiccated. It's a lot harder to dissect a dry one than a wet one. We had to wear respirators and suits."

"How do they actually do the dissection?" Nora asked.

"Small hand and mechanical saws, scissors, scalpels. Cutting into those bodies raised a shitload of dust."

The waitress caught the last few words as she returned. "Are we ready to order?"

"The steak Dunigan for both of us," said Nora. "Rare."

The waitress collected the menus and departed, and Corrie went on. "The autopsy started with an analysis of the cuts in the clothes, matching them to equivalent cuts in the body. We first did Wright, starting with a catalog of his skin injuries and then a CT scan of the entire body. Then we went on to the usual Y-section."

"You say 'we.' Did you help?"

"I assisted. I'm certified to do that—took a course at John Jay."

"A handy skill. Probably makes for good small talk at cocktail parties, too."

Corrie laughed. "We quickly determined the cause of death: exsanguination from a severed femoral artery, entry wound in the right anterior thigh. The body was covered with knife wounds—neck, face, hands, arms, chest, legs. Wright was clearly involved in a prolonged effort to ward off a knife-wielding attacker, who stabbed him all over in a crazy, almost random pattern, before finally hitting the femoral. The body showed over seventy knife wounds, not to mention many more slashes to the clothing that didn't penetrate. There was no method or skill displayed, just a mad frenzy of slashes and cuts."

"Any idea who the attacker was?"

Corrie made a face. "This is where things get crazy. Wright's blood was all over Tolland, but Tolland had no defensive wounds, no stab wounds—his body was clean. The only injury he had was a single knife wound, the knife plunged into the heart, and done with great force. It was the same knife used in the attack on Wright."

The steaks arrived and Corrie paused in her description. "God, I'm starved," she said, eyeing the thick strip and then picking up her steak knife and slicing it in half, red juices flowing out. "Just as I like it."

Nora cut into hers, and there was a silence as they took their first bites. The green chile was hot, but Corrie didn't seem to mind. It often took new arrivals to New Mexico a few years to get used to the temperature of the local chile, but Corrie seemed to have adjusted quickly.

Corrie finally laid down her knife and dabbed her mouth. "When we finished the autopsy, only one conclusion was possible."

Nora had an idea of what that was. She waited.

"Tolland killed Wright in a frenzied attack and then committed suicide. He plunged the knife into his chest using both hands, the blow penetrating the sternum in the weak area between the manubrium and body and then going right into the heart, causing massive hemorrhaging and death within seconds—so fast that he died with his hands still wrapped around the knife handle in a kind of death grip."

"Jesus," said Nora. She paused a moment, thinking. "Extreme hypothermia can make people do bizarre things. Many of those hikers left the tent scantily clad to begin with—too scared even to dress, or something. That would have caused their core temperatures to drop really quickly, given their exposure to the cold."

"Some shed more clothing as they ran," Corrie said. "Others tried to add to their own coverings, cutting clothes off bodies at the site of the fire."

"What's known as paradoxical undressing takes place in up to half of those suffering such severe hypothermia. Late-stage behaviors include 'terminal burrowing,' which might be what these two victims, Wright and Tolland, were doing. They were better dressed, and terminal burrowing is more common when heat loss is gradual." She paused again, more significantly. "Other common behaviors are hallucinations—and extreme aggression."

"Including self-aggression?" Corrie finished off her martini. "It's probably obvious, but stabbing yourself in the heart would take some serious mental impairment, not to mention a crazy amount of determination."

As Nora was about to deal her steak its own mortal blow, she glanced to her right at the nice older couple at the next table—clearly tourists. They did not look happy. Their faces were gray and they hadn't touched their own steaks. The man cast a swift glace at her with a horrified eye.

Oh no, Nora thought, *they've been overhearing our conversation*. She gave them an apologetic smile and resumed work on her steak.

The waitress came over. "Another round?" Her expression had changed since she first seated Nora.

"Yes, please," said Corrie, while Nora ordered a cabernet.

Then Corrie resumed. "The knife was driven in with such force into the sternum—"

Nora quickly touched Corrie's hand and nodded slightly toward the couple at the next table. Corrie stopped speaking and glanced over, realization dawning on her face.

Nora leaned forward, speaking in a whisper. "I think we're ruining their dinner."

"Oh, jeez. Right. The tables are so close."

Nora nodded.

"Reminds me of my human anatomy class back at John Jay," said Corrie, sotto voce, "where we'd eat lunch while dissecting, chopped liver sandwich in one hand, scalpel in the other. I guess we're immune to it."

They both giggled softly, and then Corrie resumed, keeping her voice low and leaning forward. "Tolland stabbed himself with such force that the lower edge of the manubrium was fractured and pieces of the bone were driven into the heart itself."

"Yikes."

"The thing is, those two victims were much better dressed than the others. Having found the cave, they might actually have been able to survive the storm."

"If they weren't already too hypothermic to resist a fight, brought on by their aggressive hallucinations."

"Do you think Tolland might have started to regain his presence of mind after killing Wright? The suicide might have been done in remorse for killing his friend."

"I've studied hypothermia and its effects pretty extensively, and I guess anything is possible. Paradoxical undressing, terminal burrowing—it's all well known and documented. But this kind of fighting, and the bizarre suicide..." Nora shook her head. "It does go beyond most of the behaviors I've read about."

"We're doing broad histology and toxicology on the cadavers, looking for a whole range of exotic drugs and poisons, along with an analysis of stomach contents. We've already ruled out the entire suite of common drugs—LSD, mushrooms, psilocybin, meth, and so forth. We looked for needle marks and scarring—no sign of drug use. The CT scan showed no evidence of brain abnormalities, stroke, aneurism, epileptic seizure—nothing that could explain a psychotic break. We've got people looking into the relationship between Wright and Tolland, prior conflicts, but so far nothing—no girlfriend troubles, jealousy, public arguments. They were good friends going back to high school in Albuquerque."

The next round of drinks arrived. "I can see why you needed a martini," said Nora. "This is nuts."

"I know. You'd think the discovery of two more victims would have shed some light. Just the opposite." Corrie set down the glass. "By the way, I haven't thanked you for finding the site of the fire and uncovering that knife."

"Didn't they search the area of the fire back in 2008?"

"I can't find a record of it in the files." She hesitated. "The mountains were snowed in and the ground wasn't free of snow until June. We're about to interview the supervisory agent at the time, a guy named Gold. That's one of the things I plan to ask him."

"Any luck with the 'MHT' initials?" Nora asked.

"We started with the idea it might have belonged to a Tolland family member, but apparently there wasn't one with those initials."

Nora shook her head.

"I'd like to ground-survey the ravine where the two other bodies were found," Corrie said, "but the mountains are snowed in. We'll have to wait until spring."

"I hope the case is solved by then," said Nora.

"The way things are going..." Corrie shook her head, her voice trailing off into silence.

28

SILVER CITY, CORRIE discovered, was a small old Western town four hours south of Albuquerque, so well preserved it was often used as a movie set. Sharp had mentioned this during the drive—that, and the fact that the town had been taken over by retirees. He'd said little else, sitting in the passenger seat and doing his lizard impression: motionless, only his eyes raising their heavy lids from time to time.

It was not until they'd driven through Silver City itself and were approaching their destination that he spoke again. "Corrie? A word of caution. Keep your professional judgment to yourself until the interview's concluded. An interview is often like a poker game: no feedback, no reaction, keep playing...in this interview perhaps more so than most."

This was the last thing Corrie expected to hear. There'd been some oblique talk about Gold from senior agents that indicated something hadn't been quite right with him since the original investigation. But she knew Sharp well enough to simply nod in agreement and not ask for more detail.

Robertson Gold's house was situated north of town, on a pretty cul-de-sac backing up against the Gila National Forest. The house, Corrie noted, was the last on the street, facing down its length—a law officer's instinctive preference for keeping his back to the wall with a full view of anyone who might be coming. A half dozen cars were parked along the street, and for a moment she wondered if these were real estate agents at an open house nearby. But as they approached, she realized they were protesters: three men and two women, some carrying signs that read, simply, TRUTH. As they pulled past the cars into the driveway, she could hear what they were chanting: "Tell the truth, no more lies! Tell the truth, no more lies!" This was embellished by fist pumps and waving of the signs.

"That's Melody Ann O'Connell," Sharp said, nodding in the direction of a woman in her mid-forties, wearing tight white jeans and incongruously high heels. "She's the stepmother of Rodney O'Connell—victim nine. The de facto spokesperson for the victims' group, Manzano Families Memorial Association."

Corrie scrutinized her, committing to memory

the expensive blow-out, black-painted nails, and a face that seemed to have received the ministrations of multiple cosmetic surgeons. She thought she'd seen her before somewhere—probably on a TV news clip.

Getting out of the vehicle, Sharp and Corrie went briskly up the walkway to the front door, triggering an increased volume of chanting.

"Hey, FBI! What are you hiding?"

"Tell the truth, you liars!"

As an agent Corrie had never been subjected to this kind of confrontation before. But she followed Sharp's lead in ignoring them. Instead of ringing the doorbell, Sharp knocked loudly, making their presence known over the din. It was immediately cracked open—so quickly that Corrie figured the inhabitant had already been in the front hall, watching the goings-on outside.

"Agents Sharp and Swanson," Sharp said.

The door opened wide enough to allow them entrance. As they stepped in, a man—Robertson Gold, Corrie assumed—quickly shut, bolted, and chained the door behind them. According to the file, Robertson Gold was sixty-eight years old. But Corrie would have taken him for at least a decade older. He was tall but bent with age, dressed in a plaid work shirt and jeans. In his lined face Corrie could see, like a pentimento, traces of a strikingly handsome man.

"Let's go back into the office," Gold said. "It's quieter back there."

He turned and led the way out of the living room, past the kitchen, and down a hall. The inside of the house was dim, the curtains drawn. As Gold walked before them, Corrie caught sight of a pistol jammed into his jeans at the small of his back.

The back office was unremarkable, with as much personality as a furniture warehouse. A computer sat on a desk of blond wood, accompanied by a printer. The only place to sit other than at the desk was a sofa against the far wall, between two filing cabinets; Corrie and Sharp settled themselves on it after a wave from Gold. There were no family photographs on display, no plaques or commendations on the wall, no personal knickknacks on the desk. A bookcase stood behind the desk, mostly bare save for books on the JFK assassination and histories of the naval battles of Midway and the Coral Sea. Beyond was a plate-glass window with drawn gauzy curtains that looked toward the mountains. There was absolutely nothing to show that the man had spent decades in the FBI.

Even at the back of the house, the noisy chanting of the group was more than audible.

Gold offered them water, which they politely declined. "What's with the gun?" Sharp asked mildly.

With a faint smirk, Gold reached around, pulled

out a well-used Browning Hi-Power 9×19 Parabellum, and laid it on his desk. "It was my father's," he said.

When this was greeted with silence, he continued. "Don't worry—I'm not planning to take any potshots at those idiots outside. But a man's home is his castle, and I won't abide intrusion on my property. Besides, I made my share of enemies on the job."

"Haven't we all?" Sharp replied.

Gold nodded. "It's been—what? Fourteen years? But you haven't changed a bit, Clay."

"I'm surprised you remember my name."

"Oh, I remember a lot more than that. I remember when you first joined the Albuquerque FO. Caused a lot of speculation around the watercooler back then. Where you came from was a real mystery."

"That was a long time ago," Sharp said, apparently anxious to shift the conversation elsewhere. Corrie's curiosity was piqued, but Sharp clearly wasn't interested in talking about it.

"It's funny, the things you remember. You, for instance. And that thing with the snake." He chuckled.

Corrie broke the brief silence that ensued. "Snake?"

Sharp shifted. "Let's not—"

"Agent Sharp," Gold interrupted, turning to her,

"had only been in the Albuquerque office a month or two."

Sharp looked displeased and Corrie realized she'd just made a mistake.

Gold went on. "This package got delivered to the third floor—addressed to a secretary, chosen at random, I suppose, the FBI wasn't especially popular at that time—and the idiots in the mailroom hadn't checked carefully enough. Inside, under some fake paperwork, was a poisonous coral snake. And it was pissed. The woman screamed so loud the walls almost blew out, and she threw the package and snake into the walkway outside her cubicle. There was a huge ruckus, and that snake could have slithered away in a wink and we'd have been looking forever—but Sharp here snatched it by the tail and cracked that son of a bitch just like it was a whip. Head, eyes, brains, tongue...its whole front end snapped off." He shook his head. "Kind of made the office's day, if you know what I mean."

Corrie looked at Sharp, who now looked even more displeased. She wanted to know more but bit her tongue.

After a beat, Sharp said evenly, "The good old days... But we're here to talk about the Dead Mountain investigation that you led. May we proceed?"

"Of course," Gold replied. And something in his

voice made Corrie suspect that snake anecdote had been a way of stalling.

"Good. I'm glad to see your memory is as sharp as ever."

"That case…" His face clouded. "That case." He gestured toward the front of the house, where the muted chanting could be heard. "Did you hear that? Calling me a liar, heaping abuse on me right in front of my neighbors—when I devoted fourteen months of my life to seeking answers and ruined my life."

"You want me to post a detail?" Sharp asked.

Gold shook his head. "No. I can take care of myself." He cast a glance at the gun on his desk.

"We've got all the files," said Sharp, "so why don't you just tell us about the case in your own way—an overview, as it were."

"When I got the word I was to be lead," said Gold, "I was happier than a tornado in a trailer park." He shook his head. "You never saw a man go to the guillotine with a bigger smile on his face. But first, I'd like to hear more about what you found up in that cave. I only know what I hear on TV and read in the papers. Who did you find? Rodney? Paul? Gordy?"

Corrie could hear the sudden urgency in his voice, and she had a sudden sharp mental image of a younger Gold leading the investigation, poring over interview transcripts, walking the mountains, doing everything he could think of, and then doing it all over again.

"Fair enough," Sharp said, and briefed Gold on their investigation while the old man listened, frowning.

"Good God," Gold murmured as Sharp finished. "They fought, you say?"

"Tolland stabbed Wright to death and then took his own life."

"Jesus." Gold looked stunned. He had sat forward in his chair, hands clasped tightly. "I can't make head nor tail out of that, can't connect it to anything that makes sense."

"So," said Sharp, "let's hear your tale."

Gold began to tell his story—pretty much everything Corrie already knew, but with an injection of rage and grievance Gold had obviously carried on his shoulders ever since. The Dead Mountain case ruined his career and his peace of mind. As he spoke, Corrie hoped to hell she wouldn't end up in the same boat, with an unsolved case and a wrecked career, practically before it had started.

"And that's all there is," said Gold. "I took my retirement early and retreated down here, the case went on ice, and in time things grew quiet. Until now. I assume you read all my weekly summaries, up through ... through the last one?"

They nodded.

"Everything I know, everything I did, is in there—going over the same ground a dozen times, tracking down each lead no matter how crazy, listening to every damn false confession and moronic anonymous accusation called into the hotline."

"Thank you, Agent Gold," said Sharp. "Now, may we ask a few questions?"

"Ask away."

Sharp settled back on the couch and looked at Corrie, a clear indication for her to take the ball. She quickly flipped to her prepared questions in the notebook she'd brought in with her. "The tent site was compromised, but what about the improvised campfire where the three bodies were found?"

"What about it?"

"Did you do a survey?"

"There was a couple feet of snow at the site, but we did what we could. The search and rescue teams were in such a hurry. A few days had passed—we still had hope we'd find some of them alive." He paused. "If you've read the reports, you'll know that the discoveries...of the bodies, of the remains of the campfire...it all took a while to put together. The discoveries overlapped. It was only later we were able to reconstruct what might have happened there. The big mystery was why those bodies were burned the way they were—feet, heads even."

"And after the snow melted? Did you survey the area then?"

Gold looked at her for a long moment. "There was no reason to."

Corrie glanced at Sharp. She recalled his warning: poker face. Now she understood—don't do anything to put the man on the defensive. But the answer was odd and almost, it seemed to her, deceptive.

"Okay," she said. "I know this question might sound a little strange. But did your sixth sense... well, pick up on anything that maybe didn't, or couldn't, go into your reports? Something you might not have thought appropriate to put in writing?"

Gold hesitated for what felt like a long time. "The answer is no: hard facts, hard evidence, verified statements went into those reports. No speculation. I mean, every jackass has a theory. My goal was to keep my head down and focus on the facts."

Corrie turned a page. "One thing we're curious about in particular were the tests for radiation—why they were ordered, who sent the samples."

"I have no idea."

"Where did the results come from—what lab?"

"No idea. The file folder had no ID on it, no cover information. And then, just like that, the report was suddenly withdrawn—classified. No one would answer my questions, even though I had a security clearance, of course."

"Can you be more specific about the withdrawal of that report?"

"A day after the results came in, two spooks showed up. Very polite. They spent some time in our lab, some more time in the evidence vault, and then they came up to me and my team and asked that we give them all the files pertaining to the tests and their results. Next thing I know, the thing was classified at the highest level."

"So who were the spooks? You must have asked for identification."

"No badges of any official governmental branch, just generic IDs, which we confirmed with Justice. They were the real deal—no question."

"But word about the radiation leaked out anyway," Corrie prompted. "How did that happen?"

"We investigated that leak and got nowhere. I'm pretty sure it didn't come from the FBI. Maybe Justice, maybe the military. Too many people had already seen the results to put the genie all the way back in the bottle." He paused. "Have you learned any more about the radiation in your own investigation?" There was a curious tone in his voice as he asked the question, edgy, almost sarcastic.

"The results were a precise match to the tests done on the original samples fifteen years ago." This information had, in fact, just come in, along with the additional toxicology tests on Tolland and

Wright—which had been depressingly devoid of anything interesting. "Let's move ahead to the following May, when two more bodies were found."

Gold nodded. "Lynn and Luke."

"Your reports describe the condition of the bodies in detail but offer no solid conclusions as to what happened."

"No viable scenario presented itself to us. It was clear that the two, who were better clothed than the first four, had tried to dig a cave for warmth in an area of deep, drifted snow near the top of a ravine. What wasn't clear—what, to be blunt, we had no answer for—was why they were crushed in such a traumatic fashion."

"Avalanche?" Corrie asked.

"We looked into that, of course. We called in a local expert on winter mountaineering; it's in the reports. Avalanches require a slope of at least twenty-two degrees to form, and the slope above the ravine was fifteen. In addition, they were at the very top of the ravine, where avalanches don't usually form. We had the expert review the topography—he ruled it out. In the absence of an avalanche, we were unable to determine how they'd been crushed like that, with no broken skin. Any more than we knew how some of them suffered third-degree burns."

"So your final report read," said Corrie.

"Let me just correct you there, Agent Swanson.

There was a *last* report, as I said—but it wasn't final. It was interim. The pressure to solve this case was incredible. God knows there were plenty of half-assed ideas floating around. I could have chosen the least crazy hypothesis and written it up as our presumptive official theory. But that's not the way the FBI works. At least, not how it's supposed to."

"So when you found no theory that fit, no answer that could explain the circumstances, you—as the lead investigator—gave no answer at all," Sharp said.

"Exactly."

And so the case was left open, Corrie thought. *And that only further fueled the controversy. And led to Gold's fall from grace. At least he was honest.*

Aloud, she asked, "Did you survey the ravine area, where the two bodies were found?"

"We collected evidence, of course."

"I mean a survey of the archaeological kind, subsurface."

"Pointless," said Gold. "Even in May the ravine was still full of snow. You saw the photographs. Our ERT did a meticulous job collecting evidence."

He stopped speaking and shifted in his chair, the chanting outside filling the silence. In his eyes, Corrie saw lonely despair; defiance; anger; and frustration.

"I have no more questions," she said, closing her notebook.

Ten minutes later they were back in their SUV, the small band of protesters taking up positions on both sides of them now, chanting energized by their departure. The strophe and antistrophe of their chorus faded as they accelerated away, the front door of the house closed and the blinds shut tight.

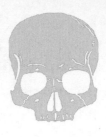

29

As they began the long drive back to the FO, Corrie found herself sharing Sharp's disinclination for talk. She had too much to think about. She'd been hoping to uncover some nugget, some discrepancy, some clue everyone had overlooked, that would blow the case wide open. But all she'd gotten out of the interview was despair and failure. Gold was—no pun intended—played out. Everything he'd witnessed, everything he'd done, was in the files she'd already looked at. Instead of the revelation she'd been anticipating, she'd had a revelation of a far different kind: what it looked like to be given a monster of a case ... and remain unable to bring it to a satisfactory conclusion.

She had a creeping suspicion that Gold—a hardworking, accomplished, and honorable agent—hadn't quite been up to it. He'd gone into the case with high hopes, a stepping-stone to greater things.

But instead, he had retired under a cloud, and the unfinished business had gnawed at him ever since. And it seemed to her that he had not followed up, or had given up too soon, on some obvious lines of inquiry. Instead of a mother lode, she'd found a sad and disturbing scene—made worse by shrill protesters invading his very place of retreat. *Tell the truth, no more lies!* It was awful. They were awful. She quickly reminded herself they were the families of the victims—but did that excuse it?

Tell the truth, no more lies! The voices echoed in Corrie's head as she merged onto I-25 just south of Caballo. But Gold *had* told the truth—that was the problem.

Could what happened to Gold happen to her now? Or Sharp?

What kind of agent had he been? Competent, honest, but unimaginative. The regimented mindset he'd revealed was unsuited to such an exotic problem. If ever there was a case that demanded out-of-the-box thinking, this was it. The more she thought about it, the more it seemed Gold had searched for answers by asking only the most obvious questions. When normal investigative paths led nowhere, he'd just gone down them again...and again. For example, he couldn't understand why the bodies around the fire were so badly burned on their feet, legs, and heads. To him, it was a mystery. To the public, it was proof of aliens or secret weapons. But to Corrie, the answer seemed so obvious she was almost afraid to voice it.

And Gold hadn't surveyed the fire pit: something Nora did before Corrie thought to ask her. And she'd recovered a knife with initials on it. Perhaps not a valuable clue, but still... Then there was the ravine. Nobody had surveyed that. An avalanche could not have taken place—she felt Gold had reasonably established that—but what other possibilities had he failed to consider? Some weird weather event? Falling rocks? What else could have crushed those bodies so completely?

She drove another twenty minutes in silence, wheels turning in her head as well as on the road. Then she turned to Sharp. "About those burns on the victims...?"

"Yes?"

She hesitated. "I'm not a winter backpacker, sir, but I think I know how they got burned."

"Let's hear it."

"Okay, consider this, sir: You have these nine people, mostly undressed, who've fled their tent into a storm. They've run in the snow almost a mile, then lit a fire. That must have taken a half hour or more. According to Dr. Kelly's survey of the fire area, it was a big fire."

"Go on."

"So by the time the fire is going, they're already freezing to death. They've got hypothermia. Their feet and hands are badly frostbitten. They're losing their grip on reality."

"So you think they stuck their feet, hands, and heads into the fire?"

He made it sound so stupid. But she went on. "Well, yes, in fact. Think about it. That fire, big as it was, couldn't keep them from freezing. The meteorological report says the winds were forty to fifty miles an hour, temperatures ten below zero. They got too close to the fire in a desperate effort to extract warmth from it."

"And actually burned their flesh?"

"They couldn't feel it! The burns were on their feet, shins, forearms, and heads. Those are the very areas that were exposed. Those extremities were frostbitten; they were huddling so close to the fire they were too close to the flames, maybe even *in* the flames, and they were freezing to death at the same time. The first three died anyway, then the rest cut off their meager clothes and went on northward, realizing the fire couldn't save them."

"This is a new wrinkle."

"It seems obvious." She abruptly stopped. Maybe she had pushed her point too far.

"Obvious? Yet none of our experts drew this conclusion."

"Agent Gold knew it wasn't an avalanche that collapsed the tent. He said he'd called in an expert on winter mountaineering."

"A local expert."

"But he didn't say anything about calling a doctor who specialized in hypothermia. Or a real expert in avalanches."

"No," said Sharp slowly, drawing out the word. "But perhaps you should."

"I will, sir."

She couldn't tell from those sleepy eyes what he really thought. But he did authorize her to hire experts. She made a mental note to find the most qualified avalanche expert she could—the case, and the victims, demanded no less.

"Another thing?" she ventured.

The eyelids rose.

"Do you think we could arrange a tour of Kirtland?"

The senior agent was slow to stir himself. "Kirtland?"

"I'd like to ask the military to give us a tour. I don't mean the typical visitor's tour, but a tour of the mountainous area in the east."

"May I ask why?"

"The radiation contamination, the whole classified business Gold talked about. Kirtland stores the nation's nuclear weapons. That's an obvious connection."

"Another 'obvious.' Okay. Now, give me an anodyne reason that I can put on paper...one which might stand a chance of getting through military bureaucracy."

Corrie was silent a moment. "Kirtland's southern border is about five miles north of the cave where Tolland and Wright were found. You were the first one to tell me that the location of the bodies trend in a beeline north: from the tent, to the fire pit, to where the fourth body was found, to the ravine, to the cave. That direction leads to the southern Kirtland border. I'd like to see that portion of its fence."

"And look for what?"

"Maybe the ninth person cut through the fence, and there's evidence of that still."

"I'm not sure the air force would appreciate being linked to the Dead Mountain investigation. We might not be welcome."

"We don't need them to welcome us with dancing girls and champagne...just a Jeep and a driver. Present it as routine. Dotting the i's and crossing the t's."

"They are likely to point out this seems rather far-fetched."

"I don't think it's random that every one of those

victims were heading in the same direction. They left the fire with a goal in mind, some goal we don't yet know. Maybe it was just the base itself and the hope of finding a patrol. But it stands to reason if the ninth camper, O'Connell, survived longer than the rest—and we haven't found his body anywhere along the route—he might have made it to that fence and onto the base. He was only one of two with both his boots on and fully dressed for outside."

"I won't insult your intelligence by pointing out that had he gotten into Kirtland, his body would have been discovered long ago."

"But it's the one place we haven't been able to search. And that radiation—you've got to admit it points to Kirtland. I don't recall from the files that Gold or anyone else followed up on that possible lead."

Sharp was quiet for so long that Corrie grew sure he'd nixed the idea. And so it was with surprise that, as they were passing the desiccated whistle stop known as Luis Lopez, she heard him say, "Okay."

"Okay what, sir?"

"I think it's a good idea."

"Thank you."

"Don't thank me yet. When we get back to the office, let's schedule a visit with the Kirtland commander to discuss it. He'll have the final say. And Corrie?"

"Yes?"

"Step on it, will you? I'd like to get back before dinner."

And while Sharp plumped and prodded his seat like a dog preparing for a nap, Corrie—already going seventy-five—pressed her foot on the accelerator, adding another fifteen miles per hour. She was, after all, in no danger of getting a speeding ticket.

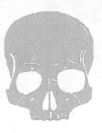

30

WINTER HAD SETTLED in along the Rio Grande. A freezing wind whipped a few stray flakes of snow across the mesa that overlooked the river, flowing sluggish and brown. The mesa top was barren save for a few twisted juniper trees, and the sky the color of zinc. Nora looked around curiously as people assembled for the burial ceremony. While she had attended a number of Pueblo dances, she'd never participated in anything like this, and she knew it was a privilege to be there. Few were in attendance—less than two dozen. Two side-by-side graves lay open, dirt piled up nearby. Next to them stood a folding table covered with a baize cloth, on which were placed two small painted boxes carrying the bones. Laid out next to the boxes were the few artifacts recovered: the broken golden micaceous pot, gleaming dully in the gray light; several spearpoints; and a fetish made of carved shell. A line of Isleta elders in traditional Pueblo dress stood in a solemn row next to the gravesite, along with a singer with a drum, waiting motionless, the wind ruffling their hair and clothing. Nora, bundled in a down jacket, a hat, and gloves, thought they must be freezing, but they showed no signs of cold.

Skip stood next to her, also in a puffy down jacket, hands shoved into his pockets, looking dour. Skip's attorney, Edward Lightfeather, was beside him. The last to arrive was Darren Tenorio, wearing an Isleta-style shirt with a cowboy hat and leather vest, who came over from the parking area. He greeted her with a nod and a handshake.

"Glad to have you here," he said.

"Thank you for the invitation."

Tenorio leaned over and grasped Skip's hand. "You too, Skip. I'm glad you could come to see us put these remains to rest—especially after the price you paid."

"Thank you," said Skip, "I really appreciate that. That bastard Hawley—"

Nora nudged him, hard; now was not the time to go on another tirade about the crooked sheriff.

Tenorio turned to Nora. "This mesa top is our traditional burying ground. Most of our people today are Catholic and they're buried in the mission graveyard, but we don't bury prehistoric remains there. Those who aren't Christians can be buried up here, if they choose."

"It's got an amazing view."

"Yes. You can see the entire pueblo. Isleta was originally built on an island in the river, which is why the Spanish gave it that name four hundred years ago. You can see the scar of the old river channel behind town. Its real name—our name—is Shiewhibak."

Nora could see where the river had once been, having evidently shifted into its present channel sometime in the past. The dusty adobe and prefab homes of the pueblo were surrounded by irrigated fields, with strips of bare cottonwood trees along the river. The Manzanos rose up in the east, a wall of mountains from north to south as far as the eye could see, their upper slopes covered with fresh snow, peaks lost in the winter clouds. In the opposite direction, to the west, stood layer upon layer of desert mesas in shades of brown, orange, and russet. It was an austere, windswept vista.

At the last minute, a Ford Explorer emblazoned with a sheriff's logo drove up and a young man got out, wearing a black cowboy hat. Nora immediately recognized, to her surprise, that it was Sheriff Watts. He came striding over on lanky legs.

"Glad you could make it, Sheriff," said Tenorio, as they shook hands.

"Honored to be invited." He leaned over and took Nora's hand, then Skip's and the lawyer's, greeting them all.

"What are you doing here?" Nora whispered.

"I'm a friend of the tribe," he whispered back. "Our office has been able to, shall we say, help them with a few matters."

With this mysterious pronouncement, the hour arrived, and they fell into silence. Watts removed his hat. The drummer began to beat a mournful rhythm, long and slow, on the painted cottonwood drum tightly covered with hide. After a moment, several singers broke into a high, quavering song that rose and fell in the wind.

After a few moments an elder, wrapped in a woven blanket, with long white braids down his back, came forward and sprinkled pollen and cornmeal from a small painted pot over the two coffin-boxes. The singing rose in cadence and the beat got louder, remaining at the same slow pace. The old man stepped back, covered the pot with a piece of sandstone, raised it up, and placed it back in a leather satchel.

The singing slowly died away as the drumbeat softened, then ended with the shake of a bone rattle.

The elder stepped forward and began speaking in the Isletan language, which Nora understood was Southern Tiwa. It wasn't so much a spoken requiem

as it was a low, repetitive chant, with a funereal into-
nation. His quavering voice was whisked away by
the cold wind, sometimes louder, sometimes softer,
but always elegiac. As the chanting continued,
Tenorio and three other council members stepped
forward and grasped the green straps around each
coffin, which they used to raise up and carefully
lower the caskets into the two holes, first one and
then the other. The few grave goods—including,
Nora saw with dismay, the micaceous pot—were
then lowered into the graves. Each council member in turn took a silver spade and tossed in a bit of
earth from the piles. The elder gestured for everyone else who was present to come forward and add
their own spadefuls of earth, as the chanting dirge
continued.

And then it was over. Everyone shook hands with
each other in silence, and they headed back to their
vehicles, while some remained behind to finish filling in the graves.

Watts fell alongside of Nora and Skip as they
walked back to the car.

"Sorry to hear about the Hawley incident," said
Watts, shaking his head. "He's an embarrassment to
the state."

"You're not kidding," said Skip. "I got everything
on video, but I guess he's erased it by now."

"Of course he has."

Lightfeather joined them and they stood next to the car.

"What do you know about him?" Skip asked the sheriff.

Watts paused. "Well...We had a little dustup once. It's a long story. All I can say is, I'm glad you got yourself a good lawyer." He grinned and laid his hand on Lightfeather's shoulder. "I'd love to see you put one over on old One-Bally."

Lightfeather nodded, a twinkle appearing in his eye.

Skip leaned forward. "One-Bally?"

"We know him as One-Bally Hawley."

"Why?"

Watts gave a low chuckle. "This isn't the time or place to talk about it. For now, I'll just say this much: Hawley's a real son of a bitch, and you'd better be prepared." He donned his hat, stepped into the sheriff's department vehicle, then gave them a little wave as he pulled away.

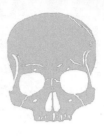

31

CORRIE WALKED INTO her apartment and set her laptop and notebooks down on the worktable. What with the Gold interview and the drive there and back, it felt like a long day even though it was just half past four. High-profile or not, the Dead Mountain case was still full of humdrum work: checking off every lead, filling out paperwork, following up on useless tips. Bellamy, O'Hara, and the others had been out in the field all day, doing exactly that: currently, they'd moved on to interviewing people even tangentially connected with the case. Meanwhile, now that they'd spoken with Gold, she had assigned herself the problem of the knife.

Once she'd learned the initials "MHT" matched nobody in the Tolland family, she began looking farther afield. She'd hit upon the idea of calling the registrar at NMIT, to learn if there were any students with those initials around the time of the

Manzano tragedy. She had managed to catch an administrator just before the registrar's office closed, and it had taken a little standard-issue FBI pressure to loosen the bureaucracy, but in the end she'd been rewarded with a class list of students roughly contemporaneous with the fated nine. One name stood out: Matthew Hartley Tanner, who'd graduated in 2010 with a PhD in biochemistry. He now worked at a company outside Stanford, specializing in the vetting of new pharmaceutical applications for the FDA.

She put some water on to boil, then, checking her watch, turned on the TV. Amid the flood of streaming content, she'd accidentally found a local channel that, as if thumbing its nose at a dystopian present, stubbornly devoted afternoons to airing reruns of chestnuts like *The Dick Van Dyke Show*, *The Lone Ranger*, and *Hogan's Heroes*. These brought back good memories to Corrie—afternoons when she got home from school, before her mom finished work, and she enjoyed their background murmur. Besides, she'd had a youthful crush on Clayton Moore—with his black mask and white-handled pistols—that hadn't entirely gone away.

Corrie opened her laptop and updated her case log to reflect the work she'd done that day. Then she went over her notes and turned down the TV—just as the Lone Ranger was ordering Tonto, in a most

un-woke manner, to ride into town—and made a
call on her cell phone. She checked her watch: quarter to five, near the end of the workday—a good
time to call.

"Tanner," came the crisp voice on the other end
of the phone.

"Is this Matthew Tanner?"

"This is Dr. Tanner. Who am I speaking with?"

"Dr. Tanner, my name is Agent Corinne Swanson. I'm with the FBI, and we're investigating the
recent developments in the Manzano case."

There was a brief pause. "You mean the two
bodies."

"Yes."

"Were they really two of the missing?"

"Yes. Beyond that, I'm afraid I can't go into
detail. The reason I'm calling is that a knife with
the engraved initials 'MHT' was found in a location
where some of the victims died. Since you attended
New Mexico Institute of Technology around the
time of the tragedy and those are your initials, we
were wondering if you knew anything about this
knife."

Another pause. "What can you tell me about the
knife? What did it look like?"

The guy sounded wary, but naturally so under
the circumstances. "It's a folding knife, with a lock-
ing blade roughly four inches long. The initials are

engraved on a small silver plaque on the side, inset into a wooden handle."

"Was it a classic Buck?"

"Yes."

"Then it's mine, all right. My dad gave it to me when I became an Eagle Scout."

"And you took it with you to grad school?"

"Yes."

"What happened to it?"

"I thought I'd lost it. You're saying you *found* it with the bodies?"

"Yes."

"Wow."

"Dr. Tanner, did you know any of the victims on that expedition?"

"I did. Two of them, Mike and Amanda, lived in my dorm. I mostly knew them through my roommate, who was in the engineering department with them. I was in the chem department."

"I see. And did you loan either of them your knife?"

"No."

"Did you loan anybody your knife?"

"No." A hesitation. "I wouldn't have loaned it out. It meant a lot to me."

"Could one of the party have taken it without your knowledge?"

"I guess so—you know what it's like living in a

dorm; people were always borrowing CDs or stealing cookies." Another hesitation. "That was a pretty traumatic time for all of us at the university."

"You said your roommate knew some of them well. Who was that?"

"Alex. Alex DeGregorio. He was really torn up about it."

The name didn't ring a bell. She was pretty sure he hadn't been interviewed in the case the first time around. Maybe he'd taken the knife and given it to one of the hikers.

"I'd like to send you a photo of the knife to get a positive ID. May I do that?"

"Sure. Of course." He hesitated. "Is there any way I could get it back?"

Corrie assumed he wanted the knife for sentimental reasons. Made sense, under the circumstances. "Right now, it's evidence. But I can look into returning it later on, once the case is closed."

After another brief exchange, she thanked him and hung up. Now she had an owner to match the -initials on the knife, but it hadn't really gotten her anywhere. Somebody on the expedition had borrowed or stolen it.

I mostly knew them through my roommate. So the roommate—Alex DeGregorio—had known the victims well. Two agents had been assigned to work

their way through a list of interviews at NMIT—
academic advisors of the victims and close friends—
but they didn't know about Tanner or DeGregorio.
As long as she was checking off leads, she might as
well finish this one.

Glancing through the class lists she'd obtained
from the registrar, Corrie located an Alexander
DeGregorio who had been on campus around the
same time as Tanner. His record was less complete
than Tanner's—perhaps he'd transferred somewhere else. A check of the FBI's database furnished
her with an address and phone number in Fal-
mouth, Massachusetts. It appeared to be a business
address, but it was the only one on file. She made
the call.

"Prometheus Libre Associates."

"May I speak with Alexander DeGregorio?"

When Corrie was finally transferred to DeGregorio's office after going through an alarming number of assistants, his secretary informed her that
DeGregorio was in the field at Nirwana, Indonesia,
and temporarily out of reach.

Corrie left a message for him to call her back.
It was now past six, and the reruns on her muted
TV had given way to local news. As she reached
for the power button, an info ticker crawled across
the bottom of the screen, telling of a gangland-style

execution—of someone with the odd name of Cheape—that had taken place in Socorro.

Socorro: that was Watts's territory. She turned on the sound and learned that Cheape, a retired maintenance worker from Kirtland AFB, had been bound with duct tape in his own living room and shot through the back of the head. That would be a noteworthy case for Watts, she thought, which might be interesting to hear about at their next meeting. And there was Kirtland—again.

Her mind temporarily strayed to Watts and his curly hair and white teeth. She quickly pushed these out of her head and turned back to her computer. As she did a deeper search on DeGregorio, she found out the guy had done well after leaving grad school— built up and sold a bioengineering company for a couple of hundred million by age thirty-five, then started a foundation to improve the treatment of Neglected Tropical Diseases, or NTDs, endemic to South Pacific countries like the Marshall Islands, Malaysia, Brunei, and Borneo, where he'd spent the first part of his life as a navy brat.

Nirwana, the secretary had said. Corrie googled this and discovered it was a beach community on the island of Sulawesi. The photos on her screen showed an unspoiled idyll of turquoise water, white sand, and lush palm trees.

If you're going to start a foundation, might as well start one in paradise, she thought. Standing, she wondered if all FBI agents were this cynical—or if that was something else she had Medicine Creek to thank for.

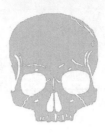

32

THE PRESS CONFERENCE was held on the broad
steps of the Albuquerque Field Office. A podium
and stanchions had been hastily assembled, and
the press had gathered in the parking lot directly
in front. As Sharp strolled up toward the podium
in the afternoon light, Corrie—following him at
a slight distance—was shocked by the vast sea of
cameras and boom microphones, the scores of eager
faces that made up the gathered media.

Corrie had known the case was big, but looking
at the call signs emblazoned on the video cameras—
CNN, FOX, MSNBC, various network and cable
channels—she realized not only that these people
had come from all over the state, but that a lot of
them represented national news. She'd seen press
vans and gaggles of reporters around town—one
had even parked outside her apartment a few morn-
ings ago, forcing her to leave by a back exit—but

this was a far cry from the impromptu media brief-ing she'd conducted eight days before.

Earlier, Sharp had, without preamble, let her know he'd be handling this one—and she'd felt relieved. Behind Sharp stood an impressive, blue-suited row of big shots. Garcia was in the middle, silent and stern, hands crossed in front, the other agents on the case, including Corrie, flanking him on either side.

Briskly, without a pause to test the mike or clear his throat, Sharp began. "Ladies and gentlemen," he said, voice echoing lazily across the lot, "we've called you here to present our initial findings in the ongo-ing Dead Mountain case. Our purpose is to present such facts as we know, answer your questions to the best of our ability, quell any rumors, and in so doing uphold our duty to inform the public."

He'd brought along no notes to refer to, so after a quick glance around he continued. In a calm, almost conversational tone, he reviewed the earlier history of the case, then proceeded to summarize the new discoveries so quickly, and so masterfully, that the group fell silent in order not to miss a single word. He sounded surprisingly frank and forthcoming—naming the two victims who'd been found—except he did not mention that Tolland killed Wright and then stabbed himself in the heart.

When he was done, he swept the audience with

his heavy eyes. "We'll now take a brief number of questions. Please be direct and to the point."

He glanced over the audience. Everyone, it seemed, raised their hand at once. He pointed. "Ms. Fleming."

Corrie, looking in the indicated direction, was astonished to see one of CNN's major anchors.

"Where were these new bodies found in relation to the campsite?" the woman asked.

"Roughly three miles to the north. The specific location has been secured, and let me warn the public and press to please not attempt to access or approach it."

"One member of the expedition is still missing?" another reporter asked.

"Yes—Rodney O'Connell."

"Any idea where he might be?"

"Unfortunately, no. But we're searching."

"Were these victims undressed, like the others?"

"These had greater protection against the cold, but by no means sufficient for the conditions."

The voices began to shout over each other. A skeletal woman with blonde hair made herself heard. "Some of the victims found earlier—many, in fact— were in a strange condition, burnt feet and hair, missing eyes and the like, that has never been satisfactorily explained. What was the cause of death in these newly found victims?"

"You described the condition of some of the bodies as not being 'satisfactorily explained.' That remains the situation today. There are certain deaths for which we still lack clarification. Once we have that evidence, we won't hold it back."

Sharp waited for the commotion to die down, then he selected another raised hand.

"When this tragedy first came to light," asked a man beside a camera labeled *Tripp NewsNational*, "many theories were brought forward. Has the discovery of these two bodies pushed any of those theories to the front?"

"Not yet. As I said, we're still analyzing the evidence."

"A lot of time has passed since the tragedy," said another national anchor. "There's been a huge improvement in forensic technology in those intervening years. Can we assume the discovery of these two bodies caused a fresh examination of the original evidence?"

"We would be remiss if it had not."

"And has any of that technology revealed new leads?"

"Yes, but it's too soon to say what those are."

"What's going on with the ancient Indian bones that were also found in that cave?" yelled somebody else.

"The bones have been repatriated to Isleta Pueblo

and buried, under the auspices of tribal leaders, on sacred ground. For more information, you'll have to speak with the tribe itself."

"What about the radiation?" came a new voice. "Were the new bodies contaminated like some of the others?"

"We're looking into that," Sharp said. Not a white lie, exactly, but—since the answer they'd already received was positive—an omission of detail.

"Where did the radiation come from?"

"Again, we're actively pursuing that question."

"As everyone knows, strange moving lights were seen in the mountains the night of the hikers' deaths," another voice called out. "Have you considered the possibility of some sort of alien attack or encounter?"

"Those aliens I've spoken to deny any involvement."

A murmur of amusement rose up. Corrie marveled at how Sharp was playing this unruly crowd like a conductor taming an orchestra.

"What about the Boston Project?" came a shrill voice.

"The Boston Project?" repeated Sharp.

"The secret project launched in parallel with the Manhattan Project! The one involving biowarfare and genetic engineering."

Corrie's heart sank as she recognized Melody

Ann, the leader of the Manzano Families group she'd seen gathered in protest outside Agent Gold's house the day before.

"The so-called Boston Project," said Sharp mildly, "was thoroughly and completely debunked years ago. We do not believe there ever was such a project."

Melody Ann was surrounded by the same people as before, only this time there were more of them. Several were again holding signs that read, TRUTH. Corrie wondered how that mob had gained entry to a press conference—then realized it would be awfully difficult to turn away family members.

"I represent the Manzano Families," Melody Ann continued, "and we believe there's a cover-up in process here: one that's been in the works since our children first went missing. How can you be so sure that the Boston Project isn't real?"

"Thank you for the question," said Sharp, addressing this woman as if she were a professional reporter. "I mentioned that we're reexamining all aspects of this case, new and old. It's important that we keep an open mind." He paused to let this sink in. "So let me direct my response to all the various Dead Mountain theories that stray into the realms of the exotic or unusual."

He looked around. "We have, in fact, considered every single one of these: aliens, a Yeti attack,

Russian espionage gone awry, North Korea, ghost hyenas from the asteroid belt, and, of course, the so-called Boston Project you mention. We have found absolutely no evidence so far to support any of these. But let me repeat, so as to be very clear: until such time as we actually solve this case with solid, tangible, irrefutable evidence, we would be doing the victims a disservice if we did not keep our minds completely open."

"You claim to have investigated, but we don't believe it!" cried Melody Ann. "This whole thing is a smokescreen, a misdirection. *You!*" she said, pointing at Corrie. "What are you hiding? What are *all* of you hiding?"

Corrie felt as if she'd been suddenly tossed a bundle of rattlesnakes, but Sharp didn't miss a beat. He leaned into the mike, and the power of his amplified voice rang loud and clear, overpowering the strident woman. "You have my promise that we will make ourselves available again as soon as we know more. Thank you for coming, and good day."

And with this he turned, nodding at Garcia and motioning for Corrie to precede him back into the field office. A fresh volley of questions rolled over their shoulders, along with a group of voices—Melody Ann's included—chanting the names of the victims: "*Henry Gardiner . . . Luke Hightower . . . Andrew Marchenko . . . Lynn Martinez . . .*"

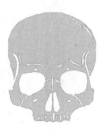

33

SPECIAL AGENT BRENDAN O'Hara paused at the summit of Wilson Peak, his breath condensing into clouds of frost in the cold mountain air. It was a stupendous sight, with views both east and west. The peak was flat, a large expanse of unbroken snow ending in steep cliffs. Snow had accumulated to about a foot, but the wind had stripped most of it off the high ridgeline, making snowshoes unnecessary. He hadn't been happy with the assignment—it seemed like a waste of time, searching these snowy mountains for human remains—but now that he was up here, he was glad. O'Hara was a hiking aficionado, and he decided to treat this not as a time-wasting assignment but as a day off from work.

The view northward showed the broad summit narrowing to a ridge that continued along the spine of the mountains, leading to another peak that stood up like a shark's tooth in the distance. He checked his GPS app on his phone—Lagarto Peak, right on the border of the Kirtland AFB property. It was less than two miles away, and the hike to its base looked easy. Beyond that, it was steep.

Agent Bellamy came up behind him with two people from the Evidence Response Team, carrying packs with their usual equipment and containers—although it didn't seem likely they would gather any evidence in these snowy mountains.

"That peak's our destination," said O'Hara, checking his phone again. "Two miles. The Kirtland fence goes across the summit."

"Right," said Bellamy, panting. "And what exactly are we supposed to be looking for?"

"Caves, overhangs, rocks, any places where the final victim might have tried to shelter."

"Needle in a haystack," Bellamy said. "The body could be anywhere in these mountains—or nowhere at all if the coyotes and bears got to it. It's been fifteen years, for fuck's sake."

O'Hara was getting fed up with Bellamy's complaining, which had been going on since the drive up. "It's a four-mile round-trip hike—two hours. No big deal."

"Can you believe they gave a mentee the number two slot on this case?" Bellamy said, as they found their hiking rhythm.

"You mean Agent Swanson?"

"Yeah. Why her? This is a huge case."

O'Hara didn't answer. He didn't feel like engaging with Bellamy on the subject.

"I'll tell you 'why her,'" Bellamy went on. "Affirmative action at work. I mean, they're always making a big deal about getting more female agents, so they take a girl like her and leapfrog her over the rest of us with seniority. She's, like, barely out of the Academy."

O'Hara didn't like this talk at all. It was the kind that could get him and Bellamy in deep shit. He paused and lifted his binoculars, scouring the slopes and looking for any sign of a cave or shelter. The wind was blowing lightly, and the air was bracing. While the ridgetops were bare, snow cornices were piling up on the eastern slopes. The nine hikers had all gone north, but he couldn't imagine why. There was nothing he could see ahead but more mountains.

"I just don't think it's fair, that's all," Bellamy grumbled.

It seemed Bellamy just had to have a response, so O'Hara said, "She found the cave with the two bodies, so I don't think it's so unusual she was given second slot."

"Not if she were a guy."

"Why are you so sure she's lucky, anyway? If they don't solve it, she's screwed. Look what happened to Gold."

"That was before my time."

"Dead Mountain ruined his career. He took early retirement."

"Sharp's a smart guy, but in my opinion, Swanson's going to be a drag on him. She has no experience."

At this, O'Hara glanced back at the two ERT technicians, who were engaged in their own conversation, too far away to hear. Then he looked at Bellamy, keeping his voice low. "You need to be more careful with what you say—you know that?"

"Who's gonna hear?"

"I am."

"Don't tell me you're offended."

"I'm getting there."

Bellamy shook his head. "Sorry. She's a friend?"

"No."

"So why the bent nose? I was at the range with her, and she can't shoot worth shit. This is a serious issue, O'Hara. The FBI's lowering its standards. It's a risk to all of us."

O'Hara knew that career advancement in the FBI was highly dependent on collegiality and maintaining your fellow agents' regard. For that reason it would not be a good idea to tell Bellamy he was a first-class dickwad. He just wished that up there in the mountains, the guy would shut his trap long enough to allow him some peace and quiet to enjoy the views. The solution, he decided, was to pick up his pace—dramatically.

It worked. Bellamy struggled to keep up, thankfully falling silent as he got too out of breath to engage in small talk. O'Hara stopped from time to time to examine the slopes with his binocs and check his GPS. The ninth victim, if he really got this far north, really didn't have a choice but to follow the mountain spine, as the slopes fell off so steeply on either side—except a ridge ahead that branched off to the right, curving eastward, that was fairly level. It disappeared behind Lagarto Peak. He took out his phone and looked at the GPS, displaying a USGS topo map of where he was. The ridge sloped downward slightly and went behind the Kirtland AFB property before ending in a warren of savage and impassable canyons, marked on the map as the Knot. If the ninth victim had gone that way, he'd certainly have gotten lost and died in that labyrinth.

He wondered about the ninth victim. It was at night in a blizzard. He must have had a headlamp, otherwise he'd never have gotten anywhere...But a headlamp wouldn't see very far in the snowstorm, which meant that unless there was shelter close to the ridgeline, number nine would not have found it.

He tried to recall the name. Rodney O'Connell— that was it. Irish, like himself. The victim's family hadn't been on his interview list, and he wondered if they were still around. He and his wife had just started trying to have a baby, and the thought of their child vanishing into thin air seemed like the worst nightmare in the world.

He continued hiking briskly, taking long steps. The ridge was scoured of snow and it was easy going. Lagarto Peak loomed up. They were making good time. O'Hara was glad he stayed in good shape. Bellamy, on the other hand, was falling behind, and he could hear the agent breathing hard.

The ridge descended gradually to a saddle. At the bottom, he paused to look up, Lagarto Peak rising like a pyramid above him. He now had a clear view of the ridgeline to the summit. He stopped to survey it with his binoculars.

"See anything?" Bellamy asked.

O'Hara, ignoring his partner, could see no good route up the ridge of Lagarto. There was no trail, and various bands of rock along the ridge would have to be scrambled up, some looking fairly serious, maybe class 3 or even 4. And trying to climb them at night, in a blizzard...? No. There was no way O'Connell could have scrambled up that. Which meant one of two things: either he had perished before he got to Lagarto, or he had gone some other way. The eastward-curving ridge was the only other way he could have gone. It was a relatively gentle route until it ended abruptly in those canyons.

There was no point in continuing up Lagarto Peak. It would be a bear of a climb, and O'Connell hadn't gone that way. That warren of canyons to the east might be an area to search later.

"We're not going to climb that son of a bitch, are we?" Bellamy asked, looking up at the peak.

"No," said O'Hara. "It's getting late. We're going back."

"About fucking time."

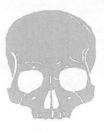

34

THE JEEP APPROACHED the foothills of the Manzanos along a straight dirt road, Colonel Abecassis at the wheel and driving fast—too fast. Corrie had a whole list of questions she wanted to ask, but she was finding it hard to focus as the Jeep tore across the desert at sixty miles an hour. Meanwhile, Abecassis was reciting the history of Kirtland and the role it played in the nation's nuclear defense, occupying fifty-two thousand acres and employing twenty-three thousand people, including forty-two hundred on active duty, home to the 377th Air Base Wing—her wing—the 498th Nuclear Systems Wing, the 58th Special Operations Wing, ten groups and seven squadrons, and on and on, with Corrie nodding and murmuring encouraging words and gripping the armrests with white knuckles.

In their initial meeting, Corrie had been surprised to find the vice commander a woman, and

then she chided herself for holding the same unconscious assumptions she decried in others. She had
written in her notebook her tongue-twisting name
and title: Colonel Maryam Abecassis, Vice Commander, 377th Air Base Wing. She was the person
at Kirtland in charge of, among many other things,
base security.

Abecassis had insisted on driving the Jeep herself,
dismissing the notion of a driver. She put Corrie in
the seat next to her—openly impressed that such a
young woman was an FBI agent—while sticking
Sharp in the back with a master sergeant named
Brickell, whom she'd chosen to come along because
he knew the remote areas of the base and had been
there almost seventeen years—which would have
included the Manzano tragedy.

Colonel Abecassis was a physically imposing
presence—six feet tall, athletic, hair pulled back
in a bun, wearing desert camo and a maroon beret
at a jaunty angle, with the full-bird colonel's eagle
stitched on the front. Despite the intimidating look,
she proved to be friendly and relaxed—and talk-
ative to the point of garrulousness.

Corrie had almost canceled the tour after getting
O'Hara's report on the difficulty the ninth victim
would have faced in reaching the Kirtland AFB
fence. But she didn't, if only because she was certain
the radiation contamination must have something

to do with Kirtland and its store of nuclear weapons. While there were other possible sources of radiation contamination—medical uses, for example—the FBI lab in Quantico had reported that the radioisotopes found on the clothing included trace amounts of plutonium and uranium that could only have come from a nuclear weapon or a reactor. It seemed obvious that nearby Kirtland, the world's largest depository of nuclear weapons, must have been the source.

As the foothills loomed up, Abecassis slowed down slightly, to Corrie's relief. She managed to insert a question during a brief lull in the flow of history. "I understand you store a lot of nuclear weapons here."

"Yes. In the Underground Munitions and Maintenance Storage Complex. It's not something we talk about, but everyone knows. Exactly what's stored there, how much—that's all classified."

"There was radioactive contamination on the clothing of the two victims found in the cave." *Just like on the other six*, she thought but did not say. "Do you have any idea where that might have come from?"

"What kind of contamination?"

"The lab at Quantico tells us plutonium, uranium, and tritium, among others. Very trace amounts."

"Oh boy. That's not good."

"The report says it can only have come from a nuclear weapon or reactor."

"That's correct." She hesitated. "Let's be honest. In the days of the Manhattan Project—which we were part of—people weren't careful. Quite a lot of minor contamination occurred. People just didn't know how dangerous radioactivity was or how to handle it properly. Sometimes they disposed of radioisotopes like you would garbage. Up at Los Alamos, I hear they just tossed the stuff into the canyons. Incredible, right? That seems to have happened here as well, to a much lesser extent. We've had to conduct some remedial efforts cleaning up stuff on the base."

"What about outside the base? In the mountains where the victims were found?"

"That's highly unlikely. I'd say impossible, in fact. We receive and ship nuclear weapons, of course, but they're completely sealed."

"No idea, then, how contamination might have gotten into the mountains south of here, where the bodies were found?"

"None at all. But if I had to guess, I'd say the bodies brought the contamination to the mountains—not the other way around."

They had now reached the base of the foothills, and the Jeep slowed further as the road wound up a draw.

"What can you tell me about the history of weapon storage here?" Corrie asked.

"The first bombs were sent here in 1945 and guarded by Manhattan Project military police, at a place then called the Manzano Base. Kirtland absorbed the base as it expanded. In 1947, they excavated a storage facility in the Manzano Mountains and moved the weapons inside. They were stored in steel bunkers. Those early Mark V bombs had to be assembled in case of war. They also created an emergency relocation center for President Eisenhower in 1953, where he could retreat in case of nuclear war—a command and control bunker complex, specially built for him and select military staff."

"Really?" Corrie was surprised by this. "A presidential bunker? Here in New Mexico? Is that generally known?"

"It's legendary. Most everyone in New Mexico knows the story."

"Is it still in use?"

Abecassis laughed. "A classic case of anachronistic military overspending—but you didn't hear that from me. Less than ten years after its completion, when the Russians unleashed the Tsar Bomba, they realized the bunker couldn't survive an H-bomb strike of that size, so they abandoned it."

"So where is this complex? In the mountains?"

"The bunker was built into the mountains. The entrance was at the base of the foothills and ran in quite a ways."

"Any other entrances?"

"You mean, like a back door on a submarine?" Abecassis laughed again. "No, just the one."

"What about the current storage area for nukes?"

"The exact location is classified, but it's not in the mountains—miles away, in fact."

Corrie found this fascinating, but she noted with impatience that none of it furthered their investigation. "Another question, if you don't mind: the nine hikers made a beeline to the north after fleeing their tent—in the direction of the Kirtland property. Is there anything or any place in the mountainous part of Kirtland they might have been heading for?"

Abecassis, slewing the Jeep around a particularly sharp hairpin turn, didn't answer immediately. They had been climbing steadily and were now among ponderosa pines clinging to steep hillsides.

"When did they shut down the Manzano storage bunkers?"

"Early nineties. Like I said, the presidential bunker was closed off decades earlier, but the weapons bunkers were used until, I think, June of 1992. That's when they deactivated the perimeter alarms, the nukes were moved to the new location, and the entire complex was permanently mothballed and sealed."

"You told me that those bunkers were common knowledge around here. Do you think there's any chance the hikers could have been headed toward that complex, for shelter?"

"Not a chance in hell. The only entrance is on the flats. Where the hikers were, up here somewhere in the high country—you simply can't get down to the flats. Cliffs, canyons, ravines... it's impossible."

The Jeep bumped over a particularly large pot-hole, sending everyone bouncing.

"Sorry about that," said Abecassis, slowing down yet again. "We're almost at the fence line."

Now patches of snow could be seen among a deep forest of fir trees. A moment later, a double chain-link fence appeared on their right, tarnished but still in good condition, topped with concertina wire.

The road turned to parallel the perimeter fence. They continued on, driving alongside as the fence rose up a gradual ridgeline.

"Do any sensors or alarms remain on this section of the fence?" Corrie asked.

"Not since the bunker was mothballed. We have hundreds of miles of fence. The security perimeters around weapons storage are, of course, much tighter and much, *much* more stringent."

"If someone could cut through the fence, would you know?" asked Sharp, speaking for the first time since the tour began.

"Yes. There aren't any alarms, but we'd find out. We patrol this road weekly."

"Was there any evidence, fifteen years ago, of anyone trying to break in?" he asked. "Like a hole cut in the fence that had to be repaired?"

"I'd be glad to check our security records. Anything like that would have been noted. But nobody's likely to have broken in around this section of the fence—not unless they had wings. That area eastward is called the Knot. It's awful country, full of knobs, sharp peaks, and ravines so deep no light ever touches them." The colonel glanced at Corrie. "How far do you want to go along the fence?"

"To the eastern corner?"

"Of course."

The snow got a little deeper, but it had been packed down by the weekly patrol. The long ridgeline finally topped out on a summit, and Abecassis stopped the Jeep. "We're at the high point—Lagarto Peak. Let's get out and stretch our legs."

The air was fresh and cold, and smelled of snow, and the view was tremendous. The fence line ran across the top of the peak and down again. The slope on the Kirtland side was gentle, but on the side called the Knot lay a brutal, stony landscape that quickly ended in a steep decline. O'Hara was right; hiker number nine would never have been able to climb that slope at night in winter. And the fence here was just as tarnished and old-looking as elsewhere—no sign of an old repair or hole being cut.

286 DOUGLAS PRESTON & LINCOLN CHILD

Number nine definitely didn't enter Kirtland at this point—or any other, it seemed. A dead end.

Sharp had been so quiet during the drive that as they were about to get back in, Corrie turned to him. "Why don't we switch places so you can talk to Colonel Abecassis for the rest of the trip?" She lowered her voice. "In case you have questions..."

She let the sentence trail off as Sharp nodded. "Glad to."

They got back in, Sharp in the front and Corrie in the rear with the sergeant. Master Sergeant Brickell was an older man, bald with a fringe of gray hair around the sides, cut very short. He had intense blue eyes, a thin mouth, and a taciturn expression— the very image of a soldier.

As the Jeep continued down the road, Sharp and Abecassis chatting in front, Corrie wondered what to say to this old man. "So, you've been at Kirtland a long time?"

"All my career," he said, in a gruff voice that discouraged further questioning.

"What's your role here?"

"Security."

"When the Dead Mountain tragedy happened, was there much talk at the base about it?"

"There was talk all over."

"What do you think happened?" Corrie asked.

At this, Sergeant Brickell seemed to hesitate. "I've no idea."

"But everyone's got a theory, right?"

"I think they were high."

"What makes you say that?"

"Kids were always taking drugs back then."

"Were there rumors at the base about the incident? Is that what people were saying—drugs?"

"There was talk about everything—ignorant talk. Like you said, everyone had their theory."

They came to the fence corner. The land fell away steeply beyond into a horrific maze of canyons, ravines, arroyos, and knife-edged ridges.

"Whose land is that?" Corrie asked, looking down into it.

"That's part of the Manzano Wilderness," Brickell told her. "The colonel mentioned it. Called the Knot, because it's so twisted up."

"But what about that valley down there, way on the other side? I can see buildings and a road in." Her heart leapt: maybe that was where O'Connell was headed.

"Rancho Bonito. A new luxury dude ranch."

"How new?"

"Four, five years. Built on a private land inholding in the national forest."

"So it wasn't there at the time of the tragedy?"

"No."

Corrie, disappointed, breathed deeply of the cool evergreen air. The sun glistened on the snow, the fir trees sighed in a faint wind, and the eastward plains were etched crisply against the blue sky. Beautiful—but the trip had been a bust. There was no way victim number nine would have been able to navigate those canyons or get up Lagarto Peak. It was now quite evident O'Connell hadn't come into Kirtland at all. He must have disappeared somewhere in the mountains south of the fence.

Corrie leaned forward to speak with Abecassis. "One other thing—did you hear about the guy who got murdered down in Socorro a couple of days ago?"

The vice commander furrowed her brow. "It's not ringing a bell."

"There was a guy killed execution-style, and the papers said he was a longtime civilian employee of Kirtland."

"What was his name?"

"Benjamin Cheape."

"Cheape?" She shook her head. "Sorry, don't know him. Did I mention we have twenty-three thousand employees?" She paused and frowned. "Is there some significance or connection I should be aware of?"

"No," said Corrie. "I was just wondering."

She glanced at Sharp, saw a disapproving look in his eyes.

"That particular homicide is not an FBI case," Sharp said, as if reciting her thoughts verbatim. "It's a matter for the local sheriff and State Police."

There was a brief, awkward silence. "What now, Agent Swanson?" Abecassis asked. "We can drive northward along the fence, or go back?"

"We can head back," Corrie said. "Thanks so much for your time. I've seen all that I needed."

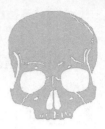

35

Driving south on I-40, Corrie almost didn't answer the call coming from a blocked number. But it was her FBI phone, so she picked it up.

"Special Agent Swanson?" came a smooth female voice.

"Speaking."

"I have Dr. DeGregorio on the line, calling from Indonesia."

Corrie hadn't expected to hear back so quickly—or even at all—from the philanthropist. But in a moment another voice came on, clear and high-pitched. "Agent Swanson? This is Alex DeGregorio. Returning your call."

Since she was driving, Corrie couldn't take notes. But she didn't want to call him back—she might not get him again. "Thank you. Sir, I'm an agent working on the Dead Mountain case—which I assume you're familiar with."

"Unfortunately, yes. I was good friends with some of the victims."

"Since we've reopened the case, I was wondering if I could ask a few questions?"

"Now? Over the phone?"

"It's voluntary and, naturally, if you'd feel more comfortable with an attorney present—"

"No need for that," DeGregorio said. "I'm happy to assist any way I can. But how can I possibly be of help?"

"We recovered a knife with the initials 'MHT' on it at a place where several victims were found. We've connected it to Matthew H. Tanner, your former roommate at NMIT. He said what you just confirmed: that you were close to some of the victims."

"Very much so. Especially Rod—Rodney O'Connell, the one still missing. He was about the best friend I ever had. If I may ask—any leads on finding his remains?"

"Not yet. We're actively looking."

"It really affected me at the time. I...well, I had to take a term off from my studies."

Corrie moved into the slow lane so she could concentrate better. "Dr. Tanner wasn't able to say how his knife ended up with one of the victims. He didn't recall loaning or giving it to anyone. Do you have any recollection of that matter?"

A brief silence. "No. In fact, I don't recall Matt

having a knife at all, although I'm sure he must have. He was an avid outdoorsman."

"The nine hikers appeared to be heading northward in the Manzanos, possibly toward a refuge of some kind. Do you have any idea of what that might have been?"

Another pause. "Sorry. None at all."

Corrie decided to change tacks. "What was Rodney like? Was he an experienced mountaineer?"

"Very experienced. Adventurous, fit, ran every day."

"And the others? Did you know them all?"

"I knew most of them, more or less. We were grad students together in the engineering department. It was pretty small—at least back then." He laughed a little ruefully.

"What was the group studying?"

"Just about any flavor of engineering we could find—computers, civil, nuclear, aerospace, that sort of thing."

"Nuclear?" Corrie felt a sudden twinge.

"That was Rod's area."

"In what way?"

"He had the hope of working up at LANL—Los Alamos—after graduation."

"So he was going to be a nuclear bomb designer?"

"No. At least, that wasn't his intention—things can change once you get your doctorate. But he was mostly interested in reentry systems, ballistic missile design, not actual warheads."

This would definitely be worth looking into further, Corrie thought.

"Did you know about the hiking trip before they left?"

"Oh, sure. They talked about it nonstop."

"Were you invited?"

"No. I enjoyed climbing mountains as much as any of the others, but I had no winter experience."

No winter experience. A picture came unbidden into Corrie's mind of the slope-shouldered body that went with the high-pitched voice. It hadn't stopped him from making a fortune before he turned forty. It occurred to her that she was running out of questions. "You knew the victims—do you have any idea what might have happened?"

"I must have mulled that over a million times. Every theory I come up with always has at least one hole in it—usually several. I'm certain something terrified them, but I have no idea what, or how. And the business with the radiation contamination is really nuts."

"Thank you for your time, Dr. DeGregorio. Before we hang up, is there anything more you'd like to tell me, or that you think I should know?"

"I can't think of anything, but if I do, I'll call."

He paused. "I really hope you can solve the case this time around. I mean, I'm not a relative, just a friend...but it's been a real burden on me nonetheless. Not knowing, I mean."

"Thanks again." Corrie hung up just as she was leaving the freeway for the exit ramp to Socorro.

She arrived at Martha's Black Dog Café early and decided to drive around the block a couple of times so she wouldn't look too eager. As usual, she felt a little nervous whenever it came to Homer Watts, and this morning it mingled with a deep sense of unease and discouragement about the case. Eleven days had passed and they'd made no real progress. Over the past few days Sharp had seemed more quiet and sleepy than usual, which seemed to her a warning sign.

When she parked and went inside the café, she saw Sheriff Watts already seated in the back, cowboy hat on the table, coffee mug next to it. He rose as she came over, stooping to shake her hand with the usual bashful air, his deep brown eyes crinkling with a smile.

They both sat down. "Got here early," he said. "Already ordered coffee, sorry."

"No worries."

The waitress arrived and filled a mug for Corrie. She dumped in three sugars and a heavy pour of half-and-half, stirred, and took a big gulp. "So," she said, "what have you got?"

"Good stuff," said Watts, with a grin displaying his white teeth. "Starting with this guy Cheape."

"Lay it on me." She leaned forward and Watts did too. She could smell his aftershave.

"Cheape was a civilian employee of Kirtland pretty much all his life, in the maintenance department. He started as a janitor, although even to do that he would have needed a security clearance. Ended up a supervisor. Totally unremarkable career, one minor commendation on his record, not much advancement. Retired at fifty-five, lived a dull, quiet life since."

"Commendation? What'd he do?"

"Didn't say. Maybe he shined some pilot's shoes extra well. Have to dig out the letter, I guess."

"Who might have killed him?"

Watts shook his head. "The hit appears to be professional, single shot to the back of the neck with a .22 no less, silencer used, no fingerprints or other evidence. You know how everyone now has video camera doorbells looking out onto the street? The State Police collected lots of it—nothing. The killer avoided all that—we're not sure how, but it shows a level of sophistication beyond the ordinary."

"Strange," Corrie said.

"But there's a twist. Cheape had recently put

a down payment on—and taken delivery of—a hundred-thousand-dollar Tesla."

"Really?"

"Yes. In cash."

"Oh boy."

"Yeah."

"His bank statements?"

"Nothing out of the ordinary. He was a frugal guy, divorced, two kids grown up and gone, bank accounts showing no unusual expenses or deposits. No record of money flowing through it to buy the Tesla."

"How much was the Tesla deposit?" Corrie asked as their breakfasts arrived—eggs, bacon, and toast for him, omelet for her.

"Ten grand. Cheape had no money in the bank to pay the rest of the ninety thousand when the car was delivered. So we think he had at least a hundred grand in cash stowed away somewhere."

"Was he robbed?"

Watts gave her a slow smile. "At first we thought the house was tossed as a cover, because a lot of valuable stuff was left behind. But this Tesla thing leads us to think the cash was taken. Because it's not there now."

"Any idea where the cash came from?"

"We're looking. Cheape's life looks dirt-free. No

drugs, debts, gambling, women, family conflicts, disputes—no speeding or parking tickets even."

"So maybe it wasn't an execution-style killing? Maybe it was just a robbery and murder?"

"Maybe. But where did the cash come from? And how did the thieves know he had it? That's what we're working on now."

Corrie fell silent, feeling vaguely disappointed. This was seeming less and less connected to Kirtland or the Dead Mountain case. It felt like Sharp had been right after all: the murder of Cheape was not an FBI matter.

"Thanks for sharing this with me," Corrie said.

"I've got more. I did a little poking around on the Dead Mountain families," said Watts. "Did you know that the missing victim's father, Harry O'Connell, *also* worked at Kirtland?"

"How did I miss that? What kind of work did he do?"

"I don't know. I was going through some old *Albuquerque Journal* articles about Dead Mountain, and there it was—Harry O'Connell, the father of one of the missing, lieutenant colonel, retired, Kirtland AFB."

"Too bad he's deceased," said Corrie. "His widow is a piece of work. Melody Ann, the stepmother who never met her stepson. She'll never talk to me, unfortunately—thinks we're engaged in a cover-up."

"The one raising hell about the investigation? I saw her on the news."

"Don't I know it. She disrupted the press conference the other day with demands for the truth. She's gone down the rabbit hole, big time." She paused. "I'm surprised we didn't already know about the missing victim's dad being in the military."

"It's probably written on some tiny note, buried in fifteen-year-old paperwork."

Just another fact Gold had probably turned up, but that hadn't led anywhere. "Even so, it makes me curious. I'll see what I can find on my end—but would you mind looking into the O'Connell family from a local angle?"

"Sure."

"Thanks. I owe you one, Homer. I really do."

"If you say so." He leaned back with a smile and waved over the check. "You remember the Bosque del Apache, where we watched the sun rise over the river a while ago? That grove of cottonwood trees along the river?"

Corrie nodded.

"Let's get fresh coffees and go back down there and hang out. It's Saturday, we're both off work—what do you think?"

"And do what? Watch the river flow?" Corrie

suddenly found herself coloring, embarrassed by the dumb, unintended implication.

"We'll think of something." His face still held a wry, dimpled smile.

Now her heart was pounding. God, what was wrong with her? She swallowed. "Okay."

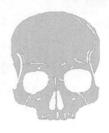

36

SKIP PULLED INTO the parking lot of Gallina's Peek, letting the dust settle as he sourly eyed the flickering neon sign of a nubile Indian woman peering coquettishly out from a wigwam. This pun on nearby Gallinas Peak wasn't any more promising than the establishment itself appeared to be. But he'd already stopped at half a dozen roadhouses that afternoon—one more wouldn't hurt.

He'd gotten a late start on the day—although not that late, considering he'd been up half the night scouring the internet for dirt on Sheriff Hawley—but he'd headed out with enthusiasm. Hawley, he believed, was enough of a natural douchebag that Skip's own experience couldn't be unique. There had to be others out there he'd mistreated, who hated the sheriff's guts—and among this august group, one or maybe several would know some scuttlebutt Hawley wouldn't want made public. In a day or two of searching, he hoped to gather enough shit on Hawley to build a cow-pie colossus bigger than Rhodes...and when Lightfeather dumped the damning evidence before Hawley, he'd drop the case so fast Skip could almost feel those fat lips kissing his aggrieved ass.

Except it turned out not to be that easy. He'd first tried a couple of country clubs and fraternal organizations, posing as a journalist writing a history of Torrance County; he figured coming in with a neutral approach on Hawley, the man, would be the best way to smoke out anyone willing to talk trash about him. But it hadn't gone as expected. He'd heard through Nora that the county was Hawley's personal fiefdom. And from the way the retired golfers and community big shots sang his praises, it was clear Hawley had spread his crooked largess far and wide. Skip would have to sink his muck rake into a lower stratum of citizenry.

So he'd tried the barbershops and diners in and around McIntosh, Estancia, and Encino. People in these establishments didn't speak of Hawley in quite such worshipful tones—no longer was he an incarnation of the risen lord—but there was also a deep wariness, even fear, and Skip couldn't find anybody interested in dishing dirt.

It was, at last, in bars and roadhouses that Skip began to sense he might have better luck. The farther south he went, it seemed, the more Hawley's influence waned. He now jettisoned the journalism story for the injustice of a wronged man: Hawley had boned his sister while her boyfriend was doing a tour of duty overseas. He'd kept it on the down-low, not making a big deal about his grudge but letting it eventually bubble to the surface as he bought drinks for those around him at the bar. He was encouraged by a few knowing scowls and sympathetic grunts. He'd heard some interesting tidbits, but nobody was willing to get specific beyond vague declarations that Hawley was a shitbag.

Gallina's Peek, though, felt like a place where he might hit pay dirt. One old geezer had rolled his eyes at the mention of Hawley, and Skip's *droit du seigneur* story about the sheriff and his sister (God help him if Nora ever got wind of that) was received with a chorus of groans.

"So old One-Bally still has it in him," the fat, balding bartender cackled as he pulled a pint of Michelob Ultra for a customer.

"One-Bally?" Skip recalled hearing this nickname being mentioned at the Isleta burial ceremony. "What's that mean?"

The bartender laughed again. "You didn't know? Hawley's the biggest, baddest pistolero in all New Mexico. Broke up a bank stickup and got into a gunfight with the robber. Shot him, too—even though he got winged himself." He slid the pint down the bar. "Oh, he's real proud of that. Took a bullet in the line of duty."

"Just don't ask him *where* he got winged," said somebody nearby, "unless you want to spend a night in the drunk tank!" There was general laughter.

"Another inch or two to the left," the bartender said, "and that shot would've killed him."

"Depending on how tight his pants were that day!" said the other, to more laughter.

Skip began to get the idea. "Where was he shot, exactly?"

"Jesus, kid, is it that hard to figure out?" the barman replied, pointing downward with one finger from his belt buckle.

"So Hawley got shot *in the balls*?!" Skip laughed uproariously. "Oh God, I love it!"

Suddenly, a huge form rose from one of the tables in the recesses of the roadhouse. He had a buzz cut and was wearing a leather jacket. He loomed over Skip, who was leaning back on his stool, laughing.

"Shut the fuck up," he said to Skip and the bartender. "Both of you."

"I'll say whatever I damn please in my own establishment," the bartender retorted.

Skip, meanwhile, was so delighted to learn his nemesis had an Achilles' heel that he couldn't keep quiet. "*One-Bally Hawley!*" he chortled. "Ha ha ha ha—"

His laugh was cut short as a fistful of knuckles bounced off his teeth. As he went down, the biker leaned over him and, grabbing the bartender by the collar, hauled him up with one hand and punched him in the face with the other. Another patron leapt on top of the big man, and others rushed to join in. Skip, lying on the floor half-dazed, started crawling away from the fracas, dimly hearing the sounds of thuds and broken glass. He'd almost reached the door when someone yelled, "There goes the guy who started it!" Skip rose to his feet and prepared to run, only to be clocked upside the head.

The next thing he knew, he was lying on the floor, all was quiet, and two deputies stood in the entryway. Several men, some bleeding, were standing in a line before the bar. Skip tried to rise—only to find that his wrists were cuffed behind him.

"What the hell?" he said, blinking his eyes into focus.

"Hey!" said one of the deputies. "Sleeping Beauty's awake!" A chorus of laughter followed.

Skip noticed he was the only one wearing handcuffs. "Wait a minute! I didn't start the fight. I didn't even throw a punch. Take these things off me!"

"This has nothing to do with a bar fight," said the other deputy, who was busy writing something on a notepad.

"What, then?"

"Violation of conditions of release," the deputy replied. He spoke in the slowest drawl Skip had ever heard. He was chewing gum, and perhaps that—combined with writing and speaking—was proving difficult.

"That's crazy!" Skip said, struggling against the cuffs. "I didn't violate anything. This is New Mexico!"

"That's right," said the first deputy, "but it ain't your home county. Bail regulations state you can't leave Santa Fe County—but here you are, hell and gone at the ass end of Torrance. But don't worry—Sheriff Hawley's on his way right now, and I bet he'll take good care of a little lost lamb like you."

The man laughed. But this time, only the other deputy joined in.

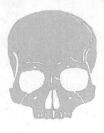

37

I'M LOOKING AT the photographs now," said Evan Gross, his face looming in the Zoom window on Corrie's computer. Corrie could see the avalanche expert seated at his desk in his sunny Colorado office, with a view of snowy peaks through the window behind him.

Once Sharp had given her the green light to talk to an avalanche expert, she thought it might be difficult to find someone truly knowledgeable in such a field. It turned out to be surprisingly easy: the University of Colorado had arguably the finest experts on avalanches in the world, and Dr. Gross headed the list. He'd been willing to talk to her—in fact, happy to do so. It seemed that, unlike politicians, scientists were eager to talk about the nuances of their work.

Via the Zoom window on her computer, Corrie

could see that the photographs she had emailed him were spread out on his desk, along with the autopsies of the two crushed victims—Lynn Martinez and Luke Hightower. Gross was surprisingly young, with a long ponytail and beard, looking more like a ski bum than a PhD scientist. Perhaps he *had* been a ski bum—one who'd managed to turn his avocation into a successful career.

"It's really very interesting," he said, moving the photos around. "I haven't had a problem quite this intriguing in a long time."

"Dr. Gross, may I record this call?"

"Of course."

"Could you please state your name and credentials for the record?"

"Sure. I'm Evan Gross, and I have a PhD in geosciences from the University of Colorado, where I'm now a research professor. My specialty is studying structure, transfer of mass, and movement of heat in snow."

"Right," said Corrie. "And this means you're an expert in what areas?"

"Among other things, avalanche forecasting. Avalanches are all about snow structure and mass transfer."

"Thank you." Corrie felt a twinge of anticipation. The mystery of the two crushed bodies had tripped up Gold in the initial investigation and added fuel to the plethora of conspiracy theories about UFOs, Yeti attacks, secret weapons, and the rest. Gold had hired someone, too—someone who concluded an avalanche wasn't possible on the slope where the two crushed victims were found. Whether or not that was the case, his investigation had not been able to determine what exactly had happened to the two victims.

"Let's start with the autopsies you sent me," said Gross. "I'm not a medical doctor, but I have a lot of experience in avalanche fatalities and body recoveries. The first victim had a chest fracture so extreme—severe flail chest—that it caused fatal trauma to the heart. The second, in addition to chest trauma, suffered a skull fracture so drastic that it drove cranial splinters into the brain. Both injuries were immediately fatal."

"Yet whatever happened to them didn't break the skin," Corrie said. "It's bizarre."

"Not really. These injuries are not atypical for avalanche victims."

"But there was no evidence of an avalanche."

"Yes! You're quite correct. That's because there *wasn't* an avalanche. The slope is too shallow, and the area too close to the ridgeline. These pictures tell another story entirely—a tragic one."

He began shuffling through the photographs he'd printed. "Here are the bodies as they were found by the searchers." He held up an image Corrie immediately recognized, showing the two bodies lying facedown in the creek, crossways, one on top of the other—Hightower below, Martinez on top.

"You can see they're lying in a shallow, rocky streambed, partly immersed in the water. Now, here's a photo of what remains of the apparent snow cave they were building. You can see the fresh boughs they had cut, which they'd laid out on the floor. In this photo, they're all churned up in the snow."

"The previous investigators did conclude they were building a snow cave."

"And they were right. The two victims burrowed into the snow on the lee side of a ridge. Unfortunately for them, they were tunneling into a cornice that was directly above a live stream. The snow was very deep in that area at the time—over twenty feet."

"So early in the season? October 31?"

"Absolutely. Those cornices can develop very quickly in high winds and reach depths of fifty or more feet. What they didn't realize was that the cave they were building sat right above the cavity formed by that stream. You see, that stream didn't freeze in the winter—and the deep, insulating snow above was one of the reasons. Since the stream was always a few degrees warmer than freezing, however, a cavity was formed directly above its length."

He held up a few other photographs of the area, showing the ridge above and a depression formed by the stream.

"At some point, the bottom of the snow cave collapsed into the cavity. It threw the two tunnelers maybe five feet to the rocky bed of the stream, and the snow above them came down on top—crushing their bodies into the rocks and creating the massive injuries you see in the autopsy."

Corrie hesitated. "It's hard to believe a five-foot fall would be enough to crush those bodies."

"Normally it wouldn't be. What caused the injuries wasn't the fall, but the fifteen feet of snow that came down on top of them. Here, let's do a little math. The snow they dug into wasn't normal snow: it was hard, wind-drifted, cross-loaded snow, which is three to four times denser than fresh-fallen snow. That kind of snow typically weighs between six hundred and a thousand pounds per cubic yard. Multiply that times fifteen feet, or five cubic yards, and you get around five thousand pounds of snow dropping on them from above and crushing them against the rocks of the creek bed. Trust me, that's going to cause a lot of damage."

Explanation complete, Gross sat back. "And that, Agent Swanson, is the solution to your mystery."

Corrie stared at him. "How sure are you about this?"

"Close to one hundred percent positive."

"What about the missing tongue and eyes?"

At this, Gross shook his head and chuckled. "That's even less of a mystery. They were lying face-down in a stream. There are all kinds of little critters living in that stream—caddisfly larvae, stonefly nymphs, mosquito larvae, crustaceans, minnows. All of them will nibble on animal protein whenever they can get it. The eyes and tongues of two dead people, immersed in the water, decaying over months—what a feast that would be!"

Corrie was disgusted—and amazed. "So it's as simple as that?"

"Are you disappointed?" He chuckled again. "People love a good mystery. I'm sorry to spoil it for everyone, but this mystery is thoroughly explained by the application of a little science."

"Would you be willing to write this up in a report? We'll pay your usual fee, of course."

"Absolutely. I'll write it up this afternoon and email it to you tomorrow."

Corrie thanked him, then ended the Zoom call. She wondered why Gold hadn't sought out a real avalanche expert like Gross. Of course, she almost hadn't either, until she realized it was a part of Gold's investigation that didn't quite add up. It was, she realized, not the only part of Gold's investigation that gave her an uneasy feeling. There was something about that investigation she couldn't put her finger on ... but that just didn't feel right.

38

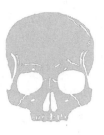

IT WAS A cold November Sunday, even for Silver City, but Melody Ann O'Connell felt invigorated at the thought of the upcoming protest. Cosmo and Cassy Wright had driven down with her. At least a dozen other people had signed up for the protest on the Manzano Families Facebook page, which would make this their biggest protest yet. Even more satisfying was the fact that a local television station, KWOW, was planning to tape the demonstration and interview her for the local evening news.

Agent Gold's street, Bluejay Lane, lay at the outskirts of town. It was a cul-de-sac that ended in a circle. Gold's house, a mid-fifties modern, stood directly at the end. The house was, as usual, shuttered up tight, all the curtains drawn, car pulled into the garage. The street would provide ample parking for everyone, as well as plenty of space to parade around in front of the house without trespassing on Gold's lawn.

Melody Ann pulled her Lexus up to the curb and got out, Cassie and Cosmo following. She went around and opened the back, removing the signs she had made and leaning them up against the car, careful not to scratch the paint. She had taken care to make sure they didn't look amateurish. She'd painted on them the messages that, in her opinion, had resonated the most: TRUTH. REMEMBER THE NINE. FBI COME CLEAN.

She removed a small folding table from the trunk, then placed a Dunkin' Donuts tray on it, and beside it a Box O' Joe with a stack of cups.

She checked her watch: quarter to noon. The others would be coming soon—in fact, they were already starting to arrive. A car pulled into the street, followed by another, and another. Melody Ann could see some curtains stirring in other houses on the street. But the Gold house remained shut and silent.

"Doesn't look like anyone's home," said Cassy Wright, selecting a blueberry donut and pouring out a cup of coffee.

"Doesn't matter," said Melody Ann. "What matters is the publicity."

Cosmo reached for a fritter and took a big bite, chasing it down with a swig of coffee. "I hope the bastard is in there," he mumbled as he chewed.

Now still more cars were arriving, people getting out and congregating around the coffee and donuts.

While this was going on, a man came out of the house next to Gold's and stood on the stoop, hands on his hips, angry expression on his face. He stared for a while.

Melody Ann waved.

The man did not wave back. Instead, he called out, "Don't you folks have something better to do on a Sunday?"

"Ignore him," said Melody Ann.

"Go bother someone else!" the man yelled. "This is a nice neighborhood!"

But nobody responded and eventually he went back inside, slamming the door.

The swelling group milled around, and there was a sense of electricity in the air that to Melody Ann felt almost festive. At noon exactly, she raised her voice, and—flanked by Cassy and Cosmo—called for attention.

Silence fell. She looked around. She counted twenty-one people, even more than she'd hoped for. The news van would arrive at 1 PM, and they planned to wrap it up at 2.

"My friends!" Melody Ann began. "The Manzano Families thank you for coming out to support us on this cold afternoon! Thank you!" She held up her hands and clapped, generating applause from the group.

"I'd like to introduce Cosmo and Cassy Wright,

the grieving parents of Gordon Wright, whose remains, as you all are now aware, were recently found in a cave in the Manzanos. Two weeks ago, the FBI announced they were reopening the case. And yet since then, we've heard nothing. At first, we assumed this was just more foot-dragging and incompetence. But then we realized something else was going on. A dark pattern was beginning to repeat itself."

She paused dramatically.

"The entire Dead Mountain case has the feeling of one long cover-up from beginning to end. Why have we heard nothing? Because they refuse to tell us anything! And that's why we're here—to call out the FBI. Demand the truth."

She pointed dramatically at the house, then spoke again in a ringing voice. "Former FBI agent Robertson Gold directed the original investigation and cover-up. *He knows the truth.* All roads lead back to him. And after fifteen long years, *we demand answers!*"

She paused. "In the past few weeks, the Manzano Families have been gathering fresh information—new and frightening information. I can't promise we have the answers—but we have some leads. And we, the families, want to share what we know—with *you.*"

Another pause.

The crowd was totally silent.

"For years, there've been rumors of a secret project, launched in parallel with the Manhattan Project. I'm talking, of course, about the Boston Project. Some of you have undoubtedly heard of it. The Boston Project centered on another kind of WMD—not nuclear weapons, but bioweapons. Specifically, what would today be called genetic engineering. The Manhattan Project was a success, of course, and led to the atomic bomb and victory over the Japanese. But the Boston Project, based at Kirtland, was not a success—not for a long time. While we are still assembling the details, we believe its goal was to create the perfect soldier. Early on, the Boston Project didn't have the necessary technology, and their crude experiments made little progress. But nevertheless it continued along in secrecy—and finally reached fruition with the advanced biotechnology tools now available. But there were, shall we say, a few hiccups along the way."

Melody Ann felt a rush of energy and excitement to see that the small crowd was riveted.

"I say *hiccups*. A more accurate word would be failures. Early on, they created freaks. Hideous, powerful, subhuman. And on the night of October 31, 2008, one of those genetic monsters escaped the base and wandered off into the storm. It opened the flap of the tent, triggering horror and panic. And in so doing, sparking a tragedy that led to nine deaths."

She looked around again, letting what she'd said settle in.

"You may ask me, Where's the evidence? A fair question. So let's go over the facts. First, it's generally acknowledged—even by the government—that something blocked the tent doorway that was so terrifying our children cut their way out and fled. A bear, mountain lion, another human being? Hardly. These were experienced mountaineers and wilderness-goers."

"Two: In going over old newspaper articles, I've noted that people reported an unusual number of helicopters and planes flying around the mountains that very night—that *very* night, before anyone even knew the hikers were missing. What were they searching for if not an escapee?

"Three: The radiation found on some of the clothing, which was intended to remain secret but—luckily for anyone who seeks the truth—managed to leak out. It's a well-known fact that medical isotopes are used in genetic engineering and identification of neurological problems."

The crowd was hanging on every word. She wasn't sure if this theory was 100 percent correct, but if you wanted to motivate people, you had to use the same tools being used against you: even bending the truth a little if it meant giving them something concrete, something specific.

"Enough talk!" she cried. "Let's start the protest!"

She got out a couple of electronic megaphones, keeping one for herself and giving Cosmo the other. The signs were quickly distributed, too, and she directed everyone to stay on the sidewalks and in the turnaround circle, moving in a counterclockwise direction. She began the chanting, and soon everyone was following along in unison as they made a slow circle in front of Gold's house, careful not to trespass on his lawn, staying on the sidewalk and street.

This went on for forty-five minutes, and then the real excitement began. Turning into the street was a big white van with a satellite dish on top— KWOW. It pulled up next to her car, and several technicians and a sound man got out, followed by the local investigative reporter, Liz Sanchez, an attractive woman in a crisp suit with a short, dark, serious haircut. Next to her was a man, gesturing and giving directions, evidently the news producer. Melody Ann peeled off from the group and came over to them.

"Any sign of Gold?" asked Sanchez.

"No, but he's in there, I'm sure," said Melody Ann. "He doesn't go anywhere."

"Okay. We're going to set up over there," she said, as the sound technician started miking up Melody Ann with a lavalier. Sanchez and the producer discussed where they were going to set up and shoot, and asked that the protesters continue circling and chanting in the near ground, with the Gold house in the middle distance.

Soon they were ready. Melody Ann shook out her frosted tips as Sanchez stood next to her with the mike.

"This is Liz Sanchez, here in Silver City with Melody Ann O'Connell, the mother of the final missing victim of the Dead Mountain tragedy. Melody Ann, can you tell us what's going on here?"

"Yes, Liz, and thank you." She took a deep breath. "We're here to protest the FBI's flagrant cover-up of what really happened to the Manzano nine."

"A cover-up? How so?"

As Melody Ann began to launch into the spiel she'd practiced, there was a shout from behind her. The news producer was pointing at the house. "Hey, get that shot! He's coming out!"

The news crew abandoned Melody Ann and rushed up the driveway, carrying their cameras and equipment, boom mikes swinging.

Gold had come out of the house, and he was yelling. "Get the hell out of here! Get the hell off my property!"

"Agent Gold! Agent Gold!" Sanchez was calling out, her mike extended.

"You crazy bastards, get out of here!" Gold

screeched, his face mottled red, eyes bulging, jacket askew. Melody Ann grew frightened—he looked totally unhinged, a man who could do anything.

"Get out!" He rushed down the driveway. "Get out!" He reached behind and pulled something out of his waistband.

"*Gun!*" someone screamed, and there was an instant chorus of shrieking as everyone fell to the ground all at once, cameras crashing down, mikes flying, as Melody Ann threw herself onto the asphalt. The screaming continued as people scrambled to their feet and began running every which way, like hysterical geese scattered by a rampaging dog. But Melody Ann remained on the ground, heart pounding even though she had recovered her wits. The man hadn't fired at them, but just waved the gun over his head—and now he was standing there, looking at his hand holding the gun like it was some foreign thing. A camera operator had resumed filming from a low position, and the producer was shouting, "*Get it on tape! Get it on tape!*"

This is unbelievable, Melody Ann thought. The station was getting footage of this FBI agent screaming and waving his gun around, as if her talk of a cover-up had forced his hand. The only thing left to make this absolutely perfect was for the guy to get arrested on camera.

Arrested on camera. That would be all over the

news. And she, Melody Ann, had made it possible. This meant vindication of all her hard work, all those years—well, months at least—of struggle and doubt. Now the FBI would *have* to come clean. This would blow the Dead Mountain case wide open.

She grabbed for her cell phone and dialed.

"Nine one one—what's the nature of your emergency?" came the bored voice.

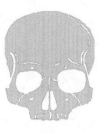

39

CORRIE NOSED THE FBI pool vehicle into a free space on San Pedro Drive Northeast, then put it in park, turned off the engine, and sat a moment, looking out at the cracked asphalt, motels, and working-class apartments that lined both sides of the street.

In the passenger seat, Watts stretched and yawned. "This is a novelty, being chauffeured around for a change," he said. "And it's a good thing you're armed. We're only—" he twisted around, looking through the rear window— "a mile and a half north of the 'War Zone.'"

Corrie smiled wryly at this reference to Albuquerque's International District, one of the city's poorest neighborhoods and certainly its most violent. "Well, let's see how it goes. Interviews are easy when you just need somebody to verify what you already know. Others—like when you don't exactly know what you want—can be tough."

"You've learned all that as an intern?"

"I'm not an 'intern,'" said Corrie, giving him a playful punch in the arm. "Another crack like that, and I'll use that cowboy hat for a Frisbee."

Watts was in a teasing mood. Corrie wondered if it was covering some lingering nervousness from their moment—she wasn't sure what else to call it—by the river the other day. What happened was unexpected. The Bosque del Apache had been beautiful, like an Albert Bierstadt miniature, and he'd nuzzled her under the cottonwood trees. She'd nuzzled back. And the next thing she knew, they were locked in a passionate kiss. One of them, she wasn't sure which, had pulled back a little in surprise...and an elderly couple strolling nearby prevented the Bierstadt landscape from morphing into *Le Déjeuner sur l'herbe*. All Corrie knew for sure was, at that moment, she'd felt white-hot with lust for Watts. But the moment had passed—and, luckily, without becoming either too drastic or too embarrassing.

What was, or wasn't, going on between them? She couldn't deny her attraction, and it was obvious he felt the same way. But it seemed too much of their time together had been tangled up with work. It wasn't that she expected some kind of nineteenth-century courtship...but a few nights out at the movies or romantic dinners or flowers would be nice. She knew Watts was a stand-up guy, not interested in a wham-bam-thank-you-ma'am fling. Maybe he was just intimidated. Or inexperienced. Well, that made two of them.

Whatever it was, it could wait—she was juggling a lot of balls right now and wasn't sure she wanted to handle two more.

"Anyway, I'm glad you're along," she said. "After all, you found her."

"You asked me to sniff around locally. Anything for a lady."

"Not that anyone's going to ask, but if they do, she could have turned up as part of your investigation into Cheape's murder."

They got out into a chill wind and crossed the road, approaching the drab residence of Winifred Luckie. Watts had already gotten her up to speed on the woman's details: born in Hartsdale, New York; aged thirty-nine; unmarried, no children; graduate of Hudson Valley Community College. She'd moved to New Mexico in 2006 and worked as a substitute teacher, employed off and on, occasionally applying for support from the New Mexico Human Services Department in between jobs.

Corrie had purposely not alerted the woman they were coming. This time, her gut told her to catch the woman off guard, before she'd had time to prepare. It was 10 AM on a holiday Monday, and even if Winifred Luckie was currently working, which her background check indicated was probably not the case, there would be no school.

Their knock was answered by a woman in a sweatshirt and black leggings. One look at her clothes and uncombed hair told Corrie she probably hadn't worked in a while.

"Winifred Luckie?" she said, holding her ID up through the door's security bars. "I'm Special Agent Corinne Swanson of the FBI, and this is Sheriff Homer Watts. Could we come inside and ask you a few questions?"

"What about?"

"Rodney O'Connell."

"Have you found him?"

"Not yet." The woman seemed in no hurry to open the door. "Ma'am, if you don't mind, could we speak inside?"

The woman hesitated long enough to examine their IDs once more, then unlocked the security door and let them in.

The apartment beyond was in a kind of curious disorder. To Corrie, it looked as if attempts had been made to stem the mess but, like an encroaching tide, it kept returning. Carefully stacked Tupperware containers on the dining room table were surrounded by a litter of Chinese take-out cartons. An ironing board in the corner, clothes folded atop it, had its legs buried in unwashed T-shirts and underwear. As the woman led them through the dining room and into an adjoining living area, Corrie noticed that one corner held a card table with a computer atop it. This area had been kept scrupulously clean. Beside it was an improvised plank bookshelf, and Corrie was surprised to see that Luckie shared her taste in both music and fiction. There were scuffed CDs of Inade and Stars of the Lid, as well as some of her childhood SF favorites by Larry Niven and Roger Zelazny, along with a handful of obscure thrillers, including the sadly forgotten *Ice Limit IV: Wormstorm*.

Luckie pushed some TV remotes off the sofa and motioned for them to sit down. Without offering any refreshment, she took the comfy office chair near the computer, swiveled it around, and looked at them expectantly.

"So," she said. "Have you found out anything more about Rod?"

"No, we haven't," said Corrie. "A new search is underway."

"So why do you want to talk to me again? I must have talked to you feds at least a dozen times back when it happened."

Actually, she had submitted to five rather rushed and perfunctory interviews, which Corrie had glanced over after Watts gave her the woman's name. Although she had been cooperative, she hadn't been able to provide any useful information.

"We'll take up as little of your time as possible," Corrie said. "In light of the recent discoveries we're reaching out to everyone involved, in case anything was missed."

The woman shrugged. "Okay."

"Thanks, Winifred—may I call you Winifred?"

"No. And please don't call me Winnie, either. Call me Helen—that's my middle name."

"Helen, then. Do you remember where you first met Mr. O'Connell?"

"Sure. At the grotto."

"The what?"

"It's what they call local chapters of the NSS."

"The National Speleological Society." Watts spoke for the first time. "You were cavers?"

"That's right. We'd go out with other members of our grotto to some of the caves around Dutchess County. New York. Rod was big into caving then, and I was a noob. He helped me through some pretty gnarly caves. Like Carson's Mistake."

"Carson's Mistake?" Corrie echoed.

"It's got this hundred-yard horizontal tube called the meat grinder. Once you enter it, there's no turning back. You have to keep going. I freaked out halfway, and he talked me through the rest of it."

She nodded toward a table at one end of the sofa, on which sat a couple of framed Ektachrome prints, much faded.

Corrie looked—and was shocked. One was of a skinny girl in a formfitting caving suit, rope slung over her right shoulder like an aiguillette. Despite the muddy outfit, and the helmet with light and chin-strap that partially obscured the face, Corrie could tell the girl was pretty. It was hard to reconcile that twenty-four-year-old image with the tired-looking woman who sat before them now. Every day, Corrie realized, was another fork in life, based on what you did or didn't do . . . and it might be years before you realized that some action, now regretted, had sent you down the wrong path. It sure as hell could have happened to herself. She pushed this aside and returned to her mental list of questions.

"So you started dating," she said.

The woman nodded.

"But you went to different schools."

"No, we didn't. I started at Rensselaer. Transferred to Hudson Valley after my first year."

Corrie tried to align the dates in her head. She'd transferred from a four-year to a two-year college, just before Rodney O'Connell graduated from Rensselaer Polytechnic Institute and went on to graduate studies at NMIT. He must have been an upperclassman when she was a freshman.

"So you followed Rodney out here?" Watts said. Corrie had been wondering the same thing, but this phrasing sounded aggressive.

"I didn't 'follow' him. We were going to be married."

"Married," Watts repeated, sounding unconvinced.

"I was pregnant!" Helen snapped.

What the hell is Homer doing? Corrie wanted to keep this interview friendly, productive. "So, Helen: Did you get to know his student friends out here? Like some of the hikers who perished?"

"A few." Helen shifted in her chair, unhappy now and growing impatient.

"Was he particularly close to any of them?"

Helen shrugged. "I guess. Gordy. Luke."

"Do you know of any animosities inside that group? Jealousy, competition, anything like that?"

"No."

"Is there anything Rodney might have told you, or you overheard or learned about somehow, that could shed further light on what happened?"

"No."

Corrie pressed a little. "Or perhaps there's something you've remembered, or that's happened, since the first times you were questioned?"

"No. I told the cops everything. If you haven't found him, then get back to looking and stop bothering me."

"Back then, you didn't tell us you were pregnant," Watts said, hazarding what Corrie felt certain was a guess.

The woman turned from Corrie back to him. "It wasn't relevant."

"It must have been relevant to you. And to Rodney. And, I'd assume, his parents. So what happened?"

Briefly, the woman's face went blank. "Nothing happened."

"Did you get an abortion? Have a miscarriage? Give the child away?"

"That's none of your business!"

"Unless you faked it," Watts went on, his eyes turning toward the ceiling as if watching a celestial tableau unfold. "Faked it so he'd stay with you. And then, after the tragedy, it didn't matter anymore... until it did."

Corrie opened her mouth, then abruptly shut it again. Watts wasn't just being aggressive, she realized, and he wasn't fishing either—there was method here, and she should let him play it out.

It seemed Helen had instinctively realized the same thing, because she kept silent as well.

"After the dust settled," Watts went on, "you meant something to the parents, Harry and Ruth. They saw you and especially the unborn child as a connection to their son."

Hearing no denials, he went on. "And then, for

whatever reason, the child went away. But even after that, you kept the link to Rodney's parents alive. They felt sorry for you, especially Harry. And he gave you money."

Helen sat up. "That's—!" She stopped, evidently forcing herself to keep silent.

"It wasn't much. Maybe a one-time gift, more likely a stipend. You played on his conscience—his fatherly mix of guilt and grief. Pretty soon, you had a nice little income stream. But then Ruth died. And Harry met Melody Ann. And when you met her, you realized the game was up."

"You can't prove any of that!" Helen said.

"No, and we don't intend to. It's on your conscience—not ours."

She abruptly sat back in the chair and buried her head in her hands. No sound emerged; no sobs racked her shoulders. Corrie, a little taken aback by this sudden reversal, didn't know if she was crying or not.

"There's no way to undo what you've done," Watts said, his tone suddenly milder, wistful rather than accusatory. "No way to make amends. I don't think you have anything to offer us, which is too bad. I mean, if you *did* know something that might help and finally bring closure to the family and honor to your boyfriend's memory, it could be a small step toward healing."

And with this he prepared to rise.

"Wait," she said, face still hidden.

Watts and Corrie exchanged glances.

"He told me never to tell anybody."

"Not tell anybody what?" Watts asked.

For a time, the woman said nothing more. Then, just when Corrie expected Watts to start playing bad cop again, she spoke. "He once said he knew a way into the bunker."

"What bunker?" Corrie asked.

"That old one. The one on Kirtland, where his dad worked. They'd built it in the early fifties to shield the president and his brain trust in case of a nuke attack. The bunker had a front entry, but it also had a secret escape route: a long tunnel that led out the back. It came out somewhere in the mountains. The back door—Harry, I mean Mr. O'Connell—he'd been in charge of securing that. He bragged about it to Rod, said he'd used his son's birthday as a code for the lock. Rod made me swear never, ever to tell anybody about it."

As Helen spoke, the emotion drained from her voice until the final words sounded like a rote recitation.

"And where was this back exit?" Corrie asked.

"No idea. Rod said he'd take me, but then he disappeared..." She trailed off.

"Didn't he give you *any* idea?" Corrie urged.

"No. Like I told you, he said the escape tunnel

was long. It went through the mountain and came out on the other side, in a flat area where a helicopter could land. He never told me anything else."

"What mountain?"

"He didn't say."

"Why didn't you tell anyone this?" Corrie asked.

"I didn't want to get Rod and Dad—his dad—into trouble." And now at last the sobs came.

Corrie walked slowly back across the street, trying to fit this last-minute revelation into the jigsaw of what she already knew. "Do you think that's where O'Connell was headed?" she asked. "That bunker?"

To her disappointment, Watts didn't look all that impressed. "I doubt it. That's an area called the Knot. Suicide to go in there in wintertime, at night, in a snowstorm."

"Oh yeah," said Corrie. "I got a glimpse down into the Knot when we got the tour of Kirtland. That and the new dude ranch."

"Rancho Bonito. They got yoga retreats, spas, massages, meditation, you name it." Watts's tone made clear how he felt about the place. "Anyway, that resort was only built a few years ago. I don't think O'Connell would go into the Knot intentionally—even if he thought a back door was hidden there."

"She said there was a flat spot—how many of those are there in those mountains?"

"It doesn't take a big area to land a chopper," Watts said.

Corrie nodded. "On another note, how did you dig up all that shit on the grifter girlfriend?"

"I know people who know people who know people," he said, with a dimpled smile. "When I found her for you, I couldn't resist putting the Cheape investigation aside for fifteen minutes and digging a little. I just had a feeling. Seems our dear Winifred, or Helen, or whoever, came into a nice income in the years after Rod's death—and stopped working. Which ended abruptly when your friend Melody Ann arrived on the scene."

As they got into the car, he added, "Well? I think that deserves at least a lunch—on you."

Corrie laughed. "All right, you get lunch. But I've got another interview this afternoon, so it'll have to be hot dogs from the food truck."

"Make it a chili dog and you've just bought yourself a boy." Grinning, Watts buckled himself in and adjusted his Resistol as Corrie pulled away from the curb and accelerated north.

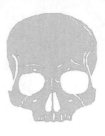

40

THIS VISIT TO the jail was different from the first in every imaginable way. There were no papers for Nora to sign, checks to write, forms to be stamped. And Skip didn't walk out of a side door, arms swinging, wearing his own clothes. This time, Nora and the lawyer, Lightfeather, had to endure pat-downs and magnetometer scans, and a long wait before passing through one locked door, then another, until they reached a small room, with a dirty plexiglass window in the far wall. There were two seats, but the space was barely big enough for both of them to sit. A minute passed, and then a light was switched on behind the glass and Skip came into view. Nora's heart immediately sank. His wrists were chained in front of him, his legs were shackled, and he walked with a prisoner's shuffle. He wore an orange coverall with PRISONER and the name of the county jail stenciled on both front and back. He hadn't shaved in a couple of days and his hair was messed up. But worst of all was the look in his eyes: of a caged animal, desperate, close to panic.

"Nora!" he said, catching sight of her. "Oh my God, *Nora*!" He rushed toward the glass, only to be stopped by a guard who grabbed and propelled him into the chair. Then, when Skip was calm, he removed his handcuffs and left, closing the door behind him after saying, "Five minutes."

"Skip!" Nora cried through a small circular grill in the plexiglass. "Are you all right?"

He massaged his wrists, then planted his elbows on the narrow metal railing in front of him and let his forehead sink onto his palms. "Sis, I'm so screwed." His voice was quavering, on the edge of tears.

Nora spread her hands over the plexiglass, repelled by its greasy feel. "Skip, are you being abused? Are you in danger?"

Skip shook his head without lifting it. "No. It's just—I can't go to prison! I just can't!"

"Skip," Lightfeather said, leaning toward the speaker grill and speaking soothingly, "you're in jail, but that's just for violating conditions of release. It's not a serious offense. You crossed the county line by five thousand yards—unintentionally. The real problem is—"

But Skip wasn't listening. "How old will I be when I get out?" he moaned. "Forty? Fifty?"

"Let's focus on the case. The DA has decided to go ahead and seek attempted murder, which is clearly an overreach, a kind of extortion to get you to plead. So you need to think about pleading—"

"I'm innocent!" Skip cried. "He started it! He attacked my sister! And then he tampered with evidence!"

"Easy now," said Lightfeather. "This isn't the place or time to confer attorney to client, but I just want you to think about pleading, okay? The sheriff's holding most of the cards."

"I'll be branded a felon the rest of my days!"

"Skip," Nora said, "please calm down and listen to Mr. Lightfeather."

"My life is ruined! So is yours! I've ruined *everything*!"

Everything Skip had kept locked inside during those dark hours behind bars was pouring out, like liquid from a broken bottle. He wasn't listening— he just needed to vent.

"Skip," said Nora, "why did you go to that bar?"

"I'll tell you why." Skip suddenly changed his tone. "I was getting someplace. I met people in that bar that I'm sure know Hawley's dirty. All we have to do is dig a little deeper—"

Now it was the lawyer's turn to interrupt. "Skip, this is not a viable strategy. Allegations from a couple of drunks in a bar aren't going to help you. Even if they were true, they wouldn't be admissible in court. Listen to me: going rogue, trying to solve this on your own, that kind of attitude is only going to harm you in court. With the jury."

"So what the hell would you suggest? Plead guilty? Assure everybody that lying sack of shit was telling the truth and didn't assault my sister? Perjure myself to save his skin—and then go to prison, to boot? No way!"

At that moment the guard returned. "Time's up," he said, leaning forward to cuff Skip once again.

For a terrible moment, Nora thought Skip might resist. His eyes widened, he called her name...but then his whole body seemed to go limp, and he allowed himself to be hoisted to his feet.

"We'll talk soon," said Lightfeather. "Think about a plea bargain."

Skip was led out of the tiny room without looking back.

Another harrowing journey through locked doors and past iron bars, and then Nora was out in the visitors' lounge once again. She looked at Lightfeather.

"He's in denial," the lawyer said. "It's common. I'll make another appointment with him, and I'm

sure by then he'll have thought things through a little better."

"But he's got a point," she said. "Doesn't being
innocent matter?"

Lightfeather sighed. "Of course it matters. But
life is fundamentally unfair. Hawley isn't going to
back down, and most of the judges and prosecutors
are either friends or else owe him a favor. They're
going to play hardball."

"Can't we request a change of venue?"

"We could, but we'd be on very shaky ground. And
if it failed, we'd be worse off than when we started.
As it is, we have to contend with the fact he violated
conditions of release, even if unintentionally."

All this lawyerly verbiage made Nora want to
scream. She couldn't get the image of Skip out of her
head—she'd never seen him look so panicked, so
beaten down. He'd gone through periods of depression during and after college, heavily lubricated by
tequila, but he'd managed to shake them off.

"Just lay it out for me," she said. "Please. What
kind of plea deal are we talking about?"

Lightfeather looked at her closely. "Attempted
murder is a second-degree felony, punishable in
New Mexico by up to fifteen years in prison. If
Skip's convicted on that, he'd probably be out in
seven with good behavior. There's a decent chance I
can plea bargain the prosecutor down to aggravated

assault...but that's still a felony, with a possible eighteen-month sentence, of which Skip would do half. And if Hawley wants to really twist the knife, he can argue for a sentencing enhancement, which would expose Skip to a longer stretch. The prosecutor's been coy on that point."

"And if Skip doesn't plea down?"

"Then he'll go to trial for attempted murder of a law officer, most likely with a hostile jury, and the judge could easily sentence him to the full stretch. Now, listen, Nora—next time I'm going to talk to him alone. Let's give him a couple of days to cool down. That usually does the trick. But later...well, he's—forgive me—a stubborn, idealistic fellow. Even though seeing you obviously agitates him, I may need your help persuading him to plead."

"Plead guilty," Nora repeated bitterly. "When we know the sheriff is a goddamned liar and Skip did nothing wrong."

"Some world we live in, isn't it? Now—can you do that for me? Stay away for a couple of days, let me see him on my own?"

Nora nodded.

"Good. Just forget Hawley. Even if Skip had dug up stuff on him, it would never be admitted." He paused. "Listen: the Isleta council is being extremely generous with my time and fees, so I have a lot of resources to work with. Don't give up hope."

Somehow, that final sentence made Nora's hopes—already slim—grow fainter. Taking a deep breath, she nodded again, thanked Lightfeather, then turned and walked out into the pitiless November air.

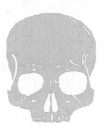

41

MASTER SERGEANT RAMSAY Brickell lived in a neat house in the Trumbull Village section of Albuquerque. Corrie had decided to interview him by herself, after Sharp had shown more than a little impatience at her continued pursuit of the Kirtland angle. Sharp hadn't exactly forbidden her to interview him—he evidently was willing to let her make her own decisions—but he hadn't tried to cover up his skepticism, either.

But Corrie just couldn't shake her sense that there had been a flicker of something in Brickell's eyes, in that moment of hesitation, when she brought up the Dead Mountain incident during the tour of the base. More to the point, as part of his investigation of Cheape's murder, Watts had obtained certain personnel files from Kirtland, and he'd passed along a single document to Corrie. As Watts had already implied, there was a minor commendation

344 DOUGLAS PRESTON & LINCOLN CHILD

note in Cheape's file. The note was uninformative
as to what Cheape had actually done that was com-
mendable. It wouldn't normally have been of interest, except for the date of the event that led to the
commendation: November 1, 2008.

The day after the Dead Mountain incident.

She pulled into Brickell's driveway, put the car in
park, got out, and went to the door. It was answered
immediately—Brickell was clearly waiting for her.
Corrie was a little disconcerted to find him wearing his dress uniform this time, decorations and
all. With a brief handshake he ushered her into the
house with great formality, and they sat down in a
modest living room. He exuded an air of military
correctness and decorum.

"Thank you, sir, for agreeing to see me."

He inclined his head. "A pleasure to see you
again, Agent Swanson. Glad to be of help."

"May I record?" Corrie held up her FBI phone.

He hesitated. "No, thank you. I would prefer you
did not."

"Fine." She put the phone away. "Just for the
record, this interview is voluntary. You're obviously
not a suspect. I'm here for information-gathering
purposes. You can halt the interview at any time or,
of course, have an attorney present if you wish."

He nodded briskly. "I understand."

Corrie took out her notebook in which she had

jotted some questions. Sergeant Brickell was sitting with military straightness in his chair, hands clasped, looking every inch the tough, unbending sergeant he had seemed on their first meeting. She sensed he was a man of strong moral principles and fixed integrity—and she was uncertain how that would play out in the interview.

"Sergeant Brickell," she began, "you were at Kirtland at the time of the Dead Mountain tragedy. I know we've spoken about this once before—I was wondering if you remember anything else specific to it."

"Not much. It was just background noise. We were busy with more pressing business."

Corrie presumed he meant nuclear annihilation, which did seem worse than missing hikers. "Did you know that one of the victims—the one still missing, Rodney O'Connell—had a father who worked at Kirtland? Lieutenant Colonel Harry O'Connell?"

"I knew Lieutenant Colonel O'Connell slightly, and, yes, I knew his son was one of the missing. It was generally understood on the base at that time."

"What was Lieutenant Colonel O'Connell's position there?"

"He was a commander in the 58th Special Operations Wing, but in what role, I do not know."

Brickell's voice was as gravelly as before, and he had what sounded to Corrie like a Texas accent. He spoke with deliberation, pausing to formulate each response. Was this habitual—or was he being extra careful for some reason?

"Did you ever meet him?"

"I believe I must have, but I don't recall any specific encounter."

"Did you know Benjamin Cheape?"

"You mean the person who was murdered in Socorro?"

"Yes."

"I didn't know him well, but our paths crossed. He was a civilian employee in the maintenance department."

He seemed to radiate an increasing tension. Was he lying? He certainly didn't look like the lying type—just the opposite.

"How did your paths cross?"

"Very glancingly and, I believe, only once. We worked on the same project—at different levels, of course. He was, as I said, a civilian maintenance worker. I am a master sergeant. There's not much mixing between the civilian and military sides of Kirtland."

"Mr. Cheape seems to have received a commendation around that time, but there are no specifics in regard to what. Do you know anything about that?"

"No."

"You mentioned you were busy at Kirtland with more pressing business during the Dead Mountain incident."

At this his face seemed to become even more like granite. "That is correct."

"Can you be more specific?"

A long silence followed this question, then Brickell spoke. "Agent Swanson, you will understand that much of the work we do is classified. I'm afraid I can't answer that question."

"So you were involved in some sort of classified business on November 1, 2008?"

"Almost all of the work I do was, and is, classified."

"And you can recall, fifteen years later, what was happening on that particular day?"

"Yes."

"Sergeant Brickell, you do realize that I'm an FBI agent, and that we work with classified information all the time. You know you can trust me with anything you might have to say."

"I'm not aware that you have a security clearance—or even if you do, what level. Certainly you can understand that most of us at a base as vital as Kirtland are under security restrictions."

Damn, thought Corrie. It was true: she didn't have a security clearance yet at the FBI—that took time. "Would you be willing to speak to an agent with the necessary security clearance?"

"Not on this subject."

"Why not?"

Brickell didn't answer. As Corrie gazed at his fine old face, with its steely blue eyes and square jaw, she realized this man would not tell her anything he didn't wish to. The key was making him wish to.

"At around that time, was your classified work connected to the Dead Mountain incident in any way?"

"No."

It felt like she was playing twenty questions with the grizzled old noncom and getting nowhere. She put away her notebook, leaned back, and gazed at him for a moment. "Sergeant Brickell, Lieutenant Colonel O'Connell served his country honorably. I know he was a fine soldier. The disappearance of his son destroyed him. He died of a heart attack—at age sixty. The grief and uncertainty of his son's fate no doubt contributed to that. If you can shed any light on what happened—"

"I don't believe I can."

"Do you have children?"

"I have a daughter."

"And your wife?"

"I'm a widower."

"I'm sorry. But imagine, sir, if your daughter vanished into thin air, and you were left with no idea of what happened to her: no knowledge of her last moments, where she was, whether or not she suffered. Can you imagine that, Sergeant Brickell?"

Brickell said nothing, but she could see the color deepen in his face.

"I ask because that's what these families have been going through, some for as long as fifteen years. My job is not only to solve this case, but to give them closure. Give them a measure of peace. If you have *any* information that would help shed light on the fate of those nine young people—classified or not—I would suggest..." She hesitated, then went on: "That you have a moral duty to share it with me now."

She saw she had finally touched a nerve. Brickell's face had grown dark. A long silence ensued—a minute or more, an eternity in a conversation. At last, he spoke. "I'm sorry, Agent Swanson, but this interview is over."

She stared back at a face of granite. "If you don't mind, I have just a few more questions."

He stood up. "Let me see you to the door."

Corrie gathered up her stuff, rose, and followed him to the door. He opened it for her and she offered him her card. "Sergeant Brickell, I'm available if you ever want to talk."

He took it and eased the door shut. As she turned to go, she heard the bolt shoot home.

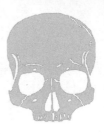

42

Before getting on the freeway, Corrie stopped at a 7-Eleven for coffee. Twilight had fallen over Albuquerque, the sky a sickly hue of mauve as she pulled into a space in front of the garishly lighted store. As she parked and went inside, she went over the interview with Brickell in her mind. She was bitterly disappointed he wouldn't talk—and at the same time, convinced he knew more than he was saying. Something had happened at Kirtland the night the nine hikers died...but the business about security clearances had tripped her up. What she needed to do was talk to Sharp about this, arrange for the required security clearance, then force Brickell to talk, with a subpoena if necessary. But how long would that take? And given his stolid façade, how could he be forced to say anything, when she had no idea what, exactly, there was to tell?

As she came out of the store carrying a large

coffee, a car pulled up next to hers and the door swung open. Brickell got out. She froze as he came around to her.

"Let's get in your car."

She slid into the driver's side while he got in the passenger seat.

"What's this about?" she asked evenly.

"Let's get one thing straight: I was never in this car. We never spoke. Nothing I tell you can be attributed to me. Can we proceed like that?"

Corrie hesitated. At Quantico, they had been taught all about handling confidential informants. It was a tricky area and there were endless rules.

"Sergeant Brickell, whatever you say I have to share with my immediate superior."

"No. You've got to swear on your word of honor that you won't tell anyone where you heard this. You're free to go out and corroborate the information elsewhere, and I hope you will. But I can't be named. Is this understood?"

Christ, how was she going to deal with this? "Um, I don't think I can agree to that."

He put his hand on the door and started to get out.

"Wait," said Corrie. She couldn't let him go. He suddenly felt like the key to everything.

He paused.

"All right. You have my word."

He got back in, took a deep breath, and let it out. He began to speak, slowly and in measured tones.

"We called it the Hallowe'en Incident," he said.

She waited.

"It happened the night of October 31, 2008. An accident."

"What kind of accident?"

"What I'm about to tell you is classified at the highest level. I doubt the current Kirtland command even knows about it. The whole business was hushed up—not to protect national security, but to cover gross incompetence by certain high-ranking officers. That's never sat well with me."

"Please tell me, sir, what happened."

He leaned back in the seat and looked straight ahead. "On the night of October 31, 2008, a B-52H Stratofortress flew out of Kirtland carrying a decommissioned Mark 17 thermonuclear warhead, en route to North Carolina for disassembly. This was an obsolete device with a yield of ten megatons—the largest in our arsenal. Most of those Mark 17s had been retired in the sixties, but there were certain commanders who wanted to keep a few around, just in case. This was one of them—but by 2008 it had deteriorated beyond any possible use. So that evening, it was placed in a special cradle in the bay of the B-52. It was heavy—twenty-one tons. The overloaded plane should never have taken off in that weather, but the order was given and the pilots obeyed. About four and a half miles south of the Kirtland control tower, at approximately six thirty PM local time, the plane encountered severe turbulence. The pilots lost control and, in a desperate attempt to lighten the aircraft, released the bomb. The plane climbed, narrowly cleared the mountain in its path, and the pilots managed to return to Kirtland."

"And the bomb?"

"The bomb fell seventeen hundred feet into the mountains. The impact set off the high-explosive shell around the primary, but not, thank God, in the way necessary to detonate the warhead. Nevertheless, there was one hell of an explosion. The resulting fire sent up a plume of smoke carrying plutonium and other radionuclides into the storm."

He paused, breathing hard. Corrie could hardly believe what she was hearing. "What happened then?"

"Kirtland immediately sent recovery teams into the mountains. The site of the drop was quickly located. Everything was covered up, the crater filled and camouflaged, the debris recovered, and over time the area was secretly decontaminated."

"And who was notified?"

"Nobody was notified. Those that knew of it eventually retired, died ... or tried to forget."

Corrie struggled to keep her demeanor calm and collected. She had taken no notes, she didn't have this on tape, and she'd given her word not to tell Sharp where she had heard it. That was against the confidential informant rules and was going to be a problem. "What connection is there between that accident and the Dead Mountain deaths?"

"I don't know. Maybe none."

"Do you think the explosion and fire might have scared the nine hikers into leaving their tent and running out to die in the blizzard?"

A long silence. "I've always wondered."

"Did anyone at Kirtland at the time investigate a possible link?"

"No. At the time, the last thing we were worried about was a bunch of hikers camped in the snow. Later, it was dismissed as a coincidence. And even if they did witness the drop, they were all dead, so it didn't matter."

"How involved were you in the bomb recovery operation?"

"I was directly involved."

"Cheape also?"

"Yes. That's the project I mentioned earlier— when we crossed paths."

"What was his role?"

"He was a member of one of several ground searching teams sent immediately into the blizzard to find the bomb location. They couldn't send up air assets right away."

"And did Cheape find the bomb location?"

"No. Another searcher called it in first. But Cheape was on the same team and they all got commendations."

"Can you show me on a map where the bomb fell?"

"Yes."

With her phone, Corrie loaded a Google Earth image of the Manzanos. "Can you drop a pin at the location?"

He took the phone, moved the image around, expanded it, tapped once, then handed it back.

Corrie stared. The bomb had landed less than a mile due south of where the nine hikers were camped. *Jesus.* This was the answer to the Dead Mountain riddle. The explosion and fire must have frightened them so badly that they slashed their way out of their tent and ran. It also explained their northward route—not to *go* somewhere, but to escape the conflagration.

"Sergeant Brickell," she said, "would you *please* repeat what you told me to Special Agent Sharp, my superior in the case? This is the solution we've been looking for—for fifteen years."

"Absolutely not. I'm retiring in a month. I've cleared my conscience and done my moral duty, as you put it. But I'm not willing to be dishonorably discharged, lose my pension, and spend my hard-earned retirement in the brig."

"The FBI can protect you. There are whistle-blower safeguards."

He looked at her, the stolid expression growing weary. "You're very young, aren't you? Do you truly believe I'd never suffer retaliation? You're just learning how the world really works, Agent Swanson, and I don't envy your forthcoming education." He paused. "Remember: you gave your word. I know you'll honor it."

"I did," said Corrie unhappily. "And I will."

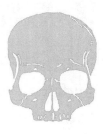

43

THE EARLY AFTERNOON sun shone brilliantly on Sandia Crest as they got on the freeway heading south. Sharp, to her surprise, had insisted on driving. He appeared uncharacteristically alert, and Corrie wasn't sure what the lack of his usual sleepy expression signaled—except that it made her nervous.

"I just want to make one thing clear," he said. "I'm going to do the talking. I may call on you to say something, but please don't speak until I ask you to do so."

"Yes, sir."

A long silence. "Let's just go over this once more," he finally said. "They're going to ask me: How do we know our confidential informant isn't a nut job? What's my answer?"

"He's in a position of responsibility. Authority. He's not repeating rumors. His knowledge of the events is firsthand. Direct knowledge."

"So why won't he go on record?"

"The information is classified. The guy's a stand-up soldier: divulging secrets isn't usually his idea of patriotism. He also thinks he'll be arrested—and that we won't be able to protect him."

Sharp sighed. For once, she could see what he was feeling: skepticism and anxiety.

"You realize this is a stunning accusation to make, with absolutely no corroboration whatsoever."

"I realize that, sir." They'd gone over this multiple times, when Corrie first briefed him on her two meetings the day before: O'Connell's old girlfriend, with her story of the bunker . . . and then Brickell's bombshell—literally.

They took the freeway exit for Kirtland and were soon at the base's gate, handing over their IDs. They were quickly let through, and five minutes later were parking in front of the command building. Two soldiers, apparently waiting for them, escorted them to the commander's office.

It was a capacious space, the vast polished desk flanked by flags. Behind it, the commander rose.

"Major General Frank Marsby," he said, coming around and shaking their hands. "And Colonel Maryam Abecassis, whom you know."

They were both dressed in formal uniforms, emblazoned with decorations. The two silver stars on General Marsby's shoulders gleamed in the bright overhead lighting. The general invited them to join him and the colonel in a sitting area, with a glass-and-chrome table and a collection of taupe stuffed chairs.

Corrie felt a nervousness that was almost over-whelming. If this was all wrong, if Brickell *was* crazy, her promising career would take an instant nosedive.

"Thank you for meeting with us," Sharp said.

General Marsby nodded. "We're always happy to help the FBI. But I have to admit, this is an unusu-ally mysterious summons, and naturally we're anx-ious to hear what's so urgent."

Sharp leaned forward on his elbows. Corrie saw that he, too, looked nervous. It occurred to her for the first time that if this accusation were false, it might affect his career even more than hers.

"I'll get straight to the point," Sharp said. "We have a confidential informant who tells us that on the night of October 31, 2008, a B-52 out of Kirtland, carrying a decommissioned thermonuclear device, dropped its payload in the Manzanos about nine miles south of the base. The warhead didn't go off—obviously—but the conventional explosives in the bomb detonated and caused a fire. The bomb debris was quickly retrieved, the area decontaminated, and evidence of any crater eliminated. The incident was then classified at the highest level."

He paused. Corrie could see in the faces of the

two listeners clear expressions of genuine shock, concern—and doubt.

"Furthermore," Sharp went on, "and of immediate concern to the FBI, it may be that this accident was the cause of the Dead Mountain incident we're investigating. The explosion and fire occurred, according to our informant, roughly a mile south of where they were camped at the time. It triggered the nine hikers into abandoning their tent and running northward, away from the explosion—where all perished." He paused a moment, then said, "That's it in a nutshell. We were hoping you might be able to shed some light on this, if it's true. Of course," he added, "our informant might be mistaken or lying, but if we believed that, we would never have brought the matter to your attention."

General Marsby stared for a moment, ran his hand over his crew cut, and then said, "Can I ask who this confidential informant is?"

"I'm afraid," said Sharp, "that they requested anonymity."

"But you believe this story?"

"The CI was highly convincing," said Sharp. "We neither believe nor disbelieve. That's why we're here, to seek clarification."

"But you think this individual is trustworthy? Not crazy?"

Sharp turned to Corrie. "Agent Swanson interviewed the informant. Could you answer the question, please?"

At this Corrie looked at the general, who was looking at her in disbelief. "Yes, I believe the person is trustworthy and reliable."

"How many people know the identity of this confidential informant?" asked the general.

Corrie nodded. "Just me, sir."

"No one else? Not you, Agent Sharp?"

"No."

"Is he connected to this base?"

"He or she. I can't reveal that, sir," said Corrie.

Now the general looked from Sharp to Corrie and back. "And you've come in here, making this serious accusation, based on *one* person's story? Do you have any corroboration?"

Again Sharp looked at Corrie.

"Well, sir," Corrie said, "the radionuclide contamination of the clothing of several of the victims—which included plutonium, polonium, and tritium—are precisely the ingredients one would find in a thermonuclear weapon, according to our lab experts."

The general stared at her. "Any additional corroboration?"

"No, but I think those radionuclides seem pretty confirmative. It's hard to explain how else they might have gotten there, sir."

"Stop calling me sir, young lady. You're not my subordinate."

"Noted," said Corrie, coloring.

Abecassis gently broke in. "If what you describe actually occurred, it would have been a major incident involving dozens of personnel, and there will certainly be a large body of classified records of it. It'll be a simple matter for us—I mean the general and myself—to either confirm or refute this story. We will investigate it immediately, and I can assure you we will know within twenty-four hours whether this incident actually occurred—or whether this story is false."

"Thank you, Commander," Corrie said.

"All well and good, but I would be astonished to see it confirmed," said the general, with a frosty look at Abecassis. "It sounds to me like a ginned-up conspiracy theory, like so many others connected to this Dead Mountain case." He paused. "Didn't I read about the police just arresting an FBI agent previously on the case for threatening some protesters with a gun?"

"The agent in question was long retired from the agency," said Sharp crisply.

"Still," said the general. "Not at all encouraging. I'm frankly quite surprised to see you bringing this story to us without more corroboration."

"Once we heard this story," said Corrie evenly,

"we felt the right thing to do was inform you immediately—and, of course, confidentially. That, we felt, was preferable to investigating the allegation behind your backs—and I should also add our interest in this only extends as far as what precipitated the deaths of those nine hikers."

"Quite so," said the general. "I understand. As Colonel Abecassis said, we'll look into this. Needless to say, this is an unexpected development, and I trust the FBI will keep this absolutely under wraps."

"The FBI routinely handles highly classified information," said Sharp. "You can be sure this will not see the light of day."

They were escorted back to their vehicle. Sharp didn't speak again until they were out on the highway. "That went better than I expected," he finally said.

"You think so?" Corrie was surprised.

"Absolutely. First, I'm convinced they had no knowledge of this incident—if it actually happened. That's good. Second, they seemed sincere in their desire to investigate it and didn't become overly defensive. Third, they promised that records would be quickly found in their classified archive— so we'll have an answer soon. Fourth, I think both of them are people of good intention. And fifth..." He smiled. "The point you made about not investigating behind their backs was a good one."

She hesitated. "And what do you think, sir? Personally?"

"Do I believe they accidentally dropped a nuke? I don't know. It's a crazy story, but God knows anything might be possible. But I feel an obligation to tell you that I'm not pleased about your mishandling of a confidential informant."

"Mishandling?"

"Next time," said Sharp, "you need to ask for the informant to supply independent corroboration of a story like that. And you must *also* insist that he tell his story to at least two agents, so there are witnesses. Otherwise the information is almost useless."

"Sir, I tried my best to do all those things. I asked him to make the statement in your presence. He absolutely refused and was going to leave. I had no other choice...unless I was willing to allow our potential answer to slip away."

"That may be. But the regulations are in place not only to protect the public, but us as well. If this turns out to be a false lead, you and I are both in trouble. The air force is not going to let it slide. You understand that?"

"Yes, sir."

"My concern now," Sharp said after a moment, "is that if it *is* true—how will the air force respond?"

44

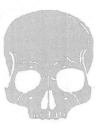

CORRIE ARRIVED IN her cubicle at seven, having hardly slept the night before. She was filled with anxiety about the case and what would happen to her—and Sharp—if the allegation turned out to be false.

Almost before she could settle down at her desk, her phone buzzed. It was Sharp.

"SAC Garcia wants us in his office. Now."

"Yes, sir."

The fact that Garcia and Sharp would even be in the office at seven in the morning set her pulse racing. They had spoken to General Marsby and the colonel at 1 PM the previous afternoon—they'd promised a prompt investigation, but surely it couldn't be this prompt.

She smoothed her hair, tugged on her suit, and walked down the hall. In a few minutes she arrived in Garcia's corner office with its view of the Sandia

Mountains, covered in fresh snow, touched by the morning sunrise.

Garcia was standing in front of his desk with Sharp next to him, and neither man looked normal. The SAC's face was dark, his thick eyebrows creased, pupils contracted into points. He didn't greet her or invite her to sit down or even look at her. She glanced at Sharp and saw that he looked uncharacteristically angry—furious, in fact, with a suppressed rage that almost frightened her.

Nobody said anything. Corrie finally stammered, "Um, good morning. Is everything all right?"

"I got a call from Raeburn last night," said Garcia. "At three in the morning."

Corrie's heart leapt into her throat. Raeburn was the director of the FBI.

"Raeburn told me—me, you, everyone in this building—to discontinue the Kirtland line of investigation."

Corrie stared at him. "What?"

Garcia made an effort to control himself. "We can no longer consider Kirtland connected in any way to the investigation."

"But—did the bomb accident happen or not? I mean, it could be the key to the whole case!" Corrie suddenly stopped herself, remembering whom she was talking to.

Garcia looked at Sharp, then back to Corrie. "I

was given no information about such an alleged incident."

"I'm sorry, sir," Corrie said. "But I'm just not following you. How are we supposed to drop such a crucial part of the investigation?"

Garcia looked exasperated. "Agent Swanson, I'm relaying orders from the FBI director himself. Those orders are clear: drop Kirtland from the case. I was given no further explanations. Do you understand?"

"No," said Corrie defiantly.

"Then I'll explain," said Sharp suddenly, his voice edged with sarcasm. He turned to Corrie, with a face the color of liver. "Obviously, your informant was right. Kirtland *did* drop a nuke. It caused an explosion and fire that, indirectly, led to the deaths of those nine hikers. They want us to suppress the investigation to cover up their incompetence."

"I don't get it," Corrie said.

Sharp went on. "When air force command heard our story, they panicked. They went up the ladder to somebody high in the government and were told to quash it. And now we've been ordered to *pretend* to investigate. Our role now is to put on a show, humiliate and debase ourselves in acting out a charade of incompetency and stupidity—just what the parents of the victims have accused us of."

"That's quite enough," said Garcia quietly to Sharp.

"It's never enough," said Sharp.

Garcia gave Sharp a penetrating stare. "Look. I hate this. You hate it. The FBI director hates it. Obviously Agent Swanson hates it. But we've been given direct orders. This came down from a level higher than the director, probably even higher than the AG."

"You mean, from yesterday afternoon to three o'clock this morning," Corrie said, "this problem went all the way up to, what, the White House? . . . And then back down to the FBI director?"

"I'd say that's a strong possibility."

Corrie could hardly believe what she was hearing. "So we're supposed to lie to the public, pretend to investigate, and intentionally let the case die?"

"Sometimes you have to carry out orders you don't like," said Garcia. "I don't mind telling you, this is the worst example of that I've ever seen. It's a hard one to swallow. *But it's the job.* Both of you will get major commendations."

"I can't accept this, sir," said Corrie.

Garcia looked at her for a long, steady moment. "Keep in mind, Agent Swanson, that an FBI agent who deliberately reveals classified information harming our national security could be prosecuted for capital treason."

At this, silence settled over the office. Sharp abruptly turned and left the office.

For a moment, Corrie didn't know what to do. Was the meeting over? Even if it was, she had one question she still wanted answered. "Did Gold also find out about the bomb accident?" she asked. "Did he get shut down, too? Is that why he quit the FBI and finally went off the rails?"

Garcia looked at her. "We'll never know, will we?"

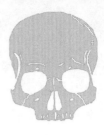

45

THE MEETING WAS over. Corrie exited the office, unsure where Sharp had gone or what she was supposed to do now. She returned to her cubicle on unsteady feet and sat down, her mind in turmoil. She felt a burning sense of betrayal that struck at the very heart of why she had joined the FBI. Her childhood had been full of injustice and the unfair use of power—from her alcoholic mother and absentee father, to being bullied at school and harassed by the local sheriff. Confronting injustice was what drove her sense of self and animated her choice of careers. But this—this was anything but justice. How could the director have agreed to it?

Now a welling up of anger washed away the feelings of betrayal. It was more than a betrayal. From Garcia on down, they'd been defrauded, undermined, demoralized...And what about Sharp?

She'd never seen him so angry. What was he going to do? What was *she* going to do?

First, she told herself, she had to calm down. She needed a moment to think through this whole fucked-up situation. They had solved the case: that much was obvious. The impact—the sound, the bright light, the tremors, whatever—had scared the shit out of the nine hikers. It explained why they had fled into the storm, why they'd run northward—not toward anything, but just away from the disaster...and into another, final one. And now they were supposed to keep pretending? How, exactly?

That much was obvious. She suddenly sat up. She could feel her head clearing. Was it really *that* obvious? Or had the excitement of this huge discovery blinded her to the whole picture?

You saw the photographs. She could almost hear Gold's words, whispering to her again.

She gathered up a sheaf of eight-by-ten photos of the original tent site and went through them slowly. Then she stared off into space, thinking, as minutes went by. Forty minutes had passed since the awful meeting in Garcia's office. It was now eight o'clock and she could hear the workplace filling up, agents arriving for the day. What to do now? She went through the photos again and selected a small number of them, along with an inventory of the objects found with Tolland and Wright. She tucked them all under her arm and rose. Stepping out of her cubicle, she nodded perfunctory greetings to her colleagues as she headed for Sharp's office.

The door was shut and she knocked.

No answer. Was he in there? She leaned close to the door. "Agent Sharp?"

A moment later, she heard the door unlock. When it opened, Sharp stood there, saying nothing. He nodded her toward a chair, shut and locked the door behind her. His demeanor was rigidly composed.

He sat down, clasped his hands on the desk. "When you joined the FBI," he said, "I don't imagine you ever thought something like this might happen."

"No, sir, I didn't," Corrie said.

"Neither did I," said Sharp.

"What are you going to do about it?"

He shook his head. "Agent Swanson, before I joined the FBI, I did some things for my country that…" He paused. "Let's just say I wasn't happy to do them, but there was no question: they had to be done. But this is different. I think of those families never knowing what really happened. And us, making a pretense of investigating… making promises… It goes against everything I believe in as an FBI agent." He shook his head. Corrie could hear the disgust in his voice. "I…"

He paused and she waited, but he didn't complete

the sentence. After a long silence, he said, "I'm very sorry, Corrie, this happened to you. Soon, I'll have finished my twenty. But you...you're just starting out."

Did that mean he might resign? "You can't abandon me," she blurted out.

He looked at her, then shook his head. It was an ambiguous gesture, and she wasn't sure if it was meant to be reassuring—or otherwise.

She took a deep breath. It was now or never. "Sir, there's something about the case I'd like to talk to you about."

He looked at her steadily. "Yes?"

"I'm not sure we've actually solved it."

His stare deepened.

Corrie brought out one of the photos. "Here's an image of the tent as it was initially found by the searchers." She slid it toward him, then chose another. "And here's one from another angle."

But Sharp did not look at the photos. He continued looking at Corrie, hands folded on the table.

"Um, you'll see, sir, that there's a vestibule at the front of the tent. They were using that area to cook on their backpacking stove—you can see the stove in there, and some packets of freeze-dried food and instant cocoa."

Finally, he took his eyes from her and looked at the photos, saying nothing.

"You can see, the front door of the tent leading into the vestibule is unzipped, and the vestibule is also staked partway open. Probably to allow the cooking fumes to ventilate."

He finally spoke, and his voice was cold. "So?"

"The point I'm making is that there was a clear way out of the tent. But instead of running out that open door, they nevertheless slashed their way out the side."

"On the side away from the blast."

"True. But...well, here: please take a look at these photos of the slashes, one from the inside and one from out."

She pushed the two additional prints over. "You see how they had to cut through two layers, the inner tent and the fly? And there are multiple slashes, some not long enough, and some not hard enough. They had to slash that ripstop nylon multiple times to make an opening big enough to get through. You see? It wasn't easy to cut their way out. On top of that, the disorganized and scattershot way it's slashed seems to indicate real panic."

He remained silent. His eyes rose from the photo to meet hers.

"Think about it, sir. They're in the tent. They're boiling water for dinner, with the flap open. Suddenly, out of nowhere, there's an explosion to the south. The sky lights up. But nothing happens directly to *them*, because the explosion is a good distance away. These hikers are experienced mountaineers—they know the storm outside is deadly. They know going out in bare feet, or unclothed, would be suicide. How long does it take to pull on a pair of boots and grab a coat and hat? Look at this photo of the inside. You can see the coats and hats and boots all there, carefully lined up, ready to be put on. Do you really think they'd rush out to certain death without bothering to pull on a coat or boots? And why waste time slashing their way out when it would have been much faster to just go out the front?"

She paused, but he remained still.

"Sir, all along our investigators have assumed that something appeared in the doorway, blocking their exit—and terrifying them beyond the power of reasoning. Bomb or no bomb, there's no reason to revise that assumption."

Pausing, she was disconcerted when Sharp chose to remain silent.

"And then, what about the murder-suicide in the cave? We've uncovered no evidence of tension between Wright and Tolland. Why would Tolland stab Wright to death and then kill himself in such a bizarre way? How can the explosion and fire explain that?"

Sharp now began shaking his head, slowly, back and forth.

Corrie began to hurry, afraid he would cut her off. "Look, here's the list of articles that Tolland and Wright carried. They both had lighters. Why didn't they light a fire in the cave, like the drunken frat kids did? And why didn't number nine, O'Connell, stay in the cave with Tolland and Wright? Why did he—as far as we can tell—keep going in the storm? None of this is rational behavior...and the more I think about it, the less I believe the bomb accident explains it all."

She halted, breathing hard.

Sharp unfolded and refolded his hands. "Are you done?"

"Yes, sir."

He spoke in a tight voice. "What do *you* think was going on?"

"I don't know, sir."

"And what do you propose to do about this?"

"Two critical pieces of evidence are still missing—the camera and the journal that the group had been jointly keeping. They weren't in the tent, and they weren't found with any of the bodies, or anywhere along the path they took. O'Connell, as the official chronicler of the expedition, would likely have had both of those with him. And since his body was never found, I think it could be in that bunker his girlfriend mentioned. Think about it: O'Connell knew the code to the emergency exit. And he knew where it was. North of the tent—precisely the direction all the hikers were headed."

Sharp was silent for a long, awkward moment. Then he said, "Agent Swanson?"

"Yes, sir?"

"What just happened this morning?"

"They told us to quash the case. But how can we do that when there are all these new leads? Take Cheape, for example. We know he was one of the searchers. He did something that triggered a commendation—but the reason for it was omitted from the files. And then when the case was revived, he suddenly came into big money...and was murdered. Doesn't that sound fishy to you?"

"And your solution to all these new leads is...what?"

"Go to Kirtland and get them to authorize a search of the bunker."

Sharp grimaced. It looked almost as if he were in pain. "Let me ask you again: *What just happened this morning?*"

This time, Corrie said nothing.

"Agent Swanson, I'm deeply impressed at your tenacity. You care. But you have to let this go. I could rebut much of what you just told me: for example, we don't know O'Connell is in the bunker; we don't know he has the camera; we don't know if the film is still viable; and in particular it seems unlikely it contains anything useful, especially if you're right that they were too busy running to even get dressed. But I'm not going to go in that direction, because the situation is really much, much simpler than that. If you continue to pursue this case, you'll destroy your career at the FBI. You understand me? You're going to make a fine agent if you can just suck it up, keep your mouth shut, and accept the commendation they're going to give you."

"I don't think I can do that, sir."

He stood up. "You'll have to. *I'll* have to. I already explained this. People far more powerful than us have determined that national security is involved. Neither of us has a choice in the matter. We're done. *Done.*"

"Did Gold have a choice in the matter?" It was out of her mouth before she could reconsider.

Sharp leaned toward her. "I'm going to take a day or two off to digest this. You need to do the same."

And with that, he picked his coat off the back of the door, pulled it on, opened the door, and left her sitting in his office.

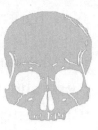

46

"ALL RISE," THE clerk of the court intoned.

Nora stood up, as did everyone else in the shabby courtroom. Nora, Skip's attorney Edward Light-feather, and another attorney from Lightfeather's firm were all sitting at the defense table on the right-hand side of the courtroom. The prosecutor and his team were on the left—the district attorney, who was personally handling the case, an assistant DA, and several others. Skip was sitting alone in the dock.

Nora had known Skip wouldn't look good—and she had steeled herself for it. Or thought she had. He was wearing an ill-fitting suit, his only one, that Nora had retrieved for him from his closet, but he had put it on carelessly, with the result skewing more toward Salvation Army than Saks. The tie was knotted awry, the top button undone, and the shirt had managed to grow wrinkled in the short time he'd had it on. The old cowlick on his head was standing up more than usual, like a cockatoo's crest, and the rest of his hair looked slept on. He was clearly terrified.

All the spectator seats were full—this was apparently a big deal in Torrance County. Nora had a bad feeling about that. She knew how popular the sheriff was on his home ground, and she worried that people would be looking forward to seeing Skip convicted, not released.

The judge came in, wearing black robes. He was a bored, weary-looking man, about sixty, with a fringe of black hair—obviously dyed—combed over a bald spot, a pug nose, and cheeks the color of suet. He had a studiously neutral face, almost slack, which Nora figured was intentionally hard to read. He positioned himself behind the bench and sat down, then the rest of the courtroom did likewise.

Nora turned her attention to the jury. She saw, or thought she saw, a cross section of working-class New Mexico—ranchers, farmers, construction workers, retail and service employees—all ordinary people. It was impossible to see into their minds, but they looked solid and fair-minded. That gave her a slender feeling of hope.

The judge went through the preliminaries, welcomed the jury, and offered some introductory remarks. He then called on the district attorney to make his opening statement.

The DA's name was Scowsen. Lightfeather had described him to Nora as formidable and more competent than one might expect to find in a backwater county: determined to win, but not crooked. Nora scrutinized him closely. He was a tall, rugged, and handsome man, in his midthirties, with curly black hair and blue eyes. He wore a gray suit and a beautiful pair of ostrich cowboy boots. Nora could sense his charisma and intelligence, which worried her even more than if he'd been corrupt. She glanced at Skip, anxiety and fear written all over his face as he watched Scowsen stroll into the center of the courtroom. Skip had never been good at concealing his emotions, and now he looked exactly like who he was: a person on trial, scared shitless, looking at fifteen years for attempted murder.

"Ladies and gentlemen of the jury," the DA began in a folksy tone, sauntering over to the jury box and laying a light hand on the railing, "I'd like to introduce myself. My name is Will Scowsen, and I am the elected district attorney of this fine county. I will be the lead prosecutor in this case. I'll be assisted by Assistant District Attorney Maureen Rivera."

Rivera stood up and nodded to the jury, giving them a quick smile.

"I'm going to speak to you for a moment about the trial and what it's about—what we attorneys call the opening statement. During the trial, I'll explain to you what the defendant did, and how we intend to prove it beyond a reasonable doubt. The burden of proof is on us, and that burden is high. Very high. It's that way for a reason—to make sure no innocent person is convicted. But as you will see as the trial progresses, the evidence here is overwhelming. We will meet that burden of proof and more.

"The defendant, Elwyn Kelly—" he turned and pointed a finger— "known familiarly as Skip, is accused of a number of felonies. I'll go over them briefly. The first is, and I quote from the statutes: 'Aggravated battery upon a peace officer in any manner whereby great bodily harm or death can be inflicted, with intent to commit obstruction of justice.' Two: 'Intentionally fleeing, attempting to evade or evading an officer of this state when the person committing the act of fleeing, attempting to evade or evasion has knowledge that the officer is attempting to apprehend or arrest him.' Three: 'Larceny in the third degree, the value of the property being over two thousand five hundred dollars and below twenty thousand dollars.' And four: 'Tampering with evidence with intent to interfere with the course of justice.'"

He took a little turn around the floor. "I know, sounds like a lot of gobbledygook. But this is a simple case. A *very* simple case. The defendant, Mr.

Elwyn Kelly, was caught stealing federal property by the sheriff of our county, Mr. Derek Hawley. When Sheriff Hawley attempted to prevent
the theft and take the defendant into custody, the
defendant violently assaulted him and threw him
to the ground, injuring him severely. The defendant
then attempted to flee. This assault was witnessed
by the deputy sheriff, Raymond Baca. You'll hear
testimony from Sheriff Hawley as to specific details,
and his version will be fully backed up by Deputy
Sheriff Baca. You'll see medical records detailing
the sheriff's injuries. You'll hear from a doctor that
the force of the assault could easily have resulted
in a fatal fracture to the sheriff's skull. You'll
hear how the defendant resisted arrest and tried
to flee.

"The defense will put up a witness, the defendant's sister, who was also present at the assault. Her
testimony—" here he took a moment to flash the
jury a smile, rolling his eyes— "will be quite different from the testimony you'll hear from our two
law enforcement officers. Your job will be to decide
who to believe: the sister who loves her brother and
wants to keep him out of prison at all costs, or our
two honorable law enforcement officers, men of
the highest integrity, who were merely doing their
jobs—men who have been protecting the good citizens of this county for a combined thirty-two years."

Nora glanced over at Lightfeather while this recitation was going on. The attorney had a grim look
on his face. Skip, on the other hand, looked like a
person openly sinking into despair, his usual bright
expression distorted with apprehension. Christ, he
already looked guilty. She felt a terrible twist of fear
in her own gut. Lightfeather had been right: Skip
was going to lose this case. He should have pleaded
down. But he'd been so damn stubborn.

"You'll hear about an iPhone, and allegations
about a video that never existed, and other claims
thrown up by the defense designed to sow doubt
in your minds. As they scatter this chaff, keep one
thing in mind: this is a simple case. The defendant
was stealing something, got caught, assaulted the
sheriff, and tried to escape. That's the entire story,
full stop.

"I would like to conclude my opening statement
with a little reminder about our sheriff. Many of
you may already know of Sheriff Hawley's heroism
in the line of duty—how, during his very first term,
he single-handedly stopped a robbery of the former
Torrance Bank and Trust, exchanged fire with the
bad guy, and took a bullet. Even as he was gravely
wounded, he took down the criminal. Ladies and
gentlemen, Sheriff Hawley is a genuine hero, and
I'm sure you will be as outraged as I am when the
defense tries to call him a liar and worse. I just want

to give you a heads-up: things could get ugly. I know you will be able to separate that chaff from the wheat, truth from falsehood, and render a just verdict. Thank you."

Scowsen retired to his table, and Nora could see him being quietly congratulated by his associates. She hated to admit it, but it had been a powerful presentation, reasonable, delivered in a steady, just-the-facts voice—short and to the point. She looked at Hawley and felt incandescent hatred for the self-satisfied, lying bastard with his meatball face, shaved dome of a head, aviator sunglasses hanging from his shirt, lips thin and tight.

Lightfeather rose up and began his opening statement, also speaking to the jury. Nora listened intently. He was very good as well, speaking in an affable voice. He talked about how what had happened was nothing as simple as the prosecution would like to paint it, how the defendant was not, in fact, stealing federal property but was authorized to remove human remains by the Isleta Pueblo Tribal Council. He was working in his capacity as an assistant archaeologist. But, he said, his voice lowering so the jury had to almost lean forward to hear him, the crucial point was this: the sheriff had assaulted the defendant's sister first, knocking her down. The defendant—Skip—had done what he did to protect his sister from further harm. This was justifiable defense in every way. On top of that, Skip had recorded a video on his cell phone of the sheriff attacking his sister. But the sheriff had confiscated the phone, claiming it as evidence, and when it was returned to them by the sheriff's department, *the video had been erased*—there was no trace of it to be found.

He paused to let this sink in, and then stated, his voice rising with suppressed anger, that the sheriff and deputy were both going to lie directly to them, the jury. The sheriff was going to deny the assault on the sister and deny erasing the video. They were going to lie about Skip trying to resist arrest. The lies and the cover-up, he told the jury, had already begun with the district attorney's well-meaning opening statement—by a prosecutor who had also been deceived by the sheriff and his deputy.

Lightfeather's opening statement was delivered in the tone of a person who seeks the truth, burning with carefully controlled indignation at the prevarications and falsehoods of those abusing their positions of authority and power. It was as well delivered as could be expected under the circumstances. But Nora, observing the faces of the jury, could already read open skepticism on some faces. How could her testimony prevail against the sworn statements of two law enforcement officers?

The courtroom recessed for lunch and Skip was

led away. Nora felt too sick to eat and excused herself to be alone. She spent the hour in a distant corner of the courthouse cafeteria—there was nowhere else to go—nursing a coffee.

The afternoon session convened at one thirty, and it was even worse. For his first witness, Scowsen called Sheriff Hawley to the stand. The sheriff told his lying story in a quiet, reasonable way, conveying an air of pained honesty. He related the "facts" with little drama, giving the appearance of even underplaying the violence and his own injuries, rendering the false particulars without embellishment. He described the attack, told of being seized by Skip and thrown to the ground. He described that as he lay on the ground, stunned, the defendant had tried to run. He told of how Baca had heroically taken him down.

The entire story was a falsehood, but Hawley had clearly prepared and rehearsed it. Every detail was internally consistent, recounted in a quiet, calm, and convincing way. The guy was good—more than good—a liar of remarkable effectiveness. Nora could see the jury hanging on every word.

Then it was time to cross-examine. Lightfeather stood up. "I have no questions, Your Honor." He sat down again.

Nora was stunned. She glared at Lightfeather. He quickly scribbled a note and passed it to her.

He's too good. Can't be shaken. To cross would only reinforce his story.

Nora felt sick. Was this how it was going to be?

Next up came an emergency room doctor, showing photographs of the sheriff's injuries—a few nickel-sized bruises and a tiny cut—testifying that while the injuries were not life-threatening, it could have been much more severe, given the rocky ground. In fact, the doctor testified, Hawley could have suffered a fatal concussion from the force of the fall, had his head made contact with a rock.

Lightfeather cross-examined the doctor and managed to get him to admit that the bruising and cut were superficial, were not medically significant, and required little more than an application of antibiotic ointment and a Band-Aid.

A government bureaucrat from the Forest Service testified to the fact that the sets of bones were federal property, even under the NAGPRA law; that the Isleta Tribal Council could not unilaterally declare that the remains were theirs without some sort of due process. On cross-examination, Lightfeather got the bureaucrat to admit that, yes, since the remains had been returned to the tribe and buried at an unknown location, the Forest Service considered the matter closed and would not pursue theft charges against anyone involved.

"Your Honor," Scowsen said, "members of the jury, it is our opinion that the number of witnesses necessary to conclude this matter is rather minimal. However, to give you a superfluity of information on which to base your conclusion, and to give the defendant the benefit of the doubt—especially given the seriousness of the charges—we will call on one or two more witnesses than we feel necessary. We beg your indulgence in this matter. The first such person we wish to call is a character witness. He was a patron at a tavern called—" here he glanced at his notes— "Gallina's Peek last Saturday, and can give a firsthand account of the violent and short-tempered nature of the defendant."

Lightfeather cursed under his breath, then stood up. "Objection. Your Honor, we were not informed of this witness during the discovery process."

"He is a lay witness," Scowsen rebutted, "and the information he presents is not directly relevant to the case—it refers more to the character of the accused."

"Your Honor," Lightfeather said, "I would like to request a sidebar."

The judge motioned both Lightfeather and the DA up to the bench. A whispered conversation ensued, which grew animated at times. Lightfeather spoke in an increasingly angry whisper. Finally, the judge ended the contentious back-and-forth with a rap of his gavel, and the two lawyers stepped away from the bench.

"In light of this new witness being called by the prosecution," the judge said, "the defense has asked for a continuance. The court will stand in recess and will reconvene at ten o'clock Monday morning." He gave another sharp rap.

As the courtroom adjourned, Nora looked up at the clock: 4 PM.

They took Skip away. Nora walked from the courtroom with Lightfeather and his assistant. They said nothing until they were out of the building, pausing by their parked cars in the cracked parking lot in front of the ugly concrete courthouse.

"It doesn't feel like it's going well," Nora said.

Lightfeather shook his head. "It isn't. I'm sorry. And this witness they're suddenly introducing worries me. They've got a strong case—why add a character witness?"

"But it gives you more time—over the weekend, at least—to work on the case. Right?"

Lightfeather did not reply directly, and Nora got the impression no amount of extra time would be of much help. "I have to tell you, Nora: the hardest job a defense attorney faces is to convince a jury a cop is lying. And in this case, we have *two* cops. I tried my best to persuade Skip to plead, but here we are. I'm going to do my best and fight this thing to the end."

Nora could feel the tears come. "But he's *innocent*. They're *lying*. Why should he confess to something he didn't do?"

"People do it every day. But that's academic— unfortunately, it's too late for that now."

"So when will I testify?"

"This new witness throws a bit of a wringer into things, but unless there are more surprises, you'll definitely testify sometime on Monday. Baca will be their final witness. Then it'll be our turn. You'll testify first. Then, if necessary, Mr. Tenorio."

"That's it?"

"We don't have any other good witnesses. We've already established that the sheriff's injuries are bullshit and the so-called theft of government property was so trivial that the government won't pursue it. When you take the stand, you're going to establish that Skip was working for you in an official capacity. Then you're going to tell your story and accuse two law enforcement officers of lying. They might cross-examine you, but probably not, since they'll already have high confidence the jury will find for them. We'll do a dry run on Sunday, but I won't kid you, Nora—that's what we're up against."

"So Skip won't testify?"

He sighed. "It's almost never a good idea to have the accused testify—and in any case I doubt Skip will make a good witness."

"There isn't any way to recover that video?"

"Trust me, we've had computer experts go over that phone with a fine-toothed comb. They've also examined the cloud account—there's no video. It's gone."

She broke down, hiccuping and sobbing. She hated to cry, but right now she didn't care.

Lightfeather hesitated and then put his arm around her. "Do you mind?"

She shook her head.

He held her while she sobbed and tried to get herself under control. Finally, she asked, "There's . . . *nothing* . . . you can do?"

"I'll do my best to break Baca. That sort of thing works on *Perry Mason*, rarely in real life. But as Yogi Berra said, it ain't over till it's over."

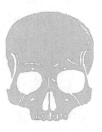

47

NORA SAT IN her car. It was now almost five, and the courthouse parking lot was empty, but somehow she felt paralyzed, unable to move.

Already, she had lightened her daily responsibilities as much as possible. She'd taken time off from the Institute, left her dog, Mitty, with a friend—even had a suitcase in the trunk, packed with a few things, in case she couldn't bear the thought of returning home, with all its reminders of Skip. Despite all this, she nevertheless found herself just sitting in the driver's seat as the minutes crawled by.

Her boyfriend, Lucas Tappan, was still in Massachusetts, trying to work the kinks out of his offshore windfarm project. They'd spoken regularly, but she hadn't worked up the courage to bring up this problem with him. He had enough on his mind already...and knowing him, he'd probably drop everything and rush back. She longed for his company, but she knew that was selfish. Besides, Lucas with all his millions couldn't solve this problem. The more high-priced lawyers they might throw at the case, the less impressed the local judge and jury would become.

Her mind kept running back to Skip. What if she married Lucas, and their kids were in junior high by the time they got to meet their uncle Skip, the jailbird? Or what if Skip fell into bad company—or got hurt in prison?

The phone suddenly danced on the passenger seat, startling her. It was Corrie calling. She answered it immediately. "Corrie?"

"Hey. I was just calling to see if you had any news about Skip."

Corrie sounded strange somehow, not like herself at all. Nora quickly brought her up to speed on the trial: there was all too little to tell.

"Christ, Nora. That sucks. I'm sorry."

Nora hesitated, then said, "Corrie, what's wrong?"

"Why do you ask?"

"I know you well enough to ask. Has something happened?"

There was a brief, tense silence. Then, abruptly, Corrie said, "Fuck it. I hate to lay my own sob story on you at a time like this, but I have to tell somebody—and at this point, you're the only one I can trust." And then, to Nora's amazement, Corrie quickly told an astonishing story: of a low-altitude bomber dropping a disarmed nuke near the site of the campers; of a mothballed presidential bunker with a back entrance; of the sudden quashing of the investigation by orders from on high. As Nora listened to the frustrated, angry voice, she was aware that she shouldn't be hearing a lot of this—if it wasn't already classified, it would be soon enough.

"So they ran because of the bomb explosion?"

A silence. "That's what I thought at first. But now I'm not so sure. I keep returning to the original riddle. Why would they cut their way out of the tent, with an open door right there? Why did Tolland kill Wright, then himself?"

"So what really happened?"

"I don't know. But I think if any answers are to be found, they'll be with the ninth body—O'Connell. I feel sure he's down in that bunker—perhaps with the missing camera and journal."

Corrie sounded really stressed. "Honestly, Corrie, I think the bomb accident is probably the answer, even if it can't be made public."

"I just had to get that off my chest," Corrie said, as if she hadn't heard. "I wanted to tell you, at least, before I . . ." Her voice trailed off.

"Before you what?"

"I'm going up there."

"Where?"

"To the bunker. I'm going to find that ninth body."

"Corrie, that's crazy."

"Crazy? *I'm* going crazy as we speak, sitting here on my hands. Do you realize what they told me to do? Cover it up. Lie. Tread water. Pretend to investigate while doing nothing! How can I keep working at the FBI, knowing what I know?"

"Well, there's one thing I can tell you for sure. It's mid-November. What do you know about winter mountaineering? You're going to get your ass frozen, and then we'll have ten victims instead of nine. On top of that, you don't have any idea where to go."

"That emergency bunker exit is supposed to emerge at a flat area used as a landing pad. It's outside the base perimeter in an area called the Knot. And it has to be north of where the cave was. They were all headed there—but only O'Connell made it."

"Or so you think. Is that all you have to go on?"

"This isn't getting us anywhere. Nora, I just wanted to say good luck with Skip, and I'm really sorry I couldn't have done more. I'll talk to you later."

"Corrie, *wait!*" Nora shouted before the agent could hang up. "Do you have any topo maps? Snowshoes? Compass?"

"I've got maps on my phone."

"Jesus. What about a snowmobile? Do you even know how to drive a snowmobile?"

"No."

"So you're screwed before you start—in more ways than I can count. Listen: I'm experienced in winter terrain. I have maps, I have snowshoes, I have the gear, and I have a snowmobile. Let's talk like sane people for a minute. Can you get a Jeep out of the FBI motor pool? I mean, one equipped for all-terrain travel? One that can haul?"

"Yeah. I guess so."

"Look. I'm at the Torrance County courthouse. I can be there in an hour. We can download the maps, look for this flat area you're talking about. Through my account at the Institute, I've got access to proprietary lidar terrain maps that might be useful. If we find what you're looking for, we can go up there tomorrow."

"Wait a minute. Are you asking to come along?"

"I'm not asking. I'm the only chance you have of finding anything."

Corrie's tone changed to one of concern. "Hold on. This is dangerous—and you're a civilian."

"*Now* you're worried? It's too late for that. You don't exactly have a choice. Look, Corrie, you roped me into this whole goddamned thing, and now I'm committed."

"Nora, I don't know—"

"Well, I do." She sighed. "Corrie, I'd consider it a favor. Anything's better than sitting around here in a parking lot, going crazy thinking about my brother rotting in a cell. I'll be at your place by six. Order some pizza."

"But..."

The rest of her sentence was cut off as Nora ended the call, took a moment to push all thoughts of her own drama from her head, then started the engine and peeled out of the parking lot.

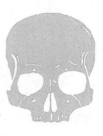

48

Nora took the hour's drive to Albuquerque to pull herself together. Right now, there was nothing she could do for Skip—she had to trust Lightfeather. It was Wednesday. Four days until the trial recommenced. If she went home, she'd only stare at the walls and slowly freak out. This way, at least, she'd be busy helping Corrie—even if the mini-expedition seemed like a fool's errand.

When she arrived, Corrie had pizza and beer waiting. Pulling out her laptop, Nora accessed her Institute internet account and downloaded a slew of data—old aerial photographs; satellite imagery; Google Earth images of the Manzano Mountains; and lidar maps. They focused on the Knot: the maze of canyons and ridges east of the Kirtland AFB fence. In her years at the New York Museum of Natural History and later at the Santa Fe Institute, Nora had developed expertise in remote sensing of archaeological sites from space. On one expedition to Utah, she had worked with a scientist from the Jet Propulsion Laboratory, using synthetic aperture radar to discover an important prehistoric ruin in the remote canyons north of Lake Powell. She now used her expertise—and her access to the restricted imagery databases—to see if they could locate any small alterations to the landscape of the Knot that might have resulted from building the bunker exit or flattening an associated helicopter pad.

Corrie had said the presidential bunker was built around 1953, when Eisenhower was inaugurated, so Nora focused on any changes in the topography before and after that date. The bunker had been decommissioned eight years later, after the Soviets detonated the infamous Tsar Bomba, the largest thermonuclear explosion in history—its almost incomprehensible power immediately rendering the bunker complex obsolete.

As they went through the aerial and satellite images, doing A/B comparisons across time, Nora was able to winnow down the possibilities to three. One site looked particularly promising. A 1951 topo map showed a small, natural-looking ridge on the side of Escarabajo Peak, about a half mile east of the Kirtland fence. The earliest aerial photo Nora could find of the site was from 1963, and relatively fuzzy, but it seemed to show a cleared area on that ridge:

a circular place devoid of fir trees. And a 2021 lidar image showed a small, unnaturally flattened area on that same ridge, although the trees had begun to grow back.

She had marked this promising location on her working topo maps as T1, for Target 1. The two other areas—not nearly so promising—she labeled T2 and T3.

They had also identified a possible jumping-off point north of the Knot, the deluxe dude ranch called Rancho Bonito. While it was closed for the winter, it seemed likely it would have a caretaker and the road would be plowed out.

They went to bed at one in the morning and rose again before sunrise. The day dawned clear and cold. Gathering up the marked-up maps and some relevant printouts, they went to the FBI office, where Corrie signed out a Jeep with a trailer hitch from the motor pool. Then they drove to Nora's place, hooked up her snowmobile and flatbed, loaded some winter hiking supplies, and set off for the mountains. And finally, Corrie called Rancho Bonito and spoke to a caretaker, a fellow named Puller. He was helpful and was expecting them. They'd use the ranch as a point of departure into the Knot, about five miles away.

By the time they reached the foothills, it was past eleven, and a mackerel sky was spreading in from the west, indicating the approach of a storm. The day was forecast to be cold and windy, with snow starting at sunset and temperatures dropping into the low teens. The current snow depth in the high country was about eighteen inches—plenty for a snowmobile, but not so much that one couldn't get through it on foot.

As the Jeep crept higher into the mountains, Nora stared again at her map and the circle she had marked as T1. She felt a certain sinking feeling. In the cold light of day, the entire plan seemed like a long shot. If they did find the bunker and, even more improbably, a body inside, the case would still be under embargo, quashed for good. Nothing they discovered would make a difference...because they'd never be allowed to reveal it. So why were they even bothering? What did it matter? Even as she asked the question, she knew the answer. It *didn't* matter—compared to Skip facing fifteen years in jail, it was irrelevant. Her brother was a decent, well-meaning person, a little impulsive but with a good heart. To think of him rotting his life away in prison over a bunch of lies was unimaginable. But somehow a long, agonizing weekend of enforced idleness, not knowing what his fate would be, felt almost worse.

The Jeep kept climbing. They hadn't reached the snowline yet and the road was clear and dry. Nora was curious about this Rancho Bonito. She recalled its construction in a national forest inholding, and how the location within a wilderness area had caused some fuss several years ago.

The drive seemed interminable, one hairpin turn after another, the piñon and juniper trees giving way to ponderosa pines and then Douglas firs. They passed the snowline, with patches of white turning into continuous cover. Nora's cell reception declined until at last a message popped up saying she had lost service. She put the phone into airplane mode to conserve its battery and made a concerted effort to focus on the upcoming expedition. All looked good: the weather was holding, the snowpack was excellent for snowmobiling, and it wasn't too cold.

They finally reached the ranch gate, built from ponderosa vigas, its crossbar announcing RANCHO BONITO with an elk skull and antlers. The caretaker, as promised, had left the gate open for them. After a quarter mile the lodge came into view: a structure of massive timbers and red-painted metal roofs, surrounded by split rail fences, corrals, a horse barn, cabins, and outbuildings situated in a broad, park-like valley dotted with trees. A smooth expanse of fresh snow glittered in the pale light even as a shadow of the approaching storm passed over the landscape.

They pulled into the reception area. Immediately

the door opened and a man came tumbling out. Corrie rolled down her window.

"Greetings!" the man said. He was wearing a red-and-black-checked jacket and had a round pink face, two blue eyes peering from underneath a stained cowboy hat. "You must be the FBI folks!"

"Right," said Corrie, showing him her badge. "I'm Agent Corinne Swanson, and this is my associate, Dr. Nora Kelly."

"Sam Puller." He stuck his hand in the window. "Nice to meet you both. I won't ask what it's all about. You warned me already—mum's the word!" He laughed.

Nora could see a woman standing in the doorway of the lodge, wearing paint-spattered clothing and holding a roller. "That's my wife, Jo," Puller explained, clearly enjoying the rare chance at company. "It's just the two of us here, we don't get many winter visitors, and it's always a pleasure. You want a cup of joe?"

"Sure, thank you," Corrie said.

"We'd like to show you some maps," Nora added. "Get your advice on what the best route might be."

"Happy to help!" He glanced at his wife. "She's been painting, as you can see. There's always something to do around here."

They got out of the vehicle and followed Puller into the lodge, Nora carrying a folder of maps. They walked into a magnificent two-story space with a gigantic stone fireplace, the walls decorated with antlers and Navajo rugs. "Spread those out here," Puller said, "and we'll get you some coffee."

"Thank you." Nora laid out a few maps on the giant wooden coffee table. Puller disappeared and returned a few minutes later with mugs of coffee, cream, and sugar.

"How familiar are you with the country, Mr. Puller?" Nora asked.

"Oh, pretty well."

"We want to visit these three spots on the map," said Nora, pointing out the markings she'd made. Her finger stopped at T1. "Ever been in that area?"

Puller peered down at the topo map, pushing his glasses up on his nose. "That's in the Knot," he said. "We almost never take guests that far south. But I've hunted elk in the area."

"Any thoughts on the best route to get there?"

He held the map up and scrutinized it. "I don't know that exact spot, but you'll clearly need to follow the ridges." He pulled a pen from his pocket. "May I?" he asked, laying the map back down.

"Please."

"Okay. You're gonna drive to the end of the plowed road through the ranch, about half a mile, to here." He drew a line. "There's a parking area that's plowed out and a trailhead. Park there and take your machine through the notch. Follow the ridges, here, here, and here. Take it slow; there'll be downed timber." He continued drawing a line across the ridges, ending at T1. He hesitated. "Um, I know this is confidential and all, but...that's kind of a strange place to go to. Godawful lonesome country. I can't think of what might be there."

Corrie smiled. "I'm sorry, Mr. Puller. I wish we could tell you more."

"Right! You're good until sunset, when the snow and wind will start picking up." He hesitated. "You don't plan to be out past dark, do you?"

"Hell no," said Corrie.

"Good. These mountains are pretty but they're not so friendly."

"We might also want to visit these other locations," Nora said, pointing at T2 and T3.

Puller scrutinized the map again. "Those are gonna be a lot harder to get to. You bring snowshoes?"

"We did."

"With crampons?"

"No."

He shook his head. "You'll need snowshoes with crampons for traction. I've got some here."

He disappeared, returning in a few minutes carrying two pairs. "These are Drifter Plus All Mountain, medium size, just about right for both of you. Pack those on your snowmobile, just in case."

He proceeded to trace paths to T2 and T3. "I'm not sure if you can get to either of those two places and back out by sunset. What I'd recommend is if your first spot is a miss, you come straight back here. We'll put you up for the night, and you can investigate the other two on Friday morning."

"That's really kind of you, Mr. Puller," said Corrie.

"You can thank me by getting back before dark," he said. "The sun sets at five. You sure as hell don't want to be stranded out there overnight in a snowstorm."

49

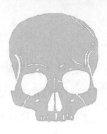

Supervisory Agent Clay Sharp sat in the living room of his house in the High Desert section of Albuquerque. The room was furnished with such spareness it might have been a monk's cell, if it weren't for the large, high ceiling and the single painting on one otherwise bare wall. The painting was a Rothko from the artist's early "multiform" period, extravagantly expensive. Sharp had decided one perfect specimen of art was better than a dozen inferior ones and had used his entire lifetime art budget on this single splurge.

Ornette Coleman's *Free Jazz* was playing, at a rather high volume, from speakers set into the walls. Sharp was not a devotee of jazz, and the music of someone like Coleman was particularly anathema to him, but he'd set the album-long piece to repeat again and again as a kind of counter-irritant. It wasn't helping, and now he reached for a remote,

switched off the music, and resumed staring mood-
ily at the painting.

He'd told himself over and over again his only
choice was to accept what had happened. The air
force certainly had good reasons to cover up an
accident like that. Revealing it would have caused a
scandal, brought comfort to America's enemies, and
frightened the American people. It made sense that
the government would be eager to suppress it.

But somehow, having good reasons wasn't
enough—not in this case. Something else was going
on here: a crime, or several crimes, that had been
festering for years. Sharp believed in national security: in fact, it lay at the foundation of his own moral
principles. But on the other hand, the Dead Mountain victims had the right to justice. Revealing
the accident would be bad publicity—but it could
be contained, and it did not in any way compro-
mise the security of his country. On the other hand,
he was now being forced to lie to citizens of that same
country—the families of the victims—and, perhaps
worse, pretend to investigate a case that was already,
or very nearly, resolved. It went against everything
he believed in.

His thoughts turned to Gold. The man had been
second in charge of the Albuquerque office and one
of the most decorated FBI agents in the Mountain West. A year or so after taking on the Dead

Mountain case, he'd resigned—and then his life had gone downhill. Had he, too, figured out what happened—and been quashed? The more Sharp thought about it, the more he felt it was likely. It would explain a great deal—not just Gold's failure to solve the case, but the many avenues of investigation the man had inexplicably neglected to follow. If he'd just followed orders, pretended to investigate...then all the things he did—and didn't do—fell into line. And being forced to follow such perverse orders destroyed him.

Sharp's father had been a decorated marine; his grandfather and great-grandfather had both been full-bird colonels in the Corps; there had been a Sharp among the marines aboard the *Bonhomme Richard*. And so although Sharp himself had grown up more interested in art history than combat, he had dutifully enlisted. It was during his training that the Corps discovered he was not only a superb marksman, but also intellectually and emotionally well suited for intelligence and counterintelligence duties.

The beginning of his actual service coincided with the Iraq War. After two years of HUMINT work, with his shifting from one nameless sub-agency to another, the war abruptly escalated, and Sharp found himself temporarily seconded to a task force, in support of Marine Recon Snipers, during the acute lack of manpower that followed in the wake of Operation Phantom Fury, the Second Battle of Fallujah.

Sharp had already killed enemy combatants and spies in the line of duty. But now, following a series of tactical missteps from HQ, he found himself unexpectedly defending a weakened American flank, sniper rifle in his hands, fighting off repeated assaults by the AQI, the IAI, and Iraq's Secret Army. In fifteen minutes of the first, intense engagement, he'd shot half a dozen insurgents. Within twenty-four hours, he'd lost count.

At last, after successive waves of reinforcements and heroic sacrifices on the part of the U.S. infantrymen, they had prevailed. The spider holes, IEDs, and Jersey barriers were cleared, and the surviving enemy had retreated. But two months later, when he returned to his previous work, Sharp found himself a changed man. What he had seen and done in Fallujah was classified, as of course was all of his work. He couldn't speak of it—and he couldn't unsee it. The waves of zealots, disintegrating in hails of 850 rpm .50 caliber bullets from entrenched M2s. Grandmothers and children, used by the enemy as two-legged shrapnel devices. Faces losing shape as they melted under sheets of white phosphorus. Friends he'd made—the instant friendships formed in the heat of battle, former strangers now trusted to watch your back and save your life—dying hours or even minutes after their first shaking hands. And so he'd left the service, with a Silver Star, at the first honorable opportunity. Both his parents had died while he was overseas, and he'd inherited a significant amount of money. Not knowing what else to do, feeling rudderless, but with a clear understanding that—for his own emotional well-being—he had to find an all-consuming occupation, and quickly, he'd joined the FBI. And he'd remained there for seventeen years, rendering exceptional and at times secretive service—and keeping his personal life, and personal baggage, locked up tightly inside himself.

Now he looked at the clock. In disgust he noted it was only noon. He stood up anyway, went into the kitchen, opened the liquor cabinet doors, took out a bottle of Johnnie Walker Blue Label, and poured himself three fingers, tossing half of it back. He felt the liquid burn down his throat. He retreated back to the living room, drink in hand. He'd acquired a taste for single malt scotch while overseas, and while the idea of blended scotch appalled him, he found the notion of "age statement" blends, which used expensive whiskies in an attempt to re-create flavor profiles from a century ago, amusing enough to pick up a bottle of Blue. And, goddammit, he liked the stuff...even though it cost as much as three bottles of Lagavulin.

He sat down and took another slug. But not even the liquor seemed to help.

He thought of his first and only mentee, Corrie Swanson. She was smart, persistent, idealistic, fearless, and, at times, a pain in the ass. Most good agents were pains in the ass. She'd done excellent work with the case, and even learned how the two bodies had been crushed—something that had remained a mystery for fifteen years. What a clusterfuck that this should happen so early in her career. He'd be able to retire in a few years—although until now, he'd had no intention of retiring until the mandatory age of fifty-seven. But Corrie was just starting out. He'd never mentored anyone before, but he approved of her strong idealism and sense of duty. And now—Christ, to be ordered to lie to grieving families? How was that going to work out for her over the next nineteen years?

He knocked back the rest of the drink.

He shouldn't have been so hard on her in that last conversation. God knows, he hadn't meant to be. Abruptly, a feeling that had lain dormant almost twenty years had washed over him in the wake of meeting with Garcia: pinned down in a hot-war situation, with no acceptable exit strategy. He'd tried to tamp it down, but Corrie coming up, worrying and worrying at the bone of the case after they'd been told to stand down—well, he'd responded with a kind of emotion he hadn't felt since Fallujah.

The accident pretty much solved everything. Of course, as with any case, there were details that remained puzzling. That murder-suicide in the cave, for example. But people did crazy things when pushed to the extreme. If he wasn't sworn to secrecy, he could cite hair-curling examples of that by the dozen.

But that business about the hikers slicing their way from the tent instead of simply fleeing out the door . . . it was true that didn't quite square with the accident. And why wouldn't they take the few seconds necessary to put on their coats and boots? As he sat in his silent retreat, he had to admit Corrie made some good points. But what good was any of that when the case had been permanently quashed? Nevertheless, he felt a twinge of guilt for being hard on her. She was still his mentee, despite everything, and she needed him now more than ever. Of course, he could never tell her the real reasons he'd erupted like that: it was not only a former self briefly reappearing again, but it was also the frustration of tilting at windmills. The windmills always won.

Nevertheless, he really should check in with her, see how she was doing, let her know—tactfully—that he understood exactly how she felt. He picked up his FBI cell phone and dialed.

The call immediately clicked over to voice mail.

He looked at the screen of the phone, a prickling feeling on the base of his neck. Although she might be pretty disgusted with the FBI right now, she was never under any circumstances allowed to turn off her work phone. Which meant she was probably out of range.

After a moment's thought, he dialed Nora Kelly.

Again, the call went straight to voice mail.

Now he sat up. What the hell? Had they both turned off their phones... or were they both out of range?

He placed a call to the dispatcher at Albuquerque FO as an uneasy thought formed in his mind. "Hi, Gloria," he said. "Did Agent Swanson check out a vehicle today from the pool?"

"As a matter of fact she did, Agent Sharp. A four-wheel-drive Jeep Wrangler. Said she might be driving in snow."

"Thank you."

Sharp lowered the phone.

What about Corrie's friend Sheriff Watts? Maybe he knew something about her whereabouts or intentions. He raised the phone and dialed Watts. His call was answered immediately.

"Sheriff? It's Agent Sharp..."

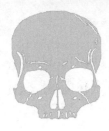

50

BY THE TIME they'd unloaded the snowmobile, packed it with their equipment and supplies, stepped into their monosuits, and donned their helmets, it was one o'clock. Gray clouds now scudded across the sky and the temperature was dropping.

"Temperature mid-twenties," Nora said. "Wind moderate, snow cover good. I'd say we're fortunate with the weather—so far. But we better hurry."

Corrie nodded.

They had reached the end of the road and parked in a plowed circular area at the far end of the valley. On their right stretched a row of small peaks, along with a notch through which their route lay, as Puller had marked on the map. Nora slipped into the saddle of the touring snowmobile, and Corrie got in behind her. The monosuit was snug and warm. The route on her map indicated a trip of five miles to T1.

If all went well, they should be there in half an hour or less.

"You've ridden a snowmobile before, right?" Nora asked.

"In Colorado. It didn't, ah, go all that well."

"We'll take it slow and easy. Just hang on tight, keep your weight forward and centered. Okay?"

"Got it."

Nora started up the machine, put it in gear, and eased it forward. They moved slowly across the open expanse of snow and into the fir trees. The conditions were good: plenty of snow, the sun behind clouds spreading an even gray light across the landscape. Nora eased the machine among the trees and through the notch. They continued along the shallow side of a hill through a forest of big firs, far enough apart to make their way easy. The trees soon gave way to a ridge, with heavy snow and cornices on one side and nearly bare ground on the other. Still moving at an unhurried pace, Nora guided the machine along the strip of firm snow in between, stopping from time to time to consult her map and the GPS on her phone. Nora didn't trust Corrie's ability to map-read in the wilderness, so she insisted on doing both the driving and the navigating.

Once they were out on the open ridgetop, the wind picked up a little, and that, combined with a layer of fresh powder, generated some flying snow as they drove, but it was light and dry and they had good electric helmets that kept it from sticking. Nora was able to average a steady ten to twelve miles per hour.

The views were stupendous. On their left lay the Knot: a crazy warren of canyons, ravines, and pinnacles, choked with fir and pine trees, with nary a flat place in sight. To their right rose the central spine of the Manzanos. Puller had routed them well, although in a few spots they had to negotiate downed timber and some steep slopes. The trail descended along ridges into the Knot, and in half an hour, just as Nora predicted, they had arrived at T1.

Nora pulled up the last length of ridge and stopped the snowmobile as the terrain leveled out. "We're here."

"Nice going, Evel Knievel."

Nora got off, brushed the loose snow from her lap, and looked around. The ground rose gradually above the Knot, covered with tall firs. A definite clearing had been made here some years ago, with many young firs now growing up. The ridge had been flattened, cut into the hill at one end and graded flat.

"That doesn't look natural," said Nora.

"This could be it," said Corrie. She took a few steps in the snow, sinking up to her thighs.

"We need snowshoes," Nora told her.

They quickly strapped in and grabbed the poles. The little trees around the clearing were loaded with fresh snow, and they pushed through them, knocking off powdery clumps as they went. Nora headed toward a spot at the far end of the ridge, where it appeared to have been cut across the ridge and leveled, creating a flat, circular area. Any opening into the mountain would be along that cut somewhere—unless it was a hatch in the ground. In that case, it would be hidden under a layer of snow and much harder to find.

They reached the far end, where the cut ridge had exposed a wall of rock.

"Let's examine the area from north to south," Nora said.

The little trees were especially thick along the rockface. They pushed through them, getting covered with loose snow.

"Hey, check this out," said Corrie.

Nora looked over. Corrie was pointing to a cylindrical cavity drilled into the side of the rockface—the remains of a blasting hole.

Nora couldn't help but feel surprised. Part of her had assumed this would be just another of Corrie's wild-goose chases. But a blasting hole, here in the middle of nowhere—that was the real deal.

They continued exploring the face of the rock, pulling back small trees and clearing off overhanging vegetation, looking for some sort of entrance. And suddenly, there it was: a small steel door, painted in camo to blend into the rock.

"My God," said Nora. "I can hardly believe it."

"Believe it!" Corrie said excitedly.

They searched for a keypad. The door was set so naturally into the rock that it was hard to follow its outlines, but Nora ripped down some hanging vegetation and exposed an old-fashioned mechanical keypad with buttons.

"The code was Rodney O'Connell's birthdate," Corrie said. "April 3, 1986."

Nora watched as Corrie keyed in 4386. Nothing. She tried 431986. Still nothing. Then she punched in 04031986. At the press of the last number, this time Nora heard a muffled click. Corrie heaved against the door with her shoulder, with no result.

"Maybe it swings outward," said Nora.

Feeling around the edges of the door, Nora discovered a small handle, also camouflaged. She gave the door a pull and, with a screech of metal, it opened an inch.

"Let's clear this stuff away," Corrie said.

They stomped down some baby trees and shoved snow away with their boots, clearing an area for the door to open. They heaved again. The door opened six more inches with another screech, then stopped.

"Let's tie a rope to that handle so we can both pull," Corrie said.

Nora returned to the snowmobile and grabbed a length of rope, picking up their two packs at the same time. She looped the rope through the handle, then they each took an end and pulled. With a final screech of protest, the door opened wide and they stumbled backward. A black passageway revealed itself, exhaling a warmish, dead-smelling air.

"Oh, Jesus," said Nora, backing up and waving a hand before her nose. "You bring a canary with you?"

"I've got a candle lantern," said Corrie, "and a carbon monoxide alarm I took from my apartment."

"Good thinking."

The open door had a spring to it, which wanted to pull it shut, so Nora took the rope and tied its free ends to a stout tree. Then, to make sure, she pried a rock from the cut nearby and wedged it in place so that the door, if it somehow slid free of the rope, could not swing fully shut.

They donned their packs and put on headlamps. Corrie took out her candle lantern, lit it, and hooked the CO detector on the back of her pack.

They stood a moment on the threshold. The beams of their headlamps stabbed into the darkness ahead. The corridor looked to Nora as if it went on endlessly, straight into the mountain—a featureless tunnel of concrete, like the path to some golem's lair.

She took a step forward, but Corrie placed a hand on her shoulder. "Me first—okay?"

"Be my guest."

Corrie stepped inside and Nora followed. She turned and, raising her light, saw another keypad on the inside of the door. "I wonder . . . ," she began.

"You wonder if there's a different code to get out than to get in?" Corrie finished the sentence for her.

"Yes."

"And you're also wondering if, maybe, O'Connell didn't have that second code?"

Nora looked at Corrie's face, pallid in the artificial light. "Exactly."

51

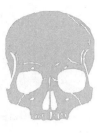

As Corrie moved farther and farther down the passage, she began to feel like a character from some dreadful *Twilight Zone* episode: trapped in an endless tunnel of concrete, destined to walk down it forever and ever. It was featureless, stained here and there by water but free of cracks even after three-quarters of a century. The air, while stale, was warm and moist. The candle kept burning brightly and the CO detector didn't go off.

From time to time, she glanced back down the corridor. The light of the exit dwindled into a tiny dot of light and soon vanished completely.

Feeling warm, she partially unzipped her mono-suit. "When is this going to end?" she whispered to Nora.

"God knows. If the bunker is on the far side of the range, this tunnel might go all the way through the mountain."

"Must've cost a fortune to build," Corrie whispered.

"Why are we whispering?" Nora answered, with a short laugh. "There's no one here."

Corrie snorted. "You're right. Only the dead... maybe."

"You really think we're going to find the body?" Nora asked.

"Yes. And along with it, the real solution to the mystery."

Ahead now, a door became barely discernible in the beams of their lights. As they approached, it seemed almost to materialize out of the darkness: a gleaming mahogany door with a polished brass knob of the kind that might grace an elegant mansion—weirdly out of place in this concrete rathole. Corrie reached out and grasped the handle, hoping to God it wasn't locked.

The handle turned almost effortlessly. The door made a squeaking sound as she eased it open, sounding uncannily like a small animal being hurt.

Corrie took a step forward, then halted in amazement. Their lights revealed an elegant marble hallway, its walls lined with gilded mirrors. A large crystal chandelier hung from the ceiling, refracting their headlamp beams and casting rainbowed flecks of light in all directions.

The corridor ran perhaps thirty feet before ending in a T. On the far wall of the T stood a niche with a plinth that had apparently once contained a statue, now empty. There were additional plinths on either side of the corridor that were similarly empty, along with blank rectangles on the walls between the mirrors, where paintings had evidently hung. Dust lay on every surface and motes drifted in the beams of light.

"Looks like they emptied the joint when they shut it down," said Corrie. "This must've been quite a place."

"Fit for a president," said Nora.

They left the door open and moved to the end of the hallway. A perpendicular corridor, also decorated with marble and chandeliers, led both left and right. Elegant doors lined either side, and gilt-covered benches, upholstered in red brocade, stood at intervals against the walls.

"It's the White House!" Corrie exclaimed.

"I was thinking the same thing," said Nora. "Just like pictures I've seen of the White House, only smaller. So the president would feel at home, I guess."

Corrie picked the right-hand corridor. "Let's try this one first."

This corridor had three doors on both sides, all shut, and ended in another empty niche. Corrie stopped at the first door on the left, grasped the knob, then opened it. A small shower of dust settled onto their shoulders. The lights revealed a small sitting room, with gilded chairs, brocaded sofas, an antique sideboard—and at the far end, an upturned tea table and two chairs that appeared to have been deliberately broken up, the legs and arms removed and stacked nearby. Strewn on the floor were pieces of a china teapot and some broken cups.

"Rats?" Corrie asked.

"No sign of rats," said Nora. "Or any animals. And rats don't break up chairs like that."

They both fell silent and retreated back into the main corridor.

Corrie opened the next door, revealing what appeared to be a dining room. This, too, had been trashed. The chandelier had fallen from the ceiling onto the table, splitting it in two. Shattered china plates and wineglasses lay scattered on the carpeted floor. Once again, the chairs had been broken into pieces, arms and legs and fragments of gilded wood lying everywhere. The sumptuous wallpaper was peeling and dangling off the walls, and in some areas it looked as if it had been deliberately stripped off and taken away.

"This looks more like vandalism than furniture removal," Nora observed.

Corrie said nothing.

They shut the door and proceeded to the third and last room on the left side of the hall. It was a small annex, ending in an archway that opened onto a kitchen.

"Jesus, what a disaster," said Nora.

The kitchen looked as if a cyclone had come through. All the cupboards had been thrown open, drawers pulled out, knives, silverware, pots, and pans scattered across the floor—along with a single tin of food, its top cut open. An old bulbous refrigerator had been thrown to the floor, where it lay open and vacant.

Corrie felt an unpleasant creeping sensation in her gut.

"It looks like somebody searched this in a great rush," said Nora. "Or maybe in a panic."

"Yeah," said Corrie, "as if desperate for food." She bent down and picked up the tin can. "Peas." She dropped it with a clatter and looked around for more, but there was nothing—no other sign of food, no cans, flour sacks, or tins. Nothing beyond the single can of peas. A small pantry lay beyond, but it was empty.

"But when they got there, the cupboard was bare," Nora murmured.

"When they shut the place down, they clearly took every last bit of food and perishable items. Missed a can, it seems, and all those mirrors—but that's it." She took a deep breath. The more they explored, the more she was formulating a mental picture of what must have happened here, fifteen years before.

They returned to the hall and opened the door directly across. It gave onto a living room, spacious and grand. Unlike the kitchen and dining room, it was in a decent state of preservation, with no broken chairs or vandalized wallpaper. A marble fireplace stood against the far wall, and a sofa had been pulled up close to it.

"Looks like somebody used that sofa for a bed," said Nora quietly.

Corrie shone her light on it. Two pillows had been propped against the sofa's arm and two blankets lay crumpled nearby, one on the sofa itself and the other on the floor next to it. Her eye moved to the fireplace. On the hearth, she could see the remains of a fire, made with partially burned pieces of gilded furniture: chair legs and arms, evidently wrenched from the broken chairs in the dining room. Next to the fireplace was a stack of chair legs and arms, ready to feed the fire.

On the opposite side of the living room, Corrie could see a set of closed double doors. "Let's try those," she whispered.

They walked across the thickly carpeted room and opened the matching doors. Another whisper of hinges. As Corrie swept her light around, she saw this was obviously the master bedroom. A king-sized bed dominated the center of the far wall. The bed looked as if designed in a past century, with a tall frame and gossamer silk curtains drawn closed. On either side stood small tables, and opposite was a small secretary desk of polished wood with a closed hutch. Two closed doors were in the back. The walls were painted in light blue with white trim, and the floor was carpeted in dark blue with a yellow design.

Corrie stared at the bed with its drawn curtains, then glanced at Nora. She hesitated. Nora nodded encouragement.

"It's your show," she said.

With trepidation, Corrie walked over to the silk curtain, grasped the material, and began to draw it back. But even as she touched the rotten material it dissolved in her hands, parting along the warp and generating a cloud of particles and bits of drifting thread, dazzling in the light beam.

It took a moment for Corrie to pull herself together and examine the scene. A man lay on the bed, hands folded across his breast, looking more like a corpse laid out for viewing than a person who, it seemed, died in an agony of hunger or thirst. His face was desiccated: the eyes sunken, lips dried and drawn away from even, white teeth. The mummi-fication did little to hide numerous signs of starva-tion: the skin drawn tight across the bones of the face, the body shrunken, the clothes sagging and loose on the limbs. The fingers of his hands were entwined on his breast, shriveled to dried vanilla beans. His neck looked impossibly skinny. He could not have been older than twenty or thirty, and the body issued no smell beyond a faint and not unpleasant scent of dust.

On the bed, next to the man's right hip, lay a journal and pencil. And on the other side was a camera.

52

For a long time, Corrie simply stared. She seemed unable to pull her gaze from those withered fingers, interlinked with each other. It was as if the man—and it had to be Rodney O'Connell—had meticulously laid himself out for death . . . which, of course, was exactly what he had done.

So her long-gestating speculation had proved right. Victim nine of the Dead Mountain tragedy had made it to the bunker, gotten locked in, and then died. How long would it have taken? Without water, she knew that death by dehydration would take less than a week. Death by starvation took much longer—forty days, perhaps.

"Poor guy," said Nora, echoing Corrie's thoughts. "What a way to go."

Corrie tried to sort through her emotions: anguish at the pathetic figure in the bed, mingled with vindication, repulsion, sorrow.

"You were right," Nora said.

Corrie nodded. She reached out for the journal.

"Are you sure you should touch anything?" Nora asked. "Shouldn't we leave it as is?"

Corrie hesitated. "Normally, I'd say yes. But if I don't read what's in that journal, and do it right now, I may never see it again. They'll cover all this up—you *know* they will. You see that pencil?" Corrie pointed at the bed. "He was writing in that journal, probably right up to his death." She lowered her voice. "I want to know what really happened. I *need* to know. Even if it's just for myself."

She reached out and—carefully, carefully—picked up the journal, then held it under her headlight. It was a small volume, with a tooled leather cover and a leather thong to hold it shut. The thong was broken, the leather of the cover rubbed and worn.

She slipped a finger under the cover and opened it. In carefully drawn letters, the title page read:

Manzano Expedition Journal

Being an account of ten fearless mountaineers Who ventured into the wilderness October 27 to _____ 2008

Corrie stared. Was this a mistake? Ten mountaineers—not nine? She kept reading.

*To which we have each solemnly affixed
our respective John Hancocks:*

Alex DeGregorio

Henry Gardiner

Luke Hightower

Andrew Marchenko

Lynn Martinez

Michael Mastrelano

Rodney O'Connell

Paul Tolland Jr.

Amanda Van Gelder

Gordon Wright

Corrie stared at the first name on the list. DeGregorio? What the hell? DeGregorio, the wealthy roommate of the knife owner…he'd been on the expedition?

If that was true, it meant he'd been the only

survivor. Yet he had told no one he was there—
including her. For some reason, he'd hidden the fact
of his participation, covered it up...but what was
he covering up? And why?

"Are you all right?" Nora asked.

Corrie pointed. "You see this name?"

"Who's Alex DeGregorio?"

"He was Matthew H. Tanner's roommate—
'MHT,' the initials engraved on the knife."

"I'm not following."

"I'm not following it myself. I'm not following
it at all." She grasped the journal, as if willing it to
speak. "There were only nine on the expedition—
at least, that's what everybody always thought. But
look, here, there's a tenth name: Alex DeGregorio."

She opened the journal, flipped through the
pages. The handwriting changed from entry to
entry, as different members of the expedition wrote
their own additions. References to Alex DeGregorio were sprinkled throughout—there was no mis-
taking that he'd been on the expedition. But why
had he kept it a secret all this time? Had he been
too traumatized, or afraid perhaps of being the only
survivor, thrust into the limelight? Or had he kept
silent out of guilt—abandonment of his expedition
mates, cowardice, committing an offense against
them...or worse?

Impatiently, she skipped ahead, turning pages

until she reached one dated October 31. Holding the book with trembling hands, Corrie began to read aloud.

> *Oct. 31, 10 am. Andy writing. Happy Halloween!! We're getting an early start, hoping to beat the weather. Good luck with that! The plan is to camp early, batten down the hatches, break out the Everclear, mix us up some instant daiquiris, and have a little party. The weather outside may be frightful, but we'll be snug in our tent! Okay, we're off. Ciao!*

Below that journal entry, Andy—that would be Andrew Marchenko—had drawn a group of stick figures hiking on a mountaintop with heavy packs. Corrie moved to the next entry.

> *4 pm. Amanda here—We decided to camp even earlier than planned. Alex was really insistent about it. The snow started falling around one and now it's coming down like crazy, and the wind is picking up. Andy thinks we maybe went off our route a bit coming up Talaya Peak, but we found a good campsite in the wind shadow of the ridge, where the snow's deep enough to*

hollow out a good cavity for protection. We set up the tent in record time, as the blizzard intensified. We'll figure out where we are tomorrow when the snow clears. It's blowing like a banshee, the tent's rattling and snapping like crazy, but it's staked down well and we're cozy as can be...

This was followed by ordinary descriptions of firing up the stove, cooking dinner, and—for some reason—sharing a diligently copied recipe for Mrs. Van Gelder's famous meatloaf. Corrie skipped over these entries.

6 pm. Amanda again—Alex talked us out of the daiquiri party. The storm is really howling and he said it would be a bad idea to get buzzed and maybe have a tough time handling some unexpected shit like the tent ripping. Or an avalanche. Luke, self-proclaimed avalanche guru, says there's no chance of an avalanche because the slope's too gentle and we're close to the top of the ridge anyway. But Alex's advice made sense. To make amends for laying down the law, he brewed up some amazing rainforest hot chocolate for all of us. Now we're cooking dinner—Mountain House freeze dried chicken tetrazzini—yum! (Not.) I thought the storm was raging before, but now it's really kicking ass.

That entry ended on the top half of a right-hand page, and the rest was left blank. Corrie flipped to the next page and was taken aback: the writing looked crabbed and agitated, wandering all over the page, with numerous crossings-out and words written over each other.

Thank God for the fire. Comforting. At least I'm alive.

The voices are fading. I think. At least they're going deeper into my head. It's like that cliché, the nightmare that never ends. It hit me so hard. I have a tough time even remembering what it was like to be free of the voices, those terrible images. Hallucinations, I guess.

I'm pretty sure it was Alex. The fucker's probably dead now. The others too, or at least some of them. I don't know. I wish I could remember. It's like my memory is a shattered mirror, shards heaped up reflecting different things. No way to put them back together. No way to know what was real and what was not.

That son of a bitch. What was he thinking?

Calm down. WRITE.

Okay. I'm going to put what I know into the journal as best I can. I think my hands are frostbitten in addition to my toes because I'm warmer now but it's really painful and hard to write. So it all began with the explosion. That happened around 6:30 p.m., half an hour or so after we all drank Alex's cocoa. I was boiling water for the freeze-dried pouches when we heard the sound.

THE SOUND...!!!

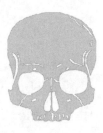

53

Sam Puller checked his watch: almost two. The sun had long vanished behind a layer of dark clouds that had moved in from the east, and a dull pewter light lay over the mountains. The storm seemed to be approaching faster than expected. Figures.

"You worried about those FBI agents?" Jo called from the kitchen, washing her rollers in the sink.

"Damn right I am," Puller replied. "I wonder what the heck they were looking for out there in the Knot?"

Jo came into the living room, drying her hands on a towel. "Quite the mystery."

"Maybe it's something to do with that lost gold mine they claim is hereabouts somewhere," said Puller. "But that wouldn't explain the hurry."

Jo snorted. "Every mountain range in New Mexico supposedly has a lost gold mine. I just hope they know what they're doing. The older one with the hazel eyes, she looked like she knew something about the mountains. The younger one—what was her name? She didn't seem quite so experienced."

"Agent Swanson," said Sam Puller.

"Right. I knew it made me think of TV dinners."

"Maybe it has something to do with that case they opened up again—those dead hikers."

"You know, that's probably it," said Jo. She paused. "So what should we do if they don't come back?"

"If I don't see them by four thirty, I'm going to take the Cat out and follow their trail."

This brought a look of apprehension to Jo's face. "They should've waited till after the storm."

A chime rang in the kitchen, indicating a vehicle had come through the gate. Puller stuck his head out the front door of the lodge and saw a black Hummer approaching slowly. "Looks like we got some more feds."

"Thank heavens for that. Let them look after their own."

Puller went outside and waited while the vehicle drew up. It stopped next to him, and the smoked passenger window slid down.

"Howdy," said Puller to the men inside. "You with those two FBI gals that came through here a while ago?"

"Sure are," said the driver. "Where'd they go? We're worried about them."

"I am, too. They hauled their snowmachine to the end of the road and headed over into the Knot."

"The Knot," said the man. "Right. When was this?"

"About one o'clock. You going after them?"

"We hope to."

"You're going to need a snowmachine."

"We were hoping we might rent some of yours."

"Rent? Hell no, I'd be glad to let the FBI borrow them. Over there in the garage, second bay—two of them, all gassed up and ready to go. I keep them in tip-top shape." He hesitated, glancing at the two men in the front and three in the back. None were properly dressed. "There's a rack of monosuits there, too. You know how to drive a snowmachine?"

"Absolutely," the driver said, with a friendly smile. "Is there anyone else on the premises?"

"No, just my better half, Jo." He nodded toward the house.

"Thank you so much, Mr. . . . ?"

"Puller. Sam Puller."

"Supervisory Special Agent Sharp. And these are agents from the Albuquerque Field Office, assisting in the investigation. Good to meet you, Sam, and thanks for supporting law enforcement." The driver reached over his companion and stuck out his hand, and Puller shook it.

"Oh, I'm sorry," said the agent named Sharp. "I realize I haven't shown you any identification."

"No need," Puller said, but the man was already reaching under the dashboard. His hand came up holding a gun. The last thing Puller heard, to his vast astonishment, was the sound of the point-blank shot into his face.

Four men jumped out of the Hummer. One pair grabbed the body of Puller, rolled it up in a plastic tarp, and threw it in the back. The other two ran into the lodge. A moment later there were two shots in rapid succession, and not long after the two men came back out carrying another body wrapped in plastic, which they also heaved into the rear.

The man with the gun had stayed in the driver's seat. He now leaned out the window. "Make sure the entrance gate is closed and locked."

"Yes, Dr. DeGregorio," said one of the men.

DeGregorio pulled the Hummer over to the multicar garage, on the far side of the plowed reception area. Everyone exited the vehicle. One pulled up the door of the second bay, revealing two snowmobiles, with half a dozen monosuits and helmets hanging on a nearby wall.

DeGregorio pulled down a suit for himself and gestured for the others to do the same. "Let's move," he said, yanking himself into the suit.

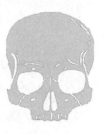

54

Even before that, though, we'd started to feel seriously weird. High, like. Not the usual high like weed or alcohol…at first I thought maybe shrooms. I knew something was fucked up with the way my brain was processing the world, but I couldn't put my finger on it. I thought it was just me. Then Amanda said, Is anyone else feeling strange?

We all started talking. We did feel weird. More than weird. The tent was shaking from the wind and I kept feeling like I was being sucked up into a storm, tugged by an invisible hand, like Dorothy in The Wizard of Oz.

Then we heard a strange whining sound somewhere in the distance. It got louder really fast, incredibly fast, until it was just roaring, totally drowning out the storm. I thought maybe it was a big plane, flying low. It sounded so close, like *it was going to crash into the tent. But then it passed overhead and, just as the roaring began to fade, there was a huge flash of light.*

It was like a monstrous flashbulb going off. Just light, no sound. I thought it might be me, hallucinating. But then a gigantic explosion lifted the whole tent off the ground before dropping it down again, and a howling wind pressed down the roof so hard I thought the tent was a goner. I swear I still don't know what was real and what was just some fucked-up vision. It was so weird, everything seemed to happen in sequence, not all at once like real life. There was the noise, the light, the wind. One after the other. And after the wind died away, I could hear a whole bunch of explosions, like giant cannons echoing again and again through the mountains. Despite what Luke said, I thought for a while maybe it was some kind of freak avalanche. But it wasn't anything natural. It went on and on and on.

All of us were feeling weird, and really scared. All that otherworldly shit, the sounds and the lights and the explosion…it triggered something. I can't speak for the others—most of them were screaming and yelling nonsense anyway. But I was suddenly, like, absolutely stricken with terror.

At this point, right after the explosion, the hallucinations just crashed in. They weren't like peyote or acid—not even on the worst trip you could imagine. My mind went to a dark place full of voices. Family, friends—even the dead. I heard my grandma haranguing me. And strange voices, too—all talking at once. At the same time, it felt like...I don't like to think about it, let alone try to explain...like my body was being turned inside out. The organs were clinging to the outside, my skin rolling up on the inside, like a glove.

For a long time after the explosion, everyone was crouching in terror. Amanda finally said, SOMEONE LOOK OUTSIDE. Alex and I were the only ones fully dressed. I moved a bit, and my organs came back together and my body closed up. I figured maybe the moving helped. So I looked out. The storm was fierce as shit, but through it I could see a huge glow. Out there floating in the darkness and whirling snow, a weird color, an incredible color, like a deep orange. I thought I was freaking out again, but someone else saw it too. I could hear someone yelling UFO! UFO!

Paul was the first to totally lose it and freak out. I think it was the voices. He was hearing them, too. They made him paranoid, maybe, or something worse. He grabbed the cooking knife and started waving it around, talking gibberish, accusing us of something incoherent. Gordy persuaded him to put it away and we huddled in the tent, freaked out by everything that had happened but most of all by that strange glow. Everything else had gone away. But the glow stayed.

Then Andy went crazy. He started shrieking, pulling out his hair. I saw his scalp tear and the blood run down his face. He was punching himself, scratching himself. It was awful. But watching it made the weird shit in my head grow a little quieter. For a time.

Alex was the only one not freaking out. I can remember now that he wasn't acting crazy. He was worried. He tried to calm us down. Promising it would pass. Telling us to ride it out, we'd be fine in the morning.

Up until that point, I'd been trying to keep it together. Despite the sounds and the wind and the weird fucking light and the organs hanging outside my body, I'd been able to maintain some shred of normal consciousness. But it was sometime around here I lost even that. All I have from that time are broken impressions.

Except one memory.

I don't know what to call it. So I'll call it the

ALIEN. That sounds crazy, and I'm not saying it was actually an alien, and I was high on some terrible shit, but that's how it seemed at the time. It's the one clear memory I have from that time, and I don't think it was a hallucination. It happened like this: Outside, over the storm, we heard a sound. Like a bear growling. And then the tent flap was thrown back and the ALIEN was in the doorway.

We all saw it. That much I know. Seven feet tall, all white, covered in skin wrinkled like an elephant, giant arms and no face—just an oval that looked like wet ice. It expanded and contracted, bulging, maybe breathing. After a moment, it stepped inside and reached for us with its gigantic, wrinkled arm.

Paul started screaming and scrambled back. He grabbed the knife again and slashed at the tent. Everyone panicked. Others began following him, ripping and tearing. My body had turned inside out again and I was having trouble telling nightmare from reality. But I could see bodies, my friends, screaming and forcing their way out. Falling down in the snow, struggling, while the ALIEN tried to grab them. Only Alex wasn't screaming. He was shouting. Shouting at us, telling us not to run, trying to get us to stop. But nobody was listening.

I was fully dressed, because I'd been cooking in the vestibule. Alex was too, he'd just been outside to take a piss around the time of the explosion. Wright had put on his boots to see what just happened outside the tent. But most of the rest had taken off their jackets and boots and were wrapped up in their sleeping bags. Nobody hesitated, nobody listened to anyone, they all just ran off into the night wearing whatever they had on. I guess I was running, too, because I have flashes of staggering through the snow, running from the tent, the weird glow, the...

Like I said, my memories from that time don't even deserve to be called fragments. But I've been trying to put them in order. We reached the tree line. Somebody yelled that we had to start a fire. We stumbled around trying to collect wood and somebody climbed a tree to break dead branches for dry wood. But the fire wasn't enough. Those with the least clothes were crowding around, practically sticking their limbs in the flames, setting their hair on fire, anything to keep warm. I could smell them burning. Andy and Michael died first. Then Hank started taking off his clothes, stripping down naked.

But there was no Alex. At least, none of the shards of memory I've collected have him in them.

Maybe the brutal cold or some sense of self-preservation broke through my insanity, because around that time I remembered the bunker. I had told everyone about it earlier. Not where it was, or the code, but the weirdness of it being there. I had enough sense then to tell the others that we could go there, find shelter. To follow me. That's what I seem to recall had happened. It's the only reason they would have followed me.

I'm not sure how many were left. Five I think, not counting me and Alex. But after a few minutes Amanda stopped and said she was going to lie down, and we tried to pull her up but she was raving. So we abandoned her. Then Lynn and I think Luke halted. They said they were going to build a snow cave. We kept going, me, Paul, and Gordy. I know that for sure. It was Paul and Gordy.

Then we found a cave—a real cave. Sheer luck. No need to search for the bunker. We crawled in. I was going to build a fire. Maybe by that point I was a little less crazy than the others. The shards of memory aren't so broken, so full of nightmare images. I went out, trying to collect wood, ignoring the voices in my head. Dead trees had fallen in the ravine—there was lots of wood. I was climbing back in when I saw. Paul had gone crazy. He'd brought along the cooking knife and he had it out, screaming SHUT UP at Gordy, attacking him. Gordy had crawled into the back of the cave, trying to get away, and Paul just kept stabbing him while he screamed. I dropped the wood and tried to stop him, but he slashed at me. He killed Gordy, his best friend, right in front of me. Stabbed him to death in a blood frenzy. His best friend. Paul was totally insane, cutting, whacking, stabbing, all the while shrieking out SHUT UP, SHUT UP, SHUT UP.

I must have figured I was next. Anyway, I took off.

I went north. Thank God I was fully dressed. As I ran from that tent, I'd managed to grab my pack with compass, map, and camera. Instinct. I headed north, struggling. You can't believe how hard it was. Hours went by, I think. Then the storm began to clear. My head started to clear a little more, too—just enough to do what was necessary. The moon was three-quarters full. I could see without my headlamp. I finally hit the Kirtland fence, followed it to the south-east corner. I found the bunker entrance where my Dad said it would be. The code worked. I went inside. I fell down and cried with relief.

And now I'm here. It's not cold, thank God. I found the presidential suite. It must be morning by now. But I'm too exhausted to move and anyway I don't trust myself yet. My hand hurts from writing. I'll deal with things in the morning.

* * *

Good morning.

If it is morning. God knows how long I slept. One thing I don't have in my pack is a watch.

I'm feeling almost normal again. Except that I woke up with a raging thirst. First thing: water. Then finish the story.

* * *

<u>*Back in my lair.*</u> *I found a kitchen, turned on the taps. Nothing. Nothing in the refrigerator, nothing in the pantry. No food, no water.*

Not a problem, I thought: I can collect snow. I retraced my path to the bunker door and punched in the code. Nothing. I tried again and again. That's when I realized there must be a different code to get out. I spent an hour punching in variations on my birthday, my father's, my mother's, my grandparents', and addresses of where we'd lived, famous dates of history…Anything my father might have thought of. Nothing.

Meanwhile, fragments of memory were starting to come back. Not just the nightmare mind-fuck I'd gone through, but real memories, too. At least I think they're real. I'm <u>afraid</u> they're real.

I started thinking about Alex. He was the only one who didn't go crazy, get all fucked up. It was when the rest of us ran off, scared to death— only then did he start to panic. He loved daiquiris. Why the cocoa? Why the fucking cocoa? He'd bragged more than once about what a good pharmaceutical engineer he was, how he'd formulated a psychoactive drug and tested it on himself. I remember him getting mad when my roommate and I just laughed and teased him for trying to be the new Albert Hofmann, the guy who discovered LSD. What a bullshit artist.

He made us that cocoa. So solicitous about it. Jesus, was Alex testing something on us? Did he <u>drug</u> us?

My thirst is so bad I'm having trouble thinking clearly. It's a funny thing—when you're thirsty, you don't get hungry. Right now I'm not hungry at all, even though I probably haven't eaten for more than a day. I'm going to search this place top to bottom. There's got to be something here. Got to be.

* * *

Okay, first round a failure. At least I found the tunnel leading to the front door of the bunker. It's got to be a mile long, at least. Man this bunker is deep. The front door is like the back one, only larger: painted steel with a keypad. Once again I tried a thousand possible combinations. I banged on the door. No one came. I found a length of metal pipe and pounded on the door. NO. ONE. CAME.

There's weird stuff abandoned in here, like a grand piano. But no food or water. My headlamp was getting dim. I can't let it go out—otherwise fire would be my only source of light. So I came back and lit a fire in the fireplace, and turned off the headlamp. I'm going to save it for an emergency. At least I have a lighter and a canister of waterproof matches—and there's plenty of wood around here. But I've got to do something about the thirst.

* * *

Later. I slept for a while, and when I woke up the fire had gone out. My thirst was just awful. I had to find water. So I made some firebrands *out of chair-legs, string, and toilet paper from the bathrooms. (No water in the toilets.)*

I searched the kitchen again. Thank God!! Behind a broken pantry shelf, I found a can of peas in water. I opened it and drank the water and ate the peas. Need more.

But the peas gave me hope. I searched every last nook and cranny of that kitchen and pantry, then the closets, storage areas, tunnels—everything. There has to be a cache of supplies somewhere, but I can't find it. Back in the kitchen, I tried all the taps. I traced the water pipes and turned on all the cocks. I even excavated into the stucco of the walls to get at the main water pipes and punctured them. DRY AS A BONE.

I'm now sitting on the sofa in the living room, in front of the fire, writing. Three days have passed. Maybe four? The drug has completely worn off. I've gone back over this and corrected stuff that I scrawled earlier, half out of my mind, and tried to make a narrative that's somewhat cohesive.

If I don't find water soon, I'll get too weak even to search. I wonder—could I really <u>die</u> in this place? Rescue parties will find the tent. And then what? There won't be a trail leading

away—not with that blizzard. And what about the explosion? The ALIEN? Paul, murdering Gordy? I'm sure I can separate the hallucinations from the reality—at least, I think I'm sure.
CHRIST IM SO THIRSTY.

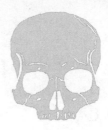

55

CORRIE CAME TO the end of a page. She stopped reading and glanced over at Nora. The archaeologist looked stricken. "How awful," she said.

"Do you want me to keep reading? There's not much more."

Nora nodded.

Corrie went back to the journal. The writing had increasingly deteriorated into a scrawl.

SIX DAYS? SEVEN? LOST ALL TRACK OF TIME

CALM DOWN. WRITE. Chronicle. Someone will read this.

Headlamp dead. No water. I never imagined how awful it could be without. You can't think, can't sleep, no longer human. Just a monstrous craving thirst-beast.

Tongue is cracked, bleeding. Eyelids sticking. STICKING. Drank piss.

* * *

ALEX DID THIS. Some experiment. Everything else must be hallucinations—crash. murder. explosion. light.

* * *

Tried keypad till fingers bled.

* * *

Journal + camera = PROOF. Develop film.

Once again, the rest of the page was blank. Corrie turned one page, and then another, to find a final, terrible scrawl.

DONT DIE IN DARK — LIGHT FIRE BEFORE.
   TOO WEAK

The rest of the journal was blank.

They stood in silence at the bedside, the desiccated corpse lying peacefully in the tomb it had arranged for itself.

"What an end," said Nora, choking with emotion. "Oh my God."

Corrie felt sick. But her mind was racing ahead on its own. "It all fits together," she said. "Alex DeGregorio was a graduate student at NMIT. A pharmaceutical engineer."

"And that's what pharmaceutical engineers do—design drugs."

Corrie nodded. "That's where he made his fortune—close to a billion dollars. Looks like he was messing around and, after trying an experimental drug on himself, tested it out on some friends. And it all went very wrong."

"Reckless at best—mass murder at worst."

"That's why he lied to me. Covered up his presence on the expedition." Corrie closed the journal and laid it down on the bed.

"And the alien?" Nora asked.

"Probably some guy in a radiation suit," said Corrie. "We know a bomb was jettisoned to prevent a plane crash. Search parties were sent out for retrieval and cover-up. Meanwhile, those nine students were tripping out of their minds, thanks to DeGregorio's experiment."

"The shock of the explosion," Nora said, "must have

made their hallucinations worse. And then somebody in a radiation suit appeared, freaking them out to such a degree they lost their minds." Nora paused. "But who was the guy in the suit? And why wasn't it reported?"

Good questions, Corrie thought. One possible answer that came to her mind also tied up another loose thread.

"I think," Corrie said slowly, "it was Cheape in the suit."

"Cheape?" Nora asked. "How so?"

"He got a commendation for something he did on that night. Maybe it was for being on the team that found the bomb location—he was one of the searchers. He came across the tent."

"So why didn't he report it?"

"I'm not sure, but it also might explain where he got the money for the Tesla—and why he was murdered. After all, DeGregorio was the only sane one—and he didn't run off like the others."

"He and Cheape must have had some sort of interaction," Nora said. "There at the tent. Cheape knew DeGregorio was on the expedition. When the Dead Mountain case was revived, Cheape probably decided to cash in. Back then DeGregorio had no money—but now he was rich."

Corrie nodded. "That's it. Cheape got greedy, tried to blackmail DeGregorio, and got killed for his trouble."

"It certainly looks that way," Nora said. "But here's the real question: What now?"

What now, indeed? Corrie felt conflicted. They'd solved the Dead Mountain case for real. It wasn't just an accidental bomb drop, but something much more—negligent homicide, if not actual murder. They'd found the guilty party—a powerful pharmaceutical-entrepreneur-cum-philanthropist and...it seemed likely...killer. Given this new slant, the government couldn't just suppress the whole thing—could it?

She finally spoke. "I'll lay it all out for Sharp and Garcia. Give them the camera and journal. And then we'll wait to see what happens. Nora, they'll *have* to do something. They can't let a killer like DeGregorio just go free."

"But what if they *don't* do anything?" said Nora. "It's hard to imagine the guys who classified this just suddenly getting all transparent. What if they keep their boot on the case—and deep-six the camera and journal?"

Corrie shook her head. She had no answer. At least not yet.

Suddenly Nora held up her hand. "Did you hear that?" she whispered.

Corrie listened intently. At first she heard nothing. And then she heard a distant, familiar sound—a squealing, like a small animal in pain—that she'd first heard when they opened the main door into the presidential suite.

They stood, frozen in place. Faint sounds, magnified and distorted by the tunnels, reached them at the edge of audibility. Low voices, a muffled footfall.

"*Someone's in here,*" Corrie whispered.

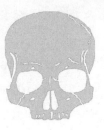

56

THEY REMAINED IMMOBILE by the bedside, scarcely daring to breathe.

Immediately, Corrie's mind turned to Sharp. He was the only one who could have deduced she would be there in the bunker. She considered calling out, revealing her presence. But then again, it might also be military personnel from Kirtland. Sealed off or not, maybe the bunker was still alarmed—and they'd set it off.

She and Nora exchanged glances, saying nothing. Then Corrie heard another faint creak—a door in the hallway was being cautiously opened.

She slipped the headlamp off her head and snapped it off. Nora followed suit. Abruptly, they were plunged into absolute darkness. In the ensuing silence, Corrie heard, or thought she heard, a faint clink of jostling in the kitchen.

Nora leaned close to her ear. "We need to get out of here," she whispered.

They had to be able to see. Holding the headlamp in her cupped hand, Corrie turned it back on, allowing a mere sliver of light to escape between her fingers. She put the journal in her pack, while Nora picked up the camera and draped it around her neck. They waited, listening. And then, another creak—whoever was in the bunker had opened another door in the hall.

Instinctively, she placed a hand on her sidearm, reassured by its cold solidity. Touching Nora, she pointed toward the doors in the back of the bedroom suite they had not yet examined. One of them might just serve as their exit. But first, she had to determine who had come into this maze of passageways.

Using the sliver of light as a guide, Corrie crept along the wall until she reached the door that led back into the living room. She flattened herself against the frame and then, shielding the light completely, peered around. At first the room appeared to be empty . . . but as she stared into the blackness, she saw a faint gleam. A slim beam of red light played around in the hall outside the living room door. A moment later, a dim figure appeared in the doorway. It was a big man—not Sharp. He was dressed in unusual camo that no FBI agent or military team would use.

These weren't FBI. And they weren't military. Who could it be? DeGregorio? It didn't seem possible. DeGregorio was in Indonesia...or was he? How could he be up here? But he was the one person who had everything to protect, and he knew about the bunker and the journal that would incriminate him. They had left an easy-to-follow snowmobile trail. If his role in the expedition came out, his life would be over. He had every reason to stop them.

The figure moved cautiously into the room, shining the pencil light to and fro. Another figure followed him. Both had military-style Colt .45s at the ready. They moved like professionals, mercenaries or hired soldiers, intent on searching every possible hiding place.

Quietly, Corrie moved away from the living room and into the bedroom, being careful to keep her light low and out of the door's line of sight. She gestured Nora to follow her toward the closed door in the rear of the bedroom.

Soundlessly crossing the deep pile rug, they reached the door. Corrie grasped the knob. Ever so slowly she began to open it. The faintest creaking sigh broke the stillness, and she froze. But there was no reaction in the hallway.

The door, to Corrie's dismay, led into a large

walk-in closet hung with a scattering of musty suits, coats, and other clothes. All the pockets had been turned inside out, obviously by O'Connell. She momentarily considered using the closet to hide, but then dismissed the idea: it would be the first place they'd search.

Quelling a wave of despair, she stepped back from the door, signaling Nora to follow. There was one more closed door to its right, bigger than the closet door. They had to move quickly now—she could hear movement in the living room, furniture being pushed aside. They would enter the bedroom at any moment.

The large door opened smoothly—thank God—and she saw, with a surge of relief, that it led onto a corridor. They quickly slipped through, then Corrie eased the door shut and turned on her headlamp.

They tiptoed down the corridor to a vestibule with two doors set opposite each other. Corrie opened one, probing the space beyond with her light. It was a salon turned into storage: she could make out an old grand piano, several folding screens, boxes of bric-a-brac, filing cabinets, many overturned in disarray in what had clearly been O'Connell's desperate attempt to find water.

At the far end of the room was another door.

Shutting the door to the corridor, the two moved past the piano and through the maze of filing cabinets and overturned boxes to the far door. It was unlocked and exposed yet another empty tunnel, this one curving sharply to the left. Fifty yards on, as they rounded the curve, the tunnel ended in another door.

Nora stopped. "Any idea who's in here?"

"I think it's DeGregorio's men."

"Shit." A moment of silence. "Look," Nora continued at a whisper, "we need a plan. We can't just keep going through doors and taking tunnels at random. If we want to get out of here, the only thing to do is outflank them. Get around behind and then go out the way we came in."

"Good idea. But I'm totally lost."

"Really?" Nora shook her head. "Me too."

"That leaves us only one option: keep going until we find the exit." Corrie grasped the knob, turned it, and eased the door open a crack. To her surprise, the door opened into an elegant space, clearly still part of the presidential suite. As she peered out, she guessed they had entered a room somewhere on the left-hand corridor—the one they hadn't taken initially.

This might help get them past the searchers. Cupping her light again, Corrie slipped through the room and to the door opening onto the main hallway of the suite. She could see down the mirrored corridor a distant reddish glow coming from an open door, which she realized must be the bedroom area where the men were still searching. They had come around in a circle.

Nora poked her shoulder, then pointed across the corridor to a door that was plainer than the others. With the palm of one hand, she mimed a large, gentle turn to the left. Immediately, Corrie understood. Nora, with a keener sense of direction, was indicating that the door might just lead back in the direction of the exit tunnel, completing a circuit of the presidential complex.

They scurried across to the door and Corrie opened it.

"Hey! There they are!" a voice cried from the hallway beyond. A red beam, held by a man at the far end of the corridor, spotlighted them.

"*Son of a bitch.*" Corrie backed up, almost stumbling in her hurry, and slammed the door. "Run!"

They ran, backtracking across the hall and into the curved tunnel. They heard the door crash open behind them, followed by pounding footsteps and shouted voices, echoing strangely through the confined spaces. They burst into the room with the piano, ran past the litter of papers and boxes, then out into the vestibule beyond. Opposite them was another door, which Corrie opened and dived through, Nora following close behind.

The thudding footsteps of their pursuers were

growing closer. "Stop!" one of them called. "We're not going to hurt you!"

Beyond the door was a small screening room, with seats, a sloped floor, and a stage. They ran down the center aisle and onto the stage.

Suddenly, gunfire—shatteringly loud after the whispers and patter of feet—echoed through the chamber, the rounds smacking the proscenium above them and spraying plaster dust and chips. Corrie yanked Nora behind a nearby curtain, pulled her 9mm SIG, ducked back out, and fired two rounds at their pursuers.

"That'll slow those motherfuckers," she said.

Behind the stage was a dark, narrow space, with open doors leading into a green room, a dressing room, and a hallway that led off into gloom, arcing back in the direction they'd just run from: not exactly the way out they were looking for.

Corrie turned to face the stage, gun extended, ready to make a stand. She could hear thudding footfalls and raspy breathing. The noise abruptly stopped on the far side of the curtain.

"We're not going to hurt you. We just want to talk," said a voice.

Neither Corrie nor Nora said anything.

"You have the camera—right? And the journal? Give us those and we'll let you go."

"Fuck you." Corrie aimed and fired through the curtain.

But as the echo died away, she heard Nora cry out a warning from behind, turned instinctively back toward the dim passage—and felt a massive blow to her head, followed by a loud buzzing sound, then nothing.

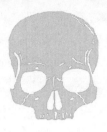

57

CORRIE SWAM BACK into consciousness. Her head pounded with every beat of her heart. Although it was dim, she became aware of people in the room around her: shapes moving, an angry voice. As her vision stabilized, she recognized the antlers, table, and gigantic stone fireplace of the day room of Rancho Bonito, the place where Sam Puller had given them coffee and advice. She tried to move, realized she was duct-taped to a chair. Through the lodge windows she could see a leaden dusk, with snow swirling past. She looked around, keeping her head upright to help steady the whirling sensation. She saw Nora, also taped to a chair, on the opposite side of the table. There were several men in the room, all armed.

"Hey, Doctor," came a voice from behind. "She's awake."

She tried to turn her head, but a sudden pain

stopped her. She closed her eyes, tried to steady herself. She and Nora had been captured. They were back in the lodge. Where were the Pullers?

"Open your eyes."

She opened them. The figure of a man loomed in front of her. He tapped her face with his fingers. "Hey. Wake up." He gave her a slightly harder slap.

She tried to focus on his face. Now he slapped her hard, sending pain shooting through her head. *"Hey!"*

Instead of spinning her back into a sickening dizziness, the pain and rough handling helped clear her head. She concentrated on the face in front of her: hollow, prominent cheekbones, thin lips, narrow eyes. Early forties. She didn't recognize the face, but the voice was familiar. Corrie realized it was Alex DeGregorio, whom she'd spoken to on the phone.

"What," she mumbled.

"Pull yourself together," he said. "We've got business." Another slap. "Paying attention now?"

Corrie stared at him. "It's all in the journal," she managed to say. "You...you did it."

"You mean this?" The man held up the scuffed leather journal, tossed it on the table. "Where's the *camera?*"

Corrie glanced over at Nora. She was awake and staring back at her. Her mouth had been taped so she couldn't speak, but her eyes were wide. She could now see that, in addition to herself, Corrie, and DeGregorio, there were a total of four other men in the room, looking back at her with grim faces.

"Where are the Pullers?" she asked.

DeGregorio glanced over to the doorway to the kitchen. Corrie followed his gaze and saw a heavy spattering of blood across the doorframe, congealing into a large pool on the floor. Sickened and aghast, she turned back to him.

"You *killed* them?"

He leaned closer to her. "I want the camera. Where is it?"

Corrie stared at him in confusion. Then she looked at Nora. She remembered the archaeologist slinging the camera around her neck—or did she? It wasn't around her neck now. Her pack was lying on the floor, open, contents strewn about.

Where *was* the camera?

"No idea," said Corrie.

At this, DeGregorio struck her across the cheek so hard it wrenched her head around and caused her vision to momentarily falter. She gasped, drawing in air, as the throbbing slowly diminished.

DeGregorio removed a gun from his waistband and pushed the cold steel muzzle into her ear. A couple of the other men moved closer.

"Where's the camera?"

"I'm not lying. I really don't know."

Another blow. As she recovered her senses, she heard DeGregorio's voice, as if at a distance. "Next time, it'll be a bullet in the knee."

Corrie fought to keep the whirling sensation from coming back. "What...," she stammered. "What was the drug you gave them?"

At this, DeGregorio looked alarmed. "What... Does the FBI know about that?"

Corrie didn't answer.

He slapped her, hard. "Talk to me, bitch."

"Tell me what the drug was," said Corrie, "and I'll answer some questions."

He looked at her. "So that's how it's going to be?" He suddenly grinned. "Why not?"

With that statement, Corrie understood clearly that they both were going to be killed.

Meanwhile, DeGregorio pulled up a seat and sat down beside her. "I was working on a new antidepressant—not an SSRI, but a completely new drug, based on the venom of the desert toad, *Bufo alvarius*. I synthesized a version of it that seemed to work fine on lab rats. I tested it on myself multiple times, and there were no side effects, except for tachyphylaxis—'diminishing returns' to you unanointed. It had incredible potential. Almost a third of the population is resistant to all antidepressants—including myself. I needed to test it for possible side effects on a larger sample, and I didn't have a few hundred million bucks for clinical trials. So I joined that expedition at the last minute and decided to test it on them. It was exactly the controlled, experimental setup required: isolated subjects, with no way to interact with the outside world. I knew Lynn and Mike had issues with depression; most graduate students do. I had tweaked the formulation to counteract the tachyphylaxis. Amazing how such a tiny change could trigger such alarming results. You know, the human mind is a great deal closer to the brink of madness than you ever imagined. They all suffered far worse negative effects—bad trips, as it were—from the new formulation than I'd expected. Paranoia, panic, hallucinations—even psychosis." He paused, shaking his head. "Even so, if it hadn't been for that bomb drop, and Cheape arriving in a clown suit, nothing bad would have happened. Nobody would have died. It was the fault of that clumsy bastard, Cheape, bursting into the tent like that, yelling at them to leave. They were so high, so freaked out, he must have looked like an alien in his radiation gear—he could have stayed mum and they still would have run, cutting their way out of the tent and running away practically in their birthday suits."

"But you weren't 'freaked out.' You realized what had really happened."

"He wanted to apprehend me and bring me in. I was forced to explain to the dumb shit that, when the brass learned he'd blundered into the tent and sent everyone scattering to their deaths, it would look as bad for him as it did for me."

"And so you killed him."

DeGregorio scoffed. "Years passed. I got rich. When Gordy and Paul were found, Cheape had the bright idea he could shake me down after all this time. It was his fault that they ran. *And* the military—I didn't ask them to drop a bomb in our laps."

"His fault? The military's fault? *You* were using your friends as guinea pigs!"

He leaned in. "Let me tell you something. The company I founded developed that drug into Impremazol. It's the most effective antidepressant ever formulated. It's helped millions of people."

Corrie was amazed to hear a surge of pride in his voice.

He gently screwed the muzzle back into her ear. "I'm sorry for what happened to them, I truly am, but it *wasn't my fault*. Enough useless chatter. Where's the camera?"

At this, Corrie heard a muffled sound and saw that Nora was struggling, trying to talk.

"Take the gag off that bitch." From the angry tone, Corrie sensed Nora had already pissed him off somehow.

One of the men tore off the duct tape. Nora gasped and took a couple of deep breaths. "She doesn't know where the camera is. I do."

"Fine. Where?"

"I hid it someplace."

He stared at her. "You *hid* it?"

"The camera contains proof you were on the expedition. If it ever comes to light, you're fucked."

DeGregorio ground the muzzle of the gun into Corrie's ear. "Well, it just so happens I've got a simple solution to that. Tell me where it is, or I'll blow your girlfriend's brains all over the wall."

"She's no girlfriend of mine. But that doesn't matter—if you kill her, I'll never tell and you'll have to kill me, too."

"Okay, fine. Tell me where it is, and I'll let you walk. Both of you."

"You're going to kill us anyway," Corrie said. "We know that. Which means you've got no leverage."

She felt the barrel of the gun move from her ear to her knee.

"I've got as many bullets as she has joints," DeGregorio said, still looking at Nora.

"Wait," said Nora. "Look, before you—"

"No more talk!" DeGregorio shouted angrily. "I want the camera. What did you do with it?"

"I'll tell you—just don't shoot her."

"Count of three. One—"

Corrie felt the barrel press into her kneecap.

"Two—"

"Don't," said Nora. "I'll tell you where it is. It's hidden in the bunker. I'll take you there."

"Tell me *where*."

"You have to promise not to shoot her."

"I promise."

Nora hesitated just a moment. "In the grand piano."

DeGregorio raised the gun from Corrie's knee to her head. "No need to kneecap you now. Happy trails."

Corrie managed to quickly close her eyes on the world just as she heard the boom of the gun.

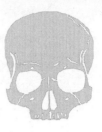

58

Nora watched in horror as Corrie lurched backward in her chair.

At almost precisely the same moment, DeGregorio spun around, gun flying from his hand.

A split second later, the lodge door burst open and a fusillade of shots rang out. Two figures rushed in, moving so fast in the stormy darkness that Nora could not immediately locate them. They fired fast and furiously, catching DeGregorio's mercenaries completely by surprise. Two were struck with bullets before they could even draw their weapons, and the other two were gunned down as they were trying to get off a shot.

And then, as suddenly as it had begun, it was all over. DeGregorio and his men lay sprawled across the floor and draped over the leather furniture, some motionless, others groaning or coughing up blood. The two who had burst in, Nora saw with something like disbelief, were Sheriff Watts and Agent Sharp. The sheriff holstered his six-guns as they were still smoking and rushed over to Corrie, who was lying on her side, still taped to the chair. He pulled out a knife to cut her free and then, grasping her body gently in his arms, laid her out on the nearby rug. There was blood on her head, and the wooden back of the chair had been pierced and splintered by the bullet.

Meanwhile, Sharp cut Nora free. With a cry, she dashed over to where Corrie lay. Watts was cradling her head and inspecting the wound. He pulled a bandanna out of his pocket and gently wiped at her temple.

"It's just a graze," he said. "Thank God!"

Heart pounding, Nora knelt beside him. "I thought she was dead."

DeGregorio must have been hit an instant before he'd squeezed his trigger, Nora thought. The round had only grazed Corrie's temple before going through the back of the wooden chair.

Now Corrie's eyes fluttered and opened. She stared up at Watts. "Homer? What...are you doing here?"

"Everything's good, and the bad guys are dead. Thank God you're okay." Watts looked so hugely relieved, so enormously thankful that Corrie was alive, that tears started running down his face.

Nora suddenly realized: *He's in love with Corrie.*

"Bad guys?... What bad guys?"

"We'll talk about it later," Watts said. "You're okay—the wound is superficial."

"I'm *wounded*?" Corrie raised a palm and touched her head, then looked at the blood on her fingers. "Oh shit."

"You seem to have a slight concussion," Watts told her. "We're going to get you to the hospital. Okay? Ambulances are on the way."

Sharp, in his turn, knelt beside Corrie on the other side. "Agent Swanson?"

Corrie looked at him, surprised once again. "You here, too? God, I feel like Dorothy waking up from the dream. What's going on?"

"When I couldn't get you or Dr. Kelly on the phone, I guessed you might have come up here looking for that bunker—especially after signing out an all-terrain Jeep."

"That's when he called me," Watts said. "I knew about this lodge. Seemed logical that you'd use this place as a trailhead. Agent Sharp verified that by calling the lodge caretaker, and he said you'd just come through."

Corrie winced. "Okay, now it's starting to come back..." She took a deep breath. "The caretakers—?"

Sharp's face creased. "I'm sorry—dead. When we got up here," he continued, "we found the gate locked. So we went in on foot and saw a vehicle by the garage—not yours. Two dead bodies were in the back. So we crept up to the lodge, using the storm for cover, saw and heard what was going on inside—and rushed in."

"Just in time," said Nora.

"I'm afraid that's all too true. Watts is damned fast with a six-gun—it was his shot that saved Corrie."

"Hell yes," said Watts. "You remembering things now, Corrie?"

"It's all coming back," Corrie said, and Nora could see her face was clearing. She looked at Sharp. "Sir, there was more to this than just the bomb accident."

Sharp nodded. "Yes."

"It's all there," said Corrie, pointing to the journal lying where DeGregorio had tossed it.

"There's also a camera," said Nora, "with undeveloped film containing important evidence. It's in the bunker, inside a grand piano, where I hid it while we were running from these goons. I put it there hoping to buy us some leverage, if those bastards caught us."

For a moment, all was quiet. Then Corrie turned to Sharp. "What's going to happen now?"

He returned her gaze but said nothing.

"We're going to go public with this—right? This *can't* be suppressed. The bloodbath up here.

DeGregorio's crimes. Cheape's murder. The truth, finally, about the Dead Mountain case!"

Sharp said nothing for a long moment. When he finally spoke, it was slow and gravelly. "It's not up to you." His gaze swept Corrie and Nora in turn, and he lowered his voice. "Nor to me."

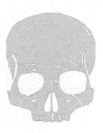

59

"A<small>LL RISE.</small>"

Once again, the judge entered the courtroom, more lugubrious than ever, hiked up his robes, sat down behind the bench, and called the courtroom to order. Skip sat once again in the dock, miserable and scared and worse than ever after four days of waiting, his suit more wrinkled, his hair sticking out. Nora was exhausted. She ached all over, and she felt like she'd slept no more than four hours in the last four days. But she couldn't miss this last session of her brother's trial—and her opportunity to testify.

The jury, on the other hand, was alert and refreshed from the weekend, and the spectator section was once again full.

Lightfeather had explained to Nora that unless something freakish happened, today—Monday— would be the last day of the trial, and Skip's fate would be determined. The prosecution had decided not to call their surprise witness from the fight at Gallina's Peek after all; Lightfeather told Nora he'd learned that the fight had broken out over an impolite nickname of Hawley's, one that the sheriff decided he didn't want to make public. Deputy Baca, Lightfeather went on, would be the last witness to testify for the prosecution, and then they'd have an opportunity to cross-examine. After that, Lightfeather would mount Skip's defense. He was planning to call two witnesses, Nora and Tenorio. He was not going to call Skip, as he had concluded— rightly so in Nora's opinion—that Skip would not testify well.

As the court settled in, the judge called on the DA to continue the prosecution's presentation.

Scowsen stood up. "I would like to call as our final witness Deputy Sheriff Raymond Baca."

Baca entered the courtroom in uniform, immaculate, badge gleaming with a fresh polish, black hair combed back. He took the witness stand and was sworn in. Nora glanced at Hawley, sitting at the DA's table; he had a satisfied smile on his face.

Scowsen strolled over to the witness stand—he had an unhurried manner, studied or not—and greeted Baca. "Deputy Sheriff. How are you today?"

Baca nodded.

"Your answers," said Scowsen, in an affable tone, "should always be spoken so our court reporter can be sure to get them down on paper."

"I'm fine," said Baca curtly.

"Excellent. This should not take long. Now, I'd like to direct your memory back to the events of the afternoon of November 5. I understand you were guarding the recently discovered cave site when some people arrived. Could you tell us about that?"

"Yes, sir. The defendant, there, Skip Kelly; his sister, Nora Kelly; and another fellow arrived around two PM. Mr. Tenorio arrived at the same time in another vehicle."

"And you knew them from before?"

"I knew them, yes, from a previous visit to the cave."

"And what happened next?"

"They told me they were going to remove the two Indian bodies. I said I'd better check with the sheriff first, but they ignored me and went ahead with the digging."

"And you checked with the sheriff?"

"Yes. It took a while, because I had to get into my vehicle and drive partway down the mountain to get service. I called and the sheriff said he was coming right up."

"And then what happened?"

"The sheriff arrived about an hour and a half later, just as they were taking out the first of the two in a body bag."

"And who was 'they'?"

"The defendant, Skip Kelly, and his sister, Nora. I was waiting for the sheriff in the parking area. When he arrived, we started down the trail to the cave. That's when we encountered them coming up carrying the body."

"And then?"

"Sheriff Hawley informed them that the bones were government property. When they ignored him, he tried to stop them from carrying the body bag to their van."

"And then?"

It seemed to Nora that Baca's face had darkened slightly. He hesitated.

"What happened then, Sheriff Baca?" the prosecutor urged.

"The sheriff blocked their path and told them to put down the bones."

"Can you describe for us that exact scene? It will help the jury form an accurate picture in their minds. I assume someone was carrying the bag in front, and another from behind?"

"Yes. Um, Skip Kelly was in front and Nora Kelly was behind."

Nora almost rose from her seat. She managed to

stop herself, then turned to Lightfeather. "That's a lie," she whispered. "I was the one in front."

Lightfeather laid a restraining finger on her forearm. "Just listen. Don't react."

"Please go on, Deputy Baca," Scowsen said.

"So when the sheriff blocked the path, Skip said something like 'Get out of our way.'"

"To whom?"

"Sheriff Hawley."

Nora felt the blood flush to her face. The lying had started in earnest. She couldn't believe how this man, a sworn officer of the law, could lie so brazenly—in front of a judge, a jury . . . not to mention those watching who knew the truth.

"And then?"

"The sheriff repeated the order to put down the body. He said it was federal property." Baca took a deep breath, and the rest all came out in a rush. "Nora Kelly said something about NAGPRA law and how she was working for Isleta Pueblo. The sheriff repeated that the bones were federal property and she was engaged in theft. Then Skip Kelly started yelling about how this was a sacred Native American burial. He insulted the sheriff. He was, uh, angry and when the sheriff wouldn't move out of his way, he dropped the handle of the body bag, seized the sheriff by the shoulders—catching him off guard—and violently threw him to the ground.

Then he bolted. I ran after him, apprehended him. The defendant tried to hide his phone but I took it from him. I cuffed him and read him his rights."

"And the sheriff?"

"He was on the ground. Stunned—the ground was covered with sharp rocks. Anyway, after Sheriff Hawley had recovered enough to function, we took the defendant in handcuffs to the police vehicle and drove off."

"And the sister, Nora Kelly? What did she do?"

"She was hysterical. Screaming. Followed us to the parking area until we drove away."

"At any time during this confrontation, did the sheriff touch or make any other contact with Nora Kelly?"

"Never."

"Did Nora Kelly fall down?"

"Yes. She tripped as she was running up the path after us."

"Did the defendant, Skip Kelly, take video or pictures at any time?"

"No."

"Why did you confiscate the phone?"

"Because he was trying to hide it in what I deemed a suspicious manner."

"Were the contents of the phone examined?"

"Yes. We got a warrant."

"And what did you find?"

"Incriminating evidence."

"What sort of evidence?"

"Pictures of the defendant, his sister, and the two others with them, engaged in illegally excavating the Indian burials."

"So confiscation of the phone was justified from an evidentiary point of view, correct?"

"Yes, that is correct."

Nora—forbidden by Lightfeather from reacting—had kept her eyes riveted on Baca. Now that he'd unloaded all his lies, which she was certain he'd carefully rehearsed, the dark color of his face lightened somewhat and he exhaled, deflating like a balloon.

The DA took a folder from his table. "I'd like to enter these photographs taken from the defendant's phone into evidence. Mr. Baca, I want to thank you for your testimony, and your service to this county and this country. I have no more questions."

It was Lightfeather's turn. He waited until Scowsen had seated himself. Then he rose to his feet, picking up a book from his table as he did so—a small book Nora hadn't noticed before. "Permission to cross-examine the witness, Your Honor?"

"Please proceed."

He strode up to the witness stand and stood directly in front of Baca. His movements had suddenly grown a shade more aggressive than before, and he leaned in toward the deputy closer than seemed appropriate. He stared wordlessly until Baca began to squirm, and then he spoke.

"Deputy Sheriff Baca, did you take an oath before God to tell the truth before you took the stand?"

Immediately, Scowsen was up. "Objection! We all saw him take the oath."

"Sustained," said the judge.

Lightfeather held up the little book, which Nora now saw was a Bible. "Do you recognize this book?"

"Objection!" cried Scowsen, on his feet again. "Irrelevant!"

"Sustained," said the judge again.

Lightfeather plowed on. "Deputy, do you consider yourself a Christian? Are you familiar with the Ten Commandments? One in particular seems important, perhaps life-altering, at the present moment: *Thou shalt not bear false—*"

But Scowsen was back on his feet. "*Objection! Mr. Lightfeather is badgering the witness!* Your Honor, can you please instruct defense counsel to confine his questions to the facts at hand? The witness's religious views have nothing to do with the matter!"

The judge turned a stern eye on Lightfeather. "Mr. Lightfeather, I'm sustaining the objection. I would note it is the third such objection in a row I have sustained. You, sir, are out of line. One more irrelevant question like that and I will hold you in contempt of court. Is that clear?"

"Yes, Your Honor."

"Proceed."

Lightfeather, seemingly shaken up by this, tried to compose himself, smoothing down his suit, running a hand over his hair. He took an inordinately long time, while the agitated Baca clasped and unclasped his hands.

Nora glanced again at Hawley. The bastard was still sitting there, a smug smile of contentment creasing his meatball face.

Then Lightfeather's head snapped up. "Mr. Baca, sir, I have only one more question. But it is an important one. Your truthful answer to this question will determine the fate of this young man, Elwyn Kelly. But I want you to realize something else: your answer, as recorded in the greatest court of all, will bear on the fate of *another* person's immortal soul—"

Scowsen leapt up, furious. "Objection! *Objection!* Your Honor, this is harassment, pure and simple. The defense is using these insinuations to threaten the witness!"

The judge banged his gavel. "Sustained! Mr. Lightfeather, I'm now holding you in contempt of court and fining you one thousand dollars." *Bang* went the gavel again. "Now ask your final question sir, with no more commentary, and be done with it."

He turned to the jury. "You will disregard the entire line of Mr. Lightfeather's previous questioning."

Lightfeather looked at Baca for a long time. "My question is direct, it's simple—and it's profound. Mr. Baca, *have you told us the truth*?"

There was a long silence. Baca was still wringing his hands and seemed unable to speak. The deputy's obvious anguish and his apparent inability to answer the question transfixed the courtroom. The tension in the room swiftly increased as Baca's silence went on. Skip had lost his hopeless, resigned expression and was staring at the deputy. Nora herself could hardly breathe. Hawley was no longer smiling.

"Mr. Baca," the judge urged. "The court is awaiting your answer."

"No," said Baca at last.

"You mean 'no' in what way, exactly, Mr. Baca?" Lightfeather asked gently.

"I mean *no*. I haven't told the truth."

"Would you like to take this opportunity to clear your conscience, before God, and tell the truth— here and now, in this court of law?"

"Objection! *Objection!*" Scowsen rose in another fury. "More threats and harassment, Your Honor!"

"Objection overruled," said the judge. "The witness appears to have something to say, and it is this court's duty to hear it."

Baca was breathing hard. He struggled to get himself under control.

"Nora Kelly was in front," he began, in a low, monotonal voice. "She was carrying the body. The brother was behind. The sheriff blocked her way. The brother started videotaping with his phone and the sheriff lunged at him, knocking down the sister in the process—"

"What the hell?" Hawley erupted, springing to his feet. "Baca, what are you doing?"

"Mr. Hawley." The judge banged his gavel. "Sit down, sir, and cease disrupting the proceedings."

"Baca, you little prick—"

Bang, bang went the gavel. "Sit down this instant or I will have you removed from this court, sir!" the judge said.

The sheriff continued standing and staring at Baca, swaying slightly, while the deputy stared back, his face a mask of anguish, sweating profusely.

"*Sit down, sir!*" the judge thundered.

The sheriff sat down and then muttered, in a voice loud enough to be heard across the courtroom, "You'll pay for this, Baca."

"I will not tolerate further disruption from you in my court!" said the judge. "Bailiffs, remove Mr. Hawley from the courtroom."

Two bailiffs rose and came over to Hawley,

positioning themselves on either side. Hawley was trembling all over and his face was dark red. They tried to take his arms, but he shrugged them off with a curse. "I'll walk on my own," he said.

They escorted him from the room, the sheriff turning his head and glaring balefully at Baca on the witness stand up until the moment the courtroom's doors closed behind him.

"Mr. Lightfeather," said the judge. "You may continue questioning the witness."

"Thank you, Your Honor." He turned to Baca. "Now, I believe you were telling us the sheriff knocked down Nora Kelly, the defendant's sister, is that correct?"

"Objection!" cried Scowsen. "This witness is totally unreliable, he's lying, he's confusing the jury—I call for a mistrial!"

"Overruled. May I remind you, Mr. Scowsen, that *you* called this witness, not the defense. There are no grounds for a mistrial. Mr. Baca, please continue with your answer to the question."

"Yes, sir," said Baca, his voice quavering. "She hit the ground pretty hard. That's when the defendant grabbed and pushed down the sheriff." His voice began to grow louder, more certain. "Also, the defendant didn't run off. The sheriff took his phone and we arrested him. When we got back to the car, we locked him in the back. Then the sheriff erased the video as we were driving out."

"What about the testimony you gave earlier?" said Lightfeather. "Where did that come from?"

"The sheriff coached me on what to say, how the story should play out."

An electric silence fell in the courtroom.

"Thank you, Deputy Baca," said Lightfeather. "No further questions."

Scowsen jumped up. "Permission to examine the witness again, Your Honor."

"You may do so."

Scowsen turned and approached Baca. "So, Mr. Baca, it seems the jury has heard two different stories from you today. Are you now telling us that the first story was a lie?"

"Yes."

"In other words, you are a self-admitted liar."

"I guess so."

"If that is the case, as a confessed liar, how do you expect the jury to believe this second story? Why not tell them a third story? Or a fourth?"

"All I can say is, I'm sorry for having lied. But now I've told the truth."

"I see! And having lied once, having *confessed* to doing so, you *now* expect us to believe you?"

"I hope so."

"And, I assume, you also hope the jury should believe your word over that of Sheriff Hawley, the trusted, honored, and duly elected sheriff of this community these past twenty years, who is a hero to everyone in Torrance County?"

"He's no hero to me."

Scowsen's voice dripped with mock incredulity. "So you dare claim that the sheriff, who took a bullet in the line of duty, is not a hero?"

Scowsen's obvious contempt seemed to stiffen Baca's spine. "I think he's a bully."

Infuriated, Scowsen swiveled to the bench. "Your Honor, I object to the slandering of Sheriff Hawley's good name! I ask that you sanction the witness for making such a statement!"

The judge returned Scowsen's furious look with a weary one of his own. "Your objection is overruled. The witness's statement of bullying is explanatory to his motive for committing perjury before this court." He paused. "Do you have further questions for the witness?"

This response seemed to render Scowsen almost speechless. "Uh, no. No, Your Honor."

"Mr. Baca, you are excused from the witness stand."

Baca climbed down and stiffly made his way out of the courtroom.

Scowsen, after a moment of pure paralysis, finally

mumbled to no one in particular that he was resting the people's case. The judge called on Lightfeather to present his defense.

Lightfeather stood up. "I call Nora Kelly as a witness."

Nora went up to the stand. She sat down, took the oath, and stated her name.

"Dr. Kelly," Lightfeather said, "you heard Deputy Baca's testimony. Both the first testimony and the second, which contradicted the first. Which is true?"

"The first was a lie, the second is the truth."

"You saw your brother making the video?"

"Yes."

"The sheriff knocked you down trying to stop him?"

"Yes. He hit me like a linebacker."

"The sheriff testified that the ground was dangerously hard and stony, correct? So you might have been seriously injured?"

"Yes."

"Were you in fact injured?"

"No. Actually, yes, I was. I got a scratch and a bruise—very similar to the injuries that sent the sheriff rushing to the emergency room."

This elicited a flurry of titters from the audience.

"Your brother then grabbed the sheriff and threw him down?"

"He sort of checked him with his shoulder and pushed him down."

"Why?"

"I believe he was trying to protect me."

"What happened to the phone?"

"The sheriff got up and confiscated it."

"So the sheriff wasn't lying on the ground, stunned, as has been asserted?"

"No. He jumped right up."

"When the phone was returned to you several days later, was the video your brother took still on it?"

"No. It was gone."

"Did Skip try to run away when the sheriff apprehended him?"

"No."

"Did he resist arrest in any way?"

"No. He cooperated fully."

"No further questions," said Lightfeather. "The defense rests."

Nora returned to her seat, glancing over at the jury with apprehension. It was clear they were astonished by what had just transpired. But what were they thinking?

Scowsen gave a thunderous summation that focused on the heroism of Hawley and the lying, craven, prevaricating, unreliable, compromised nature of his deputy, Baca. In contrast, Lightfeather's summation was calm, quiet, and so brief it lasted less than five minutes. He reminded the jury of Baca's testimony, asked them to consider which of the two stories they believed, and requested they decide Skip's fate accordingly, as was their duty under the law. The judge then charged the jury, and they filed out of the courtroom. At that point, the judge called for a break. He seemed to expect a quick verdict.

And he was not wrong. Twenty minutes later, before Nora had even been able to finish the lousy cup of coffee she'd ordered in the courthouse cafeteria, the jury came back in and declared Skip not guilty on all counts.

EPILOGUE

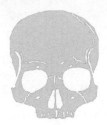

CORRIE HAD SLEPT late, as she always did on vacation. What made this particular vacation unusual, however, was that she woke to find a cappuccino on the bedside table and a copy of the *Albuquerque Journal* propped next to it. She saw the headline and sat bolt upright, suddenly wide awake.

Homer Watts was lying stretched out on a divan at the far side of their yurt, legs crossed, grinning. Sunlight was streaming in a window that looked out over Abiquiu Lake and the red buttes of Ghost Ranch.

Corrie looked back at the paper, then seized it and read, astonished. The headline screamed in an almost tabloid fashion:

ACCIDENTAL NUKE DROP REVEALED

Dead Mountain Mystery Solved
Pharma wiz gravely wounded in shootout
with FBI, arrested for murder

"Holy shit," said Corrie.

It was all there—everything—attributed to a "confidential and highly placed source, backed up by documentation independently confirmed by the *Journal* to be legitimate."

Somebody had spilled the beans. There was a comprehensive description of the entire story, with all its twists and turns: the emergency jettisoning of a bomb to avoid a crash; the clandestine drug experiment on the hikers; their hallucinatory, panicked flight after encountering a searcher in a hazmat suit; how they died; the discovery of the journal—along with a sidebar about an earlier cover-up that destroyed the career of the previous chief investigator, Robertson Gold.

The commander of Kirtland AFB had been asked for comment and—while issuing a statement in obvious consternation about violation of classified information—had not exactly denied anything. SAC Garcia of the Albuquerque FO had refused all comment, as had Supervisory Special Agent Sharp, in charge of the Dead Mountain case. Nora Kelly of the Santa Fe Archaeological Institute, who had played a key role, was away with her brother in Marblehead, Massachusetts, and could not be reached by press time. Socorro County sheriff Homer Watts and Special Agent Corinne Swanson, also deeply involved in the case, were unable to be reached for comment.

Corrie grabbed her phone and looked at it. Nothing. Of course—they were off grid. She turned and stared at Watts. "Did you know about this?"

Watts was laughing. "I swear I didn't. I got up early and went to Bode's to get us some breakfast burritos, and saw the headline. I just about fell over."

Corrie continued to read, amazed. There were related stories as well, one involving the murder of Cheape, another covering a statement from Melody Ann O'Connell of the Manzano Families Memorial Association, insisting the whole thing was just another cover-up and that the Boston Project was clearly to blame.

"My God," Corrie said, continuing to read the various stories that dominated the entire front section of the paper. "It's all here—documents, pictures, everything! Who did this?"

"The very question I asked myself." Watts laughed again, hands behind his head, apparently as amused as hell.

Corrie looked at him. This was the guy who had the skill and nerve to take out DeGregorio a split second before he would have put a bullet in her head. The man who'd saved her life. Movie-star handsome, his amber eyes crinkling with amusement—and all hers. How lucky was she? Life was strange indeed. After all this time she'd spent—worrying about what Watts thought of her, what she should do, how she should act, what their professional relationship should be—he'd invited her to spend four days with him in a yurt in the middle of nowhere. Without thinking—without needing to think—she'd said yes.

"Who did this indeed?" Watts was saying. "You don't need to be Sherlock Holmes to use the process of elimination. Could it have been ... Garcia?"

"No way," said Corrie. "He's too by-the-book."

"You?"

"Don't be funny."

"Nora?"

"Impossible."

"O'Hara or Bellamy?"

"No. One's too straight and the other too dumb. They didn't have access to all this information anyway."

"Director Raeburn?"

"No way. He ordered the quashing to begin with."

"Sheriff Hawley?"

This of course was a joke. The sheriff had been indicted for perjury, obstruction of justice, and witness tampering. He'd been forced to resign, with worse apparently to come. "Ha ha, good old One-Bally? Can't be him—what a dumbass."

At this, Watts said, "Who's left?"

Suddenly, Corrie caught her breath. "Not Sharp."

Watts merely grinned.

"No," said Corrie. "No way."

"'When you have eliminated the impossible,'" Watts quoted, "'whatever remains, however improbable, must be the truth.' It was you who taught me that line."

Corrie thought about it. Sharp? The more she pondered it, the more she realized he *must* have done it. Nothing else made sense. He had access to everything. He was in charge of the case. More to the point, she'd never seen him so disgusted and angry as when the case was suppressed. He'd been appalled and furious all over again when, less than twenty-four hours after the shootout at the lodge, the case was quashed again. The orders came down: Everything that had happened in the Manzanos— the bunker discovery, the journal, the camera, the murders of the caretakers, DeGregorio's involvement, the exchange of gunfire—would be classified to the max, on direct orders from on high. *Everything* they'd done, all they had discovered, would be deep-sixed to protect the air force from embarrassment. When Corrie learned that, she thought Sharp might resign. But instead, after initially expressing anger, he'd gone as calm and lethargic as ever—and ordered her to take a two-week break.

Instead of resigning, she realized, Sharp must have played the role of Deep Throat. And come to think of it, wasn't the original Deep Throat, the guy who'd exposed Watergate, also an FBI agent? She felt a sudden surge of pride in the FBI: despite everything, the working agents of the Bureau had displayed patriotism and integrity.

"Wow," she said. "You're right. It's gotta be Sharp."

"He's a good man. Took real balls to do this."

"But, you know, there's going to be an investigation of who leaked this," said Corrie. "I'll be one of the suspects. So will you. So will Sharp. It could get ugly. They'll figure out it was him."

"No," said Watts. "He's got more guts than you could hang on a fence. Smart, too, despite that lizard-in-the-sun act. There's no slack in his rope. If he did this, you can bet he did it with the utmost care. They might *suspect* him—but they won't prove anything."

He got off the divan, came over, and sat down on the bed. "But you know what, Corrie? I'm pretty sure things are going to go in a different direction altogether. There'll be an investigation—just not of the FBI."

"What do you mean?"

"Why take blame when you can take credit? That's what the FBI will do: take credit. As they should. You'll all get commendations, including Sharp, and if anybody gets investigated, it will be the air force. I mean, they messed up—although it's probably old enough now that nobody will actually get punished. But the FBI—you all kicked ass. You in particular. They're going to make you a hero."

Corrie stared at him. "You really think so?"

He leaned over her and kissed her. "I do. You *are* a hero."

"So are you. You saved my life."

He kissed her again.

Corrie said, "Sheriff Watts?"

"Yes?"

"Are we on federal land?"

"Technically, yes."

"That puts me in command."

"Huh?" He grinned. "Are you gonna invoke the Hobbs Act on me, Agent Swanson?"

"Not exactly. Take off that shirt."

He took off his shirt.

"And the pants. That's an order, mister."

He took off the pants.

"Now everything else."

He obeyed.

"I'd tell you to present arms, but it appears that command won't be necessary. Get in this bed, Sheriff—on the double."

"Immediately, Agent Swanson." And he slipped in beside her.

Authors' Note

We wanted to share with our readers an interesting story about the inspiration behind *Dead Mountain*. As you may know, one of us—Doug—writes occasional nonfiction pieces for the *New Yorker* magazine. In the May 17, 2021, issue, he published an article entitled, "Has an Old Soviet Mystery at Last Been Solved?" (Full disclosure: it was one of the most popular articles in the magazine that year.) The piece investigated the strange fate of nine cross-country skiers in the Ural Mountains who died in 1959 under bizarre circumstances on the slopes of a remote massif called Height 1079.

Doug sold film rights to the story, but the day the contracts arrived for his signature, Russia invaded Ukraine. Not surprisingly, the production company immediately pulled out—in protest, among other reasons. Not long after, as Doug was complaining to

Lincoln about the irony of the situation, Linc suggested it might actually be a stroke of luck. "How's that?" Doug asked. "Because now," Linc said, "we can take this fantastic true mystery—and make our own thriller out of it!"

Which we did. Using the old Soviet story as inspiration, we began brainstorming—and researching. We moved the story to the Manzano Mountains of New Mexico, picked because deep inside them is hidden the largest depot of nuclear weapons in the world. The Manzanos also contain a bunker complex built for President Eisenhower and his staff as a place of retreat in case of nuclear war, now sealed up and in disuse. And finally, we drew inspiration from a very real nuclear accident: on May 22, 1957, a B-36 bomber accidentally dropped a forty-two-thousand-pound hydrogen bomb in the Manzanos. The high explosives blasted a crater, but the H-bomb itself didn't go off—luckily for Albuquerque and a great many New Mexico residents. Armed with Doug's research, Linc's outré and fevered suggestions, and both our imaginations, we came up with a fresh mystery for Special Agent Corrie Swanson of the FBI's Albuquerque Field Office and archaeologist Nora Kelly of the Santa Fe Archaeological Institute to solve. And we conceived a solution hopefully both original and surprising—the capstone, we'd like to think, to a story that might have its footings in a real-life mystery, but that we've taken pains to make uniquely our own.

We hope you enjoyed the novel!
Doug & Linc

About the Authors

The thrillers of **DOUGLAS PRESTON** and **LINCOLN CHILD** "stand head and shoulders above their rivals" (*Publishers Weekly*). Preston and Child's *Relic* and *The Cabinet of Curiosities* were chosen by readers in a National Public Radio poll as being among the one hundred greatest thrillers ever written, and *Relic* was made into a number-one box office hit movie. They are coauthors of the famed Pendergast series, and their recent novels include *The Cabinet of Dr. Leng, Diablo Mesa, Bloodless, The Scorpion's Tail,* and *Crooked River.* In addition to his novels, Preston is the author of the award-winning nonfiction book *The Lost City of the Monkey God.* Child is a Florida resident and former book editor who has published eight novels of his own, including such bestsellers as *Chrysalis* and *Deep Storm.*

Readers can sign up for The Pendergast File, a monthly "strangely entertaining note" from the authors, at their website, PrestonChild.com. The authors welcome visitors to their Facebook page, where they post regularly.